Diana threw herself onto her hard little bed and let the tears come. Oh that she might fly to the ends of the earth away from here! Anything, anything would be better than this!

She sat up and wiped her eyes, looking about her bare room. There on the chair was the mysterious parcel. Who could it be from? She reached out and with trembling fingers tore open its wrappings, then gently lifted the cover of the box. Ah! A breath from a heavenly land was wafted into her face and her weary senses drew it in with sheer delight! Suddenly the sorrows of the last two weeks dropped away from her. She looked, her eyes filled with wonder.

Carnations! Myriads of them. Her mystery flowers had come to find her!

Tyndale House books by Grace Livingston Hill.
Check with your area bookstore for these best-sellers.

Grace Livingston Hill

MYSTERY FLOWERS

LIVING BOOKS ®
Tyndale House Publishers, Inc.
Wheaton, Illinois

This Tyndale House book
by Grace Livingston Hill
contains the complete text
of the original hardcover edition.
NOT ONE WORD
HAS BEEN OMITTED.

Printing History
J. B. Lippincott edition published 1936
Tyndale House edition/1991

Living Books is a registered trademark of Tyndale
House Publishers, Inc.

Library of Congress Catalog Card Number 91-65551
ISBN 0-8423-4613-9
Copyright © 1936 by Grace Livingston Hill.
Cover artwork copyright © 1991 by Rick Johnson
All rights reserved
Printed in the United States of America

98 97 96 95 94 93 92
 8   7   6   5   4   3   2

DIANA Disston stood at the window watching for the postman. Before her the wide velvety lawn sloped to the tall hedge which hid the highway from view. A smooth graveled driveway circled the lawn and swept down to the arched gateway where a little stone cottage, formerly the porter's lodge, nestled among the trees. It was up that driveway the postman would come.

Beside her in the wide window just between the parting of the delicate lace curtains stood a little table bearing a tall crystal bud vase with three pink carnations. Their fragrance filled the room. The girl turned and looked at them whimsically, an almost tender light coming into her eyes, her lips parted in a wistful smile, reminding one of a child dreaming over a fairy tale. Suddenly she stooped and took a deep breath of their fragrance, closing her eyes, and half shyly touching her lips to their fringed petals, laying her cheek softly against their delicate coolness.

Then, laughing half shamedly, she straightened up and took another look down the road. No postman yet! She glanced at the tall old clock in the hall beyond the arched doorway. It was fully five minutes beyond the time he usually came. Why should he be so late this particular morning when she wanted especially to know just how to plan for the day? There would surely be a letter. Or if there wasn't a letter she would know her father would be at home in an hour.

If her father was coming she wanted to dress and be ready to meet him. Perhaps he would suggest that she should go down to the office with him, and they would take lunch somewhere together. That was what he often did when he had had to be away for a day or two and leave her alone in the house with Maggie. Lately, though, he had always seemed so busy, or so absent-minded when he got back from a business trip. She puckered her brows with the worry that had disturbed her more or less ever since he had been away. Somehow he didn't seem just as he had been after her mother's death. He had been so thoughtful of her, so almost tender in his treatment of her. He understood how desolate she was without her precious mother. And of course he was desolate, too! Dear Father! It must be terribly, terribly lonesome for him. Such a wonderful woman for his wife, and to lose her! But of course Father was reticent. He never said much about his own sorrow. He was just thoughtful for her.

And yet, what was this haunting thing that troubled her? Surely it could not be business cares that worried him, for when they had sold off such a large portion of the estate, dismissed a retinue of servants, cut off a good many unnecessary expenses, and even rented the little cottage at the gateway, he had told her that all his debts were paid and they had enough to live on quite comfortably for the rest of their lives, provided of course they did not go into any great extravagances for a few years while his business was picking up. Investments were doing well and there was no reason for him to worry. He had given her a larger allowance and told her to get herself some new clothes. No, it could not be money.

And yet, was it really anything? Was it not perhaps merely her own imagination? She had been so close to him during the first intensity of her sorrow that now that he was getting back into his usual habits of life she had grown too sensitive. That was it, of course, and she simply must put it out of her mind. When he came, *if* he came this morning, she would not let herself think of such a thing. She would rush out and meet him as she always had done, and she would show him how glad she was to have him back again, but she would not let him suspect that she had been worried about anything. She was silly of course to allow imaginings to return and make her uneasy.

She turned her eyes once more to the flowers and touched them lightly with her hand. Sweet flowers! So mysterious and lovely! Coming in such a magical way. If she only knew who dropped them, one every morning in her path just where she went down the driveway to take her daily walk. And so fresh and perfect they were! Not old ones that had stood in a vase in a warm room. Not as if they had been thrown away after having been pinned to a coat. A single perfect bloom lying in almost the same spot every morning! It couldn't have *happened*. Not three times just alike!

And if it had, if somebody had been carrying an armful of them and it could just happen three times that one slipped out and fell right in that spot, where would the person carrying them be coming from? Where would he—they—*SHE* be going? That driveway belonged to the Disston house and nobody would have any business going down it every morning. Not since the butler was gone, and the other servants, and only

Maggie in the house. Of course, there was the milkman and the grocery boy, but they always came in at the back entrance, never the front, and what would milkmen and grocery men be doing with pale pink carnations early in the morning? They certainly wouldn't be throwing them away one at a time, nor dropping them carelessly. Diana reasoned that young men who delivered milk and groceries would not have so many hothouse flowers that they would be careless about them anyway, certainly not three days in succession. What could be the explanation of the mystery? Probably it had some quite commonplace explanation, but Diana dreamily touched the petals of the flowers again and smiled. She preferred to think there was some delightful romantic magic about it. And since an explanation seemed quite out of normal expectation why not indulge her dreams? At least it would be fun to see whether a fourth carnation lay on the drive tomorrow. If it did there would be a real mystery, and she would have to begin investigations. But perhaps it would stop at three times, and then she could just cherish her dreams and not worry herself by the troublesome suggestion of her conscience that perhaps she ought not to have picked them up. They had lain there in the drive, fresh and sweet, demanding to be rescued from a chance passing wheel, and just in the one spot she could not possibly see from the windows of the house, because a great clump of rhododendrons spread out gorgeously and hid the road.

Well, at least she could find out one thing. She could get up very early and see that no one went down the drive from the direction of the house. Or, could she? Might not the flowers have been placed in the drive before dawn? Her eyes melted into the dreaminess of speculation.

If Father came this morning perhaps she would tell him about the flowers. Would she? Or should she take them up to her room and wait to see if another would come tomorrow morning?

Then suddenly she saw the postman carrying a single letter in his hand that he had just taken out of his pack. She sprang to the door to meet him, her eager eyes on the letter. Oh, would he be coming this morning, or would she have to wait another day or two? She sighed at the thought of continued loneliness. And then as she took the letter, recognized the handwriting, and saw how unusually thick it was, her heart sank. He could not be coming or he would not have written so long a letter!

She flung an absent-minded smile at the postman in answer to his good morning, and went in with the letter in her hand.

Diana was in a peculiarly lonely position just at present. Her mother had been dead only a little over a year, and for two years before that she had been more or less of an invalid. Diana had delighted to be with her constantly, as much as her school duties would allow. She had attended a nearby college for a couple of years until the invalid needed her more and more, and so, dropping out of her classes for what at the time had seemed to be only a temporary absence, she had dropped out of the lives of her young friends, and become more or less of a recluse. After her mother's death she found herself left out of the youthful gaiety of which she had been a part in her high school and early college days, and without a strong desire to enter it again.

It was not that she was too shy, or gloomy, it was just that the precious last days of her companionship with her beloved mother had somehow set her apart from the little world where she had moved so happily when she was a child and a growing girl, and had made her more thoughtful, more particular perhaps about her friendships than she might have been without the refining experience of sorrow.

Oh, there were a few of her old companions who came dutifully out to call. Some of them had even tried to drag her back into young gaiety again. Others had written her lovely notes, and sent flowers, but somehow her place among them seemed gone. They were interested in new affairs, some of them were married, most of the rest engaged, chattering about social affairs in which she had no part, and almost no interest, and she hadn't felt eager to follow them back.

Later their mothers had called, and there had been quite a good many invitations recently. Diana had accepted some of them and found a strange distaste for the life which she had once so enjoyed. The conversation seemed to her vapid, the activities sometimes almost stupid, and the excesses in which some of her former companions now indulged did not tempt her. She found herself revolted at the way some of them talked, the way they drank at their parties, just as a matter of course, the way so many of them spoke of sacred things, lightly, flippantly. Was she growing morbid, she wondered, or was this just growing up? Certainly her old friends had changed. Perhaps they had grown up and she had just stayed a little girl. But she was twenty, and she had become rather intimate with death and sorrow. Still death and sorrow were not meant to sour one on life, to make one a recluse. So, from day to day she had tried to reason it out, had forced herself to go more and more among her acquaintances.

There were several of her young men friends who had begun to come to the house of late, but none of them especially interested her. They were nice boys, she told herself, some of them were quite grown up and dependable. There were even a couple who did not drink—at least not much, just politely. But she had never thought seriously about any of them. She told herself that it would make little difference to her if they all stayed away, though she smiled whimsically as she said it and realized that she would probably feel forsaken if nobody ever came. It was a significant thing that in puzzling over the carnations she had never questioned if any of them could possibly have dropped those flowers in the drive for her. It was a thought that her mind rejected when it was first presented as a solution of the pleasant mystery. There were several who might have sent flowers formally, a whole box full, but not just a single blossom dropped on her pathway daily.

So Diana came in with her letter, intending to sit down by the window and read it. Then suddenly she wanted to take it to her room. Perhaps some premonition warned her that she would want to be uninterrupted as she read, would not even want Maggie coming in for the orders of the day. As she turned back toward the hall she paused and caught up the crystal vase, carrying it with her up to her room.

She put the vase on a table in her own pretty room, a room whose windows looked out on the same sweep of lawn and drive and nestling cottage among the trees, where she had just been watching for the postman. She sat down beside the table to read her letter, but even as she tore the envelope open, again a premonition warned her. This was such a thick letter! Was he having to stay another week and leave her alone? Her heart sank. And then she began to read.

My dear daughter:

Somehow the words seemed more formal than his usual, "Dear Di," or "Dear little girl." How silly she was. It must be true that she was growing morbid! Then she read on.

> I have something to tell you which may surprise you, and perhaps will even shock you a little at first, but which I hope will prove in the end to be a great happiness to you, as it is to me.

Diana lifted frightened eyes and looked quickly about the familiar beauty of her own room—the sweet room that her mother had planned for her before she went away—as if to reassure herself that nothing could hurt her, nothing destroy the home and the steady things of life that the years had built up about her. She gave a little gasp and closed her eyes as if she were afraid to read on, then drew a deep breath taking in the spicy perfume of the flowers before she went on with her letter.

> I have had this in mind for some time, and several times have thought to tell you, but the way did not open and it seemed rather a delicate subject to talk about—

Ah! Then there was something! There had been something that had worried him. It had not been her imagination after all! Oh, was it money, in spite of what he had said? Well, if it was money she would just be thankful that it was nothing worse. Even if both of them had to go out and do hard manual labor and be very poor, she would not care. They would have each other.

She drew another deep breath and tried to take courage as she read on.

> And so I have thought it better to write it to you before I come home that you may get used to the thought of it, and be ready to be glad with me—

Her trembling hands suddenly dropped with the letter into her lap and she relaxed in her chair. Oh, would he never come to the point? Must there be this long preamble before she knew the worst? Yes, the *worst!* She felt sure now it was going to be something terrible, else why would he not have enjoyed telling her face to face? Her eyes went back to the letter.

How words could stab! She felt she never would forget the sharpness of the pain that came as she read the next words.

> It is just this, Diana, I am going to be married again. I hope it is going to be as happy a change for you as it is for me. I have felt for a long time that our loneliness has been too great to endure. I am sure I have seen this in you also. Your mother would never have wanted us to go on alone—

Alone! Did they not have each other?

Diana steadied herself tensely to take in this awful cataclysmic thought. Her father was going to put another woman in her mother's place! How could he? Oh, how could he!

This *couldn't* be true! She was dreaming!

Her eyes wildly sought the letter again to extract some word of hope somewhere from what yet remained to be read.

And so, Diana, I am doing what I feel is best both for you and for me. And now, you needn't get excited and think I am trying to make you accept a stranger in place of your mother, because the best part of this is that the woman who has honored me by promising to be my wife is more nearly your companion than mine. She is only a very little older than you are, and will therefore, I hope, be most congenial to you, and we shall have a delightful home together. I am sure that you will be glad that she is not a stranger to you—

Diana wildly began to go over the list of their acquaintances, rejecting each one as impossible, while she swept the sudden tears away that blinded her eyes so that she could not read the rest. Then, desperately she read on.

In a sense she really belongs to us because there is a distant relationship, though very distant of course, and that only by marriage. I am marrying your mother's cousin, Helen Atherton, my dear, and I hope you will rejoice with me, and make her most welcome in our home and life, and that we shall all be very happy together—

But suddenly the letter dropped from Diana's nerveless fingers and she gave a terrible wild little cry, the tears pouring forth in a torrent!

"Cousin Helen! Oh, *not* Cousin Helen!" she gasped aloud in quivering sobs, shuddering as she wept. "Oh, he can't, he *can't*,—he *wouldn't* do that! My f-f-father—w-w-would-n't—do *thha-at!*"

The great house was still and only echoed back her piteous cries hollowly. Suddenly she was aware how empty the home had become—and how *dear* it was! And now her father was going to destroy this home for her forever, destroy it so fully that she would not even want to think of it nor its pleasant memories because it would be so desecrated!

She staggered to her bedside and dropped down upon her knees. Not that she was thinking to pray, only that she must weep out her horror over this new calamity that had befallen her.

Kneeling there and weeping in her first abandoned grief she seemed hardly to be able to think. "Oh, God!" she cried again and again, until it seemed that God must be there somewhere listening, though she hadn't been conscious of Him before. Yet it seemed somehow to comfort her to think that perhaps God might listen to her trouble.

There were no words in her frenzy, but scene after scene in her girlhood in which this cousin Helen had figured went whirling through her mind, as if she were presenting pictures of what happened for God to see and remember, to remind Him how unbearable a situation it would be with Cousin Helen in her mother's place.

"Oh, Father doesn't understand!" she sobbed out. "He never knew how hateful she was!"

Instance after instance of unfortunate contact unfolded before her frightened brain, beginning with little things in her childhood, too petty perhaps to notice now, since they were both grown up. She had been only a baby when Cousin Helen took her precious best doll and singed her hair all off with her curling iron, blackened her face and made a minstrel out of her, with red and blue cambric shapeless garments and a paper collar and hat. It had been a desecration of something precious to the little girl. But the fourteen-year-old cousin had laughed impishly and flung the doll aside, breaking its lovely face and then had run away laughing.

Diana, even in the midst of her weeping, recognized that it would not be fair to judge the woman by an act of a partly grown girl. But there had been so many ugly things. Every time she had come to visit, each day had been full of trial and torture to the finely strung child.

There was the time she hid Diana's essay that she was to have read in school that afternoon. She let the whole household search for it frantically, and Diana finally had to go and read from the original scraps of paper on which it had been written, only to find the neat manuscript lying on her desk on her return from school with a placard beside it scrawled in Helen's most arrogant handwriting, "April Fool!" Diana had been fourteen then, and Cousin Helen old enough to know better. Cousin Helen had left for home that morning before Diana got back from school. Diana's father had taken her into the city to the train. He had missed the whole excitement about the essay. Perhaps no one had ever told him the outcome. So he didn't understand. Diana's wild thoughts glided over dozens of other unhappy times when Cousin Helen had gaily, almost demoniacally, committed some selfish depredation upon something Diana counted precious.

There was the affair of the green taffeta dress, Diana's first real party dress. How her mother and she had delighted in it, selecting the smooth shimmering silk with care, having it made in the style most becoming to her slender form, how happy she had been when she tried it on the last time before the party. Mother loved it so, and she felt as she looked at herself in Mother's long mirror, as if she were a child in a fairy tale. A great part of the anticipation of that party had been in the thought of the lovely dress she was to wear, her first really long dress.

And then Cousin Helen had arrived! On the very morning of the party day she had arrived. She had a way of arriving at inopportune times like that, and it always annoyed Mother. Though Mother never had said a word about it, Diana somehow knew that Mother did not enjoy Cousin Helen's visits. She wondered now—was it—could it have been that Cousin Helen so often absorbed Father's time and interest when she happened to have no other admirer near? Somehow Diana's eyes were being opened quickly to several things that had happened in the past.

But not even Cousin Helen's advent had quite dimmed the thought of that wonderful party. And so the day had slipped by in glad anticipation until it was time to dress.

Cousin Helen had gone upstairs immediately after dinner, telling them someone was coming to take her to the Country Club that evening for an affair. She had been dressed for evening when she came down to dinner, but while Diana was in her mother's room getting something done to her hair that only Mother could rightly do, Cousin Helen had suddenly appeared in the doorway with a gay rustle and called out nonchalantly:

"Well, folks, how do you like me? Don't I look delicious? I found this up in a closet and liked it so much better than my own that I put it on. Hope you don't mind!"

And there stood Cousin Helen in Diana's lovely green taffeta party dress smiling impishly, her eyes showing that she had full knowledge of the confusion she was occasioning.

Diana remembered her own indignation, how she had cried out in horror:

"Oh, that's my party dress! I'm going to wear it to a party tonight! You can't wear that, Cousin Helen!"

And Mother had turned quickly, the brush in her hand, and protested firmly:

"I'm sorry, Helen, but you couldn't wear that—"

And Cousin Helen had just given a gay laugh, whirled about, and flung back:

"Sorry, Kitten, it's too late now. You'll have to wear something else. My boy-friend is downstairs waiting for me! Tata!" and was half-way down the stairs before they could get to the door.

Mother had followed her indignantly to the head of the stairs and called down sharply:

"Helen! Come back here! You *can't do* that! You really *can't!*"

But Helen only laughed and called back, "Can't I? See if I can't!" and went out the front door slamming it gaily after her. They could hear the sound of a motor starting before they fully comprehended what had happened. That was Cousin Helen! And Father was going to marry her!

There had been other depredations as she grew older, acts utterly disloyal to her family when she was their guest, borrowings from others, unasked, of things far more important than dresses. Diana recalled dimly discussions between her father and mother concerning intense flirtations with other women's husbands in which Cousin Helen had utterly alienated some of Mother's best friends because of her calm way of taking possession of their husbands.

Diana suddenly remembered that most unaccountably Father had always taken Cousin Helen's part in these discussions. He said she was only a kid, and was "a cute little piece," and "a pretty child," and insisted that she had no idea she was doing anything to hurt anybody. Insisted that she was entirely guileless and only having a good time.

Even in the matter of the green taffeta he hadn't been able to see that there was anything more than an innocent prank.

"What's one dress?" he said amusedly. "Let Diana wear something else. She has plenty of clothes, hasn't she?" They couldn't seem to make him understand that she hadn't any real party dress that would be suitable for the occasion. That this had been her first really grown-up dress, and it had meant so much to her. He had smoothed her head caressingly when she had dissolved in tears and refused to go to the party at all, and told her she was silly to stay at home just because she couldn't wear a certain dress. Also he had insisted that nothing should be said to Cousin Helen.

Even when Cousin Helen came home with a tear in one of the taffeta ruffles and a great spot on the front of the skirt where she had spilled ice cream, and no apology but a gay laugh, Father dismissed the whole matter as a trifle. Oh, had Cousin Helen even then begun to get her hands on dear Father to pull the wool over his eyes? She had that faculty whenever she chose to use it. She had never bothered to do it with Mother and herself.

There had been many times later when Cousin Helen had demanded a great deal of Father's attendance. And it was all done so prettily. Father was always gallant to every woman, though he had ever been most devoted to Diana's mother. But the girl remembered now those evenings when Helen had dragged Father off to an entertainment she was bent on seeing. Diana more than once on such an occasion found her mother in her darkened room in tears. Mother said she had a headache, or something of the sort. But now Diana began to have a feeling that Cousin Helen had a lot to do with those headaches. Helen would steal a man's heart as easily as she would borrow a party dress!

And Father hadn't realized it. No, Father wasn't one of those men who enjoyed going off with other women, no matter how pretty and young they were. Father loved Mother deeply always. But now that Mother was gone—! Oh—! And now Helen had made him think he ought to marry her! Oh, he mustn't! He *mustn't!* She must stop it somehow! She must save him from Cousin Helen! He didn't know! He didn't realize! She must do something about it at once. Even if she had to tell him all the little silly annoying things from her childhood up, she must make him understand what a calamity it would be if he married Cousin Helen!

She caught up the letter again and began to read once more. She must find out if he was coming home that morning.

So she read on.

> We are to be married at once and will come right home for a few days before we go on a wedding trip. Helen feels that there are changes she will want made in the house and those could be made while we are absent, different furnishings and decorations. But I am writing to you now to make a few suggestions about our home coming. You will want to have a nice dinner ready of course, and the rooms in order. Perhaps Maggie will want some help about special cleaning. You will know how to look after that.
>
> But there are a few little things that you can do for me before I get there. Please go through my

room and take away anything you feel might be annoying to Helen. Your mother's picture and any little things that were especially hers. Just put them away out of sight. You have nice tact and I'm sure you will understand what to do. Helen has a very sensitive nature you know, and might feel it if anything were left about to remind her of the past.

Helen seems to think you would rather not be present at the wedding, and being a woman of course she probably knows how you would feel about that, so I will not suggest that you come on. In fact by the time this letter reaches you it would be too late for you to start. But I am sure you will understand that I have refrained wholly for *your* sake, from asking that you come on. And of course when we get home we'll all have good times together—!

Diana caught her breath in a great sob. Good times! Would there ever be any good times again? A panic seized her! She must get in touch with her father right away! She must not waste another minute. She must somehow stop this terrible catastrophe which was about to happen to herself and her father!

She glanced at the letterhead to get the name of the hotel at which he was stopping, and hurried to the telephone. Oh, would he be there? Would she be able to talk to him if he were? What should she say? How should she begin?

2

IT was two full hours before Mr. Disston was finally located in the distant city hotel to which she telephoned, and Diana spent those two hours alternately walking the floor in desperation, and flinging herself on her bed to weep her heart out, then springing up again to listen for the telephone.

During that two hours every tantalizing deed of Cousin Helen Atherton's came back in vivid form to torture her imagination. When she finally heard her father's beloved voice over the telephone she was almost too much wrought up to speak.

"Oh, Father!" she cried with a great sob in her voice. "Don't, *don't* do this dreadful thing! Don't marry that terrible woman!"

"Why, Diana!" said her father sternly. "You don't realize what you are saying!"

"Yes, I do, I do! Oh, Father, I *do!* She is *terrible!* You don't know! We never told you everything. We thought it would annoy you. But Mother almost hated her. I'm sure she did!"

"Stop!" said Diana's father in a tone she never had

heard him use to her since she was a little child and had been guilty of extreme naughtiness. "Diana, I cannot believe my senses! To think that you should speak such words! To think that you should charge your lovely sweet mother with ever having hated anybody, much less one who has often been an honored guest in our home!"

"Oh, Father! You do not understand. Helen is deceitful! She does the meanest, most underhanded things, and just laughs, and you have to stand whatever she does! She doesn't care how she hurts you! She doesn't care what she ruins or how she spoils other people's plans! She often made Mother cry. And she used to take my things and wear my clothes without even asking if she might and—"

"Oh, now, Diana," said her father in a soothing voice, "you have gotten yourself all excited over the memory of some of those little childish things that happened when Helen was a mere child herself. You can't forget that foolish party dress! I know that was a little hard for you to bear, but you were a mere baby yourself, and of course you must realize that she is grown up now. I didn't think you had it in your sweet nature to hold a grudge so long about such a trifling thing as a dress. Of course I expected you to be a little surprised, perhaps even somewhat startled. But I never dreamed that you would allow your lips to utter such bitter words about another fellow creature, let alone the woman you know your father is going to marry—"

But Diana's spirit was goaded again into a frenzy.

"That's it, Father! You *mustn't* marry her! Oh, Father, *Fath*-er, *please* don't do it! Anyway wait until you can come home and let me tell you all about her. It isn't alone for my sake I'm asking this. It's for yours. If you knew how hateful she can be you wouldn't *want* to marry her! Why, Father dear, even before Mother was gone she tried to get you away from Mother!"

"*Diana!*" Her father's voice was angry now. "Don't attempt to say another word to me! You are beside yourself! I certainly did not foresee any such demonstration as this or I should have prepared you beforehand for what I have been contemplating for some time. I am sure when you get by yourself and have a chance to think over what you have said you will be ashamed of yourself and be quite ready to apologize. In the meantime it is not good to talk about these things over the public telephone. We won't say any more about it. Just please remember, when you come to your senses, what I have asked you to do, and if I do not find it done, and well done, as I know you *can* do it, I shall consider that you have given me a personal affront. You know, Diana, I am really making this move partly for your sake, that you may have a richer, fuller life, and it ill becomes you to carry on like this even for the first few minutes until you get used to the idea. Now, child, just go and calm yourself, and do the things I have asked of you, and let us say no more about it. Certainly not over the telephone!"

"But Father—!" Diana's voice was full of desperation. "I must talk to you. I *must* tell you something—Father, *dear! Won't* you come home even for a few minutes? Won't you take the next train and come to me quick? I *must* see you!"

Her father's voice was cold and displeased as he answered. It made her shiver to listen to him.

"That is quite impossible, Diana! My plans are made and I have no time to take the long journey home just now. Be sensible, and forget your former little jealousies and prejudices. Believe me, we are going to have a very happy time now if you do your part."

"No! *No!*" protested Diana, the tears raining down her cheeks. "No, Father! I could never stay here in this home if you brought Helen here. I *couldn't!* And she would not want me! You'll find out! Oh, Daddy, Daddy! Don't do this!"

"Diana, would you want your father to be lonely the rest of his life?" came the question after a brief pause. His tone was almost placating, gentle.

"Daddy, you wouldn't be any more lonesome than I would. We would have each other," the tone was very sweet and pleading.

"But, little Di, you don't realize that pretty soon you'll be getting married yourself and then where would I be?"

Diana recognized Helen's fine strategy in that argument.

"I? Getting married? Who would I marry, Daddy? There isn't anybody in the world I would rather be with than you. There isn't anybody I care for. I'll promise *never* to get married if you won't. I'll stay with you always. And we'll have such a happy home!"

The man's voice was sharp with almost a hint of sudden pain as he replied.

"Diana, stop this nonsense. Get hold of your self-control and put these wild opinions out of your mind. You think you won't get married now, but you don't realize that such ideas change——"

"Oh, Father! *Father!*" sobbed Diana, feeling the utter futility of what she was trying to do. "Please don't marry her. If you must marry somebody, get somebody else, not *Helen*. I know Mother would tell you so if she were here."

"That's enough, Diana!" said the father angrily. "Your mother would be the first one to advise me to marry. In fact we talked about that once. She did not want me to be lonely——"

"But not Helen! Oh, not Helen, Father *dear!*"

"It is time to end this discussion," said the father sternly. "I am marrying Helen tomorrow and we'll be home the next evening for dinner. By that time I hope you will have some control over your silly feelings and be ready to meet us in the proper manner as a true daughter should do. Till then *good-bye!*"

The receiver hung up with a click, and Diana felt her heart sinking down, down, till it seemed that she could not stand up any longer. Slowly she hung up her receiver, and sank down in a chair feeling as if the worst thing that life could ever bring had happened to her. Her own father, speaking to her in that tone! Utterly refusing to hear her pleading! Determined to bring in this separating element into their lives! It seemed too horrible to be true. Her young frightened spirit fought and struggled within itself, rebelling utterly against what had happened.

Suddenly she heard a sound of the dining room door opening from the butler's pantry, and she knew Maggie must be coming. Swiftly, silently she rose and flew up the stairs. She did not want Maggie asking her questions. Not yet. She would have to tell her of course, if this awful thing were really true, but not yet—not until—well at least until she could think it out and get some degree of composure. Not until she had given her father time to think over how cruel he had been. Not until there was no more chance that he would call her up again and say he would come on and talk it over. Oh, something, *something* would surely happen to change the terrible fear into calm and peace again. It could not be that such a horrible happening could come to her, Diana Disston! It had been so hard to lose her mother, to try and get along for life with Mother gone. She had thought that she would never be able to take an interest in life again after her mother was gone. She thought that she had suffered the ultimate sorrow when death came; but now she saw there was something infinitely worse than death, and her young heart gazed into her future appalled.

But a peremptory tap on the door interrupted her sorrowful meditations. Maggie announced that the milkman had come for his money.

"And what's fer dinner the night, Miss Diana? We'll need ta be gettin' in the orders, especially if yer feyther is comin' the day."

Diana suddenly recalled from her seclusion, summoned the self-control that had been the habit of her life before others, and answered, though with a somewhat shaky voice:

"Yes, Maggie, I'll give you the money. Just a minute. And I'll be down very soon about the orders."

Maggie was a canny woman. She heard the shaky voice, and she peered keenly at Diana as the girl opened the door a crack to hand out the money.

"Ye'd best come at once," she said shortly. "We'll na get the best cuts o' the meat ef we don't get oor orders in soon."

"All right," said Diana drawing a deep breath and trying to sound cheerful. She went to the washstand and dashed cold water over her face to erase the signs of tears.

In a few minutes she was downstairs trying to wear a nonchalant air, but the canny old servant saw through her subterfuge.

"Father won't be home today," Diana spoke slowly, steadily, as if she were addressing her own soul. "He—won't be here till—Wednesday night—!"

But suddenly her lip quivered and without warning the tears brimmed over and rolled down her cheeks. She turned instantly away from the room and stared hard out the window, trying to hide her tears from Maggie. But it was too late. Maggie had known her since she was a child. She could not be deceived when something was troubling her bairn.

"There, there, child!" she said in sudden tenderness. "Yer not ta greet because of a couppla days. The day and the day's day will pass that quick you'll na meet it before it's gone."

But the sound of sympathy completely broke Diana's self-control and she put her head down on the window seat and gave herself over to weeping for the moment. Then suddenly she gained control again and raised her head, fiercely brushing away the tears.

"Oh, but Maggie, you don't know the half," she said with a long shuddering sob that shook her whole young frame. "Father's going to be married again, Maggie!"

There was an ominous silence while Maggie took in this new disaster, and a view of her kindly old face would have shown a number of emotions chasing themselves across her countenance like clouds and storm and sunshine across a summer sky. Storm first, a fury of angry clouds that the father of a girl like this and the husband of the wife he had married, could be willing to put another in his dead wife's place; compassion for the girl, then a search for comfort for sunshine in the dark view.

"Aw, but perhaps it won't be sa bad, my bonnie dear!" she said pitifully. "Perhaps he'll bring ye a nice gude wumman who'll mother ye and make it homelike again. Don't take it sa hard, my dearie. Yer feyther's a gude mon. Seems like he would pick a gude wumman. Look who he picked the first time!"

Maggie ventured a cheery little rising inflection to her voice.

But the girl shook her head.

"No, Maggie, that's the worst of it. He won't. Maggie, it's Cousin Helen Atherton!"

Maggie's blue eyes blazed at Diana in amazement and her cheeks flamed redder than their usual apple-red.

"That hussy!" she exclaimed, her eyes beginning to snap. "You can't mean it, Miss Diana! Your feyther wouldn't do the like o' that to ye!"

"It's not his fault!" sobbed Diana. "I know it's not his fault. He doesn't understand! He just doesn't know what she's like. Helen never did those horrid things when Father was around!"

Maggie's eyes held inscrutable thoughts, and her thin lips were pursed incredulously.

"Mebbe not!" she said in a noncommittal tone, though her eyes belied her tone. "Aw, but these men is that stupid when it comes ta judgin' a pretty wumman, especially if she has a bright way with her and knows how ta work her eyes. Ah! But the puir mon'll rue the day he ever saw her if he ties up ta that hussy! Ye no think ye can try ta tell him, my lamb?"

"Oh, I have, I *have*, Maggie! I've just been talking to him over the telephone. I've begged him to come home and let me tell him everything, but it only made him very angry. He says I have always misjudged her. He believes everything she says, Maggie, and he was really very displeased with me. And oh, I don't know what to do!"

Maggie suddenly came over to the girl like a little protective hen, every feather bristling, to guard a chick, and laid a work-roughened hand on Diana's bright bowed head.

"There, there! You poor little lamb!" she crooned gently.

Diana suddenly turned and flung her arms around the servant's neck and put her face on her shoulder, weeping with all her might. For a moment the Scotch woman held her in her arms, her own tears falling upon the girl's head.

"There! there!" crooned the woman patting the heaving shoulders gently. "Mebbe it won't be so bad as you think! Mebbe your feyther'll be able to manage her rampaging ways when he gets to know what she is!"

"No," said Diana sadly, "he won't find out." There was a hopeless ring to her voice. "You know what she is, Maggie. You know how she'll go about it. She'll tell him everything in her own way and make it appear that it is all my fault. She always did that, and now I won't have a chance in the world to make him see the truth. She's begun to pull the wool over his eyes already. She's told him I wouldn't want to be at the wedding!"

"The hussy!" breathed Maggie under her breath. "She would! But he'll find out, puir mon! Give him time an' he'll see what a mistake he's made!"

"But that'll be too late!" wailed Diana.

"Mebbe not. Mebbe you won't find things so hard. You must just stand up for your rights, child, and not let her get the upper hand. Remember you're a wumman grown now!"

"But I haven't any rights here now, Maggie," said the little stricken voice of the girl. "She'll be mistress here!"

"You've the rights of a daughter of the house!" said the servant grimly. "You mustn't forget that. You'll have to let her see that you don't mean to give up your rights as a daughter in this house. You've a right to the same place you had when your own mother was alive!"

"But I couldn't stay here, Maggie! Not with her! You know life would be unbearable! You know what she does to everybody around her!"

"Would you let a thing like her bein' here drive you out of your own home, Miss Diana? I'm surprised at the way yer talkin'. You was here first, an' it's here you belong!"

Diana shook her head and lifted a hopeless, tear-stained face.

"You know I won't belong when she gets here, Maggie. You know what she'll do, what she always has done, just put me in the wrong at every turn. No, Maggie, I'll have to go. It's probably what she has planned."

"Aw, my lamb! I can't think that! Ye'll mebbe make out ta get along fer a wee bit while till something turns. And ye'll be gettin' married soon an' have a home of yer own, ye know. She can't touch ye then!"

"Married!" said Diana bitterly, "who would I marry? I don't want to marry anyone, and no one wants to marry me!"

"Don't be so sure, child!" said the woman, trying to speak brightly. "There's many a lad would be glad to if ye'd give him half a chance. There's that young Tommy Watrous that's been comin' of late, what's the matter of him? He's well fixed and what would he come fer if he's not thinkin' of askin' you, my lamb?"

"Oh, Maggie!" cried Diana with a little shiver of dislike. "He's got a mouth like a fish! Would you want to wish any such fate on me as to marry him?"

"Well, child, he's not the only one. There's young Arthur McWade. I hear he's doin' verra weel in the law, an' he certainly is a fine upstanding man. He minds me of yer feyther sometimes, he's that grave and quiet."

"Yes," said Diana with asperity, "he's like an old man, and he's awfully set in his way."

"But mebbe it's a gude way, child, and he seems dependable. But then there's that Bobby Watkins. He seemed that disappointed when you weren't home last week. They do say he'll inherit his uncle's estate, and there's none better in these parts. He's that cheerful and witty, you must admit that, dear child."

Diana turned wearily away.

"Oh, don't let's talk about marrying now, Maggie, I'm not wanting to get married. Not now anyway. Marrying makes a lot of trouble. Oh, Maggie! How can I bear it!"

But suddenly the grocery boy arrived at the kitchen door with an order that had been given the day before, and Maggie had to answer his knock. Diana made a quick escape up the back stairs to her room again, and Maggie wisely left her alone for a little while.

But the interval, and the opportunity to speak her heart to another human being, had helped Diana so that she could face her immediate problems more sanely. And there was her father's request about putting away her mother's things! She must attend to it at once and get it over. It would be the hardest thing she had to do. She turned with swift steps and crossed the hall to her father's room, the room that had been her mother's also through all the years. How terrible it was going to be to have Cousin Helen have the right to be there in her mother's place! Her heart contracted with a sickening thud as she stood in the doorway looking across at the lovely portrait of her mother by Sargent that her father had had hung there where he could look at it in his first waking moments.

And now he was willing to have it stored away out of sight! Oh, what had Cousin Helen been able to do with him already! Ah, she would wind him about her slender little finger and give that amused smile to his tortured daughter, and that would be all!

Diana went and stood beneath the portrait and looked up into the calm serene eyes.

"Oh, Mother, Mother, *Mother*," she sobbed softly.

"Do you know what is happening to Father and me? Do you *know?* And don't you care any more? Is everything so wonderful where you are now that you don't care any more? Or perhaps in heaven you can see so much more and understand so much more widely than we do down here that it doesn't seem as dreadful to you as it does to me. Oh, but Mother, I know you understand how I feel—"

Diana raised her arms and lifted the great frame from its hanging, holding it close in her arms and looking into the painted eyes with tender yearning, her own brimming over till the tears splashed down the length of the portrait. She laid the painting down upon the bed and tenderly dabbed the tears away from it, as if their saltiness had been a desecration.

Then came the pain of the thought of putting the picture away out of sight. Must she? How could her father be willing to put her precious mother's picture away out of his room and his life, that picture of which he had been so proud, which had seemed to be such a comfort to him in the early days of his bereavement? But then what should make him willing to bring another— and such another—into his beloved's place? Well, it was all a terrible mystery that she could not solve.

She wondered if she dared to hang the picture in her own room? How she would love to have it there, and very likely her father would be glad to have it there, also. It was the natural place for it now of course. Then suddenly there came a rush of memories. The broken doll, a fragile cup lying in fragments on the hearth where Helen had thrown it in pettishness because she had spilled some of its contents on her hand and scalded it, a precious book that her mother treasured and loved to read, slashed from start to finish, every page disfigured, and Helen's only explanation: "Because I didn't like it! Because it was a silly book. It was too goody-goody!"

In sudden terror Diana took the picture in her arms once more and bore it to her own room. If she should leave that picture around and Helen should take a dislike to it she would not hesitate to take a carving knife and slash its painted canvas as she had done the pages of Mother's devotional book. Diana's face grew hard. Her eyes flashed. That should never happen! She would do something with the picture to make it safe.

Swiftly she went to work, laying a sheet of cardboard from among her drawing materials over the painted surface, soft cotton above that, and then wrapping the whole thing in a big old quilt, and tying it securely. And where should she hide it that it could not be found? She pondered the question anxiously as she went back to the big pleasant room across the hall that had been her father's and mother's all her young life. How empty it looked now with Mother's picture gone. The blank space on the wall seemed to reproach her as she entered and looked about, bringing bitter tears to her eyes again.

But there was need that she act quickly. There was much to be done, and now her work began to assume proportions that she had not realized at first.

She hid the picture back in the dark end of her closet with garment bags hanging in front of it. That would do for the present though she was by no means satisfied with its safety. Then she went to work in good earnest, gathering out the precious things from her father's room until she was satisfied there was not a thing left to remind of her mother. She was standing in the doorway surveying the finished work. There was not even an embroidered bureau scarf, nor a delicate satin pincushion to speak of the former occupant. Then suddenly she was aware of Maggie standing grimly behind her in the hall holding a broom and dustcloth in her hands.

"I'll just finish redding up now," she said with an air of authority. "You get you to your room and rest yersel' awhile."

Maggie's sandy eyelashes were wet with recently shed tears, and her lips were set thinly, defiantly, but she would do her duty to the end.

Diana turned with a start.

"Oh, thank you, Maggie," she said wearily, "that will help a lot. But I can't lie down now, I've a lot to do. I've other things to—" she hesitated shamedly and added, "put away."

"Yes," assented Maggie, "ye can't be too careful. Mind yer mother's pearls! And her brooch! The diamond brooch."

Diana gave her a startled look.

"Oh!" she gasped sorrowfully. "Yes, of course. I hadn't thought."

"She'll be after thae pearls!" the old servant commented sagaciously. "I mind her coaxin' yer mommie once ta let her wear 'em."

"She never did let her have them?" Diana asked the question half fearfully as if she would discover a precedent that might give her courage.

"Not she!" said Maggie. "She knew her well, that Helen. The pearls would never ha came back ef she'd once got her hand on thae."

Diana hurried away and hunted up a little chamois jewel bag in which she deposited the precious jewels, strung it on a slender chain about her neck and dropped it inside her dress. Then with a light of battle in her eyes she went forth through the house to cull out and gather into safety all precious things for which she feared.

There were a few fine paintings that had been her

mother's delight, small ones done by good artists. There were some bits of statuary, a few pieces of carved ivory and crystal. They were curios associated especially with her mother. Her father would not think of them nor notice their absence if they were gone, but they might incite the new mistress of the house to destroy them if she at all suspected that they were precious to either Diana or her mother.

When Diana was through with her work the house bore a bare severe air as if all feminine trifles were done away with forever. She stared about in dismay. How was she going to live with so much gone that had made a great part of the background of her childhood's home? And yet, they were only trifles she was carrying away, just a small basket full of pretty trifles.

Then she went to the dining room and linen closet and gathered out all the articles that were mono-grammed with her mother's initials. A great deal of the silver, too, that was marked with her mother's maiden name. Mother had always said they were to be hers. So she carried them, a basket at a time, up to the attic and packed them carefully away in an old haircloth trunk, with a pile of old magazines on the top, and shoved it back under the eaves with plenty of things in front of it. At least for a few days Helen would not go to searching, and it was safe there until she could talk with her father and find out his wish in the matter. Still, as she thought over each article she had packed, nearly everything really belonged to herself if she cared to claim it. She had a right to put the things where they would not be seen, a right even to take them out of the house if it became necessary.

The idea crossed her mind that she might even take a small room in a storage house and have some of her own things taken there if she found Helen was likely to make trouble. And yet could she do that after the new mistress had once arrived?

Puzzled, troubled, weary and perplexed, she worked, stopping for a sketchy lunch at Maggie's most earnest insistence, and then back to work again.

When she went to her room after a brief meal which Maggie described as dinner, she looked about at her own little haven with a sense of coming to a refuge. This room at least was her own. Here she had her things about her and here she could live her life perhaps, if she could once induce Helen to let her alone. She would try it at least. She couldn't go away and leave her dear father. For his sake she must stay. She must endure it somehow.

She looked around miserably on her own precious things. She would have to keep her door locked, she supposed. She couldn't call a thing her own unless she did, not if Helen took a fancy to it!

The leaden horror of what had befallen her settled down upon her young soul unbearably. The tears fell once more. She was standing by her table where stood the little crystal vase containing the flowers. Their delicate color seemed to stand out in the shadows of the room and lean toward her as if to comfort her, and with sudden impulse she bent over them and laid her tear-wet face against them, her lips on their fringes, her burning eyes half closed and brushing across them, their fragrance drenched with her tears. And suddenly, startlingly, they seemed to be human, their petals almost like cool living flesh, their touch like to the touch of a mother, and she buried her face once more in their sweetness and let their tenderness flow over her tired soul. Oh, if she only knew where these flowers came from. If only some unknown pleasant friend had left them there, some friend to whom she might go, and weep, and tell her trouble. Their cool impersonal touch soothed her disturbed being and rested her. If there were only a friend somewhere like those flowers, who would understand, and help and comfort! Perhaps God was like that! But God seemed so far away! And she didn't know God!

3

IT was early when Diana went to her bed and burrowed her face in the pillow to weep. It could not have been more than half past eight. She did not hear the doorbell ringing, nor Maggie's steps along the hall as she went to open the door. Her ears were covered by the pillow.

But Maggie's hand upon her shoulder made her start up, feeling as if all her worst fears were come upon her without warning.

"It's Mr. Bobby Watkins come to call!" announced Maggie with deep satisfaction in her voice. "Ye'er ta get up the noo an' put on yer prettiest frock and go down. It'll cheer ye up a bit."

"Oh, Maggie, I *can't!*" wailed Diana. "You tell him I've retired. Tell him anything. Tell him I'm not feeling well if you want to. That's true."

Diana, even in the dim room lighted only from the hall, was a woebegone enough young creature to touch the heart of her severest critic, and Maggie was anything but that. Her eyes were swollen, her nose was red, and her cheeks were dripping tears. But Maggie stood her ground relentlessly:

"Now, Miss Diana, that's no way to go aboot it. Yer not ta be unkind ta the nice little mon. He's come ta call an' ef ye don't see him he'll be that hurt! An' ef ye've got a hard thing ta bear in the eyes of the worruld ye'd best tak it facin' it, an' not lyin' doon. It's doin' ye na gude ta lie there an' greet. Ye'll only be sick the morn's morn an' give that hussy a chance ta gloat over ye. There's na point in lookin' like a ghaist. Get up quick an' put on yer pretty frock an' coom down the stair an' meet life. Bobby's a gude wee mon an' he'll make ye laugh an' that's half o' bearin' things, at least in the eyes of the worruld."

"But Maggie, I'm a sight!" said Diana despairingly.

"A gude dash o' cold water 'll mend that!" encouraged Maggie. "Where's that new frock with the big white collar? I'll get it for ye while ye wash up, an' give yer hair a bit lick."

So Maggie encouraged and urged and prodded, and finally Diana dressed and went down to her caller.

Bobby Watkins was a round-faced little man, not much taller than Diana herself. He was good-natured and kind-hearted and rich but Diana had never been especially interested in him. Now as she went down the last steps it suddenly occurred to her that here was a possible way out of her difficulty. She might marry Bobby. Bobby hadn't actually asked her to marry him, but her intuition told her that he had come very near to asking her on more than one occasion. It had been her own fault that he had not actually done so. Well, now, suppose she let him ask her, and suppose she should accept?

The thought repelled her, yet forced itself upon her wrought-up consciousness, and as she entered the big living room and Bobby rose to greet her with his round red face shining, and his thick lips rolled back in a wide grin of welcome, she saw him in a new role, that of a possible husband. Could she stand it? Could she ever get used to having that bland self-satisfied childlike smile about her continually? Was it conceivable that she could ever grow fond of him?

She gave a little shiver of dislike as she entered the room, trying to smile in her usual way and be pleasant, conscious of her recent tears, aware suddenly of the strangeness and bareness of the room from which little homelike touches seemed to have utterly fled as the result of her activities that afternoon. She gave him her hand in greeting and winced at the grip he gave her. His hand seemed so big and powerful, so possessive!

She lifted her face and it was well she did not know how lovely she was with that hint of tears about her lashes, the troubled light in her eyes, the flush on her cheeks left over from her weeping.

He had brought her flowers and she was glad to withdraw her hand from his greeting and open them. Gardenias in their stiff loveliness, a lot of them. He was prodigal in his buying. She could have anything she wanted if she belonged to him! The thought stabbed her with the memory of Maggie's words that morning. But again her soul recoiled from the thought. She was in trouble and sorely needed someone to comfort her, but she could not conceive of finding comfort on Bobby's broad plump shoulder. She couldn't even think of being willing to tell him what had happened to upset her world.

She heard the jokes he was telling as if she were far above him somewhere up by the ceiling, looking down on him and not really listening to what he was saying. His loud boisterous laughter grated on her sensibilities and made her wish to turn and fly upstairs again and get away from the thought of him. Oh, why had Maggie put that suggestion in her mind? Bobby had been just a pleasant rather tiresome friend before, one who didn't matter much either way. Now he seemed to have come to torment her in her misery. Why hadn't she just insisted that Maggie should go down and make some excuse for her?

But she smiled graciously and thanked Bobby for the flowers. Her lips seemed stiff with suffering, and her whole face too weary to smile, but she managed it. And perhaps Bobby noticed the misty sweet look of aloofness as she sat down. Certainly he was impressed by something in her manner, for he said with a boisterous laugh, "You're certainly looking your best tonight, Di! It must be what you're wearing. That white about your shoulders is very becoming. Makes sort of an aura about you, or isn't that the right word? Perhaps halo is the word I mean, only that is over the head, isn't it?" and Bobby laughed as if the joke were very great indeed.

Diana sat in the chair opposite to him, stiffly, with the box of gardenias in her lap and looked at him. She tried to imagine herself confiding in him that her father was about to marry a perfectly impossible woman. She tried to imagine his blunt embarrassed reaction to her confidence if she should attempt it, and felt almost hysterical over the probable result. It was with difficulty that she controlled the sudden desire to laugh, with laughter that was near to tears.

Then she heard the telephone ringing, and she sobered suddenly, her face turning perfectly white, and fear coming into her eyes. Oh, could that be her father? Had he telephoned at last? Perhaps there was relief in sight! Oh, God! If only that could be!

She half rose from her chair with a gesture almost as if she would fling the gardenias from her, box and all. Then she heard Maggie's faithful hurried steps in the hall and she knew she would answer and call her, and she dropped back again with the box still in her lap realizing that she must not appear to be anxious. So she sat with a frozen smile locked upon her pale lips, waiting in a perfect fever for Maggie to come and set her free to go and talk with her father, wildly hoping all sorts of lovely things, that her father had seen what an impossible thing he was about to try to do, and had called her up to soothe her fears and tell her he had reconsidered, tell her he loved her, tell her he hadn't realized.

But the seconds went by and grew into minutes and she heard Maggie go back to the kitchen without calling her. Oh, could it be possible that Maggie had told her father she was busy with a caller, could Maggie have dared to presume to do that? Or had she taken a message and was waiting till the caller was gone to deliver it? Oh, had she missed talking with her father? The thought was agony. She must find out. And finally she lifted miserable eyes to her guest's and interrupted a long eager description of an almost accident he had suffered driving with a friend in his new car.

"Bobby, excuse me just a minute. I heard the telephone ring, and I've been expecting a call from Father all day. I must see if that was he."

She arose hastily, deposited the box of flowers in her chair and fairly flew to the kitchen.

"Was that Father calling?" she asked Maggie breathlessly.

"No, it was just some simple person had the wrong number," said Maggie, vexed that Diana had not trusted her. "Go you back to yon lad. I'll call ye ef yer wanted on the phone."

So Diana, weak from excitement and disappointment, went back to Bobby and her flowers, and presently Maggie came with a vase of water and she could busy her shaking fingers placing the flowers while Bobby talked on dully enjoying his own conversation and feasting his eyes on the lovely girl. Bobby was having the time of his life. Diana was shying away from him as she usually did, and he wasn't keen enough to know she simply wasn't even listening to him.

For a new thought had occurred to Diana. Perhaps her father would come back tonight to talk it over with her. He had said he couldn't, but perhaps he had thought it over and decided to come anyway. If so it was about time for his train and he might arrive at any minute.

But Bobby was only flattered at the sweet attention she seemed to be giving him. That distant look in her eyes seemed to him to be a real interest. A new interest that he had never been able to rouse in her before. He took new heart of hope and went on to further relate an incident of his boyhood, rejoicing in the dreamy smile with which she fixed her eyes upon his face, while Diana, all tense, sat and listened for the sound of her father's step.

Then, startlingly the doorbell rang and Diana jumped a little and caught her breath, her eyes suddenly seeking the hall door. He had come perhaps——! He might have left his latch key at home by mistake. He often did that.

She started to her feet, but Bobby motioned her to sit down.

"You don't need to go," he said blandly, "Maggie is coming. I hear her."

And Diana dropped back into her chair again, weakly, now beset with a new idea. What if they were married already and had come ahead of the time planned? That would be like her father to hasten to her when he knew she was in distress. But oh, if he brought Helen——now——! Her eyes sought beseechingly the round bland face of her caller. She would have to tell him! Father would bring his new wife in, perhaps, and introduce her. Then Bobby would tell it all over the countryside. Bobby never could keep a secret. And the world would have to know, and then all would be over. Oh, if Father would just come first and let her talk it out with him! But if he waited till they were married it would be too late!

Over and over like a chant it rang through her brain during that extended period while Maggie was walking the length of the hall to the front door. Then a breathless moment during which Bobby occupied the air with his incessant talk and she had to strain her ears to hear the low voice at the front door. Diana caught the words "Sign here!" and her heart gave a leap. A telegram perhaps. Her father might be calling her to come on to the wedding. In which case she would go—not to the wedding but to her father—and try with all her might to get him to give up this terrible idea of marriage!

She sat with her hand on her heart and her eyes fixed fearfully upon the doorway as if she saw a ghost.

Bobby stopped in the middle of a sentence and followed her gaze and they both saw Maggie come by the door with a large florist's box in her arms.

"Maggie!" Diana called, unable to maintain her silence any longer. But her voice was faint and frightened.

"It's juist some more flowers, Miss Disston," said Maggie formally and it must be owned a bit importantly. "Wud ye like me ta open them an' put them in the water?"

Then a wild idea seized Diana. Perhaps her father had sent flowers. It would comfort her greatly if he had. But if so she wanted to open them herself.

"No, you needn't mind, Maggie," she said, trying to put up a tone of indifference. "I have lovely flowers here, enough for the present. It won't hurt them to leave them in the box."

Bobby looked at her gratefully, a sudden effulgence of joy in his round red face. His flowers were enough for her. She was wanting him to know that she was especially pleased with his flowers. He took heart of hope and bloomed into good cheer.

"I'm glad you like them, Diana," he said in a tone of exuberance.

"They are lovely!" said Diana again, wondering just how many times she had used that phrase that evening with regard to those gardenias. But Bobby seemed well pleased. He was not critical. He felt that suddenly fate had turned the sunny side of life to him, and he came over and drew a chair up closer to her.

"Diana, I came over very especially to ask you to go out with me Wednesday evening," he began, puffing a little in his excitement. Heretofore Diana had always managed to evade his invitations on one score or another, but now he meant to press his vantage while she seemed to be favorable to him. He gave her no opportunity to reply but hurried on. "I've tickets for a very fine concert in the city, and I thought we'd go in early and take dinner together. I know it is short notice, but I wasn't sure I could get tickets until tonight."

But a frightened look was coming into Diana's face. Wednesday night! That was when they were coming home—if Father really did as he had said he would!

For an instant she considered the idea of going with Bobby anyway. Even Bobby's company would be better than that awful meeting with a stepmother for the first time, and such a stepmother! Then almost instantly she knew it would not do. Her father would consider it an affront to both of them. He would never forgive it. No, she could not do that. Not the *first* night, anyway. And perhaps, perhaps there was a chance—oh, she didn't dare think of what the chance might be—but she could not pledge herself to be away until she knew. Her eyes clouded and a troubled pucker came in her brow, and instantly Bobby's face froze into disappointment. He had so often met with disappointment before, just when he had hoped to gain a little with her.

"I'm sorry, Bobby," she said, "I'm afraid Father has planned something else—" her voice trailed off into silence. She couldn't tell Bobby that Father was marrying Cousin Helen, not just yet anyway. It seemed too awful for words when she came to consider actually telling it. Bobby knew Cousin Helen. Bobby would be shocked, for Cousin Helen had always been rude to Bobby. She had laughed at his round face. She had laughed almost to his face! Bobby would be offended on his own account. He might not understand Diana's situation. She felt instinctively that he would not be able to appreciate her horror and sorrow, nor to tenderly comfort her, but he would be indignant that a respected neighbor like her father had married a young woman who had practically insulted him on more than one occasion, and he would be so filled with his own part in the matter that he would fail to appreciate hers. No, there would be no relief in taking on a husband, certainly not if he had to be Bobby. Oh, why did she have to consider such awful problems? Marrying! Why should marrying create such sorrow?

And then she knew that she could not tell Bobby. She must not tell anyone until all possibility that it was not true was passed. Surely yet there would be some word from her father, or he would arrive on the early morning train. Never before in all her life had he failed her when he knew she was in trouble. Surely, surely he would not do this terrible thing!

Then she realized that her caller had asked her a question.

"You weren't listening!" he charged her crossly. "I asked you if I might not see your father and talk it over with him. I'm quite sure he would be willing to let me have you for Wednesday evening. You don't go out half enough. I've heard several of your girl-friends say that. Won't you call him, Diana, and let me ask him?"

"He isn't here," said Diana. "He's not coming back till Wednesday sometime. And no, I can't reach him by telephone now, not unless he calls up. I don't know where he is tonight. But you see he called up this morning and—gave me directions. He's—bringing someone—a lady—home to dinner. That is he thought he might—and of course you know I would have to be here."

"Not necessarily!" said Bobby, quite vexed now. "Don't you have the least idea where I could call him?"

"No," said Diana, "I don't."

"Well, will you let me know as soon as you find out whether you can go?" persisted Bobby.

"I could do that," said Diana with a troubled look. Oh, why did she have to be bothered with Bobby, now?

But at last he took himself away, having extracted a promise that she would let him know as soon as her father came home if there was any chance that she could go with him, and she drew a sigh of relief, reflecting that she could send him a note as soon as she was sure, and she meant to be sure one way or another that she could not go. She was definitely certain that marrying Bobby Watkins would be no way out for her. If she could not endure him for one short evening how would she ever get through a lifetime in his company?

As soon as Bobby was gone Diana flew to the box of flowers and opened them. She did not look at the flowers themselves but drew out the little envelope and looked at the card it contained, hoping against hope that it would bear some message from her beloved father. But no, it bore the card of Arthur McWade, another of the young men who from time to time came to call upon her, and occasionally asked her to some party or entertainment with them. He was a nice kind man, but very formal in spite of his brilliant intellect. Diana always felt rather overpowered in his company.

She pulled the wax paper aside and glanced at the wealth of red roses he had sent. They were beautiful, yes, and with a deep musky perfume. She ought to enjoy them, but somehow she had no heart tonight. She did not even bend her head to get a whiff of their perfume. They didn't interest her tonight. She drew a deep sigh and went off upstairs to her room leaving the abandoned roses to Maggie's tender mercies. If only her father had sent them! But somehow she felt Cousin Helen's hand in all this. With keen intuition she knew that he had probably reluctantly admitted to her that his daughter was not pleased, and she had likely advised him to let her alone, promising that she, like the proverbial sheep of little Bopeep would soon come home wagging her tail behind her. She could almost see the naughty gleam in Cousin Helen's eye as she said it to Father. Strange Father never seemed to understand what that sinister gleam meant. He trusted her so. That was the hopelessness of it. Helen would tell him a gay version of anything that happened and he would trust her beyond his own daughter! How was life ever going to be endurable again?

She went into her dark room and found her way to the window that looked out across the lawn and down to the hedged highway. Off to the right she could see the twinkling lights in the stone cottage through the trees. There was a light upstairs in the gable room, and she could see someone moving around. It was pleasant to have lights in the cottage again, it had been closed so long, since they could not afford to have a retainer occupying it any more. These people were a mother and son, Maggie said. She had sent Maggie down with coffee and sandwiches the day they moved in, and Maggie had come home delighted. The people were Scotch like herself. They were from Edinburgh and knew the street where she used to live. Maggie said they were quality folks and said she wished Diana would call on "the nice old buddy" as she called the mother. "The son he's got some kind of a job in the city and he goes back and forth every day," Maggie had said, "and she's that lonesome, the puir wee mither! She's lived a' her life in Scotland, an' it's a' quite strange here fer her!" And Diana had promised and meant to go that very day had not this terrible catastrophe befallen her. But now—well, "the puir wee buddy" would have to get along as best she could in the company of her son. At least she had her son. She wasn't all alone as she, Diana was. The thought brought a sudden gush of tears. Would she ever be able to think a continuous thought again without crying?

But then like a flash she remembered that probably that son would get married like all the rest of the benighted earth, and then where would the poor mother be? She felt a quiver of pity for the unknown mother. Oh, life, life, how cruel everything was! But she had no time now to think of calling on strange lonely people. Her heart was too heavy for comforting strangers now. Down there across the dark lawn among the trees where twinkled pleasant lights of friendly folk how many of them all had some deep new sorrow such as she had to bear? How many of them knew that feeling of being stricken by some happening that seemed worse than death? Oh yes, there were things in life far more bitter than death.

Diana drew nearer to the window pane, and the little crystal vase with its three carnations swayed and would have fallen if Diana had not caught them. Some of the water splashed out, and the flowers slid out and brushed her hand as they fell. She gathered them up and laid them against her burning eyelids, and then against her lips and let them once more typify comfort and understanding as if behind them were a rare human love.

Those flowers downstairs, the roses and gardenias were richly beautiful, probably far costlier than these three single blossoms, but somehow they didn't comfort her like these mysterious flowers that had come to her so impersonally that they almost seemed like the breath of heaven, as if they might have been dropped from an angel's hands as he passed on his way to some sad heart.

If these had come from either Arthur McWade or Bobby, she knew she wouldn't want to put her lips against them. But it wasn't conceivable that either of them would have dropped them on her casual path as she had found these. She liked to think that it was without intention, just a happening, and yet the one who had dropped them had become in an indefinable sense a friend, and the only friend in whom she would care to confide her troubles.

So she laid her lips against the delicate fringes of the petals and breathed her sorrow into them.

Downstairs Maggie had come upon the abandoned flowers and stood for a minute looking down at their rich beauty.

"Ah! Puir wee thing!" she murmured, brushing away the quick tears with the corner of her apron. Then she trotted away into the living room and took a glance at the gardenias in their silver bowl in state on a polished table, abandoned also. Neither suitor could divert her from her trouble.

"Ah, puir wee thing! Puir wee thing!" she murmured again softly as she trotted back and put the great sheaf of crimson roses in water. Strange and sad and significant that both these floral tokens had come in one evening! Then, her work done, Maggie stood with her hands on her hips surveying the flowers and her mind reverted to a tiny crystal vase she had seen upstairs in Diana's room.

"*Thae* flooers?" she said meditatively, interrogatively. "Where did thae flooers come frae?" and her eyes narrowed thoughtfully.

"Ah! The puir wee thing!" she said with another sigh. "What would her bonnie mither say ef she knew it?"

4

DOWN at the little stone cottage by the great iron gates the "puir wee buddy" who was the new tenant was welcoming her son back after the day's absence.

"You're late, Gordon. I've been worried about you. I was afraid something had happened. I'm always worried when you go off on those long motor trips with someone else driving. I was sure you had had an accident. You've always been so good about telephoning when you're late."

"I know, Mother. I'm sorry. We had a flat tire away out in the country where we couldn't get word to a garage, and we had to fix it ourselves with inadequate tools. It's strange to me what risks some men take, when a few little tools would put one on the safe side. There wasn't a telephone near us, and when we got to a town if we had stopped to telephone I should have lost my bus out from the city, and I knew you'd rather I'd hurry on and catch it than to have to wait up till all hours looking for me, as you always will even if I telephone."

"Yes," said the mother half sheepishly. "I like to, you know, dear son."

"Yes, I know you do," said the son stooping and giving her an affectionate kiss, "and I ought not to find fault with you. I'd be mighty lonely if you weren't here to watch for me. I'm pretty fortunate to be having a mother that likes to watch for me, I know. But say, you didn't have the forethought to save a bite of dinner for me, did you? I'm starved. We had lunch at twelve o'clock, and not a minute nor a place to stop to eat again. I just barely caught the bus as it was."

"Of course I saved the dinner, son. You didn't think I'd forget how you love home dinners, did you? Go wash up and I'll have it on the table by the time you get down again."

She hurried away eagerly, a soft roseleaf flush on her cheeks like a girl, her eyes alight, a glad look of relief on her face. She really had been worried. She had been so worried that she had been praying about it.

So presently her tall son returned just as she was setting a steaming silver platter down before his plate.

"Mother!" he exclaimed. "Chicken! Are we celebrating something tonight? And I don't believe you've eaten a bite of it! Mother! And it's all of nine o'clock! Two legs, two wings, a whole breast," he leaned forward with the carving knife in his hand and pretended to count the members of the bird. "Why, Mother, even the neck and the back and the gizzard are all here. Now, Mother, that won't do! You'll get sick going without your food so long. You've got to stop doing this way."

She smiled.

"Oh, I had a cup of tea and a biscuit just to stay my stomach till you came. Besides, when you're anxious it's not so good to eat, you know."

"There you are, little Mother MacCarroll, what'n all am I going to have to do with you? And I can't help being late sometimes no matter how hard I try. Sometimes it's impossible even to telephone."

"Oh, I'll be all right," said the mother with a happy smile. "You always get home eventually and then we have such happy times! It's worth waiting for!"

"But not worrying for, Mother dear! I thought you had faith in your heavenly Father! Why can't you trust me in His care?"

"Well, I do!" laughed the mother. "I always trust you there. I was just bearing you up in prayer."

A tender look came over the young man's face.

"And where would I be, Mother, if you didn't do that?" he said with a smile like a benediction.

He bowed his head then reverently with a "Lord, we thank thee for each other, and for Thyself, and for this food which Thou hast furnished us tonight."

There was chicken with dumplings, light as feathers. How she managed it none could say unless she had an uncanny intuition just when to put them in, or some trick about not uncovering the steamer till they were ready to be taken out and eaten, but there they were, not a soggy one among them. And mashed potato too, not sulking as mashed potato knows how to do when it has to wait too long to be eaten. There was plenty of gravy, and little white onions creamed, and a quivering mound of currant jelly left over from last winter, with sugar cookies and coffee to top off. It was a supper fit for a king.

And when they had both been served and were seated enjoying everything Gordon said:

"Well, Mother, what's been going on at our estate today?"

It was a joke between them, when they took this tiny beautiful little cottage on the edge of the wide lawn, that the whole was their estate, and they spoke of the people at the "mansion" house as "their family." They hadn't met any of them, of course. The cottage was rented through an agent, and the new tenants had moved in without the family in the big house even knowing they were there until they chanced to notice a light in the windows one evening and remarked about it. So for some little time they did not know who were the inmates of the big house, and most assuredly the big house did not know them except by the general term of "tenants." All of which however did not hinder the tenants from being deeply interested to know who lived in the big beautiful house and to watch everyone who came and went with eager interest and a kind of possessiveness, as one would watch the scenery about a new home to become familiar with it and grow to love it. So the MacCarrolls watched and talked over their landlord's house, and felt as if they somehow had a landed right in them, and so Gordon asked his mother, "What's been going on at our estate today?"

"Well," said the mother smiling, "not much. The little lady took her customary walk as usual early in the day but she came back earlier than usual, and I couldn't help thinking she had a worried look. But maybe that was just my imagination. She didn't come out again all day, though I kept a watchful eye out. I hope it wasn't because she was sick that she didn't come. I thought maybe I'd see the Scotch woman that came down the night we moved in, but never a sight of her did I get. If the little lady isn't out tomorrow I'll maybe make an excuse to run up with a mould of jelly and enquire after her."

"Well, that would be friendly," smiled the son. "Oh, you'll get to know her yet I'm sure. No one can resist you when you once take a liking to anybody. And what did she look like this morning when she went by? Did she look pale that you should think she was ill?"

"Well, no," smiled the mother carrying out the little farce they played together to keep from being lonely in this strange land to which they had come, away from their many friends. "No, I wouldn't say pale. Perhaps just a little absorbed, as if she had something on her mind. But she was pretty and bright as ever. And she was wearing a little green frock I've never seen her wear before, a sort of knit affair that made her look like a part of the woods as she came out of them, a dryad, perhaps. It was very becoming, a mossy green, with a little green cap to match, and she carried a flower in her hand."

"A flower?" said the young man. "What sort of a flower?" He seemed unusually interested in his plate as he carefully cut a delicate bit of the breast of the chicken.

"It was a pink flower," said the mother. "I couldn't quite be sure, but it looked like a carnation. A pink carnation. She held it up to her lips as she walked along, smelling it probably, and the soft pinkness of it was like the delicate rose in her cheeks. No, I don't think she looked sick at all, only—it might be a good excuse to go up to the house and ask. But perhaps it's too soon yet to try and make acquaintance. Perhaps it's better to wait and see if she'll come here. Though maybe she wouldn't think of it. Maybe she'd think people in a cottage at the gate wouldn't be the kind she would want to know."

"Well, and how do we know that she's the kind we want to know?" smiled the son a bit haughtily. "If she would scorn people in a porter's lodge just because they lived in a cottage, we would rather not know her, wouldn't we? Perhaps you'd better bide a wee, Mother, and give her a chance to take the initiative. Personally I'd rather not know her and think she was lovely, than to get well acquainted and find out she was not. Wouldn't you?"

"Well," said the mother speculatively, "I'm not sure. Isn't that just two kinds of the same pride, after all?"

"Perhaps," said the son with a grin. "Do you want me to understand that you are calling *me* proud, too, little Mother?"

"If the shoe fits put it on," responded the mother quickly.

"Well, on the other hand, Mother, we're playing a great game, and I'd hate to do anything to spoil it, wouldn't you? At least until we get acquainted somewhere and have some real friends, we'd better not find out too much about the make-believe ones, had we?"

"Probably not," said the mother passing the second cup of coffee, "but all the same I hope she comes out to walk tomorrow. I'll not feel quite easy in my mind about her if she doesn't."

The son looked up with an engaging grin:

"Mother, if this game of ours is only giving you someone else to worry about," he said, with an undertone of real earnestness in his voice, "we'd better stop it right here and now and think up some other form of amusement."

The mother laughed.

"You silly boy. It's you who are always worrying about me. Eat your dinner and listen to the rest of my story. She had a young man caller tonight. He wasn't much to look at, too short and dumpy with a round red face. He came before it was really dark, and he brought a big box. It looked like a florist's box. And he had a fine big shiny car. I think perhaps he's up there yet. I haven't heard him drive out again. And then about a half-hour after he came, a florist's car drove in and out again. I think he left flowers too. He stayed about long enough.

She must be pretty popular. Two boxes of flowers in one evening, don't you think?"

"It would seem that way," said the son gravely. "But, Mother, Mother, I'm afraid you're getting to be an inveterate spy on your neighbors. You'll be telling me gossip next if I don't look out."

"Hark!" said Mrs. MacCarroll. "That must be his car now. He's staying a long time. I was at the window watching for you when he came. And it's almost eleven now. He must be some very special friend."

"Yes, probably," said Gordon MacCarroll grimly. "She'll be getting married on us next and then what'll we do for our romance? Come, Mother, it's high time I got you to bed. No, you sit still and I'll put these things away. You've done enough for today and it's my turn. If things keep on as well as they have today the prospect is I'll be able to get you a servant to look after the heavy work."

"Oh, Gordon," she said eagerly, "tell me about your day. How did your work go?"

He told her in detail all that he had been doing, and the bright prospects that seemed opening up before him in his chosen profession, and she listened as eagerly as any girl would have done, following his day step by step, watching his face as he talked. Her boy! Her precious, wonderful boy!

When they finally went upstairs, and before Gordon lit that light that Diana had seen from her window, he went and stood several minutes looking out on the grassy stretch between the cottage and the mansion, and then looking up at the starry sky speculatively.

"Of course," said he to himself, "I suppose I'm a fool." But whether it was about his business, or his mother, or what, he did not say, even to himself.

5

WHEN Diana awoke next morning the first thing her eyes looked upon was the crystal vase containing the three pink carnations. A sparkle came to her face as she remembered that it was a new day and there would be a possibility of another flower waiting for her. With eagerness she sat up in her bed and reached out for the flowers, drawing a deep breath of their fragrance. Then suddenly memory came on the breath of perfume and—*bang!* the joy went out of her heart and the great dark cloud loomed over her head again. Her father was getting married to Cousin Helen and they would be coming back tomorrow night! Cousin Helen was coming to stay *always!*

The sorrow settled down about her once more, beyond the power of the mysterious blossoms to cheer. She looked about her room and marvelled that the draperies could be so pleasant a color, and the sun could shine as it had in the past, when such sorrow was in the offing. And then she remembered several things she had planned last night to be done this morning, and she sprang up and began to dress. There was no time to be wasted. There were still many precious treasures to be put out of sight and packed carefully where they could not be injured. The menu must be made out for tomorrow night's dinner, things had to be ordered. Father must be pleased, whether Helen was pleased or not. But the worst of it was to remember that if Helen was pleased that was the thing just now that would most please Father! And oh, that must go on all through life! If life was really going on under such terrible conditions. It didn't seem as if it could.

The next two days seemed eons long to Diana, and yet she kept finding so many things she needed to put away or change that they grew frantically short as Wednesday evening drew nearer and she went about breathlessly making the house over to be ready for an enemy. Hour by hour she had continued to hope for another message from her father, but none came. Evidently he was not going to risk even another conversation with her over the telephone. And yet he must know she was suffering, was fairly frantic! How could he do a thing like this to her, without at least talking it over with her and trying to reconcile her to it? Not that she could ever have been really reconciled to it of course, but it would not have hurt so much if she could have felt that he was thinking a little about her in it all, that he had not just cast the thought of her his only child aside as if she didn't matter in the least. And every time she thought of him the hurt of his stern angry tones as he had talked over the wire went through her heart again with a wrench that was actual pain. Oh, now added to all the unfairnesses and indignities of the past here was this appalling loss staring her in the face. Helen was about to appropriate her father!

The roses and the gardenias occupied the big living room and wasted their sweetness alone. Not even

Maggie had time to go in and admire them. She, good woman, was intent on making the house speckless and spotless from cellar to attic before the new mistress should arrive. If this thing had to be she would leave no slightest flaw in her work. Not at first would that hussy have a chance to find fault with her anyway. Or, as she put it to herself, "The master shall have no cause to be ashamed of me, anyway."

The master was getting himself a new wife, and things might be so that she would be obliged to leave, but at least she would leave everything in good order.

When Diana came downstairs she found Maggie wiping off the windows in the living room.

"They were thot dirty!" she said frowning. "And I don't want the likes of her to be findin' fault right at once."

Diana winced at the thought, and stood staring around the room which looked bare and alien with so many familiar objects gone. Then suddenly as her glance went over the roses and gardenias she remembered the carnations. This was the time she had meant to go out and try to discover just when those carnations were dropped! She would go at once before she did anything else. Of course it might be that there were to be no more carnations, but at least she would go and see if one was there now. She would run no risk of its being picked up by anyone else. So she opened the front door and stepped out in spite of Maggie's admonition that her breakfast was already on the table.

"I'll be back in just a minute," she called, and sped away down the drive.

"Now whut can the bairn be after now?" queried Maggie of herself as she came to the window and watched Diana running swiftly as if she were going on some distinct errand with a destination.

She watched until the girl appeared in sight again and then discreetly withdrew behind a curtain until she reached the house. She was holding a flower in her hand, looking down at it with a lovely look in her face. Now where did that flower come from? Had she brought it down stairs with her? Maggie could distinctly see the flower. It was just like the others that were up in the girl's room. Where did those flowers come from? Had Diana bought them when she went on her walk yesterday? Or had some other admirer sent them? Maggie took distinct satisfaction in the flowers that had been given the girl last night. The only thing that troubled her was Diana's seeming indifference to them. Was she really as indifferent as she seemed? All those gorgeous roses in the living room, all those stately gardenias, and yet here she was putting a mere carnation to her lips as if she loved it? There seemed some mystery here that Maggie would have solved. However, she was industriously dusting when Diana came into the house. But her eyes were wide open, and she noticed that there was no flower in sight as the girl came in. Had she hidden it in her dress?

Later, when she went up to put Diana's room to rights she stood for a long time looking down at the crystal vase with its four pink carnations. Had her eyes deceived her? She was sure there had been but three there yesterday when she dusted. And Diana had run quickly upstairs before she came in to her breakfast.

On the whole Diana seemed more cheerful after that little run down through the grounds, and Maggie kept reverting to it all day long and turning it over in her mind.

Diana reverted to it also, wondering, feeling somehow comforted over the unknown friend who had manifested an interest in her just as trouble was coming her way. Of course, she told herself, those flowers might not have been meant for her at all. They might have been dropped for some utterly different reason, or just from a happening that had no reason about it at all, by someone who never saw her or even heard of her. But it comforted her to feel that they were meant for her, or even just sent from heaven now in her need. Nevertheless, silly as it was for her to make so much moment of them, it gave her a thrill to remember they were up in her room waiting for her while she worked at her unpleasant task about the house, her task of obliterating all traces of her beloved mother from the home.

Down at the stone cottage Mrs. MacCarroll watched for her in vain, and when her son came home that night she had little news of the neighborhood to tell him.

"The little lady didn't take a walk today at all," she told him over the remains of yesterday's chicken appearing now in the form of a delicate chicken pie. "I thought I spied her coming out as usual from her front door. I was upstairs making your bed and I saw her come out the door, this time without a hat, and the sun shining on her bonnie hair till it looked golden. She was walking very fast, almost running I thought, and I stopped and watched her run, she is so graceful. I watched her till she disappeared behind the group of trees, and then I went into my room thinking to see her as she came out by the gate into the street. But she didn't come out, though I watched for some time. She must have gone back another way perhaps, or have run very fast, for when I went to the back to look out she was gone. But I sighted a bluebird's nest in the tree just below your window. Did you know it was there? There are three dear little eggs in it, and the mother bird was sitting on the edge of the nest with ravellings of white in her bill."

"Oh," said Gordon, "so we have even nearer neighbors to watch now? That is good. You'll not be able to call on them perhaps but I'll warrant you'll be leaving more ravellings on the window sill for that nest. You just can't let your neighbors alone, can you, Mother?"

So the two joked away the supper hour trying to forget that there was an empty place at the table where the husband and father had sat in the old home, that would never again be filled by him on this earth. Trying to make cheer for each other, while the one went out to struggle with the world and wrest a living from it, and a prospect for the future, and the other kept the home and marked time till in the plan of God the day of reunion should come.

The day slowly wore itself away in heartbreaking nothings and Diana, just before sunset, came to stand by her own front window and look out at the long slant shadows on the lawn.

The sun was flashing silver signals of good night to the world on the upper windows of the stone cottage where she had seen the light the night before. The panes of glass looked like molten metal on fire. The light flashed through the trees sharply and quivered into flames again. She felt a poignant pleasure in the brilliancy of sunset, and in the dear familiar scene, a pleasure akin to pain it was so sharp. All this scene that was so familiar, so dear, would it be hers very much longer? Or would Helen steal this too if she knew it was precious to her?

She turned and bent her head to the carnations as she was falling into the habit of doing every time she passed them. These too, if they continued to come, Helen would somehow discover and manage to appropriate, or to turn into ridicule. She gathered them to her face and laid her lips among their coolness, her lips that quivered with the sorrow of what was about to come. For this day too had passed without any further sign from her father. And now, if he had carried out his purpose, he and

Helen were undoubtedly married. How the thought wrenched her heart! She turned away suddenly to stop the tears. She dared not weep any more. She could not face tomorrow in a storm of tears. She must be adamant. She must not let Helen see how keenly she felt this whole thing. Helen would gloat over it anyway. Helen had an uncanny way of finding out how people felt and pressing the thorn into the lacerated heart till it became unbearable.

She must not let them see her heart. There would be nobody to understand and comfort but Maggie, and if she let poor Maggie understand how she was suffering, Maggie would show her own indignation, and Helen would send her out of the house in short order. Perhaps she would anyway. Then there would be nobody to understand. For there was no hope that her father would ever understand again, not with Helen as his wife. Not as long as Helen chose to keep him blinded to her true character.

She sat down in the rosy twilight that was filling the room and tried to plan how she was to conduct herself, how to steel herself against the inevitable animosity that she would have to meet from the new mistress of the house, but in spite of herself she found no way to plan ahead.

What she really wanted to do of course was to run away before they arrived. The nearer she came to their arrival the more her heart cried out for freedom to go. But something fine in her would not let her do it. She must stand by her father even though he had not been fair to her.

The more she considered his action the more the fact stood out that the sharpest hurt of the whole matter, outside of the stunning fact itself, was that her father had made the thing inevitable before he had even intimated to her that such a change was possible. In a matter that so deeply affected her own life and happiness she felt she had a right to have been informed at least, if not consulted, before everything was determined. In a way it had lowered her father in her eyes, though she struggled against such a thought, that he had not had the courage to talk it over with her. He had thrust it upon her without the courtesy of allowing her to put her own case before him. It was not fair to her, and sometime surely he would know it, and be ashamed. Just now he was angry, and if she should run away he would only think that she was angry, and she was not. She was only appalled and hurt. More deeply hurt than she had ever been before in her life. Even her mother's death had not given her a hurt like this. It was as if all that her father had ever been to her had been erased, wiped out of her life and love. As if he had never been what she had thought she loved.

Diana was young and inexperienced of course. She forgot that human nature is never perfect. She had idolized her father, and now he had done something which showed a weakness in him. She did not know that a clever woman can influence a wonderful man to do a foolish thing, under the guise of righteousness. She had no notion that Helen had subtly worked on her prey to make him believe that what they were doing was largely for the good of sweet little motherless Diana, and that she meant to devote her life to making her happy so that when Diana went away by and by to the home of some marvelous husband she would carry a choice memory of her home. It was well perhaps that she did not know all that that wily serpent of a Helen had said on different occasions to her troubled bridegroom, until she had brought him to see Diana, and life, and even his own actions, in a new light. It was not that he had lost his love for his precious daughter, nor that another love had superseded it. It was only that his horizon and his love had widened to take in Helen that they all might be happy together. That was what the father was thinking, and he was amazed and hurt that his child could not see how beautifully it was all going to work out for everybody.

But Diana had seen only his anger, and she was hurt to the quick. Yet her conscience would not let her go away before he came. Not yet. She would stay and show him that she had done her best—if that were possible. Her best with Helen present had always been her worst in spite of her best efforts. But anyhow she must stay and face the battle at least until she was routed.

So she went down the stairs to satisfy Maggie and pretend to eat something, and then endure another night before the dawning of her evil day.

That night she drowned her pillow in tears, and when she was roused by the telephone to give Bobby Watkins a decided answer to his invitation for Wednesday evening, her voice was shaky with emotion.

"I'm sorry, Bobby. I wish I could go," she said with an honest ring to her voice. If only things were not as they were how gladly would she go anywhere with Bobby for an evening, if that could have brought back the happy past wherein she and her father lived in a charmed world of their own.

Wednesday morning dawned with a cruelly bright sun. It hurt Diana as she opened her eyes and took in the glory of the morning.

The first thought that met her waking soul was that her father was married. He had taken someone in her mother's place! It hit her in the heart, and between the eyes, as a blow might have done. But she winked back the tears that rushed ready for a deluge and shut her lips tightly. She just must not give way today at all or she could not go through the ordeal tonight.

She turned her eyes resolutely toward the carnations and drew a deep breath. Then the wonder came, would there be another flower this morning? How early were they put there? She would run out now, right away, and see. Perhaps she could catch the fairy at her work. She just must think of pleasant things until tonight was over or she would die. She felt as if she were bleeding in her heart. Controlled tears turned inward and drained the life, but she must not weep today.

She sprang from her bed, and dressing hastily, slipped out of the house before Maggie knew she was awake.

The dew was on the turf by the little path that skirted the edge of the driveway, and it caught the morning light and hung bright jewels on each particular blade of grass.

Diana could not but feel the beauty of the day as she hurried down the road, despite her heavy heart. It was as if she were going into the secret places of the morning, to the treasury of the world's jewels, where a diamond, or an amethyst, or a ruby flashed out a greeting to her as she passed, and sapphires nodded blue sparkles to the fire of opals.

Just this side of the group of trees that hid the cottage from view she thought she heard a stirring, and she walked softly, shyly, hesitating an instant. Was she coming upon the secret of her mysterious flowers and did she want to be disillusioned? Did she want to discover how they came there, if perchance the donor was passing now?

On the other hand perhaps the flowers were meant for someone else who was missing them because she had come in before and taken them. If she went on now would there be a clue that would destroy this bit of romance, the only hint of real romance that had so far come into her life?

Only an instant she hesitated, then her common sense asserted itself and she went forward. If there were so sensible an explanation of all this she would better know it now and get this nonsense out of her head. With all this trouble she was probably making too much of just a few plain carnations.

So she went on, rounding the group of shrubs that hid the place where she usually found the flowers. Then she heard the sound of a door closing back of the cottage. Was that a step? Probably just someone in the cottage shed, that opened this way.

She paused and her eyes sought the grass by the gravel path. Yes, there it lay, close by the walk, its face looking up from the grass. It was in the shadow but there was a flash of jewels all about in the dew. And—were those footprints in the dewy grass? They trailed away to a bare place around the roots of a tree, and then disappeared in a series of disconnected spots irregularly leading toward the cottage. Was it conceivable that the flowers came from the cottage? But of course not. There was only an old lady living there with her boy, Maggie had said. No young boy would go dropping flowers around for sentiment's sake, and certainly his mother wouldn't be likely to do it. Besides, those footprints were probably made by a dog, not a human, and anyway they weren't near enough to the flower to count, unless someone stood at a distance and threw the flower there.

She stood for a moment measuring the distance with her eye, calculating how it could be done. Then she stopped, picked up the flower and sped back to the house.

All day as she was working, doing last things, filled with anguish as she was, there still was an undertone of exultation, that the flower had been there again. It seemed to be the one bright thread in the dark fabric of her life. She did not want to think about it too carefully lest sane reasoning might take it away from her. She wanted to hold on to this one little cheerful thing while she was going through these blackest hours that had ever yet come her way.

They set the dinner table as soon as Diana had swallowed the few mouthfuls that made up her brief lunch. Maggie wisely saw that the best thing she could do for her young mistress was to keep her busy, and this matter of the evening meal would be the hardest of the day. It was best to get it over with since it was inevitable, so she asked in an innocent tone:

"Will ye be wantin' the best china the night?" and Diana turned a startled look on her.

"Oh, not grandmother's china!" she exclaimed in a pained voice. "Helen made fun of it once, said it looked as if it came out of the ark. Besides, Mother always said that was to be mine. Grandmother's wedding china, and not a piece broken!"

"Ye'll want ta be packin' it up then," warned Maggie with a grim look on her face.

"I ought to get a professional packer for that," said the girl with a troubled look at the clock. "I wonder if there would be time to get it done today. It will be no use to do it after she comes. She'll manage to break it or sell it or something if she knows I love it."

"No need fer a packer," said Maggie briskly. "Many's the set of china I've packed in my day and never a wee bit chipped. You bring me all the old newspapers from up the stairs, an' I'll have it out of the way in the whisk of a lamb's tail. There's a nice clean barrel or two down the cellar that will be just right, and when it's away I'll nail the head up and whisk it off in a dark corner an' she'll never know it's there."

"Oh, Maggie, you're such a comfort!" said Diana struggling with her feelings. "But—I'm wondering— you don't suppose Father will notice that we haven't it on the table, do you? We always used it on very special occasions, you know. He might think I was insulting her by using the every day dishes."

"He said fer ye to put away yer ain mither's things that might mind his new wife of her, didn't he? Well, then he can't blame ye. But anyway, he'll not notice. He'll have enough on his mind without takin' on the dishes also. Come, away with ye and bring the newspapers. We'd best get the dishes out of the way first."

So Diana got the newspapers and then came back to help Maggie take the dishes down from their top shelf and carry them all down cellar. Maggie wiped off the cupboard shelves, put fresh papers on them and arranged other dishes of which there were many not in daily use so that the grandmother's set was not missed. Then they went down cellar and Diana wrapped cups and plates under Maggie's direction, and in an incredibly short space of time the barrel was filled and rolled off into a dark corner and they came up to set the table.

"Ye'll not be wantin' flooers for a centre piece?" asked Maggie.

"No!" said Diana in a bleak voice. "No flowers!"

"Ye could take out a few roses from the livin' room an' niver be missed," she suggested speculatively, "but I wudn't ef I was you."

"No," said Diana crisply, "no flowers at all. This isn't a festive occasion. I don't feel it right to make it so. It wouldn't be appreciated if I did. Let the flowers stay where they are."

"Yer right," said the old servant. "Ye're not called

upon to do more than yer feyther suggested. She's not one would ever miss the blossoms, not ef she didn't get them herself."

So the table was set with a fine new tablecloth and napkins that had never yet been monogrammed, set with formal precision and care, but with no festive touches, and Diana hesitated a long time whether to set a plate for herself. Would it not be better taste to let them eat by themselves this first time? It would be much pleasanter for her not to have to be present.

But Maggie shook her head.

"It's yer right ta be at yer feyther's table, an' I'm sure he would consider it an unnecessary affront. He'll find oot soon enough what a bitter mistake he's made without yer hastenin' it."

So Diana let the place stay and went away to her room to face this new thought about the dinner. How was she going to eat dinner under the circumstances? The food would choke her. And if she didn't eat, her father would be annoyed and speak of it and Helen would laugh with that look of a naughty little devil in her eye. If she only had someone to advise her and help her through this hard time! For an instant she had a wild thought of asking Bobby Watkins to come to dinner, and then immediately she knew that would not do. For, in addition to the fact that he hated Helen and considered her very ill-bred, and that Helen always made fun of him to his face, there was the fear that both her father and Helen would of course think that Bobby had become something more to her than just a friend, and Diana realized that that would be most repulsive to her. It would be equivalent to announcing that she was engaged to him! Inviting him that way in an intimate family party the first night her father brought his new wife home. And of course she didn't want them to think any such thing as that. Bobby would take such significance out of it also. No, she couldn't invite Bobby, even if she wanted him, and she didn't.

The afternoon went all too swiftly at the last for the numberless little things that were to be done. Diana felt as if she had lived through centuries since she had received that awful letter from her father. It seemed as if she had passed through every phase of human feeling that there was. And at last she stood by the window in the living room looking out down the drive, just as she had done that morning when the letter came. But there was no crystal vase with carnations by her side. She had hidden it in her closet. Helen should not get a sight of the carnations not if she had to burn them up. Her romance would turn into ashes if once Helen found out about it.

Diana was dressed plainly in a slim black dress with nothing to brighten it. She would not give the impression of having dressed up. She had knelt down beside her bed before she left her room and prayed to God that He would help her to behave in a right way in this new and trying situation, but it had not done her much good. She had never learned to pray in anything but a formal way, and she had no heart in her prayer now, but it seemed that she needed some help somewhere lest she overstep the bounds of justice in the present part she had to play in the tragedy that her life had become. She had no desire to do anything which would be unjust to either her father or Helen, but her love for her father and her indignation for what he had done, and her hatred for Helen's ways were so mixed up in her frantic young mind that she wasn't able to discern just where was the borderline between right and wrong, so she went to God, feeling that if it were something He really cared about He might in some mysterious way help her. That was all she knew of God.

So Diana stood in her slim little black frock with great dark circles under her eyes and weary lines around her young lips, and watched down the driveway for her father and her new mother to come.

It was growing dark and there were cheery little lights twinkling from the cottage through the trees. She watched them enviously. It wasn't likely that the cottage housed any such tragedy as had come to her. A mansion didn't bring happiness. How glad she had been that they had been able to keep their own big house that had been home so many dear years. But how gladly would she tonight surrender the big house and go and live in the little cottage by the gate, just she and her father together, if only they might have each other and not Helen!

And then, just as she felt tears smarting into her eyes again in spite of all her best efforts, another light flashed out from the group of trees and came rapidly on around the curve of the drive. A taxi! They had come, and now she must meet them! A panic seized upon her and she longed to flee to her room, lock her door, and refuse to come down, but she stood her ground and the taxi came on, swept up in front of the door and stopped. The new mistress had arrived!

6

GORDON MacCarroll brought home a little cheap car that night and housed it in the speck of a garage that used to be a barn. There wasn't much room for anything else in the building when the little car got in, but Gordon's mother came out to admire the shabby little car and to beam upon her son with pleasure when he told her what a bargain he had made in buying it.

"There are just one or two things that need fixing up and I know how to fix them," he said gleefully. "The fellow that sold it is going abroad and he has no use for it any more. He just got his orders to go and he hadn't much time to sell, so he was willing to let it go at a bargain. And now, Mother, I shan't have to be dependent on trains and buses any longer."

"Yes, but you'll be very careful, my son," said the mother eyeing the car dubiously. "I've always felt afraid of them. Of course I know you are a careful driver, but it's other people I'm afraid of."

"Well, Mother, I guess we can trust that to God, can't we? Aren't we as safe one place as another if we're following His guidance?"

"Yes, of course," said his mother timorously, and then more firmly, "Yes *of course!*"

He laughed and drew her arm through his.

"Now come in. I'm hungry as a bear, and I want to tell you the result of my day and what I'm to do tomorrow. I've got a chance at a big proposition if I can make good. I've got to start early in the morning however in order to see my man before he leaves for a week's absence. I wish I could take you with me for it's going to be a beautiful drive and I know you would enjoy it, but I can't tell how long I'll be, and I may have to go farther and be very late getting back, so I guess I won't risk it this first time. But pretty soon now we can have some good long rides together after I get this buggy tried out. There comes a taxi. They must be having guests at the great house."

"It'll maybe be the master returning," said the mother looking toward the taxi as it came on. "The Scotch woman said he was away on business."

"Then he's brought someone home with him," said Gordon turning to look at the car as it sped by. "There's a lady with him."

"Some relative, probably. I haven't seen any of them today. They must have been getting ready for company."

They entered the immaculate little kitchen with its pleasant odor of some sweet pastry baking, mingled with cinnamon and cooking apples.

"A baked apple dumpling, Mother, am I right?" said Gordon eagerly. "Nothing could be better. I hope you made plenty of gravy?"

"Yes, there's plenty of sauce," laughed his mother, and stooped to take out the fragrant steaming dish. "And I've made a wee salad out of some bits of chicken I saved, and there are roast potatoes. Here's the fork. Take them out, and don't forget to crack them and let out the steam."

A moment more and they were seated at their pleasant supper table, their heads bent in thanksgiving. While up at the great house the taxi had deposited its travelers and presently went speeding by on its way back to the station.

Diana had turned from the window when she saw them get out of the car, and she stood there frozenly awaiting them. She had a strong impression now that she should go into the hall and meet them, say something, do something appropriate, but somehow she had lost the power to move. It was as if she had suddenly become petrified. The power of speech seemed to have gone too, for when she heard her father's voice saying in vexed tones "Well, I wonder where she is," the cry with which her heart wanted to greet him died in her throat. He seemed a stranger, an alien, and not her father whom she loved so dearly.

Then a light laugh with a sneer in the tail of it like the venom of a serpent stung her with the old deadly hatred and she swayed and would have fallen had she not reached her hands back and clutched the window sill with her cold frightened fingers.

A step and they were in the doorway scanning the room, her father's eyes upon her where she stood. Her face was white with anguish, her eyes dark and tortured, her sensitive lips trembling.

He looked at her questioningly, his glance changing into sternness. Then his voice, stern and displeased, spoke: "Well? Diana, is that the way you welcome us?"

With a cry like a hurt thing now Diana sprang forward, her eyes on her father, threw her arms about his neck, drew his face down and kissed him hungrily, then buried her face on his shoulder and burst into tears, as she clung helplessly to him.

His arm stealing softly, almost gently about her, in the

old familiar way upheld her for the moment and steadied her quivering shoulders that shook with her sobs.

Then that light mocking laugh fell on her senses again and the pain stung back into her heart.

"Oh, my word! Diana," trilled the bride in a penetrating voice that found her senses through her sobs, "are you still such a child that you have to go into hysterics? A great big girl like you to be acting like that! I should think you'd be ashamed."

The comforting arm that had held her close for an instant in such a reassuring clasp, and the caressing hand that had been laid on her sorrowful young head, suddenly ceased their tender contact, and her father put her from him as one would a naughty child.

"For heaven's sake, Diana, be a woman, can't you?" he said in low vexed tones that showed plainly that he was displeased that she should be laying herself open to criticism right at the start.

His words stung her into silence. She felt shamed and sick that she should have given way. She drew her quivering breath in and realized that she was alone against these two and she need no more expect her father to be on her side in anything. It had come just as she had foreseen it would, only she hadn't thought it would come so soon.

She lifted her head and stepped back, brushing the tears away with her hand and lifting a proud young chin that no longer quivered.

"I'm sorry!" she said coldly, and gave her father a look as alien as his own. Then, with sudden self-control she added, as if they were stranger-guests, "Dinner is ready to serve whenever you wish it. Will you go upstairs first?"

"No!" said Helen decidedly. "We'll eat at once. I'm starved. We'll go upstairs after dinner. I want to give a few directions before we leave. We're not staying here tonight you know. Come!"

Diana gave her a bleak glance, and they went out to the dining room, Helen leading the way as if she had always done so. She was still wearing her hat and she drew her gloves off as she went.

Diana watched her take the mistress' place at the table as a matter of course, and reaching out change the position of several dishes as if they offended her. Then she gave a quick glance at the table as a whole and a mocking smile came on her lips.

"I'm glad you didn't put on those hideous old dishes that you always considered the company set. I've always secretly wished to take those out and smash them, and now I think that will be one of the first things I'll do."

She laughed as she said it, flashing her little white teeth between her red, red lips, and twinkling her eyes at her husband amusedly in the way she had of saying outrageous things and making them pass for a joke before those whom she wanted to deceive.

Mr. Disston answered her look with a grave worried smile. It was evident he saw nothing in her words but pleasantry. But Maggie, coming in at that moment with her tray, heard and fully understood, and the red flamed into her cheeks, and her blue eyes with the wet lashes of recently shed tears, angry tears, flashed fire, as much as blue kindly eyes could flash. But she shut her thin lips and went about her serving.

Diana had slipped into the third seat and was trying beneath the tablecloth to keep her trembling hands still, and her lips from quivering. She found her teeth suddenly inclined to chatter and she had to hold herself tense to keep from trembling like a leaf.

Helen, after the first taste of her fruit appetizer, gave her attention to her new stepdaughter.

"For heaven's sake, Diana, you haven't gone ascetic on us have you?" she asked flippantly. "Why such sombre garb? I don't object to black of course. It's smart just now, but that isn't smart that you have on. It's just a dud. It isn't your type and not a bit becoming. I'll have to get at you and reconstruct your wardrobe I see. We can't have you around looking like that."

Her father looked up and surveyed her critically.

"Yes," he said, "Diana, it does seem as if you might have dressed up a little more festively on an occasion like this." He gave her a cold look that was meant to show her how disappointed he was in her, and Diana suddenly choked, and for an instant was on the point of fleeing to her own room.

"Don't speak to her, Stephen, she's got the jitters," laughed the new mother in an amused tone. "Let her alone till she gets her bearings. Can't you see she's all upset, just as I told you she'd be? Let's talk about something else. What time did you say that train to the shore goes? I want plenty of time to give Diana my directions after dinner."

Diana regained a semblance of calm and went on pretending to eat and the meal dragged its slow progress to the end, the conversation a mere dialogue about trifles between her father and the new wife. Diana sat there listening and realizing more and more how utterly out of things she was intended to be from now on, hardening her heart to the thought, struggling to look as if she did not mind. Perhaps it was the knowledge that she was affording so much wicked amusement to her new step-mother that made it so much harder to bear even than she had expected.

Diana felt as if she were a long way off looking at herself, analyzing her own feelings, reasoning out things, trying to look dispassionately at the whole situation and create a philosophy about it that would make her able to live in spite of it all. She fixed her eyes on the olive dish and tried to say to herself what a beautiful dish it was, how well it set off the dark green of the olives, what handsome olives they were, anything just to keep her mind away from what was happening, and get her through the ordeal until they left. Oh, she was glad, glad, they were going away that night. She was tired, so tired with emotion and hard work that she could hardly hold her head up. She wanted to close her eyes, to lie down and rest from the unshed tears that hurt her so much more than if they had been shed. She wanted to get rested enough to think out what had happened to her and try to get where she could do the right thing. That was what she had prayed for, that she might do the right thing. Where was God that He had not answered her prayer?

Well, perhaps such prayers as hers had no right to be answered. Probably God hadn't time for little personal troubles.

She tried so hard to sit up and look pleasant, but only succeeded in being dispassionate. Her hurt eyes looked out upon the two, the one who was so dear and the one who was not, with torture in them, and met no comforting glance to help her back into a normal attitude, and when they rose to leave the table her father said in low displeased tones:

"I certainly am disappointed in you, Diana!"

It needed only that word to make Diana feel that life and happiness for her had come to an end, and the only thing she could possibly hope to do was to get creditably through the rest of the evening and then crawl into a hole somewhere and die. She felt as if she had received her death blow from her father's attitude and words.

"Now, we're going upstairs!" said Helen. "Come, Diana, I want to get this over and get off!"

Diana wanted to get it over too, so she followed silently up the stairs after the bride, who tripped up lightly, gaily, as if she were enjoying herself.

"No, not in there!" she said sharply, as Diana swung the door of her father's room open and switched on the light. "I never liked that room. I'm going to take the room across the hall when I come back."

"Oh, but that is my room," said Diana quietly.

"I know," said Helen amusedly, "I have a perfectly good memory. But it's going to be my room now. I've got it all arranged. Your father and I talked it over and we decided to give you an apartment on the third floor. Then we can take this whole floor ourselves, and you can feel more independent. We're doing the whole house over soon anyway. And then you can arrange the third floor as you like, and have a place to receive your friends and entertain as much as you like without inter-fering with us."

"I wouldn't care for that, Helen," said Diana with sudden spirit. "I'd rather keep my own room. Mother had it done over for me just before she died and I feel more at home there than anywhere else."

"Oh, indeed!" laughed Helen amiably. "Well, you'll have to get used to feeling at home somewhere else then, for that's the room I'm going to have. In fact I'm using the whole second floor myself, so you may as well understand it. I shall have lots of guests and shall need every inch of space, so that's that. Take it or leave it as you like, but you rate the third floor."

Helen stepped across the hall and swung Diana's door open, glancing about the lovely room with satisfaction.

"You can leave this furniture and hangings just as they are. They're not so bad! I may use them entire for a guest room. It's rather a good color scheme. And you can take the furniture from your father's room up to the third floor for yourself. I never did care for it and I suppose you'll like it for its association!" She gave another mocking smile, and turned back to the other room. "That was what I wanted to tell you. You're to get a man and have everything from here moved to the third story. You can arrange it as you like of course. It'll be your domain for awhile. You'll be getting married soon yourself I suppose, but until then you can fix that floor to suit yourself."

Diana stood and stared at her, a frozen look upon her face, utterly appalled at the attitude the new mistress was daring to take toward her on this the very first night in the house. It seemed as if some enemy had her by the throat. She could not think of any reply that would be adequate. Her lips seemed to be sealed. Even if she knew what to say she felt that no sound would come from her. It was as if her vocal chords were paralyzed, as if her whole being were turning to stone. Her feelings were beyond mere indignation. This thing that was being said to her was incredible. Surely her father would interfere. And yet, and yet, so well she knew this woman who had been set over her that she felt her strength draining from the tips of her fingers. She felt as if in a moment more she would lose her power to stand erect and would fall over on her face, stiff and rigid like a statue. Then, suddenly, because she must do something she fell to laughing, a wild hysterical little giggle, ending in a real paroxysm of laughter.

Helen gave her a startled stare, then took hold of her arm and gave her a fierce smart shake until Diana's teeth chattered.

"Stop that!" said Helen. "You needn't think you can get your father's sympathy by any such carryings on as that. He'll see through that ruse, and you can't get your way by carrying on, no matter how many hysterics you have. And another thing. It's time you stopped kissing your father like a little girl! It's ridiculous! You! A great big girl! Besides, I don't like it!"

Diana yielded herself to the shaking, relaxing into a hall chair, the laughter ceasing as suddenly as it had begun. She lifted her hands and pressed them to her quivering lips. The tears were very near the surface and she wanted to fend them off. She must not cry before Helen. That would please her more than anything else. She must not let her father hear her. There must be a way to behave that would give dignity to this humbling occasion.

Helen was watching her sharply.

"Now, if you are sane again," she said keeping a suspicious glance on her, "I'll tell you the rest. We're going down to the shore tonight and I expect these changes to be all made by the time I come back. I want you to oversee them, and you'd better call up a man to move things. He ought to come early in the morning. It ought not to take long. I've had my own things sent on. They may get here tomorrow by van and they should be put right in the rooms, to save moving twice. I've marked everything, which go in the east room and which in the west. Of course I wasn't counting on the furniture in your room being so good, but you might have what I've marked for your room put in the middle guest room. And the furniture in there you might sell to a second hand man, unless there's something you want to save. I always hated that in the days when I visited here and had to sleep in that room. It gave me the horrors, so I'd like it to be disposed of out of my sight by the time I get back. Now, do you understand? You sit there like a sphinx and don't say a word! Have you heard anything I've said, or haven't you?"

Diana summoned the stiff muscles of her throat to utter three words: "I have heard," and sat quietly watching her tormentor.

"Well, see that you carry out my orders then," said Helen flinging up her chin imperiously. "I want this all done, and your things entirely out of the way by the time I get back! Now, do you understand?"

"I understand!" said Diana again gravely, watching Helen with a steady gaze. She was mistress of herself now, and her strength was coming back to her again.

"Well, then see that you attend to everything." Helen tossed her head and laughed lightly, her laughter evidently intended to reach the hall below where Diana could hear her father entering from the front door. Helen trilled another light laugh and ran briskly down the stairs. But before she reached the last step Diana heard her pause a moment and then turn and run back up again.

"Diana," she challenged, "were those flowers down in the living room sent to me, or did you buy them?"

"They were sent to *me* last night," answered Diana still in that steady grave tone.

"Oh, really?" Helen's voice expressed mingled incredulity and envy.

"You can have them if you like," went on Diana in a voice from which all expression seemed to have been extracted, "I don't care anything about them."

"Oh, *really?*" said Helen again, this time with a sting in her voice. "You think I would care for your cast-off flowers? No thank you, I can get plenty of my own. And by the way, better take yours upstairs after this so there won't be any mistake."

Diana sat still and let the disagreeable words uttered in

a silvery voice for the benefit of the listener in the lower hall, roll away from her. Her whole sensitive being quivered at their impact, but she did not reply.

Then, just as the new lady of the house turned to go downstairs again, a shadow loomed below her and Maggie appeared, her countenance like a thunder cloud.

"Is Miss Diana up the stair?" she demanded as haughtily as if she were the mistress and the other the maid.

"I believe she is," said the new Mrs. Disston coldly. "What do you want?"

"There's a young gentleman down the stair to see her!" announced the Scotch woman.

"Oh!" said Mrs. Disston with a note of curiosity in her voice. "Well, go up and tell her." Then lightly as a feather she tripped downstairs and peered into the big living room where Bobby Watkins sat impatiently on the edge of a chair awaiting Diana.

He rose eagerly as Mrs. Disston parted the portieres and faced him, and then stepped back with an exclamation of dismay.

"Oh, it's *you,* is it?" she said and backed away from him rudely without further words.

Bobby flushed angrily and stepped out into the hall after her, but Mrs. Disston was already halfway up the stairs again.

"Diana!" she called in a clear sweet voice that was quite audible both upstairs and down in the living room, "it's the fat one, dear. Don't keep him waiting, he's already quite impatient."

By which Diana knew that her father must have stepped outside again, for Helen would never have spoken so before him.

The girl's pale face flushed angrily and she felt a passing pity for Bobby, therefore she did not wait to smooth her hair nor dash cold water in her face to take away the stricken look. She arose and hurried downstairs with a set look upon her lips and a light of battle in her eyes. She would not heed the annoyances that were meant for herself, but in so far as she could she would try to make up to Bobby for the rudeness that had been dealt out to him. Oh, if her father knew what had happened it would open his eyes. But alas, it was too late! Poor Father when he should finally find out what sort of woman he had married!

"How did she get here again?" asked Bobby wrathfully, as Diana hurried into the room a trifle breathless.

"Sh!" she said under her breath.

"Why should I hush? She didn't hesitate to shout her opinion of me all over the house. She's a pest! Why does your father let her come here?"

"Don't, please!" said Diana hurriedly. "You—I'll have to explain. Come over to the other end of the room where we can't be overheard."

"No!" said Bobby authoritatively. "Come outside! She'd be snooping round the corner!"

"Oh, Bobby, please—!" Diana begged. "You mustn't! You don't understand!"

"No! I'm afraid I don't understand!" said Bobby arrogantly. "Even if she is your guest that doesn't give her the right to be protected in her insolence. Come on outside!" and Bobby drew Diana out the front door and down the drive.

"I've left my car out in the street," he said as he walked her away by the sheer force of his will. "We'll get in the car and talk. I didn't bring it up the drive because I wanted to find out how the land lay before I was announced to your father, if he was here. A car in the driveway always announces one's presence so quickly."

"No, Bobby," Diana stopped on the path and tried to draw her arm away, but he held her fast.

"But I can't go out to your car," she said. "I have to be here now. Father has just come home and he's going away again. I can only stay a minute to explain to you and then I must go in. Let go of my arm, please, you are hurting me."

"Well, then, stop trying to pull away!" ordered Bobby wrathfully. "I've stood your putting me off again and again, but I'm not going to stand your having to go in to that woman when I've come to call. And besides, I've got something to tell you!"

"But you must listen to me, first, Bobby!"

Diana's tone was quiet and collected. She turned and walked by his side, but drew her arm away from his.

"You've got to know that Helen has a right to stay at our house now. She is my father's wife!"

Diana felt as she said it that she was talking in a dream. It couldn't be true that it had really happened and she was making it known to the world! It wrenched her heart to think it and she was not half listening to Bobby. He had stopped short in the path and was staring at her.

"Diana! You don't mean that your father has been such a fool! You're trying to put something over on me."

"It's true, Bobby," said Diana sadly, "and I wish you wouldn't talk about it. It's hard enough to bear without hearing—what you think about it."

"But Diana, it can't be possible that your father would do a thing like that to you."

"Please don't!" said Diana wearily. "He thought he was doing the best for me. He really did. I'm sure he thought so!"

"He couldn't!" said Bobby righteously. "He simply couldn't!"

Diana drew away shrinking from his words as if they had been blows.

"I must go back, Bobby. I really must. My father will want me."

"Let him want awhile!" shouted Bobby arrogantly. "You come on down to that group of trees. I've got to talk to you. Let's get out of sight of the house. I've something to say and I don't want to say it before the whole world"

"Well, for only just a minute," yielded Diana hesitantly.

He drew her swiftly along and they were soon within the shelter of the thick growth of trees that hid the stone cottage from the driveway. Diana realized as they halted that she was standing almost directly in the spot from which she had picked up the carnation that morning. She glanced down and there a few feet from where she stood a white something caught her eye, a delicate flower face looking up to her! Was she seeing things?

She passed her hand over her weary eyes to brush imagination away, and looked again. Yes, there it really was, or seemed to be! Only a frail moonbeam or two penetrated the darkness, but that was certainly a flower! Could she be mistaken? Perhaps it was only a stray bit of paper. What a very fool she was! Always imagining another flower. Silly! It wasn't time for a flower to be there yet. They must have been always placed in the early morning else they would not look so fresh. And she had already had one today. It was only paper of course. But after Bobby was gone she would come back by herself and see! She certainly would!

"You are not listening to me!" charged Bobby savagely. "I am asking you to marry me. To go away with me now and get married, and then I can take you away from that woman! Your father is no longer to be considered. He has spoiled your home, and now I am asking you to go away with me, tonight, at once! You do not need to go back for anything. I can buy you a hat and whatever else you need. Let them wonder where you are! Let them search for you if they want you. Telephone and tell them they have driven you away!"

Appalled at his torrent of words Diana drew away.

"Oh, don't, Bobby! I am so tired and troubled. I can't think now. I must get rested. I couldn't go away!"

"That's silly, Diana. There'll be plenty of time to rest after we're married. We can run right down to the rectory and get it over with. I'll attend to the license. I've got a friend—! I can fix that all up afterward. Then I'll take you to a hotel in the city and you can rest all you want to, and in the morning we'll go off on a honeymoon!"

He reached out and caught her two hands and drew her close to him, folding his cushiony arms about her, his hot breath was upon her face, and his thick moist lips suddenly pressed possessively upon hers, as if he would draw her very soul forth from her body in a kiss that suddenly became to her repulsive, unclean. His eyes looking into hers in the moonlight had the selfish beastly look of a cannibal about to sate his cruel desire for human blood.

Diana shrank back in horror from the touch of his lips, but the lips followed her. She struggled and gasped and uttered a half stifled scream. Her arms were pinioned on his breast, held in a vise-like grasp of one fat hand, and the other hand was back of her head holding her lips to his as if he could not get enough. Terror and loathing filled her soul as she tried to get her hands free.

"I love you, Diana! I love you!" The hot words were breathed fiercely.

Diana managed to turn her face to the side for an instant.

"I hate you!" she gasped! "I *hate* you! If that is love I want none of it!" And then his heavy face came down upon hers again and he held her head so that she could not struggle free, while he kissed her again and again, pressing her close in his arms.

It was then she gave a real scream!

"Can I be of any assistance?" a voice spoke close behind her, and a strong blow came down on the inner curve of Bobby's elbow, making it fall away powerless for the instant.

"Who the devil are you?" roared Bobby dropping his other arm from about Diana and turning to face the interloper. "What business have you got interfering?"

But Diana, free for the instant, turned and fled!

7

DIANA arrived back at the house with a face as white as chalk and eyes that were dark with terror. Her recent experience had overtopped all climaxes in her life, and had almost made her forget for the time being the tragedy in her home. It seemed to her that the covering of decency had been stripped from life and love, and everything worth while was left stark and naked. Was love like that, and could caresses turn to so hideous a thing? She never wanted to see or hear of Bobby Watkins again.

Helen stared at her as she entered the door, narrowing her eyes and searching her face.

"Why the tragedy?" she asked flippantly.

Diana ignored her remark.

"Where is my father?" she asked. Her voice was steady and grave as if she had a serious matter on her mind.

Helen's eyes grew belligerent.

"He's in the library calling up a taxi. We're going away at once so you needn't think you're going to have time to talk with him. You might as well learn to cut out any long conferences. I don't like them. I remember how you used to do, and I don't like it, understand?"

"Oh, yes?" said Diana coolly giving her antagonist a level look and walking slowly up the stairs.

Diana went to the front window and looked out into the darkness. The lights in the cottage windows glimmered in a friendly way but Diana only shuddered as she watched them. Once it came to her to wonder who it had been that came and stood behind her and rescued her from those terrible iron-muscled arms and those fiendish moist fat lips? Could it have been some passer-by on the street who had heard her scream? Bobby Watkins! How had she ever fancied it might be possible for her to find refuge in marriage with Bobby Watkins even to escape from her present tragic situation? To think of having him around every day, with the right to kiss her—that way! How terrible!

But her meditations were interrupted by her father's imperious knock at her door.

"I've got to go now, Diana. I came up to—to—! Diana, have you nothing to say to me? You certainly have been acting in a strange way. I cannot understand it."

Diana turned and faced him and again the sternness of his tone seemed to overwhelm her so that she could not think nor speak, and her lips and chin were trembling in her effort to control the tears. Never, never since she was a little child and had disobeyed his express command not to take the ink bottle down off the desk, and had spilled ink all over Mother's new oriental rug had she ever heard her father speak to her in a tone like that. It seemed she could not bear it. It seemed that it was something irreparable!

"And so," he said eyeing her sternly with a kind of desperation in his face, "you have nothing to say. You do not want to ask forgiveness? You do not want to say you are sorry for such rude conduct to my wife?"

His wife! How she quivered at the words! Even so soon those words were separating them! But—*forgiveness*. What had she done? Broken down, yes, but that was his fault, not hers. He should have told her beforehand, talked it over with her and helped her to understand, allowed her to tell what she knew, not separated himself from her without a word and then tried to choke this terrible relationship down her throat. She longed to cry out "I was not rude to her, Father, you do not know. You did not hear what she said to me!" but she could only choke back a sob and turn her face away.

"So! You intend to keep it up, do you? You're not even going to kiss me good-bye?" His voice was more deeply angry than she had ever heard it before. "I thought you loved me! And you're not even going to kiss me good-bye!"

But Diana turned at that.

"I *can't,* Father! I can't *any more!*" she burst forth sorrowfully. "She told me not to. She said I was too old to kiss my father, and she didn't like it!"

He looked at her as if he could not believe his ears.

"And have you descended as low as that, that you will lie to me to prove her in the wrong?" His voice was grieved now, incredulous.

"Father! You know better! You know I do not lie. She said it. She took me upstairs and told me that just a few minutes ago!"

He stared at her an instant more and then his face cleared with a half contemptuous smile.

"If Helen said that you know she said it in a joke. You know she would never mean a thing like that. You are being willfully hateful to prove your point, just because years ago you took a prejudice against her on account of that silly dress. I would rather have bought you a dozen silk dresses than to have your judgment and your sweet innocent nature warped.

"Father!" cried Diana desperately, "go and ask her! She did say it. She was not joking. She never jokes. She means it. She was quite vexed. She said she did not like it and she wouldn't stand for it! Go and ask her. Perhaps she will be willing to tell you the truth about it."

"Are you implying that she also lies?" His voice was very stern again now.

"Oh, Daddy, Daddy, dear!" Diana cried out, suddenly turning and putting her head down on the broad window seat, her shoulders shaking with suppressed sobs.

He watched her a moment, his brows knit in deep trouble, and then sighing turned away.

"Well, I cannot wait any longer for you to see your error," he said sadly. "I never thought that my child would behave like this. Well—," wistfully, "I must go."

He turned and walked sadly out of the room and down the stairs, and a moment later she heard the taxi driving away. He was gone!

She flung herself on her bed and wept until it seemed her heart was breaking. Wept until Maggie came up and tried to soothe her, bathed her face with cool water, said "There, my lamb, my lamb," and tried in every way to hearten her.

At last the violent sobbing was over and she could speak to the old servant.

"I can't stay here, Maggie, I can't! I can't! She wants to get rid of me. She says I'm to go upstairs—" and she poured out all the directions that the new mistress had given.

Maggie's face was full of indignation as she listened, but at last she said:

"Well, my lamb, it's a sore trial I mind, put it how ye

wull, but I'd advise ye t' get ye ta yer couch an' sleep the night over it, an' in the morn we'll see whut ta do. Now, I'll fetch ye a sup o' hot milk fer ye didn't eat enough o' the fine dinner we had to keep a bird alive, and do you put on yer little bed goon and get ye ta yer rest. The morn will bring ye new wisdom. Bide ye till the morn. Then we'll see."

Diana was worn out with excitement and emotion and she readily fell asleep from sheer exhaustion, after the drink of hot milk. But for one in sorrow sleep does not last. It suddenly vanishes in the small hours of the night and the sufferer is left to toss and turn and see the ghosts of possibilities all go trooping by. So Diana woke. It might have been one o'clock, or it might have been later, and sharply on her waking thoughts came the memory of a flower lying in the dewy grass, staring up from almost under foot, pale with the reflection of the moon drifting through dense branches.

The flower! Oh why had she not picked up her flower! Was it really there at all or had she dreamed it? If it was there then that made six. There were three the morning the letter came, one yesterday morning, one this morning, and now this one tonight, if it was really a flower and not a figment of her imagination, not just a bit of paper, or a fragment of fluff blown about by the wind.

Somehow her drowsy thoughts hovered about that flower without touching on her troubles. It was as if her first waking consciousness was afraid to think of all that had come upon her, as if she took refuge in thoughts of the pleasant bit of romance that seemed to be dropping into her quiet life.

More and more as she grew wider awake she longed to know whether that flower were really there. It seemed as if her only hope of riding above her troubles lay in knowing whether that had been a flower, a real flower there in the dim shadows. If it had been a flower she might grasp its sweetness to her heart and go on somehow working out her strange problems. Suddenly it seemed to her that she must rise and run out there and discover for herself.

Oh, she knew it wasn't a reasonable thing to do at all. The house was dark, Maggie was asleep, all the country-side was asleep. It wasn't a safe thing for her to do either to go down that lonely drive in the night on such a foolish errand. Her father wouldn't approve. Her mother would not have approved. Maggie would cry out upon her and insist in going along if she knew. But Maggie didn't know. Maggie was soundly asleep, and snoring. And Diana knew even before she made the first actual move to rise from her bed, that she was going. She must know whether that flower was there or not. If she waited till dawn some mysterious person might come by and get it. She would never know then whether it had been there at all, and it seemed most important to know positively whether it was there now.

All the time she was flinging on garments, stepping into slippers, and throwing a long dark silk cloak about her, she was resolutely refusing to let her mind spring back and reveal to her all the sorrow and horror that was there beneath the surface of her consciousness.

When she was ready she stole down the hall and stairs with silent tread, unfastened the door and slid out like a wraith.

The moon was low in the west by now, and was casting long faint weird shadows across the grass. In her dark cloak with her silent tread she seemed like one of the shadows, a swiftly moving shadow, as noiseless as a moth, drifting along on faint pale moonbeams.

As she approached the group of trees and was about

to pass into the depth of shade they made the memory of her experience burst back upon her with full force, and she paused, frightened, looking ahead, listening. Was it conceivable that Bobby might be lingering about the place yet? She shuddered at the memory of his lips, his great possessive arms. But somehow she must go on. A power within herself was compelling her, would not be satisfied until she found the flower. And though her heart was wildly beating she went on again. There could be no turning back. Silly! Why should she be frightened? There would be no one about at this hour of course, and who would want to steal a silly little single cast-out flower in the grass—if there was a flower at all. She must know. So she went on.

She stole into the depth of the darkness and stood looking down until her eyes grew accustomed to the blackness, and suddenly she saw it, there, right at her feet, staring up at her, its fringed petals making a soft blur of light in the dimness.

With her heart beating as wildly as if she were seeing a spirit-flower she stooped and snatched it, and then turning, fled back to the house, her white face showing like the passing of a moonbeam. For now it seemed that Bobby with his hot breath fanning her face, and his fat arms reached out to clasp her, was running with great strides just behind her, and would presently win out in the race and she would be in that awful embrace again. And there would not be a stranger near at hand this time with a voice of authority to protect her.

She was like a sleep walker in a nightmare as she ran, until she reached the front door and fastened it behind her. But unlike the nightmare victim she did reach the door before she came to herself. She stood there panting, her eyes closed, leaning back against the door for a moment's respite, trying to get her breath and courage to go on and know what life had in store for her. She seemed to know that as soon as she had mounted the stairs again and entered her room her trouble in its entirety would rush upon her and take her in its grasp, sting her with its sorrow again. So she lingered till her breath came back, and then stole softly up to her bed, with Maggie still noisily slumbering in the back bedroom with the door open wide to be near to guard her bairn if anything should molest.

Back in her bed again, strangely enough the evil spectre of her troubles stood at bay, exorcised, perhaps, by the fragrant breath of the flower.

She did not put the carnation into the vase with the others, but kept it in her hand and it lay against her cheek upon the pillow and whether because of sheer weariness, or because the flower seemed to bring something like peace upon her worn spirit, she fell asleep again.

When morning came at last she slept on till Maggie, worried about her, slipped softly in to see if all was right, and found her sleeping with the flower upon the pillow just touching her lips.

She stood a moment studying the girl's sweet face, noting the deep blue shadows under her eyes, and the sorrowful droop of her mouth.

"Aw, the puir wee thing!" she said under her breath. "The puir wee thing! If her feyther could but see her the noo! But I doot ef he'd understand the while yet. He's that fey aboot the hussy! Puir silly mon! He'll be that shamed when he understands! An' he'll see it yet! He's a gude mon, only just silly for the whiles. But I doot it'll be too late fer savin' his girlie's happiness! Puir wee thing!"

Then Maggie stole quietly away and closed the door.

But a half hour later the sun stole in and cast a warm finger across the pillow, touching her eyelids and lighting up the flower and Diana awoke with a start. No bewilderings now. The whole terrible tragedy flashed across her consciousness in full force and her mind was on duty at once informing her of what was necessary to be done. Instantly the words of her new stepmother came to her about the changes that were to be made, strong hints of what might happen to things that had grown dear to the girl through the years, and she realized that if she did not save them they would go out of her care and keeping and would be sold or destroyed ruthlessly.

And now as she lay still she saw what she had to do. Whether she stayed herself or not, those precious things of her mother's must be put in a safe place. Sometime Father would rouse to the situation and enquire for the household goods. If he was ever disillusioned he would surely feel badly that they were gone. Moreover many of them belonged to Diana. Both her father and mother had spoken of this often. The ancestral dishes, the portraits, a lot of things that she had packed away in inconspicuous places, and had hoped were safe from the iconoclast, she now saw would be ruthlessly rooted out and sold or destroyed.

She did some swift thinking and decided that she would send them to a storage house. Even if she went away herself she could not take them with her until she had some place to put them, and it might take days to find the right place. It might even take weeks. She had a little money in her own checking account and could pay the storage and get along somehow if worst came to worst, but the things that were to be saved must be saved today or it would be too late. They could not be gotten out of the house after Helen came back, that was certain.

Further consideration made it plain also that the goods must be stored where they could not be traced and brought back. What Helen had not seen or noticed might not be missed, but it was certain that Grand-mother's sprigged china and many other little things would be. Well, she would not telephone to the storage house from home for that perhaps might be traceable from the itemized telephone bill. She would run down to the village, three quarters of a mile away, and tele-phone. She would tell them that they must come by two o'clock. That would give her time to get her own furniture ready to go.

Suddenly Diana arose and began rapidly to dress. There were no tears this morning. There was excite-ment, anxiety, overwhelming haste.

But just as she turned to leave her room her eye fell on the flower lying on her pillow, and she caught her breath with a great wonder in her eyes. She had jumped up so suddenly and been so absorbed in her problems that she had not noticed the flower for it had fallen away from her face over to the other end of the pillow.

She went slowly over to the bed and touched the flower, lifted it to her face, drew a deep breath of its perfume. It was real then. She had thought it a dream! Then she had really gotten up and gone out on the drive to find it! How strange! Poor little flower! It should have been in water all night! Yet it seemed almost as fresh as its mates for whom she had cared so tenderly. How did it happen that the flower was out there in the evening? Had all the others been put there at that hour? It didn't seem possible, they had been so fresh and dewy. It was a mystery flower. She could not solve its problem. She just knew it had been a comfort to her in this her great life sorrow.

Then like a flash she remembered all that she had to do today! She waited only to put her flower in the crystal vase with its mates and then she hurried downstairs.

Maggie came out into the hall with an anxious face and saw that Diana had on her hat.

"Ye're not gangin' awa'?" she asked fearsomely. "The breakfast is near ready an' we can talk whilst yer eatin'."

"I'm running down to the village to do some long distance telephoning," said Diana breathlessly, glancing at the clock. "I don't want it to go on the bill for Helen to see. I'll explain it all when I get back. I won't be long."

"But couldn't ye wait for a bite first?"

"No, Maggie, I must go at once. I want to get some people before they are gone to business. I'll be right back."

Diana dashed out the door and down the drive without waiting for further parley, and Maggie, with distress in her face, followed to the piazza and watched her out of sight.

"Now whut's the puir wee thing got on her mind this time?" she said aloud to herself, her arms akimbo, her cheeks red with worry, her mouth in a vexed line. "It's a bad business, tormentin' the puir wee bairn. Her feyther is storin' up sorrow, an' him not knowin' whut the little hussy is at, but the day'll come when he wull. Well, he'll rue the day he ever saw that flipperty-gib."

Just then the scones set up a smell of burning and she flew to their rescue.

"Puir wee thing, she'll be that hungry when she comes back," said Maggie as she set about preparing a more elaborate breakfast than she had planned.

As Diana went flying down the drive her mind was busy with her plans, but her breath was coming in long sobbing gasps. Out here in the open she felt that no one could hear her for the moment and she let herself give a long trembling moan, let the smarting tears fall for a minute or two. She felt sick and dizzy with all she had been through, and with loss of sleep. She began to tremble as she neared the scene of her silent struggle last night, and wondered at herself that she had dared come down there in the middle of the night—just for a flower! What was a flower after all? It probably belonged to someone else and all the fairy romance she had woven about it was just of her imagination. Perhaps someone had plenty of these and threw them away every now and then. Yet there it had been in the middle of the night as if it dropped down from the soft moonbeams. There for her greatest need. Well, it was probably the only one she would have found this morning if she had waited. It was likely placed there every night instead of morning and the dew kept it fresh.

Then suddenly she started back, stopped and looked down at her feet, for there lay another carnation, sweet and pink and fresh, just like all the rest. She gasped in astonishment and looked furtively about her. What could it mean? It was fully two hours before her usual time to walk that way, and yet there it lay smiling up at her.

Then she stooped and picked it up, and as she touched it to her lips the tears came rushing down again and she sobbed softly to herself as she went on her way. It certainly was strange and uncanny, and somehow it seemed as if somebody like her mother were doing this. She almost believed for the instant that the flower actually fell from heaven at her feet. It seemed so wonderful to have it come just when she so needed comfort, and she hugged it to her lips and kissed it, sobbing softly as she hurried on. As she passed the end of the cottage and neared the street she paused to brush away the tears. She must not cry in the street! And she must hurry on or she would perhaps miss the mover for the day, and those things *must* leave the house before Helen got back or they would never leave, that was certain.

She could hear Helen's laughter now if she should come even while they were leaving, and knew as well as if it had happened before her eyes how quickly she would have her father persuaded that it was absurd for them to go. Oh, Helen would never let the things go out of the house until she had investigated every one, that was certain. And she would save some of them for the pleasure of destroying them. No one who hadn't seen Helen work would probably believe that. If Diana had not suffered from her methods many times perhaps she would not have believed it herself. But she was taking no chances. The things she loved would go out of the house before Helen got there if she had to drag them out one by one herself and hide them in the barn, or the back meadow.

Such thoughts hastened her feet till she reached the village drug store and went in to telephone. Even then she had to try three storage places before she found one that would promise to come that afternoon. Diana found she was trembling when she hung up the receiver.

She waited only to get a few trifling things she would need in packing, and then she hurried back.

On her way home her thoughts were leaping ahead, planning what she would do first, counting up different matters that must be attended to before the movers arrived. In imagination she took down her pictures and curtains, folded her garments into drawers and trunks, gathered out her books from the library, tabulated on her fingers the boxes and furniture stored away in attic and cellar that must not be forgotten. It seemed as if the thoughts in her mind were like bees buzzing about in confusion to be sorted out and marshalled in orderly array. She was fairly running the last lap of the way, and arrived at home quite out of breath. Maggie had to draw her by sheer force to the dining room.

"Sit ye doon," she said vexedly. "Here have I kept breakfast waiting all this time. Ye can na work on an empty stomach. Come, eat a good breakfast or I'll na help ye a stroke. Yer porridge first. I dinna hold with the folks that puts sour fruit juices in on an empty stomach. It heartens ye ta get a good fill of porridge first, nice an' hot! And there are scones ta come with strawberry jam. Mind yer milk, too. Ye canna keep up unless ye eat. I'll wager ye na slept the night much. Ye must eat ef ye canna sleep. Ye dinna want ta give her a chance ta have ye sick on her hands."

So Diana ate a sketchy breakfast.

"I haven't time," she protested as she hastily buttered a scone. "I'm sending my things away, Maggie, the things she would smash or take away. I can't leave them here for her to destroy, and I won't let her have my precious furniture that Mother got for me."

"But where will ye send them, child?"

"To storage. At least for awhile till I know what to do."

Maggie looked startled.

"Won't that cost ye a lot? You mightta sent them to my sister's hoose, only it's sooch a wee bit housie I don't mind where she could put them."

"No," said Diana firmly. "I'm not going to involve you and your sister in my troubles. She'd just go there and get them if she found out. No, Maggie, this is the best way. It doesn't cost so much, and I can get them out any time I like of course. They'll be protected in storage, and be insured. I have a little money of my own you know. I'm quite sure this is the only way to do."

"Then coom!" said the servant determinedly. "We'll

get it off yer mind. I'll take doon the draperies and brush them. Do you put away your pretties in the drawers."

They set to work in silence, and in due time the room that had been so sweet and homelike was reduced to bare walls and desolate furniture standing about. Even the pretty bed was wearing only its springs now, the mattress being trussed around, covered with an old sheet, and neatly tied with rope by the capable hands of Maggie.

Suddenly Diana turned about and surveyed the place and a great desolation swept over her.

"I can't stay here, Maggie," she cried with a soft little wail in her voice. "I couldn't stand living in the third story and having her take my pretty room and put herself or her guests here, the kind of guests she always has when she has her way. Am I wicked, Maggie, that I feel I can't stay here? Not even Mother would want me to, I'm sure. I couldn't stay and have her always putting me in the wrong before Father! It wouldn't do him any good, and it would make endless trouble. I couldn't, Maggie, could I? I *must go!*"

She bent her head and the tears gushed forth as she stood with pitiful clasped hands and let the tears splash down on the rug at her feet.

"But where would ye go?" asked Maggie lifting her face and discovering the slow tears that for some time had been coursing over her honest sorrowful face. "Whut can ye do, my wee birdling?"

Diana stood silent for a minute, then she lifted her face and her eyes were dark and tragic as she looked at Maggie.

"I can make some visits!" she said bravely, drawing a deep breath. "I thought it all out on the way home. Maggie, I've got to be gone before they come home tonight. They'll likely be here for dinner, and I must be gone before they come. I couldn't meet her—*them*—

again, not now with Father feeling as he does against me. I've got to go. There's Aunt Harriet, a great many miles away. I can take the sleeper at midnight and be there in the morning. And there are those girls that invited me to house parties. They'll all be glad to have me visit them a few days each. I'll write them that I'm coming their way and will stop off a few days if it's convenient. And by that time I'll get settled in my mind and know what I want to do."

"But what if yer Aunt Harriet isn't at home?" queried Maggie anxiously.

"She's always at home. She's an invalid you know," said Diana. "She's often invited me."

"Ye better send her a wee wire then, sayin' yer comin'."

"No," said Diana, "I'll just go. I can't explain things in a wire and I haven't time for a letter."

"Aw, my wee lamb! Ef I only had a place of my own I'd share it with ye! I'd not let ye stray around the world all belonst this way. Ef I only hadn't of let my sister's husband borry my earnings ta buy his hoose! T' be sure I'm that wulcome, an' I doot not he'd tak ye in too, ef I'd ast him."

"No, Maggie!" said Diana. "You're very kind, but I want to get farther away. But, we mustn't stand here and talk there's so much to do. It's almost twelve o'clock and the van will be here at two. I've all my clothes to pack. I'll take a suitcase and the big Gladstone bag, that'll be all I'll need for visiting. The rest of my things I'll pack in the bureau drawers."

They went silently to work again, like two who had just read a death warrant, speaking no words that were not necessary, furtive tears stealing down their cheeks which each ignored.

At last the work was done, and Maggie insisted on

Diana's lying down a little while on a bed she had fixed for her in the guest room.

"I'll just run doon the stair an' get ye a bite ta eat an' a coop o' tea whilst ye sleep," said Maggie.

"Oh, no, Maggie," protested the girl. "I can't sleep now till it's over. Wait till the things are gone. Then we'll have lunch and rest."

"Ye'd best drink a sup o' tea!" admonished the woman, and hurried down to get it. Then Diana sat down to her little desk where she had spent so many happy hours of her life studying and writing, and penned a letter to her father. It had to be done quickly for the men would come and the desk must go, and she couldn't think of writing *that* letter anywhere else but at her own desk. It seemed as if another desk or another room might somehow snatch the meaning of her letter and turn it to a traitor use. She must write it here with her pen dipped in the love and agony of her heart, here in the four walls of her dismantled room before they became alien walls, sheltering her enemy. And she must write it rapidly too, because her heart might weaken if she took a long time and weighed her words too well. She would just tell briefly what were the facts.

And so with her own fountain pen that had been her father's gift on her last birthday, her initials set in green and gold enamel in its barrel, she wrote. Oh, she had never never thought when he gave it to her that she would write such words as she was writing now with that cherished pen.

8

DEAR Father;

I must go away. If you knew everything you
would fully understand and would think that I am
right. It would only make terrible trouble for all of
us if I were to stay. Things can never be as they
were before, and you would soon see it yourself.

At first I thought I could stay until you found this
out and then I could talk it over with you and plan
for my going in the way that you thought was best,
but several things last night showed me that that
would be impossible. There would be no way now
for you and me to talk together alone, and I could
not talk it over with Helen. So I see that I must go
at once without waiting for you to come back.

You need not worry about me for I shall be
visiting for awhile, and I will write and let you
know my plans as soon as I have had a chance to
decide what I am going to do. I shall write you at
your office. And meanwhile you can just say that I
am visiting friends and relatives.

I have not taken anything with me that did not

belong to me personally, except things that you yourself suggested should be put away. If I have taken too many you can just let me know and I will have them sent back. They are in a perfectly safe place, and insured, so I hope you will think I did right about them.

And now dear Father, I want you to know that I love you very dearly, but I could not stay here under the circumstances. And it is too late to talk about it, so I will just say again I love you, and good-bye.

Your little girl,
Diana

The movers arrived just as she was writing the last word, and Diana hastily sealed her letter, addressed it to her father, and swallowed the tea which Maggie had brought her. Then she went down to meet the movers and show them what things had to go.

How ruthlessly those stalwart men marshalled the few household articles, which had seemed so many but a few minutes before, and dropped them into the depths of that great yawning van. Diana rushed from cellar to attic to make sure everything was gone that she had intended. Then she directed that a trunk containing part of her wardrobe should be put where it would be accessible if needed while the things were in storage.

They stood in the doorway together, the servant and the girl, watching the great van rattle off jauntily down the drive and disappear, carrying with it a part of what had once been the furnishings of an unusually happy home. The old servant had her lips set in a grim line, and she was sniffing back a stray tear.

"Well," she said with a heavy sigh, "at least they'll be

safe. An' noo," she said turning back to Diana, "Coom! I've got a bit lunch ready. Sit ye doon the noo an' eat. Yes, yer no to wait. It's nice an' hot an' I'm not lettin' ye leave it ta get cold."

"If you'll sit down with me, Maggie," said Diana with a catch in her voice. "I can't sit down and eat alone, this last time."

"It's not the last meal in yer ain hame, bairnie," said Maggie fiercely. "I feel it in my bones the day wull come when ye'll be back an' happier than ever. An' it's no fittin' that a servant should eat with her mistress, but I'll bide in the room while ye eat, an' we'll talk a bit."

But Diana would have it that she should eat with her.

"You're the only friend I've got left, Maggie!" she pleaded, and so the old servant reluctantly yielded and sat down, every mouthful a protest against her sense of the fitness of things.

"Maggie, I've written a letter to Father and I want you to see that he gets it when he's alone. I don't want her to know I've written it. At least, not until he's read it. Will you give it to him?"

Maggie was silent a moment.

"I wasn't thinkin' of stayin' after you was gone, my bairn," said Maggie slowly, "but yes, I'll stay ta give it to him onygait."

"Oh, Maggie!" wailed the girl, "I'm doing you out of a place!"

"It's not you, you puir wee lamb," said the woman. "It's her. That Helen! Ye don't think I cud stomach the likes of her, do ye? I was studyin' whut I should do, fer I couldn't abear ta leave ye alane with that hussy. But I knew she an' I'd be two people from the start. We never did get along when she was only visitin', and I'd never take orders from her."

"No," said Diana sadly, "I suppose you couldn't. Oh,

I'm so sorry for Father! He'll miss your cooking so much!"

"It's naebuddy's faucht but his ain, poor silly mon! An' he'll find out good and soon I'm thinkin'. But I'll stay an' deliver yer letter, an' I'll see she don't get her hands on it till he's read it through, so don't ye worry. An' now, ye better get a bit o' rest before ye get back to work. Aren't ye almost done?"

"No, there's quite a lot of things yet. I haven't packed my bags, and there are some boxes of letters I've got to look over and burn. I don't want her to be reading my letters." Diana sighed wearily and turned away.

As she passed the door of the living room she looked wistfully toward the piano, her mother's piano! Helen wouldn't want it, would probably try to sell it or relegate it to the attic, for Helen couldn't play. But several of her associates were musicians, or called themselves so, though the music they played was jazzy modern stuff that Diana hated. Helen would probably have them playing jazz on her mother's piano—unless Helen could coax her father to buy a new one. Oh, the piano ought to have gone with the other things to storage, but she dared not take it away without consulting her father. Well, perhaps the fact that she had not taken it would work in its favor. Perhaps Helen would simply not think about it at all.

She stepped into the living room and sat down at the instrument, touching the keys tenderly, softly, recalling how her mother had sat there playing evening after evening all during the happy years, how she had received her own first lessons there from her mother. She remembered how happy she had been when she had succeeded in playing her first little piece perfectly. How her father and mother had stood there with shining eyes watching and commending her. How that piano was connected with all the pleasant happenings of life! And now she must leave it, probably forever! The tears began to gather again and she put her head down on the music rack and pressed her hands against her eyes. She must not cry again, it unnerved her so. And she had still much to do.

At last she gathered strength to lift her head, giving the old instrument one more caressing touch, her fingers sweeping the keys softly, tenderly. Then she closed the lid. She wished she dared lock it, but that would be only to rouse Helen's ire, and she really had no right to lock it even if she knew where the key was. She had no memory that the piano had ever been locked. So, she lingered a moment more moving her hands softly over the polished surface of the case, like a last handclasp with a friend, and then she turned and quickly went upstairs.

It was almost dark when she finished with her packing and dressing. The late summer twilight seemed to come unusually soon, but Diana, looking at her watch, discovered that it was almost time for the travelers to arrive if they came on the shore train which they would be likely to take. She could tell by the fragrance that came up from the region of the kitchen that dinner was in process of preparation. Maggie would have a good dinner for her last one in the old house.

Diana put on her hat, gathered up her wrap and gloves, and stood for a moment gazing about her empty room, her room that her parents had planned for her. And now she was leaving it forever. Her glance swept about its empty walls and lingered on the wide window seats where she had so often sat among cushions reading some favorite book. It had all been so dear and now she would see it no more!

Then she saw the crystal vase with its seven lovely

flowers standing alone in the other window seat, forgotten! How had she forgotten them? She must not leave those behind. They had been her comfort during this tragic hour, and there would be no more of them. Seven mystery flowers! A perfect number. No, they must not be left behind!

She took them out of the vase and dried it, found some cotton and tissue paper and wrapping it carefully stowed it in her bag. There was a piece of wax paper in the closet also, and she put the flowers in that. After a moment's hesitation she slipped them too in the bag. There was space for them, but she felt as if she were smothering children as she laid them in.

She paused a minute thoughtfully, and then suddenly searched in her suitcase for her writing case and sitting in the window seat in the fading light she wrote hastily:

> Dear Flower Person:
> I am going away and will not be able to come and find any more of your lovely carnations, but I had to let you know how they have helped and comforted me during a very hard time. I shall probably never know who put the flowers in my path, nor even if they were really meant for me, but I shall never forget them.
> Thank you and good-bye.

She slipped the note into a small envelope, addressed it "To the Flower Person" and put it in her handbag.

Then suddenly she heard the sound of a motor, and hurrying to the front window she saw the lights of a taxi coming swiftly up the drive. They had come and she was still here!

Panic seized her. She could not meet them! She must

get away! She must be gone when they entered the house, and the taxi was almost at the door! Could she make it?

She snatched up her bags, gave one last wistful frantic look about her denuded room and fled down the hall to the back stairs.

She appeared in the kitchen like a wraith, her face white, her eyes dark with excitement:

"They've come, Maggie. Here's the letter for Father! Good-bye you dear! And I'll write you in care of your sister!"

She flashed out of the kitchen even as the front door opened letting in the householders. She stole swiftly across the back lawn to a wide group of shrubs, disappearing into the midst of their friendly branches. The twilight was kindly and hid her going, the shrubs were thick and formed a perfect screen. Maggie had rushed after her to the kitchen door crying out in subdued protest:

"But ye mustn't gang awa alane. I was goin' down the road with ye——!"

But Diana was not there. Then Maggie realized that the next act was hers and she was holding the letter in her hand. She hid it quickly behind the bib of her ample apron, and went back to her cooking, assuming an air of indifference toward the world, but keeping a weather ear open to all developments, while her heart cried out for the girl who had fled. She had meant to give her all sorts of cautions, and now it was too late! But she could not run after her. That would be to give the whole matter away.

So the master and the new mistress walked into the house and went upstairs with no one to interrupt their progress.

Helen went up the stairs like a victor who has taken a

city and means to behead the former ruler. She marched straight to the master bedroom and flung open the door. She wanted to see if her commands had been obeyed. Then she stood staring for an instant at the prim immaculate neatness that prevailed. Dominated by the fine old walnut furniture that had belonged to its former mistress, bare only of the little feminine and artistic touches, and its lovely portrait, it had a forbidding look. As she stared a fury grew in her face not pretty to see.

"She hasn't touched it!" she said aloud in a tone meant to reach to the lower hall.

She paused an instant, head bent in a listening attitude, then she flounced around and flung open the door across the hall. There stood Diana's room stark and bare!

She made a sound such as is generally associated with the snorting of a war horse preparatory to battle. She stepped into the room and snapped on the light. Its brilliance flung out the curtainless window and penetrated the dense shrubbery that traveled more or less irregularly from the kitchen garden down the far side of the drive toward the entrance gate. Diana was slowly progressing toward the gate as she waited for the taxi to get out of sight before she made her dash across the open to the dense growth of trees that hid the cottage. So Diana knew that the secret of her moving was discovered. She had hoped to be farther away before they found it out.

Helen walked determinedly across the bare floor and flung the closet wide. Everything gone, the room cleaned. Not even a box nor a paper on the empty shelf!

She ran out in the hall and up the third story stairs, with an eye that boded no good to her enemy. The light snapped on at the foot of the stairs and Diana saw that too and dashed across in the twilight to the spot behind the trees, her trysting place with the flowers. But she was not thinking of the flowers now, nor looking for them.

She was crouching down beneath a huge hemlock, its lacy branches brushing her face. She was parting the branches and looking back to the house. She could see a figure walking by the hall window. That would be Helen. She was looking in every room for each window blazed out in turn. She was finding out that her new stepdaughter had not done anything she had told her to do!

Well, there was a moment's time perhaps. The front door was still closed. Diana searched out the letter from her handbag, and stooping laid it in the very place where the carnation had lain the night before, and this morning. She caught her breath in a little sob. There would be no more carnations for her. If one lay there in the morning she would not be there to find it! She was leaving everything, home and love and even her bit of mystery and romance.

Then she turned a quick look back to the house, and saw the front door flung wide, the light streaming out, and Helen standing slim and vibrant looking out into the darkness.

Diana shrank and catching up her bags fled out of the gateway and down the road, pausing in the shadow of the tall hedge to wait and listen breathlessly. It was not likely that Helen would pursue her out into the darkness on foot, but yet, there was never any telling what Helen would do. It would be hard to run from pursuit and carry all that baggage, but still it could be done. However, perhaps if she saw them coming it would be better to push the bags through the hedge and come back for them later. She considered that an instant, then peering through the thick hedge she saw the light of the doorway shut off, and distinctly heard the closing of the front door. Helen would likely have gone to consult Maggie, and it would take her some time to get anything out of Maggie if Maggie chose to be stupid and not understand.

Diana relaxed against the hedge and found herself terribly weary. There would be a bus along soon. If she might only sit down on the grass, lie down, close her eyes and rest. But of course she couldn't. She must stand alert and ready to fly if need be. She was thankful however for the momentary ease against the strong resilient arms of the old hedge. She put her head back. She could almost go to sleep here. She resolutely put away from her all thoughts of what might be going on at the house behind her. She would not think it now. She could not bear it. The tears would come if she did, and one could not get into a public conveyance weeping. She took a deep breath and shut her lips with determination.

Then behind her she became aware of a voice—or was it voices?—speaking low and gently—a voice, it was a voice speaking to someone. She could not hear the first words, they were very low and gentle, just behind her within that open window of the cottage. She turned instinctively and looked at the square of light that was the cottage window, screened by sheer muslin curtains moving softly in the breeze, and thickly sheltered by the tall hedge. It was as safely private as a bird's nest in a tall tree. Pedestrians did not creep within the shelter of hedges as she was doing. An ordinary passer-by would never have heard that voice, so reverent, so tender. She found herself soothed by the very tone.

And then the voice grew more distinct:

"We thank Thee for the care of the day, and for these gifts for our refreshment."

He was saying grace at the evening meal! Father used to do that while Mother was living, but of late it had become a mumbled formality. Who was this person?

The voice was grave, but not old. She had understood from Maggie that the woman who had taken the cottage was elderly. Perhaps after all her husband was living. Maggie had only spoken of a woman and her boy. But perhaps this was some relative taking supper with them.

The voice rose again just a little so that she heard the words:

"And Lord we would ask Thy mercy and tenderness and leading for the people up at the great house. Perhaps some of them are sad. Lord, give them comfort. Perhaps they need guidance. Do Thou send Thy light—!"

And then suddenly the bus rumbled up to the curb to drop a passenger. The bus would never have stopped at all if it hadn't been for that passenger, for Diana had been away back in the shadow out of sight. But now she came back to herself with a start, caught up her bags and hurried forward into the bus. She was whirled away, but she turned wondering eyes toward the quiet cottage with its cosy light shining softly through the tall hedge, and forgot entirely to look back upon the home she was leaving until it was too late to see anything but the long streaks of light that streamed down across the lawn from the front windows. Her mind was wholly occupied with what she had heard. It seemed so extraordinary. She would never forget it. She said it over to herself silently, conning it like a lesson of which she must not lose one precious word. "Lord, we would ask Thy mercy and tenderness and leading for the people up at the great house. Perhaps some of them are sad. Lord, give them comfort. Perhaps they need guidance. Do Thou send Thy light—!"

How she longed to know what was to have followed that half-finished sentence. Why had she not stayed to hear? Another bus would have been but a half hour longer, and plenty of time to catch her train. She glanced at her watch. Yes, she could have waited, but it was too late to go back now. It was too far to walk with her bags and she was much too tired.

Then she said the words over again, "And Lord we would ask Thy mercy for the people up at the great house." Was it conceivable that the person meant the Disston house? It was the way a servant would speak of a master's family. Perhaps the reference was to some former master's family, just being tenderly remembered in prayer, the way Maggie would do. But this voice had not been the voice of a servant. It was a cultured voice, a voice like a master's voice. How the words throbbed and thrilled along her sore tired heart! Here was someone who believed in God, believed that God was interested in individuals, even interested in individuals who were not especially interested in Him. Could he be bespeaking God's interest in her father's house by individuals? Was it really her father's house? Of course it might be some other house far away. But it soothed and rested Diana to think it was the house of Disston the voice meant.

She was too tired now to question why, it was just enough to have someone care, even in a quiet impersonal way, and pray for them. Oh, how they needed praying for—that is if prayer did any good. At least it was comforting to think someone cared to try. She put her head back against the window frame and closed her eyes on the hot tears that tried to struggle to the lashes and squeeze through. She thought of the flowers in her bag, and the prayer in her heart, and was glad she had heard those few words. They helped her anyway, even if they were not meant for her. Perhaps there was a God who cared after all, instead of just a mere impersonal creator. If one soul could speak like that as if he knew Him, he must have had some experience to make him sure God was like that. If she ever went back to her home—it was not conceivable tonight that she would, but if she ever did—she would try to seek out the people who lived in the cottage and get to know them and see if she could find out what it was that they had that would explain the tenderness of a prayer like that.

Presently she got out her pencil and a bit of card from her handbag and wrote down the words as well as she could remember them. She must not forget that prayer. She must hide it in her heart and memory. It was like the flowers.

She went on into the city to take her train. It seemed a very long ride tonight, longer than usual. She hoped the train would be ready soon. She wanted to lie down.

She hadn't bothered to look up the time of the train. There was usually one along toward midnight going in the direction of the city where Aunt Harriet lived, an hour or two more or less either way didn't matter. She forgot that she had had no dinner and very little lunch. She was not hungry, she only wanted to lie down. She felt that she was too tired even to cry.

As she neared the city and got away more and more from thoughts of home and the tragedy that made her going necessary, she began to review wearily the few arrangements she had made. She had plenty of money with her for her journey, for it just happened that her father had given her her generous allowance in cash the day he went away for his trip and she had carelessly neglected to put it in the bank, so she had not had to take time to look after that. She had fastened part of her money inside her dress, but she had enough in her bag to pay her fare and some over. There was nothing about that to worry over. Also she had paid a month's storage on her goods with the privilege of refund if she decided to take them out sooner. Somehow all these details seemed so unimportant. They had been merely things to fill this awful day until she was gone. None of them seemed to be of as much importance as the few words of the prayer which she had had the privilege of hearing. How those words seemed to float about her like a sweet protection as the bus rumbled along into the city, and the country was left behind.

Meanwhile, back at the great house, Helen had come rushing down the stairs, searching vainly in the rooms for Diana, hoping to find her at once while her wrath was hot. There was more satisfaction in serving wrath piping hot than after it had a chance to get lukewarm. But no Diana was to be found.

Then Helen arrived magnificently in the kitchen with all the air of a full-fledged mistress of the house.

"Maggie, where is Diana?" she demanded with something in her voice which suggested that Maggie might have hidden her somewhere.

"She's awa'!" stated Maggie crustily.

"Away?" said Helen in an annoyed tone, as if it were all Maggie's fault. "Where is she gone?"

"She didn't *say*," said Maggie shoving the iron frying pan across the top of the stove with a great clatter.

"She didn't say!" repeated Helen in an outraged tone. "When did she go?"

"Awhile back," said Maggie laconically.

"But didn't she tell you where she was going? Didn't you ask her?"

"It was none of my business, why should I ask?" snapped Maggie.

"But didn't she say when she was coming back?"

"She didn't mention comin' back. She said she'd be payin' visits fer some while."

"It was very rude of her to treat us that way. I

wouldn't have thought she would have dared do that to her father."

Maggie was silent, taking up the dinner, her face very red, her deep blue eyes angry with sparks in them.

"Well, what did she do with the furniture she had taken out of her room, and—other things—that I miss, around the house?"

"I couldn't say," said Maggie in a belligerent tone. "I try to mind my own business around a place where I'm workin', Miss Helen, as much as I'm let be."

Helen looked at her haughtily.

"You will call me Mrs. Disston after this!" she said icily.

"Oh, *wull* I?" said Maggie rolling the words out with satisfaction. "I'll not be callin' ye *any*thin' verra long. I'm leavin' the night after the kitchen is redd up. Ye can get someone ta call ye any name in the dictionary if ye like, but I wudn't work for the likes of ye for ony wages."

"I'll have Mr. Disston speak to you," said Helen furiously. "You can't leave a place like that without any notice."

"Oh, I can't, can't I? Well, I'll have ye ta know that I've worruked in this hoose afore ye was born, an' I'll leave when I like, an' not a day later."

"You'll not get your wages then. I'll tell Mr. Disston not to give you a cent."

"Wages or no wages I'm gaein' the nicht. But the master is not like thot. You don't ken him verra weel ef ye think he is. The master is a silly fule sometimes I'll admit, but he's honest! The master may be blind as a bat sometimes but he's a gude mon in spite of it, an' he's honest as the day is lang. I'll leave my case in the master's hands, an' wages or no wages I'm leavin' the hoose the nicht!"

Helen gave her a baleful look and turned away furious, going in search of her husband. Maggie went on calmly taking up her dinner.

"The dinner's ready," she called after the mistress, "an ye'd best eat it noo unless ye want ta wash up afterwards. I'm not stayin' late, so ye'd best coom at once."

9

DOWN in the stone cottage about half an hour before the taxi bearing the master and mistress of the great house reached the door and Diana made her hasty exit from the kitchen, Gordon MacCarroll arrived home from his long day's trip. He stabled his flivver in the little old barn and came in to greet his mother.

He had been away since dawn on a longer journey than any his new connection in the business world had demanded of him yet, and he had been greatly successful. There was a light of victory in his face as he stooped to kiss his mother, and a keen delight in getting home again after a hard day's work. He was tired and hungry and a little bit lonely too, and glad to get back where he could rest. The dinner was beginning to send out a delectable aroma from the oven where something delicious and spicy was in preparation, and the little cosy house looked good to him.

"Well, how is everything, Mother?" he asked as he went to the sink and washed his hands, wiping them on the spick and span roller towel. He was just like a boy with a playmate when he got home to his mother. There was a lovely comradeship between them.

But the mother's face clouded over a trifle.

"Oh, do you know, I'm afraid there's some trouble up at the great house," she said, turning from the celery she was washing and placing in a narrow crystal dish. "The little lady came by this morning just as usual, or maybe a bit earlier—and she was carrying a flower again, isn't that curious?—I wonder if they have a greenhouse up there! This is twice she's carried flowers— But Gordon, she was *crying!*"

"Oh, Mother! You must have been mistaken!" The young man frowned and looked at her intently.

"No, I was not mistaken. I saw her quite distinctly, though she didn't see me. I had just gone out the back door to hang out the dishcloths for a good sunning and I saw her coming through the trees. She was running along and she stooped to pick something up, perhaps she had dropped her flower. I saw her just as she was rising from stooping over, and she bent her head down over the flower. I saw her chin tremble and then her face went down right into the flower, and she was crying hard, as if she was terribly grieved. And she caught her breath in one little sob. It sounded so piteous I wanted to rush out and put my arms around the sweet child and comfort her. But I didn't stir. I even held my breath, lest she would spy me and know I had heard, and somehow I felt that would hurt her still more to know anyone had seen her. I was behind the bushes and I felt like a thief seeing her there when she wouldn't have wanted me to, but I couldn't get away, and even if I had closed my eyes I couldn't help hearing that sob. The poor sweet child. I'm afraid she is in some real trouble. I've been wondering if it is connected with some of those young men we've seen driving in occasionally? Poor child without any mother! I must really try to get acquainted somehow and see if I can't win her confidence. My heart goes out to her."

The young man gave a startled look at his mother, and then turned and looked meditatively out of the window. His mother was thickening gravy for the moment. She was putting in the salt and pepper, a bit of butter, and stirring it while it bubbled smoothly over the fire. Presently Gordon turned back and watched her.

"Did she come back again?" he asked gravely, trying to make his voice sound quite casual.

"Yes, she came back, but she had stayed away longer than usual, and she was hurrying as if she were out of breath. And then about two o'clock a big moving van came driving in and went up to the house and stayed about an hour or more. I couldn't see so well, but I went up to your window and looked out because I was troubled. I didn't know but our folks had lost all their money and were moving out. But they didn't stay long enough to move all the furniture. It might have been just some things that belonged to someone else, or that they were selling or giving away, so my mind was free about that. The van was all closed up of course when it came out so I couldn't tell what like things they were that were taken away."

"My word, Mother! You certainly are getting to be a nosy little neighbor, prying into other folks' business. I never knew you to be so curious before," laughed Gordon, albeit with a thoughtful look in his eyes.

"Well, it's not exactly curiosity you know, son," protested the mother. "I just can't bear to think of that sweet pretty little girl having to suffer. I hope it's not more money troubles. You know that agent that rented this house to us said the owner had seen reverses and that was why he was willing to rent the cottage."

"I know." Gordon was grave again.

"But there are worse things of course than losing one's house and one's money," went on the mother. "I couldn't help wondering, was the child going to marry one of those men that call on her? The fat one, or the gray-haired one, or maybe the one with the long thin face and the foppish clothes? And maybe she just isn't happy about it. Oh, I'd like to get my arms about her and get her to let me help her a bit with her decisions. You know that van might have come to take her things away to her future home."

Gordon made a quick movement with his hand and almost knocked a cup off from the table. He caught it just in time, but sent a spoon clattering off on the floor.

"Oh, I say, Mother! Aren't you going a little too far with your wonderings?"

He tried to laugh but the sober look stayed in his eyes.

"Well, perhaps I am," smiled the mother. "I think perhaps I am making a story out of it. Being a stranger here with not very much to do all day I can't help being interested in what's about me. Pretty soon we'll get acquainted hereabouts and then it will be different. Though I shall never be quite so much interested in any other people I'm sure. I somehow feel they are in a sense our own folks because we're renting from them. Now, come, the dinner is ready. Let's sit down right away. I know you are good and hungry. Hark! Isn't that a taxi coming in the drive? Maybe it's a wedding after all." She laughed gaily, but Gordon turned sharply around and looked out of the kitchen window for a long time, and for once forgot to help his mother put the dinner on the table.

There was a bit of delay after all with the dinner, for Mrs. MacCarroll had been so interested in telling the happenings of the day that she had forgotten to put the butter and cream on the table, and then she had to go back to the refrigerator again for pickles and jelly, and to the pantry for some crackers for the soup.

Gordon so far recovered himself as to get a pitcher of water and fill the glasses, and then with another glance up at the window he remarked:

"There's no sign of any great festivity up at the house, Mother, only two rooms are lit up yet. And there! There comes the taxi going away. Perhaps her father has arrived. Didn't you say he was away?"

"Yes," said the mother. "That's probably it. Come, let's get on with the meal. I'm afraid everything will be stone cold. Ask the blessing, child, and let's forget the neighbors while we eat. Besides I want to hear all about your day."

Then Gordon MacCarroll bowed his head and asked that blessing which was more than a mere saying of grace, and outside the tall hedge his heartfelt petition reached to the lonely girl waiting there in the dark, and was imprinted on her memory indelibly.

They had a pleasant time at their evening meal, they always did together, those two. They talked over the developments of the day and Gordon's work, and they laid their cheerful plans for the future, and then Gordon helped his mother put the kitchen to rights for the night.

"You'd better get right to bed, son, and make up your sleep. You look dead tired. Do you have to go very early tomorrow morning?"

"No, not till eight-thirty," responded the son cheerfully. "I'm due at the office in the morning to report, and the official heads don't care to arise at dawn to hear what I've done, so for once I can have a real sleep."

When Gordon had gone to his room and closed his door he stood for a long time looking out his window toward the great house. There were lights in plenty now, from the first floor to the roof, and in a kind of consternation he watched. Then it occurred to him that a single taxi wasn't likely to make a wedding, and he stood and laughed at himself. He was getting as curious as his mother. Besides, there, the lights were going out again!

But though he turned away and turned on his own light, trying to banish the thought of the little lady from the great house weeping with her lips against a flower, he could not get his mind at rest, and finally he just frankly opened his door and went down the stairs.

"I'm just running out to the garage for a minute, Mother," he called, and went out the back door. A few minutes later he came in with a small white envelope in his hand, and his mother put her head down on her pillow with a smile. What a good dear boy he was, and what blessed fortune was hers that she should have him when all the rest of her family were gone!

And about that time up at the big house, the new mistress having adroitly put Maggie in a very bad light before her husband, had slipped off upstairs to reconnoitre, with a gleam of victory in her eyes. She had accomplished her purpose of driving out her stepdaughter sooner than she had hoped. But perhaps she would not have been so sure of her victory if she could have seen the tired troubled look on her husband's face when he came out in the kitchen to talk to Maggie and try to get her to reconsider her rash resignation.

He looked old and gray and his shoulders drooped as he came out and stood beside the sink where Maggie was washing up her tea towels, and dripping tears into the dish water.

"What's this Mrs. Disston has been telling me, Maggie, that you're going to desert us? That surely can't be right. I told her I thought there must be some mistake. I told her it must be merely some little misunderstanding. You've been with us so long, Maggie, we won't know what to do without you. I never thought you would leave us."

"I wouldn't, sir, not fer a minute if 'twas juist yerself an' Miss Diana. I'd stick by ye till there wasn't a stroke of work left in me. But it's herself I canna abide. She an' I could never stay by in the same hoose. It was bad enough her visitin' when the missis was here ta manage, but now, her with the airs she takes, I no can bide an' work fer her."

The master's eye grew stern.

"Nonsense, Maggie!" he said sharply. "I'm afraid Diana has been putting notions in your head. Diana is a foolish child who will get over her pettishness in a day or two and everything will be all right."

"Miss Diana didna needta put notions in my head. I had thae afore she did. Ef you'd ever tried to get a meal in this kitchen with that limb o' Satan around you'd ken withoot bein' told, and I'm no bidin' an' that's a' there is tae it. I'm aenly here the noo ta give ye the letter."

"Letter?" The father turned a grave puzzled look on her.

Maggie fumbled in the capacious bib of her apron and finally brought out Diana's letter.

"I was ta give it tae ye where there was no one else by. She wanted ye should read it by yer lane. After that I've na more ta dae with it. I'm packin' noo, an' leavin' the hoose the nicht, an' ye needn't pay me the wages that's comin' tae me unless ye like. I'm gaein' juist the same."

The man took his daughter's letter in a hand that trembled and tried to make his voice stern as he searched the face of the old servant.

"Maggie, have you been helping on my daughter in this nonsense? Did you help her to go away? Did you put this idea in her head?"

"Ef ye mean did I try ta comfort her when I saw her grievin' her heart away an' cryin' her pretty eyes out by her lane, yes, I did. Ef ye mean did I help her get her bit things thegither when she said she was gangin' awa, sure I did! But fer puttin' the notions in her head, na! She had thae notions herself, an' rightly, an' ef you hadna been as blind as a bat you wud have seen it yersel' afore it was too late!"

Anger rose in the father's face and he lifted his head haughtily, preparing a stern rebuke. But Maggie went about the room doing little last things, hanging up her dishcloths, hanging the dishpan on its hook, closing the cupboard door with a finality that seemed to have a strange foreboding, and suddenly the master of the house realized that his time might be short, and he was losing another link in the chain that had made up the home life all these years. Suppose Maggie should carry out her purpose and disappear too, and he would have lost a valuable clue to finding his foolish little girl?

"Maggie," he said, and there was almost an appeal in his voice for somehow he began to realize that he *must* have this woman on his side, "Where is my daughter?"

"She didn't tell me aught aboot where she was gaein' save that she was on a visit. I gathered she might see some relatives, an' perhaps some friends too. I didna ask her. I minded it was none of my business. But ef ye're thinkin' she'll be comin' back, ye'll find yerself grandly mistaken. She'll not coom back while that wumman is mistress, er my name's not Maggie Morrison. Ye brought the hussy here, an' noo ye'll hev ta abide by yer own act."

"Maggie!" said Mr. Disston coldly. "You are forgetting yourself. You are presuming on your long connection in our home. I don't want to hear any more such impertinence!"

"Nae, I'm not forgettin' myself," said Maggie arrogantly, "I'm juist statin' fact. But I'm done noo, an' I'm gaein' up the stair tae get my bit things an' leave ye. I've naethin' more tae say except one thing. Ef ye're iver alane an' need me, juist send fer me, an' I'll cum back. But not whilst that hussy is in the hoose as mistress. I canna abide her, an' I'd na sleep under the same roof with her. She's a *hussy*, an' that's all there is tae it, an' ye'll find it oot ta yer ain sorrow soon enough! Good-bye!" and dashing away the tears Maggie stormed up the back stairs to her room, and the master went to his library with his letter and locked the door to read it.

And over across the lawn a young man, a stranger, knelt in the moonlight, with a letter in his hand, and prayed for a girl he did not know, whom the Lord had laid upon his heart.

And out through the night and the darkness, into a new country, the train was hurrying along mile after mile carrying a sorrowful girl far away from all that she knew and loved. A girl who lay with her face against a handful of pale carnations and kept them wet all night with her tears.

Anger and prayer and tears, the breath of flowers watered by bitter tears, a girl groping in terrible sorrow and darkness.

10

THE train drew in to the station an hour late, and Diana pale with weeping and the long vigil came out into the strange station and looked about her. She had traveled often with her father but very little by herself. She was not used to looking after the details of travel, and she had never been to this city where the aunt of her mother's lived. Now that she was here she shrank inexpressibly from meeting her. She had half a mind to turn around and go back, only where could she go? She was an exile from home, a wayfarer and a stranger on the face of the earth. The realization of what it was going to mean swept over her as she followed the porter carrying her luggage, and such a wave of homesickness and heartsickness came over her that she felt she simply must drop right down there on the platform and give up.

But instead she followed the porter to the taxi stand, gave her directions clearly and climbed into the cab, heartily wishing she had never come in search of this unknown aunt whose only contact during the years had been an occasional letter, and a gift of a handkerchief or collar at Christmas. Why had she come here to her?

Why hadn't she chosen some one of her mother's friends and confided in her? Why hadn't she gone even to Maggie's sister's for awhile as the good old servant had several times during yesterday suggested?

Oh, she knew the answers to all those questions. She had thoroughly canvassed the whole matter during the watches of the night, and it had seemed that this was the only refuge she could depend upon that was far enough to elude the indomitable Helen. So here she was and the immediate future had to be faced.

Yet she was unable to find any help for her mind as she was whirled through one unfamiliar street after another, out into the suburbs. It was a pleasant street into which they finally turned, a bit common, and very old-fashioned, not in the least like the wide highway on which the Disston estate was situated. Well, she couldn't expect that of course. She was an exile now and must be content with what she found.

Presently they stopped before a large old-fashioned house surrounded by a dismal yard containing a few scraggly trees. It looked comfortable enough, but a bit neglected, and as if no one had cared about it for a good many years. Diana gave a quick comprehending glance and her heart dropped several degrees. It wasn't a pleasant outlook. Still, there was a yard, and it was not a bad neighborhood. All the houses had more or less ground about them, and there were even one or two little cottages that had almost a cheerful look. This house where she was going seemed to rather dominate the street, as if its past respectability gave it the right. Yet there was nothing really attractive and welcoming to make it seem like a refuge in her distress. It was comfortable and solid and old-fashioned, that was all.

Diana's heart beat wildly while she paid the fare and got out of the taxi to look around her. It suddenly seemed to her a very great breach of etiquette that she had sent no word ahead to announce her coming. She should at least have sent a telegram to ask if it would be convenient. Perhaps even now she should drive back to the station and telephone to ask if she might come. Yet that would seem very odd to the taxi driver. Of course it was none of his business what she did if she paid him, yet he would be likely to think she was crazy. Well, she was here now and of course she must go on. She could say she was taking a trip and had stopped off to see her aunt. Strange it hadn't occurred to her to think of this before. She had been so taken up with her own troubles that this end of her journey had not been a consideration at all.

She walked slowly up to the house which seemed to grow more forbidding the nearer she drew. The taxi driver was following with her bags. She wished she had told him not to mind, and tried to carry them herself, though they were heavy. Then she would be rid of him and could even turn back if she liked.

As she mounted the steps to the wide piazza she noticed a dilapidated doll flung abandonedly under a porch chair, suggesting the recent presence of a child. A child? The aunt had no children! She was supposed to be living alone with an old servant. But perhaps the servant had a child. A child, even the child of a servant, would bespeak a little cheer. Diana drew a deep breath and told the driver to leave the bags on the porch. Then she put out a timid hand and raised the old-fashioned knocker.

The knocker was loose and echoed through the house as if it were made of sounding boards. Diana shrank away from the door and wished again that she had not come. Then she heard footsteps coming and she felt that frightened sinking in her heart again. What should she say? How should she explain her sudden appearance? How could she tell an unknown relative what had happened in her life. A stranger! This woman she had come to see was in reality a stranger! And now she remembered that her mother had said she never approved of her marriage to Stephen Disston. She had wanted Mother to marry an older man by the name of Eldridge who had two half-grown children by a former marriage and a handsome house across the street. That must be the Eldridge house over there, built of stone with elaborate casements and ornate columns. Suppose Mother had married him and lived there! Diana shivered at the thought and turned to meet the dowdy girl who opened the door. Then suddenly Diana didn't know what to say. Why hadn't she planned this all out?

But she summoned her senses and asked if Mrs. Whitley was in.

The girl was frankly staring Diana up and down, admiring her clothes. There was no mistaking that look, and Diana was suddenly conscious of her heavy heart beneath her chic garments. She had a feeling that presently the girl would see that heart too, and wonder. Then the girl came to herself and answered:

"No, she doesn't live here."

"Doesn't *live* here!" repeated Diana startled. "Why, isn't this Moreland Avenue? Isn't this number 425?"

"Sure," said the girl, "but she doesn't own this place any more. My father bought this place over a year ago."

"Oh!" Diana caught her breath. "But where did she move? Is it far away?"

"Quite a ways," said the girl complacently. "They say it takes about two hours on the bus. My father went up there once to see her about the house settlement. He said she was fixed real nice."

"Oh," said Diana, a troubled look coming into her eyes. "Do you have the address?"

"My father has. But he isn't home today. He went off fishing with a friend. He won't be home till late tonight. And my mother isn't here either. She's gone up in the country to nurse my aunt. She's real sick. Just I and my brothers are here, and they wouldn't know the address either. But you wouldn't have any trouble finding it. It's a Home, you know. One of those where you put in all the money you have and you get a nice big room to yourself and they're bound to take care of you while you live no matter how old and sick you get. My father says her room is peachy, and she's got it fixed up lovely with what furniture she saved from this house. It's up to a place called Wynnewood. You could hire a taxi, I suppose, to take you, but it would cost an awful lot."

"Oh!" said Diana again in a growing dismay, giving a glance of trepidation around the grubby-looking front yard with a sudden relief that she didn't have to stay here, even for a day.

But—! Where *was* she going?

She turned back to the girl.

"Do you know how long she has been gone from here?"

"Sure!" said the girl. "It's just a year ago last Saturday that we moved in. My father was talking about it last Sunday."

Diana gave another troubled look into nowhere.

"Well—I suppose I might as well go on, then—" the words trailed off uncertainly.

"You can come in if you want," said the girl, casting a hesitant glance at the smart pile of baggage.

"Oh, no," said Diana quickly. There was no point in going in. "But—" she paused and looked down the road. "I'm sorry I let the taxi go until I was sure whether this was the right place."

"Oh, I can call him for you," offered the girl brightly.

"He's only up the road a piece. You see he's engaged to my cousin and he takes every chance he can to stop at the house when he gets up this way. I can send my kid brother over to call him if you want."

"Oh, thank you!" said Diana, strangely grateful for this offer. But what was she going to do next?

The girl offered her a chair on the porch while she went to send the little brother on his errand, and Diana sat down and looked across the street at the ugly pretentious house that her mother did not marry all those long years ago, and thought of the lovely mansion she had left last night, the rolling lawns, the groups of century-old trees, the picturesque stone cottage by the gate, and the flowers that had lain there in the shadow on the grass so mysteriously, and sudden tears sprang to her eyes.

But the girl was coming back carrying a glass of water.

"I thought perhaps you were thirsty," she said handing over the glass, and quite frankly settling herself in an old porch rocker to examine her guest. "Ted'll be back in a minute," she added. "It's only up the road a little piece."

"Is that house across the way owned by a Mr. Eldridge?" asked Diana with sudden interest.

"Why, yes!" said the girl. "How did you know? Did you ever live in this town?"

"No," said Diana with a little shiver—she was glad she had never lived about here—"but my mother did for a little while. She used to tell me about some Eldridges across the road from her aunt's."

"Oh!" said the girl giving her another speculative glance and then looking across the way to the ugly old Eldridge house, trying to harmonize house and girl. Then her eyes came back to Diana.

"He's real old," she explained, "Mr. Eldridge. He's just buried his third wife, and they say it might be he'll marry Miss Hurst, the nurse that's taking care of him.

He's sick you know and not expecting to get well, and he's mad with all his children, so he has nobody to leave his property to. My! I wish he'd leave it to me! I'd know what to do with it." The girl's face took on a wistful look.

"They say his children was all mad at him when he married this last time, and they tried to put him in the insane asylum, but he was too smart for them, and now he has disinherited all of them."

The girl reeled the story off as if it were a fairy tale, and Diana sat up sharply and drew a deep breath. Marrying! Marrying! It was everywhere! Why couldn't people be true to their first marriage? And here were other children suffering as she was! She felt a fellow feeling for them.

"Where are they all, the children?" she asked suddenly, wondering if their state would throw any light on her problem.

"Oh, different places I guess. There's one daughter over in the next town teaching school, she's the oldest. They call her an old maid, and she's been teaching a good many years. The next girl married a farmer but they're awful poor. He's got a big mortgage on his farm and he might lose it this fall. The youngest girl ran off with a fella and they don't know where she is, and the boy's been in jail twice already."

The girl told it off as indifferently as if she were detailing the fate of a lot of squirrels, but Diana stared at the ugly old house aghast! Her life had always been so guarded! She had not realized how hard life was for many! So, she was not the only one who suffered! She had emerged out of her haven into a world where suffering and sordidness were on every hand!

"It's awful when parents get married again!" announced the girl quite irrelevantly and apathetically.

"It is!" said Diana rising suddenly as she saw the taxi careening down the road in the distance.

"I'll help ya down with the bags," said the girl taking up a shining suitcase admiringly. "Ted's in a hurry I guess. It's almost train time again and he has to be back on time or he'll lose his job."

"You've been very kind," said Diana gratefully, picking up a smaller bag and finding it taken from her hand by the grimy fingers of a ten-year-old who had likely gone after the taxi.

As the taxi swung up to the sidewalk Diana summoned a smile and handed out a bit of money to the boy, and then, shyly, gave the girl a bill.

"Just to remember me by," she said brightly and got in, thankful that she did not have to stay in that dismal spot overnight.

"Where to?" asked the driver, and Diana suddenly was brought face to face with her future again. Where should she go next?

"Wantta go back ta the station?" persisted the driver, thinking she had not heard him.

"Oh, yes," said Diana coming out of her daze. "Certainly."

"Which train ya takin'?" asked the driver.

"Oh, why, I have to enquire about trains. I'm not sure yet."

The young man Ted appeared to want to converse, but Diana answered him coolly and was glad when the station came in sight again.

"Goin' back south again?" he asked.

"That depends," said Diana sweetly, "I'm not sure yet."

Diana went and sat in the station for two long hours trying to think out what she should do. She wrote out a list of all her friends whom it would be possible for her to visit, and weighed each possibility carefully, deciding at last that it would be utterly out of the question for her to visit anyone in her present state of mind. She couldn't bring herself to the telling of what had happened to her, not before mere casual acquaintances, and that was what most of her friends had become in the last three years. No, she had got to get herself more in hand, get more balance, work out a philosophy of living that would keep her from shivering and bursting into tears at everything that reminded her of her calamity before she mingled again with people who thought they had a right to question her.

Having decided against visits, she weighed, just briefly, the possibility of marrying any of the men she knew who would be likely to want to marry her, and found the idea so unpleasant that she quickly put that thought away as not to be further considered.

Then what should she do?

If she had to provide a home for herself permanently could she do it on her own small income? She would never ask her father for money since she had left his home and shelter. And if she did she felt quite sure Helen would counsel him not to give her anything. Naturally he might think that would be a way to bring her back home, for she knew in her heart that he would miss her. No matter how much he might care for his new wife, he loved her, and naturally he would want her to return. She put her head wearily back against the station wall and thought about that. Perhaps she ought to have stayed awhile just to convince him that it would not be a happy thing for anybody if she did. But no, Helen would only have made it appear that she was always in fault. It was better as it was, only what was she going to do with herself? She was not wanted anywhere, except of course by her father, and where would be the point in convincing him that she could not stay at home? It was too late for that now. And she was tired, oh, so deadly tired. She wished everything were at an end. Yet one couldn't jump off the bridge, or wade out in a stream and drown. Respectable people didn't do things like that. Not unless they were crazy of course, and she wasn't crazy. She had to live on and somehow go on alone! Alone! What a terrible word that was!

Well, she had to do it and the sooner she started the better. Why not begin right here in this strange town? The first thing would be to find a room somewhere. Not a boarding place. That would entail other people who had a right to enquire into one's business, and she was just now like a hurt animal that wanted to crawl away from all its kind and lick its wounds in secret.

So she checked her baggage and started out.

IT was almost noon and as she passed a restaurant she realized that she could not go on long without something to eat, so she stopped and ordered a cup of coffee and toyed with a buttered roll. She drank the coffee but somehow the food did not attract her. It was the first time in her life that she had ever eaten in a cheap restaurant, but she felt that that did not matter. Any food in any restaurant would have been as uninteresting.

Then she went on her way up one street and down another aimlessly, wondering where to begin. She had never hunted rooms in a city before. She had no idea where to look for rooming houses. Finally she bought a paper and stood on a corner studying advertisements, and then went on again in search of a place to lay her head for the night.

It is safe to say that Diana never had dreamed that there were such places as some of those she saw that afternoon, following that newspaper column of advertised apartments. They were not all bad of course. Some were really attractive, but then the price soared beyond her modest income and frightened her with the cost of life.

Her search narrowed down at last to two, one on the third floor of a walk-up rooming house, its windows overlooking the roofs in the theatrical district. An ill-smelling bathroom down the hall would have to be shared with occupants of the entire floor. It was stifling hot and filled with the din of the city arising in a roar from the streets below. The other one was small, ornate, with built-in cupboards, cheap mirrors and a tiny uncertain automatic elevator to the fifth floor. A fire siren screeched all the time she was looking at it and Diana fancied a night, and the building on fire, and that inadequate elevator gone below and *staying* there! Diana fled from the spot, but a half-hour later returned and forced herself to consider the details, because it had seemed the only approach to anything like the life to which she had been accustomed. She looked out the windows and saw an undertaking establishment across the street, and a neat sign of coffins hung next door, and fled again. Back in the station she considered both places and did some figuring, and then rested her head back against the seat and closed her eyes, wishing that life was over and she did not have to consider any more possibilities. When she thought of those apartments she seemed to see herself lying alone, unknown, in a coffin.

A trainman slammed a metal sign into its frame over the station door, announcing a train back to her home city, and a great longing came over her to board it and return. Back to where she was at least known, and knew her way around. Back where she could tell the sordid parts of town from the decent respectable ones. If she must go into lodgings—and she was still determined she would not go to boarding—certainly it would be better to know what kind of place she was taking. Also, she had learned enough that afternoon to realize that she could get a room unfurnished cheaper than furnished, and by that means save the money she would be spending for storage. Also, if she was going to use her own furniture it would cost a lot to move it away up here in this far city.

It suddenly seemed to her most preposterous to try to stay here, with no aunt in the vicinity, and no point to the whole thing except to get as far away from Helen as possible. Surely she could hide nearer to home and not be found.

She remembered a woman's hotel in the home city where a friend had once stayed for a few days. Why could she not go there for a week and look around until she found the right place?

It was growing dark. The strange noisy station seemed aloof and unfriendly. The continual coming and going of trains began to weary her inexpressibly. Oh, to be at home in her own sweet room, to lie down and sleep until she was rested, until her heart did not ache so feebly. Ah! But there was no home! The room was stark and bare, and her lovely things stored in a great storage house! She had no home any more! It was entirely up to her now to make a place in which to stay, and she had no desire whatever, no interest in it at all. She opened her handbag to get out a handkerchief and the faint perfume of the carnations stole out into the sooty atmosphere of the station and carried her back on a breath to the lawn of her father's estate, and the tall trees shading the spot where the mystery flowers had lain, and a longing filled her to go back. Perhaps this morning there had been another flower and she had not been there to find it! Perhaps another would find it! Could Helen? That would be just like Helen to steal her flowers, her few mystery flowers, after she had stolen her father and her home and everything that was worth while in her life. Ah! And perhaps tomorrow there would be another flower—that is if no one else found them— But—surely by then the flower person would discover that she was gone—and that it was useless to drop any more. Would her note be found by the right one? Would it be read, and would it be understood?

What if Helen should find it? The thought seized her heart like the gripping of pain. Even there in the noisy station with the people jostling one another, she could hear that light mocking laugh that Helen would give should she find that note in the grass! Oh, why had she ever been silly enough to write that note?

Her cheeks burned red and hot at the thought. Oh, if she could only go in the night and hunt for it and find it and destroy it!

And suddenly Diana knew she was going back.

Not to her home of course. But she must get back where she knew her way about. She must find a place somewhere where her soul belonged. She was lost, lost, lost, in a great world that knew her not nor cared. There was nobody who cared now, except her father, and he was angry at her.

She went in a sudden panic to the ticket window and asked a few questions. She bought a return ticket to the home city. She went to the lunch counter in the station and swallowed a few bites, drank a cup of coffee, and was ready, standing with her bags at her feet beside the gateway, waiting for her train, fifteen minutes before the scheduled time for its arrival.

She might have been sitting, resting on one of the station benches, for she was deadly weary, but she was too restless to rest. She had to be there, ready to go out the moment the gates were open. So she stood, tense, braced, and looking with unseeing eyes about on the great dusky room with its coming and going throngs. Why had she come out here? How had she hoped to find haven even with an aunt? For now she saw clearly that if the aunt had been there as she had expected, and she had been obliged to stay several days to explain her presence there at all, it would have been torture. What she wanted was to be alone in some little quiet place where she could rest and think, and try to straighten out what this life meant that she was called upon to live, this life which she had no right to lay down, and yet which seemed to have no solution to its problems. She had got to find that out before she could go on any further. Aunts and friends or even strangers could only hinder a process like this. She must be alone to think. She must find a solution to life in order to endure it. She had always had someone to lean upon, first her darling mother, and then her loving father. But now she had neither, and she had in addition an enemy! That was the situation. She had to work it out alone, *ALONE!*

The delicacy of her face, the rippling of her hair, the deep appeal of her eyes made her a noticeable figure as she stood there alone by the train gateway, surrounded by her luggage. More than one weary traveler waiting for a belated train, or a wandering member of his household, watched her idly as one would gaze upon a flower garden in the rain. But her eyes roved over them all restlessly, not seeing them at all.

She did not know that there were heavy lines graven in her soft face where but yesterday it was smooth and fine, she did not know that her eyes were full of anguish that anyone might read. She thought herself a quiet patient figure, unobtrusively waiting for a train, and when she saw a slender figure rise from the bench across the room and come toward her she noticed her no more than if she had been the station janitor going about with his broom and long-handled pan to gather up the papers and the match ends.

But then the other girl paused beside her, shyly, sweetly, with such a friendly look in her plain gray eyes, and spoke half hesitantly:

"I brought you this," said the other girl. "I've been reading it, and I thought perhaps it would rest you to read it too. I could see something has hurt you. I'm sorry. I understood because I've been hurt too. But I found something that will heal the hurt, and you will too if you'll read this and believe it."

She handed out a tiny printed tract, just two miniature pages. There was a look in her eyes that could not anger anyone no matter how proud.

Diana brought startled eyes down to the bit of paper the other girl held out, and a shade of the Disston pride stiffened her features. Then she turned her glance to the girl who offered it and saw the gentleness in the girl's face, and her own eyes softened.

The stranger was plainly dressed, even poorly, in the cheapest kind of garments, with a little hat that might have come from a bargain counter in the ten cent store, and her hands were cased in cheap ill-fitting cotton gloves, that is one was, though the other was bare, showing that though delicately formed it was rough and hardened with work. Her shoes were shabby and her dress of common dark cotton, ill-cut and not at all becoming, yet there shone in the girl's face a light and joy that made her noticeable anywhere, and looking into her clear sweet eyes Diana could not help but trust her.

She put out her hand to take the little paper offered, and as she did so the other girl's face lighted with a joy inexpressible as if it gave her real pleasure to have this stranger accept her gift.

"What is it?" Diana asked wonderingly, looking at the paper and then up at the girl.

"It's something wonderful. I can't stay to explain. My train's called and I have to hurry, but you read it. You trust it! It helped me and I know it'll help you. Good-bye!" The girl started away, but pausing turned back and said in a low sweet voice, "I'll be praying that you'll get what I got!"

Then she was gone.

Diana watched her threading her way swiftly through the throngs, hurrying through the gate, her newspaper bundle gripped in one arm, her ticket in the other hand. One bright look she cast back and then was gone. Diana stood wondering, the little paper trembling in her hand, her thoughts utterly turned away from herself for the first time that day. This was a poor girl, hard-working, thin and not well-fed apparently. There was a look in her eyes of suffering endured, and yet how they lighted up with real joy! There was even a sparkle in her voice! Diana stood wondering, staring at the gate where the girl had disappeared till suddenly a trainman came up and slammed open the steel gate that led to her own train and called it out, reaching out his punch to her ticket, and Diana was roused to her own situation again.

She followed the porter down the steps to the train, and up into the car, down the aisle to her compartment in a sort of daze, still bearing in her hand the tiny fluttering paper, gripping it as if it were something precious. And when she had paid the porter and settled down in her seat with a weary sigh of relief, she sat still holding that bit of paper, staring out the window and thinking about the look in that other girl's face.

It was not until the train was finally moving that she turned her eyes to the paper and began to read with deepening interest.

HE UNDERSTANDS!

In large letters it stood out as the title to the tiny message. Startled, she read on, as if it had been written by someone she knew, and sent to her as a special message in her need. It would not have been any more startling if a telegraph boy had come through the train and handed it to her, and she had found Maggie's or her mother's name attached to it.

No matter what problem or sorrow is in your life today, there is Someone who understands and cares.

That was all that was on that little front page, standing out clearly from the paper in large type, as if a voice were speaking it to her soul. Diana was almost afraid to turn the tiny page lest the spell would be broken and she would find it merely the advertisement of some trickster, some beauty parlor, or new product. Then her mind became impatient and she turned the leaf tremblingly, so much she wanted it to be some real help for her need.

One reason why the Son of God came to earth and took a human body, was so that He might suffer and understand, and help us in our griefs.

Diana read that over twice, wondering if that could really be true and how the writer knew that? This then was religion, and she had been brought up to respect religion, although it had never meant anything practical to her. But these were arresting sentences and her need was very great. Her soul seemed to be clutching for the bit of a message, and seeking to draw the truth from its pages. She read on.

There is no kind of sorrow He does not know, even to having His beloved Father turn His back upon Him for a time!

Oh! Was that true? How had that been? Had God really turned His back upon Christ? And why? There were two references below in tiny type. Diana wished she had a Bible that she might look them up. Perhaps the references would explain the statement. But how wonderful that her very situation should be described! For her father had in reality turned his back upon her. She remembered that gesture of impatience when she had flung her arms about him and cried on his shoulder. How he had put her away and gone and stood by the mantel with his back half turned away.

The tears sprang into her eyes unbidden and she had to dash them away before she could go on reading. It seemed to her nothing short of miraculous that this little message should have fallen into her hands tonight, of all nights, when she so much needed it, this message that exactly fitted and understood her heart's cry.

> For as He has Himself felt the pain of temptation and trial, He is able also to help those who are tempted and tried.

There were more references here, and then the last little page went on in big letters again:

> In the darkest hour of your life remember He is a living, loving Saviour.

Three more small lines of references again. That was all. How she wished again for a Bible! She had not brought hers with her. It had never been a vital part of her life. It had not occurred to her to take it with her in her suitcase, and she could not even remember if she had packed it with the other books that were in storage. She was not sure when she had seen it last. Well, no matter, it was just a small fine print copy, anyway, and she could surely get one anywhere. Didn't they have them in hotel rooms? It seemed to her that she remembered having seen one there the last time she and her father took a trip together. Well, when she got somewhere she would get a Bible and look up the references and see if there was really anything in it to give her comfort. She could not afford to pass by any chance, no matter how frail, of finding something to ease her pain.

She read the little tract over again slowly, before she prepared for the night. As she lay down she had a vision of that stranger girl in the station, her bright earnest face, and the words she had called back in leaving. She had promised to pray for her! What a strange thing for a stranger to do. And yet, if it were all true perhaps that was the way the children of God ought to do with one another. Another time such interference by an utter stranger would have aroused her scorn, would have repelled her. But now her heart felt strangely warmed toward another human creature who had suffered herself and therefore had rightly read her own suffering.

Finally she closed her eyes and tried to think of God as looking down on her and caring what became of her and how this matter of her life turned out.

"Oh God," she whispered, softly like a prayer, "if You really know and care, won't You show me how to find You, for I need You very greatly."

She fell asleep at last with the little paper held tightly in her hand.

ABOUT that same time Gordon MacCarroll arrived home at the cottage, put up his excellent cheap little car for the night and came in to get the belated supper that his mother was keeping warm and delicious for him.

"Soup!" he said giving a pleased sniff at the atmosphere as he entered. "Good old beef soup and plenty of potatoes and dumplings. There's nothing better than that."

"Yes," said his mother with a pleased smile, "it's best when you don't know how long you have to wait to serve it. It always keeps well. Now sit down right away. I know you must be starved."

"Well, all but—" said the son. "And say, I'm tired tonight! I had a lot of difficulty finding my location today, and difficulty with my man after I found him, but I won out and got my contract signed, so it doesn't matter," he said as he passed his plate.

"That's good! Tell me all about it," said the mother with satisfaction, watching the light of content play over her boy's face.

So while they dallied restfully with the soup, and more

soup, they talked about Gordon's business, he telling little details of the day, describing the scenery along the way he had driven, the people he had met. Gordon was a great mimic and his mother was a good audience. She enjoyed to the full every bit of character sketch he gave, and followed his delight in the woods and trees and sky effects. They were good company for one another, these two.

It was not until the delicious apple pie, delicate of crust and transparent with dripping jellied fruit, was brought in, with its accompanying velvety cheese, that Mrs. MacCarroll remembered.

"Oh," she said suddenly, "I've news for you about the big house. I had a caller today!"

"A caller?" said Gordon, his eyes lighting, "someone from the village?"

"No, no one from the village yet, son, what could you expect? We haven't been in the cottage but a month and people haven't discovered us yet. Besides, we've been traveling about from one church to another of a Sabbath trying to find out where we belong, so people don't know where to place us yet. Another thing, too, we're among big estates, and we're neither one nor the other. We're not servants, nor mansion owners, and how would anybody call on us yet till they learn us?"

"Well, I don't care, Mother, only for your sake. I know you miss the hosts of friends you left in Edinburgh."

"That's all right, Gordon. I miss them of course, but real friends like the friends of a lifetime aren't made in a day. Don't be in such a rush. I'm content."

"You're a wonderful little mother," said the son with a tender light in his eyes. "You wouldn't complain if you didn't have any friends, I know. But I do want you to have a few right away so you won't be lonely when I have to be away. But I interrupted you. Who was your caller? You don't mean to tell me it was the Little Lady?"

"No," smiled the mother shaking her head with a flitting of sadness in her eyes, "I wish it had been. No, it was only the servant woman, Maggie, as she said I was to call her. She came to bring me the recipe for that pudding she promised the other day, and to bid me good-bye. She's gone."

"You mean the whole family are moving away?" asked Gordon with dismay in his face. "They haven't sold the house, have they?"

"No," said his mother with a look of having more news, "no, but the woman, Maggie, is leaving. It seems there have been great doings up at our estate, and Maggie can't stand them. The master has married again and neither the daughter nor the servant like the new mistress, and they have both left, so we won't see our little lady any more. Isn't that a pity? That must have been what she was crying about when she went by."

"You don't say!" said the young man dropping his fork suddenly and then recovering it again and taking a long time to cut the next translucent bite of pastry.

"Yes," said his mother sympathetically, as she poured another cup of coffee for Gordon. "I feel so sorry for her. Maggie says she's a wonderful girl, and that this new stepmother is a perfect tartar, really malicious you know, doing mean things just for the sake of doing them, and then laughing at her victim."

"Still," said the young man thoughtfully taking a slow bite of cheese, "you can't always tell about a servant's gossip, you know. She is probably prejudiced."

"Well," said the mother lifting her brows meditatively, "she doesn't just seem to be the ordinary servant. She's a Christian woman I should say and she loved her former mistress a great deal. She's been telling me about how lovely she was, and it does seem strange that a man who had such a lovely wife should have no better judgment—"

"That's it, Mother, he probably has, and this is just prejudice—"

"But Gordon, listen, if she speaks the truth, and I think she does, she seems like an honest woman, this new mistress is something of a freak, rather young you know, and exercising her wiles over an older man, flattering him and torturing his daughter behind his back, yet making it appear that the girl has done it all!"

Gordon frowned. Then after a moment's thought he said, as if he were thinking it out, arguing with himself, "But this woman shouldn't have told you these things of course! We're practically strangers and a really loyal servant wouldn't have told the troubles of her master's home. If she isn't loyal she probably isn't true."

"No," said the mother thoughtfully, "I don't believe that is the case with this woman. She didn't mean to tell me anything. She was quite proper when she came in with the recipe, and told me most formally that she wouldn't be here again, and that the young lady had sent word she couldn't make the promised call after all as she had been obliged to go away in a hurry. But when I said it would be all right for her to come when she returned, and that I would be looking forward to it the woman turned sharply as if she were going away, and then I saw that she was crying, and I said: 'Why, is anything the matter, my dear? Isn't she coming back?' and she just stood there and sobbed silently into her handkerchief for a full minute and then she got out the words: 'No, I'm afraid not.'

"I didn't quite know what to say and I didn't like to ask any more questions, but in a minute she wiped her eyes and turned around and said in quite a dignified tone:

"'You see, ma'am, the master is marryin' agin, and my little lady feels she can't bide in the hoose.'

"'Oh,' I said, 'that's too bad! But maybe she'll change her mind and come back later. Those things are hard to bear when they first happen you know, but time heals almost everything. Maybe something will happen that they'll get to know one another better, and then perhaps she'll be glad to come back to her lovely home.' But the woman shook her head. 'No,' she said most decidedly, 'she'll na coom. It was that hard for her to gae, but she'll na return. She knows the wumman fu' well a'ready. She's her cousin three times removed, an' mony's the time she's suffered under a visit from her. She's a hussy an' thot's true as truth! I am thot shamed tae be sayin' it, but it's true! It's why I'm na stayin' mysel'. Naebuddy could bide in the same hoose wi' her. She's a trollop! A wicked trollop! An' I couldn't blame the poor wee bairn fer leavin'.'"

The young man listened with growing sympathy.

"But doesn't her father do anything about it?" he asked sharply. "Or didn't she say anything about him?"

"Oh, yes," laughed the mother, "she said plenty after she got warmed up and started. And yet you could see she was trying to be loyal to him too. She said he was 'thot fey aboot the hussy that he couldna see straight.' She said he was 'a good mon but blind as a bat,' and she went on to include all mankind in a general statement that all men were more or less 'feckless when it came to joodgment aboot lassies.'"

"But what about his own daughter? Isn't she a lassie?" said Gordon, and there was a sharpness in his tone as if he were arguing with the father in question. His mother looked up with surprise in her eyes, then laughed again.

"Oh, she says the father is sure the daughter will come around by and by and be as much in love with her new stepmother as he is." But Gordon did not smile. Instead he ate his last bit of pie thoughtfully, almost seriously.

"It seems queer," he said almost savagely, "that a man who has lived his life up to the time when his daughter is grown up shouldn't be able to forget himself enough to think of her. It's selfishness, with a daughter like that. I can't help thinking he is to blame."

"But you don't know either of them," said his mother, surprised. "You can't tell what the daughter is, really. She looks very pretty seeing her go by, and very sweet, but you can't ever be sure."

"Can't I? Well, how long is it since you were saying almost the same thing about her, Mother Mine?"

"Yes, I know, but still—we don't really *know!*"

"Well, just in general, then, no man has a right to bring a second mother on the scene unless his children are happy about it."

"But Gordon, you know there are some lovely stepmothers—" protested his mother. "There was Aunt Genevieve! And there was Mrs. Stacey. There couldn't have been happier homes, and those children all adored those stepmothers."

"Of course there are exceptions," said Gordon. "I grant that, but they all knew and loved the stepmothers before they became their stepmothers."

"And there was Mrs. McCorkle, and Mrs. Reamer, and that dear Mrs. Bowman in Edinburgh."

"But the children were mere babes in all three of those cases and didn't know the difference, and besides, Mother, you know every one of those women were saints. This woman, you say, is a hussy!"

"I know," the mother laughed, "and I can't help being sorry for the girl, Gordon. She must feel it terribly!"

"I guess they all need sympathy," said the young man,

"and I suppose all the business we have with it is to pray for them."

"Yes," said his mother, "I have been praying all day—for the daughter. I can't get her out of my mind as she went by sobbing yesterday with that flower pressed close to her cheek. I can't help thinking what if she were my little girl out in the world alone? And the world is such a very dreadful place in these days, too."

The young man did not answer. He was carefully gathering a few crumbs from the tablecloth into a neat little heap and then scattering them again, and presently the mother arose and began to gather up the dishes, and Gordon shoved back his chair and helped her. Afterwards Gordon went out to the garage and walked about among the trees awhile thinking, and once he looked belligerently up toward the great house studying the lighted windows. The right hand front window was all dark tonight.

But back in the library of the great house the master and the new mistress were talking. They had just returned from dinner in town because the bride had declined to get dinner at home and the bridegroom had declined to call up an agency in the city and have a cook and butler and a waitress sent out from town. The dishes from the breakfast that the master of the house had gotten—a breakfast of grapefruit, dry cereal, toast and coffee with soft boiled eggs, all on a tray for the bride, and carried up to her room dutifully—were still lying stacked in the sink unwashed. Helen said she would ruin her hands if she should attempt to wash them, and besides the excitement of the night before had unfitted her for such strenuous labor. "You wouldn't want me to wash dishes, would you, not just now when I'm supposed to be at my very best? The first few days I'm a bride? Suppose we have callers and they find me washing the dishes! My first day in the house! You wouldn't want that, would you dear?"

She looked at him with that adoring, languishing glance that always thrilled him, the glance that had flattered the wistful growing-old part of him, and made him think he was young again, and he smiled sadly, indulgently at her, looked down at the tricky little stained fingernails, and sighed.

"No, I suppose not," he said.

"We're going out to lunch and do some shopping in the city, you said. You're going to buy that diamond clasp for me, you know, and we could just as well stay in the city for dinner and see a play or something, and then you think by that time Maggie will get over her huff, don't you? You said she was just angry and would be back?"

She lifted her liquid eyes so trustingly to his face and he passed his hand gently over her head, thinking what a pretty child she was and how sad it was that they should have anything to interfere with the perfect bliss of their homecoming. And then his heart would swell again with anger and indignation at the incredible way in which Diana, his devoted child, had taken all this, when he had really done it for her sake as much as anything else.

"Yes, I think—I hope she will be back—" he said and sighed deeply. "She's very fond of Diana, you know, and I suppose she's just angry in sympathy with her. I can't think what has come over Diana to act this way. It isn't in the least like her. I don't know but I ought to take the noon train, and find her and bring her back. Things won't go right until we have an understanding. It's just as I told you, dear, Diana is hurt. I think she was hurt because we didn't insist on her coming up to the wedding. I felt that all along. You know we've always been so close—!"

"And now you're thinking that I have come between you!" said the artful Helen with a quiver of her red lips and a quick brimming of tears into her eyes. "You are sorry you married me! You are! You *a-a-rre!*" and soft gentle sobs and well-trained tears, not so very wet, rolled harmlessly over the smooth cheeks. Those tears and controlled sobs went to his heart like barbed darts as she had meant they should do. He had to take her in his arms then, and comfort her, and assure her that he loved her above all things else, and that certainly he was not sorry that he had married her, and surely everything would come out all right as soon as Diana understood.

She let herself be comforted and swept off to the city to get the diamond clasp as a consolation prize. They had gone, and stayed as she had planned, and now they were come back to a cheerless dark house, with those soiled dishes still huddled in the sink, and not a scrap or sign of repentant note or telegram from the prodigal daughter, and no Maggie in the kitchen, no prospect of anyone to get the breakfast tomorrow morning. The master of the house was frantic. Nevertheless, his attitude of consolation was still required, and his role for the present was such that he must not let Helen see how frantic he was about his missing daughter.

All day Helen had kept him strained to the utmost to prove to her that she was not de trop. If he sighed so much as a breath, or let a distant look come into his tired eyes, or let his smile droop on his lips she charged him with having to work so hard to make her think he was happy with her. And then all the day's work of reassuring her had to be done over again. He felt suddenly old and tired, and somehow condemned.

He had wanted to go and hunt his child, but Helen had tenderly persuaded him that it was unwise, that she would only think she had the upper hand and there would be no harmony ever if she thought he was wrong and she was right. She had made the argument so plausible and so gentle, so delicately punctuated with tears and regrets that she had married him that he felt his hands utterly tied.

Time and again during the day and evening he had tried to slip away and telephone Long Distance to the old aunt's house where she was supposed to have gone, but always he was followed and gently questioned and urged to do the best way, just patiently wait till the prodigal returned repentant. And always he would come back with her to something she wanted to do and sit and look at her and think what a sweet, forgiving, lovely woman he had married, and how amazingly wicked Diana had been to take such a silly prejudice against her. Yet underneath all the time his heart was crying out to go after Diana and have a heart-to-heart talk with her and bring her back into the path of submission and rectitude. Why, Diana had never been like this! He was sure he could bring Diana to her senses if he only had a few minutes' talk with her.

So the harassed father and husband had gone through the hours, until now they were back in the house again, the empty house, with their problems all unsolved before them, and Helen sighing and making him feel like a veritable Blue Beard in his Castle.

It was all wrong of course. He could see it now. He should have taken Diana into his confidence. He should have had her invite Helen there or sent her to visit Helen. He should have revealed the whole matter more gradually, and been near to comfort and sustain her in the first shock. Diana was merely hurt of course. He could understand it better now since the thing was done. She evidently had had no such thought that he would ever marry again. She was a young girl, and of course perhaps it was perfectly natural that she should be shocked. Time did not move so rapidly with young people as with older ones. It seemed to him ages since the death of his first wife, and it had been so wonderful that Helen in her youth and beauty had been willing to come in and relieve the terrible loneliness that Marilla's going had made. He had always thought of it as *their* loneliness, his and Diana's, not his alone. Diana would of course profit by having a mother, who was also young enough to be a sort of companion for her. He had deceived himself into thinking, into actually believing that Diana would be glad over the addition to the household. Her attitude had in reality been a great shock to him. Little Di whose utmost delight had always been to do his will, whose most cherished plans were ready to be flung aside for anything he had to propose. It was cataclysmic for her to rebel at anything he did or wanted. Surely this would not last! Surely she would come to herself very soon, as Helen had suggested, and return to her home and be her sweet self.

So at last he submitted to the inevitable and retired to a sleepless night, trying to persuade himself that the morrow would bring good news from the penitent. Then they could really begin to live! Then he would gently try to lead Diana and Helen to understand one another!

So the weary hours crept by but no sleep came. In the morning he looked drawn and haggard, and Helen, rousing from a late beauty sleep to take the tray he brought to her again, surveyed him with veiled vexation.

"You have no business to take things this way," she said sharply, "it makes you look old and you can't afford that. You married me, and now it's up to you to keep young. And this toast is horribly burned! It isn't fit to eat!

We've got to have some servants today or go to a hotel. I won't stand for this sort of thing!"

He winced as she said that about his looking old, and a gray look passed over his face as he turned away with a sigh and went out of the room.

DIANA was really too exhausted to lie awake long that night, and she fell asleep almost as soon as she lay down in her berth. But when she awoke, quite early in the morning, her first thought was of the words she had read from the little tract the stranger girl had given her in the station. It had seemed somehow to be something strong to lean upon. She hadn't grasped it yet, nor taken it for her own, but she wondered if it could be true, and her heart reached out in longing for something outside herself which would bear her up. For just now she felt as if she were going to crumple up and die just anywhere, as if she were utterly unable to think or decide any matter.

But next her whole pitiful situation flashed over her and she realized that now in a few brief minutes she had to do something about a place to stay.

She glanced at her watch and found it had stopped in the night. She had forgotten to wind it of course. She pulled aside the curtain and looked out. It was broad daylight and she thought she recognized the landscape. Yes, there was the name of a town she had often heard that could not be more than an hour or so from the home city. She must hurry and get herself ready! And she must decide where she was going when she got there.

The little paper caught her eye as she was closing her suitcase. It had slipped down under the sheet. She picked it up carefully and put it into her purse, stole a glimpse at her flowers in their soft wrappings. They still seemed to be alive. She must get them into water as soon as possible. She did not want to lose them. They were hardy little things. Only one of them was getting a bit brown around its fringes. They were all she had left of home now, dear mysterious flowers! Then she remembered the girl and her message. Mysterious flowers and mysterious messenger. Could they be connected in some way? Was God sending them both into her life? She gave the flowers a pitiful little smile, and a touch like a caress, then closed her suitcase, put on her hat and made ready to get out.

They were coming into the city now. The rows of cheap little houses, brick and wood and stucco, reminded her of the city where she had searched for a room yesterday. She shuddered as she drew a deep courageous breath and tried to think what she must do first. She did not seem to be any nearer a decision than last night, but she must do something. She would probably have to go to the woman's hotel for a day or two anyway.

When she got out of the train and walked through the station she looked around half frightened, almost expecting to see her father and Helen standing there waiting for her. Then she remembered they did not know where she was, and took courage, glad though to take refuge in the taxi. But when she arrived at the hotel her heart failed her again, for she found that even the very cheapest room in the place was far beyond what she ought to afford in her present state of finances. She was fairly frightened to realize how much she had spent of her small hoard in just the two or three days since she had cut herself loose from home. But she must get somewhere and rest a little and freshen up before she started on another hunt.

After breakfast and a bath, arrayed in fresh garments, she felt better and started out on foot in search of a room. If she could only find a decent room where she could use her own furniture it would be so much more comfortable.

But a couple of hours' hunt revealed the same state of things that had been obtained in the other city she had searched. Rooms were either too expensive or in too sordid a neighborhood to seem at all possible.

As she went along the weary way from house to house she began to realize that either she must find some way to increase her income, or else she must give up her ideas of what was barely decent in the way of an abiding place.

Right off at the start she registered a vow that she would not ask her father for money. He had made it impossible for her to stay at home and he didn't seem to see it, therefore she would maintain herself somehow without his aid.

The matter of money had never bulked very largely in Diana's life. She knew that her mother had left her something, how much she had never bothered to enquire, or if she had ever been told, to remember. She had her allowance which had been ample for her needs, and when she wanted anything extra it had always been forthcoming. She knew that for a time their fortunes had been somewhat straitened, and she had not asked often for money. She seemed to have everything she wanted. But now, faced with the problem of providing shelter and food her allowance suddenly shrank in proportion to her needs.

Many another girl with her income would have counted herself well off, and made the allowance cover an amazing lot of needs, but Diana had no experience in such things, and was moreover bound by the traditions of her family as to what was necessary. However, she had a lot of courage and character and she faced the problems before her like a thoroughbred.

She spent the afternoon canvassing dreary boarding houses and trying to conceive of herself as being one of their regular guests, but she turned from each one with a loathing that she had hard work to conceal from their hard-faced weary keepers.

There were other boarding places of course. She tried a few attractive ones, but found them altogether beyond her price.

That night she came home with the evening papers and all day Sunday pored over the want advertisements, and columns of cheap apartments and rooms.

Three days she thus pursued her weary hunt, growing more desperate each day, until she finally located a large bare room on the third story back of a shabby row of old brick houses in a crowded street of the old and unfashionable portion of the city. It wasn't just unfashionable, it was so far away from ever having been recognized by fashion as not to be within the ken of those who lived on the substantial comfortable streets not far away. It was a street where a week ago Diana would have picked her way, looking questioningly at the rows of ash cans and milk bottles and hurried out into another block to draw a free breath again. But Diana's standards had come down a good many notches during that three-day hunt. She no longer was looking for pleasantness in surroundings, or for attractiveness in a landlady, or for culture in a neighborhood. The sole requirement she was determined upon now was cleanliness, and even that didn't extend to the street any more. She wasn't sure as she entered that last door whether she would even require cleanliness in the halls or stairs, if she could just have a spot that she had a right to scrub clean herself, where she might lie down and cry her heart out and then sleep until this awful ache of weariness had left her breast and she could go out and try for a job. For now there was no more question, she must have a job or she could not live long even in this room.

Each night when she came back to the hotel there had been the slowly fading carnations, and in her purse the little tract, which she had read over more than once and pondered as she was dropping off to sleep, but though the hotel room contained the Bible she had wished for she had been too tired and depressed to look up the references, and more and more the impression of the little tract had grown dim and left her with that lonely feeling again. Sometime when she was settled she would look into it, but she was too tired to think about it any more now. So she slept through the nights and toiled through the days, looking alternately for rooms and jobs. She had learned to unite the two in certain neighborhoods, and found each equally hopeless as to results, until she finally took that large bare room on the third story back, overlooking an alley and a row of kitchens belonging to an even shabbier row of houses on the next street. When she took the room she cast a thankful glance out of the window at its dreary mate behind, whose open window sheltered a woman in dirty negligee who looked as if her every hope was gone. Diana was actually thankful that she hadn't fallen quite as low as that next row of houses, and had them only to look at.

The room was not heated and had only one poor

electric bulb hung from a long wire in the middle, but it was still summer and she would not need heat at present, and she would just have to manage about the light.

They told her she might have possession at once, and she called up her storage company who promised to deliver her furniture early the next morning and refund half of the storage for the month.

The room didn't look very clean even to Diana's inexperienced eyes and she hated to have her pretty things come into a dirty room, so she went to the corner grocery near by, bought a bucket, a broom, a mop, a cake of soap and a couple of dishcloths wherewith to cleanse it. The woman who waited on her suggested a scrubbing brush so she bought that.

Tired as she was it was no easy task, even if she had ever done it before, which she hadn't, to scrub that rough dirty floor. She had to bring up the water from the floor below, and there wasn't any hot water nor any way to heat it. In her inexperience she sloshed on the soap and water and then had a terrible time wiping it up, and as for wringing that unwieldy mop it seemed just an impossibility. But by the time it grew dark she had the walls swept down, the floor mopped up in a sort of way, the baseboards wiped off, also the window sills. The windows would have to wait until another time. She was too tired to drag another step. With a despairing look around in the dusk she locked her door, toiled downstairs and could scarcely get back to her hotel.

That night she dreamed of the girl in the station with the happy eyes who had given her the tract, and awoke wondering if she were real or if that experience too had been a dream. She had to go to her handbag and take out the tract to straighten it all out in her mind. She was so tired she could not think, and so downhearted that nothing seemed worth while. Was there really Someone somewhere who cared? She wished she could see that girl again and talk with her a little while.

When she got to her new abode, by morning light the room looked cleaner than she had feared. At least it had lost that musty smell. The floor had dried in streaks and the ugly wall paper showed up all its defects, and they were many. She stood in the middle of the room and looked about her and tried to fancy that this was her home now, for as long as she had money to maintain it.

She went to the window and looked out upon the back yards and alley. There were two cats, a gray one with a dirty white star in its forehead, and a black one with a torn ear and an ugly sneer on its weird scrawny face, sitting tucked up on the back fence at respectable distances making faces at one another, and occasionally uttering guttural threats. There was a dirty old man with a burlap bag slung over one shoulder and a long iron rod in his hand, poking about among the ash cans. Someone flung a bit of garbage over the fence and the two cats were down in a trice and after it, but a sharp little nondescript dog went like a streak from some invisible quarter and got there first, growling his right to the tidbit. A mere baby with tousled hair was toddling down the alley with nothing on but a diminutive shirt and mud streaks over the whiteness of its undernourished body. It was scrawnier than the cats. Two women were arguing angrily over their side fence, and an old man with crutches beside him was sitting dolefully on one pair of back steps. It was not a pleasant prospect. Even so early in the morning there were flies about, swarming over a garbage can and buzzing up in a whirl now and then as if in disagreement. Diana turned from it disconsolately with sudden memory of the broad sweep of lawn in front of her father's home, and the deep cool setting of woodland behind the house. How had her fortunes changed in these few brief hours! A few days ago she was mistress in that beautiful home that had been her mother's wedding gift from the grandfather, and now here was her fortune laid, with alleycats and garbage cans and brawling neighbors. She turned from the window with sudden new sinking of heart and felt as if she could not stand up another minute in that bare room.

Finally she spread down the morning paper that she had brought with her and sat down upon the floor, overwhelmed with the stinging tears that rushed into her eyes. Oh, would that moving van never come?

It was half past ten before it arrived, and Diana still sat there waiting when the landlady knocked at the door to announce it. She had taken out the poor little flowers from her bag and sat with them coolly against her burning eyelids, trying to fancy herself back home among the shadows on the grass, picking them up one by one, and remembering how she had walked with Bobby there that night and had seen one flower, and how that stranger's voice had interfered when Bobby grew offensive. She was wondering about that voice for the thousandth time, and had almost lost her sense of her sordid surroundings.

But she sprang up quickly to unlock her door, and saw with relief two men standing there each with a chair in his arms.

They put the chairs down and hurried back downstairs, and Diana thanked the grim landlady and tried not to see the contemptuous glances of envy that she cast at the rich covering of the upholstery. After she was gone downstairs Diana stood back and looked at her beloved chairs almost apologetically. If they could feel what would they think of her for putting them into such surroundings? She felt like asking their pardon. And one was her mother's big wing chair. She could see her sitting in it now, and she put her hands softly over the covering like a caress. She was still holding the precious flowers in her hand, and she put her face down on her arms over the back of the chair and gave a little heartsick moan. It seemed as if already she had been away from her home for weeks and the sight of the dear familiar objects filled her with exquisite joy, almost as if they had been alive.

But the men were coming up again with another load, and Diana moved the chairs where they would be out of the way and went over by the window to watch.

They had brought their arms full of small articles now that had probably been stowed in the van at the last. Diana met each object with a lingering glance of welcome, and mentally began to arrange a spot where each should stand. Already the room seemed peopled, but she fancied the things stood there astonished to be brought to such a place! Yet oh, she was glad to have them!

And now the bed was coming in sections and two more men behind were bringing springs and mattress. How quickly they set it up and the room took on the look of a habitation. Then her bureau and her desk. It was well the room was large. The landlady had said she might put her barrels of dishes in the hall by her door. She was planning to put a curtain across in front of them. Some boxes of books could go there, too.

Everything was up at last, how pitifully few when you thought of home! But they elbowed one another and it would take some contriving to assemble them into living order.

The men opened some boxes for her, unstrapped a trunk or two that would go in the hall eventually, and drove two or three nails to hang the few pictures she had brought. The bureau and the wardrobe filled the widest wall spaces, with the bed in the far corner, the gate-leg table in the middle. Now, when the window was washed and a curtain up it wouldn't be so bad, and she could perhaps hang one of the superfluous curtains across that other corner and make a closet out of it.

The men stood back and surveyed it before they went.

"Ain't sa bad," said one, looking from floor to ceiling.

"She wants paperin' and paintin' bad," said the other.

Then they were gone and Diana stood alone in her new home, realizing that there was work to be done.

She took out the linen sheets, her mother's, with the lovely monograms, smelling of lavender, and smooth and fine. There was another problem. Laundry! That would be yet another expense. Oh to have Maggie along on this exile! But of course that was out of the question. She could never afford Maggie. She would have to learn to wash for herself. But where and how? In that terrible bathroom down a flight? Never! She shuddered at the memory of the unspeakable tin tub grimy with the dirt of the ages.

But when the bed was made, with its pretty spread that matched the curtains, when the bureau was dusted and its ruffled cover in place, a feeling of comfort began to steal into the room, and Diana looked up to the lovely portrait of her mother with thankfulness at least if not of joy.

The landlady came up after a time and stood looking about.

"H'm!" she remarked grimly, "I guess you're rich!"

"Oh, no," said Diana quickly, "not any more. I am really very poor, and—I'm going out to get a job. These are things from my old home."

"Ain't your mother living?"

"No," said Diana with a tremble in her voice.

Mrs. Lundy looked up to the portrait.

"That her?" she asked taking in everything with hurried eagle eye.

"Yes," said Diana softly, trying to control the trembling of her lips.

"Well, it's plain to be seen you won't stay long," she said with a sigh of resignation. "Ef I'd knowed what kind you was I shouldn't uv took you. But now 't you're here we may as well make the best of it, only I'd oughtta uv charged you a dollar more."

"I couldn't have paid it," said Diana, lifting honest eyes.

"Well, I'm poor too an' I can't afford ta let my rooms fer nothin'. I'll want my pay good and regular."

"Of course!" said Diana shrinking inwardly. Oh, to have to deal with coarse-grained people like this. How could she ever stand it under the same roof with a woman like that?

But the woman went away and Diana put her things in order as best she could, washed her one window with unskilled hands, wondering how ever she was to get it clean on the outside, and finally managed to tack up her curtain temporarily. After that she lay down and took a long nap, and when she woke up it was dark. She hadn't had any lunch nor dinner, but she shrank inexpressibly from going out alone in that region at night. Perhaps by and by she would grow more accustomed to the place and not be afraid. But this night at least she would rather go hungry than go out alone and find her way to a restaurant. There was a box of crackers on the window sill. She would eat those and go to bed.

So, quite in the dark except for weird flickers of light that came in at the window, fitfully playing over the floor now and then, she groped her way to the crackers and sat in her big chair sadly munching them, and wondering if life was always to be like this. She might have turned on the garish bulb waving disconsolately in air above her, but she shrank inexpressibly tonight from a stark unshaded glare above the dear home things. She just couldn't bear to meet the painted eyes of her mother's portrait, here, alone, tonight.

Oh, some of those girls in dismal hall bedrooms, washing out their bits of finery, and their one pair of stockings, and sleeping on a hard lumpy cot, would have thought her room a palace and her lot heavenly if they could have exchanged with Diana. But to Diana it was as if she and a few of her precious things had wandered into an alien desert land of squalor, where they were prisoners.

It was a comfort however next morning to waken with familiar objects about her, and as she dressed she tried to keep back the desire for tears and just be thankful that she was in a place at last where she could have her own things, even though the place itself was anything but desirable.

After eating a few more crackers and drinking her pint of milk for which she had left an order the day before and which she found outside her door, she sat down to count her resources. There had been a few trifling expenses connected with the moving which she had not taken into account when she calculated, fees to the men, and a larger charge for the moving than she had anticipated. It had cut down her money supply tremendously and the end of another week was approaching. If she did not get a job this week she might have to go on starvation rations. Perhaps it would be as well to visit the bank and see if it would be possible for her to get the interest on the money her mother left to her, a few days ahead of its usual time. It was customary for her father to look after such matters for her, though during his absence she had sometimes gone into the city bank herself. The bank president knew her, so it wouldn't be necessary for her to explain anything to him. He wouldn't know what had happened. And of course the money was hers, it was only a matter of a week to the end of the month and her usual instalment. If she had been at home she would have called him up and told him she wanted to draw a check a few days ahead of time, and that would be all there would be to it. The money was hers without question.

So, when she went out on her usual hunt that morning she stopped at the bank with a check she had made out for a small sum more than she knew was left in her checking account. She explained to the cashier to whom she handed it and asked if it would be all right as she wanted to use the money right away. He knew her from having seen her with her father and he met her request with courtesy.

"Just a moment, Miss Disston," he said, a trifle uncertainly, "I presume it will be quite all right but I'll have to see."

He came back in a moment telling her that the president would like to speak with her in his office.

Diana went back with a little trepidation. Was there some cut and dried law that made it necessary for her to wait the five days before she could use this money that was her own?

The president met her gravely, gave her a chair, and when he had seated himself with a little more formality than usual he said:

"Miss Disston, I'm very sorry, but we have received a request from your father not to pay you any more of your interest without permission from him. Being a trustee of your funds of course he has the right to do this. I understand he has been very much disturbed by your absence from home and has telegraphed to a number of places where he thought you might be, without finding you. He therefore has taken this method to get in touch with you. He naturally reasoned that if you had no money you would have to get in touch with him at once."

Diana sat staring at Mr. Dunham, her eyes very large and wide, and her face suddenly flaming crimson. The great man sat in his chair of authority with his elbows on its arms and the tips of his long white fingers touching one another, surveying her speculatively. He had not been prepared for the consternation that had come into her face, and he was puzzled by her sweet quiet manner. This was no wild young thing having her fling. This looked like a conscientious girl. But he had to obey his client's orders of course. However, he felt uncomfortable under the clear steady gaze of her big eyes. Also the color had receded as suddenly as it had come and left her face a dead white. There was some deep feeling behind all this. Was Disston perhaps a little hard on his child? Yet he had seemed to cherish her as the very apple of his eye. He felt almost disconcerted as she continued to sit quietly looking at him.

"I'm sorry to have to refuse your request," he said half embarrassedly, "but of course you see how it is, and I'm sure you will accede to your father's request to go home at once and all will be right. It's probably just some little misunderstanding, and with your father's permission we shall be glad to favor you with advance money at any time of course."

Still Diana did not answer. Her sweet face drooped for an instant and then lifted, with a serious gaze, as she half rose, steadying herself with the tips of her fingers lightly touching his desk.

Then she spoke, and her patrician chin was lifted just the least little bit with gentle dignity.

"I'm sorry to have troubled you," she said with a

fleeting distant semblance of a smile. Her voice was soft
and a shade husky, but she had good control of herself.

"Not at all, not at all!" said the banker, almost cordially,
"I—! You—! You understand how it is? And if you are
short of funds for getting to your home from the city, why
I understand there is a trifling sum, a matter of something
like five dollars, perhaps, in your checking account, which
you are of course at liberty to withdraw at any time. If
you'll sit down a minute I'll write you an order to that
effect and you can make out a check and cash it at once.
That will I am sure cover your fare to the suburbs."

Diana swept him a glance of haughtiness.

"Thank you," she said coolly, "that will not be necessary," and she walked from the room without looking
at him again.

It was just as the door was swinging to behind her that
he came to himself and started forward.

"Miss Disston," he said raising his voice, "I hope that
you will go straight to your home. I assure you your
father is very anxious!" He was almost shouting with the
last word. But Diana was gone, and the big mahogany
door had closed noiselessly.

What a fool he was! He ought to have got her address!
Her father would blame him if she didn't go home at
once. But of course she would! What was it about her that
made him feel she did not intend to? He strode forward
and swung the door open, looking down the passage
toward the main part of the bank, but Diana was not there.
There was a side entrance opposite his office door for his
own private use. He opened the door and looked down
the street but there was no sign of her anywhere. How
could she have got away so quickly? She was embarrassed,
stung to the quick of course, one could see that. He
stepped into the bank and looked carefully at everyone but
she was not there. Diana was gone!

14

AT first Diana did not realize where she was going. Her only object was to get out of that bank and away from Mr. Dunham. That she was hurt to the quick was manifest in the way she walked, with long fleeing strides, and the ground seemed fairly to fly under her feet. She walked as if she were going to some direct appointment, and people watched her, turned to look after her, marveled at her graceful movements. She made her way through a crowded street and it seemed almost as if the crowds divided at her coming. She slid through breathlessly, crossing streets without noticing where she was, rushing on like something wound up and not able to stop.

But her mind was smarting as if a whip were lashing it. Her father had done this thing to her! He had stopped her money and brought her to shame before his acquaintance! His banker knew she was gone, without knowing the reason! Oh, how could she ever live this down? To her inflamed mind the whole thing grew in proportion until it seemed that the worst humiliation there could be had been put upon her. So far from feeling sorry for her, her father was but anxious to get her back and bend her to his will; but wishing to punish her for having refused to try and live in the same house with Helen! Her lips were quivering as she walked, and great tears swelled out and threatened to fall, yet she held them back and went on. Her soul was bursting with sorrow. Her father had so far descended as to use her little income as a whiplash to force her back to him.

Well, never would she go back to get money, even if she starved!

And that brought her to the next thing. She must get a job at once!

She had walked until she was breathless, and weary, though she did not realize it, but suddenly she came to the end of things. A river ahead with no bridge and only a sharp turn to the left if she wanted still to go on.

She paused an instant. The river winked and beckoned to her, in bright sunny sparkles between the shipping craft and wharfs, and suddenly she came to herself and gave a sane brave little laugh. She was Diana Disston and tragedy was not to be carried on by her. If other people did crazy things she couldn't help it, but she could help it if she let them drive her to do more of them. Somehow she had to work this thing out, to get rid of the pain in her heart, and find a way to exist, without money if necessary, but not by doing anything wild.

There were few people about when she gave that laugh, just some men standing about the door of a warehouse, one or two lounging on the steps, watching a tug slowly pulling a barge out into the river. They were not looking at her, and she gave no thought to them as she took that sharp turn to the left and walked over one block turning back on the next street and starting toward the centre of the city again. But one man turned and looked her full in the face as she sped by, watching her till she turned the corner and went on out of sight. He was one of those who slouched low on the step, his gaunt ill-strung length stretched to its utmost, his gawky limbs lying absolutely relaxed, his lazy arms anchored by hands in his pockets. He had a weak chin and an irresponsible manner. It had taken the distance of a block for him to get a full recognition across to himself, and even then he wasn't quite sure. As much as he allowed his lazy mind to think he turned the matter over once or twice and then decided it didn't matter anyway, and went on sunning himself on the shackly step. If she was the girl who used often to pass his mother's cottage when he was a child, what business of his was it anyway? She wouldn't recognize Bill Sharpe of course. It likely wasn't the same girl, and why should he care? He would have smoked a cigarette on it if he had had one to smoke, but he hadn't. That was why he was here, to see if he couldn't pick up a job. He needed some money badly. His mother was dead and could no longer earn it for him doing fine sewing. He sat still and presently forgot that he might possibly have seen a daughter of the Disston House go by in this most unexpected place.

But Diana walked more slowly back on the next street. She was looking about her now with a purpose. She must find a job. And if she couldn't find a job within the next day or two she might presently find herself having to move to one of these unspeakable little tenements which she was passing, for she had but two dollars and seventy-five cents between her and starvation. True, there was the five dollars the banker had suggested she might draw out at her will, but what was that? She scorned to go back and get it. At best it would keep her but a very short time, and if there was a job somewhere she must get it now.

She was keeping her eye out for signs, but there was nothing for women. Several places had a card out "Boy Wanted," and one dirty little shop had a blackboard at the door, with a scrawled sign, "Man wanted to drive a truck," but there was nothing for women or girls till she came into the downtown region again, and there she saw a notice in the window of a common little restaurant, "Waitress wanted!"

Diana paused before the door and looked within. It was the noon hour and there was a crowd of working people, swarming in like flies, waiting behind chairs for their occupants to finish. The waitresses had highly illuminated, hard faces and untidy dress. They were knocking about among the people with heavy trays lifted high, calling out in raucous voices for room to get by. There was a heavy odor of burned grease, fried fish and onions floating on the air. A man with fulsome sneering lips and little pig eyes was directing it all. Diana stood for a full minute and took it all in. Then she turned and walked wearily away. Would she have to come to that?

It was not that she felt above such work. It seemed a thing that anyone might learn to do. But to have to live in such a noisy mess and be ordered about by a loathsome man like that! Why, Bobby Watkins was a seraph compared to that man.

She allowed herself a glass of milk and one little packet of peanut butter sandwiches for her dinner that night, but had hard work to finish even that. She was heartsick and could not eat. She toiled up to her third story room afterwards too utterly weary to think. But after a few minutes lying prone across her bed she got up desperately and went to the drawer where she had put the little tract. She must have some help somewhere or she would lose her mind!

She had bought a little cheap Bible the day before as

she passed a second hand bookstore, but had had no time to look at it yet. Now as she took it out she realized that she ought to have saved even the small sum that she had paid for it. But it was too late for such regrets. Perhaps she might even come to having to sell it again, but she wanted to get those references and write them out before it was gone. She took up the tract and read the now familiar words:

> One reason why the Son of God came to earth and took a human body was so that He might suffer and understand us in our griefs. There is no kind of sorrow that He does not know, even to having His beloved Father turn His back upon Him for a time.

She looked at the first reference, Psalm 22:1, and turned bewilderedly to her Book. She had been so long away from any intimate contact with a Bible that the books seemed to have changed places since she last knew them. But at last she found the Psalms, and suddenly a verse caught her eye: "When my father and my mother forsake me then the Lord will take me up!" What an astonishing verse for her to come upon when she was in such desperation! Her mother was gone and her father had practically forsaken her. For now as she thought over the interview in the bank she began to see clearly the fine vindictive hand of her new stepmother in what her father had done to her. She was quite sure he would never of himself have done such a thing if Helen had not suggested it, and suggested it in such a way, fairly pursuing her victim till it was done, that he simply had to do it or rebel. Diana instinctively recognized that his marriage was too new for him to rebel yet. But at least for the time, whether he realized it or not, he had forsaken her, his daughter.

And now, was it true that there was Someone who cared about all this? She would find out. She turned back the pages to the twenty-second Psalm. But when she had found the verse she could make nothing of the desolate cry, "My God, my God, why hast Thou forsaken me?" until she finally turned to the reference in Matthew: "And about the ninth hour Jesus cried with a loud voice saying, 'Eli, Eli, lama sabachthani? that is to say, My God, my God, why hast Thou forsaken me?'"

So then Jesus was forsaken! She went back to the beginning of the chapter and read the whole story of the crucifixion. She had heard it over and over again in her childhood of course but it had made little impression. It had just been a story of a Man who lived long ago Whom she had been taught was the Saviour of the world.

But now, because she realized for the first time that He was really in the position of having been forsaken by God, His Father, because He had taken upon Him the sins of the world and God could not have any fellowship with sin, she suddenly saw what had never occurred to her before, that Jesus, the Saviour of the world knew what she was going through now because *He had gone through it*. He had voluntarily accepted that separation from God which was what His death meant, and had done it for her sake, for the sake of those He was saving.

This did not come to her all at once. It took careful reading over and over, and even then it was only a dawning comprehension. Nevertheless it was enough to fill her with wonder and a degree of belief.

At last, her mind filled with the picture of Calvary and the meaning of it as applied to herself, she found the next reference, Hebrews 2:18.

"For in that He Himself hath suffered being tempted, He is able to succor them that are tempted."

It was as if a voice spoke to her soul from the printed page. She was so lonely and desolate that she welcomed the message with a throb of joy. It was like an assurance from Heaven that there was Someone who cared after all else had failed!

She thought about it for a few minutes. Able to succor! Then He had the power, an understanding power because He had been through the same experience. Ah! How wonderful! But—were there no qualifications that one must have to be worthy of such succor, except just to be in need? Was this for everybody? How could she be sure He would succor, even though He were able?

She turned to the next verse:

"I will not leave you comfortless, I will come to you."

How tenderly precious. He would come. Her father hadn't been willing to come. But this One had promised to come and bring comfort.

But stay! She still did not know whether that meant herself or not. How could she be sure? He hadn't come, had He? She had been in the direst need and He hadn't come. Wasn't there something lacking somewhere in her case at least?

But there was one more reference. She hurriedly turned the leaves. The little tract seemed so sure. Why should it be broadcast in print this way if it were not for everyone in trouble? Then she read, and it was the story of Mary going to the empty tomb to find her Lord, and finding only angels:

"And they say unto her, Woman, why weepest thou? She saith unto them, Because they have taken away my Lord, and I know not where they have laid Him. And when she had thus said, she turned herself back, and saw Jesus standing, and knew not that it was Jesus."

Diana read in astonishment. Well, what could that mean in *her* life, always supposing that this story was meant to mean something in her life? Could it be that Jesus had come to her somewhere, somehow, and she had not recognized Him? Oh, to understand, to know! But how was she to find out? She went back and read through the resurrection story, finding herself curiously interested, sympathetic with the weeping Mary, yet still perplexed, still wondering how to find Mary's Lord, and whether He would be willing to be her Friend and Comforter. It all seemed so long ago, and she here alone in a new dreadful world, wherein money was withheld as well as comfort. There was no comfort it seemed. And she had never dreamed that money bulked so largely in the human equation. There had always been enough before and she had never thought about it. But now she had to think. She must earn her way, and she was hungry! Actually hungry! But she didn't dare spend more than was absolutely necessary, and tomorrow she must get a job! Even if she had to go back to that awful restaurant, she must get one!

The money was all gone and she had actually not a cent left after the glass of milk she took for her breakfast the morning she did find some work.

Of course her room was paid for for the month. That was good. If she had to starve she could at least die decently. And of course, there were things she could sell, though she didn't know how to go about selling them, and it made her heart sink to think of it. There were the pearls! But they should be the last resort. Her mother's pearls! She laid her hand over the little chamois bag that hung about her neck beneath her dress on its tiny platinum chain and felt stronger for the contact.

"When my father and my mother forsake me then the Lord will take me up," she said softly over to herself as she started out on her desperate way. "I'll just have to trust Him, that's all. I don't know Him, but perhaps He knows me, and I'll *have* to trust He'll look out for me, for I've nobody else!"

It was just a moment later that her eye caught a glimpse of the card in the window of a small book shop, or was it a publisher's office? She wasn't sure. But there was the neatly printed card.

GIRL WANTED
TO ADDRESS ENVELOPES
Must Write Well

She stopped short and stared. She felt somehow as if her unspoken prayer had been answered. She began to wonder if her eyes were really seeing aright. Did things really happen like that?

Then she turned and went in.

It was a neat pleasant office with a sweet-faced elderly woman at its head, and a glimpse of several nice-looking women and girls at desks in an inner room, two of them at typewriters. Farther on there was another room where she could see a gray-haired man sitting at a desk and a younger man standing by him with papers in his hand about which they seemed to be talking. She learned later that this was the editorial room.

It was all so easy. She had only to write her name and address and a sentence or two. They took her at once. She wrote a beautiful clear hand and her appearance was in her favor. But her heart sank when she was told that it was only a temporary job. It might last only a couple of days, or they might even get the work done by night. They were not sure. It depended upon some lists that might come in before the day was done. The pay was reckoned on the number finished each day.

Diana sat down at the desk they assigned her in the middle room and began her work. She was glad she had brought her fountain pen along in her handbag. She could work better with her own tools. Soon she was hard at it. The manager from the front office came through the room several times and stopped now and again to look over her shoulder, noticed how rapidly the finished piles of envelopes were mounting, and smiled her approval, but beyond that nothing was said to her.

At noon the office manager stepped in and told her she might take her lunch hour now, and Diana looked up with a rising color of embarrassment

"Would you mind if I didn't go out?" she asked. "I really don't care for lunch today, and I'd like to stay and get more done, if that's all right with you."

The woman gave her a keen swift look but told her she might stay if she preferred. "Although," she added, "I always think it's better for the girls to get out for a breath of fresh air and a little something to eat even if it isn't much. You can of course bring your lunch if you prefer. There's a dressing room just up those steps to the right where you can eat it. But do as you prefer. Of course we're anxious to get these envelopes finished as soon as possible."

"Then I'll stay," said Diana with relief, "I—had breakfast rather late, anyway," she added, and drove her pen rapidly on in clear graceful writing.

The manager looked a bit troubled but turned away and most of the workers went out by twos and threes for their noon hour. Only two others remained and presently they went up to the dressing room with their neat little packages of lunch. One of them came down with a luscious pear in her hand, and came over to Diana shyly.

"My sister put two pears in my lunch box today and I couldn't possibly eat them both. I wondered if you wouldn't like to help me out? I noticed you didn't go out to lunch and I do hate to carry it back home again."

It was on Diana's lips to give a haughty "No thank you!" but she lifted her eyes to the girl's face and found such kindly good will that the words died on her lips and instead she smiled. After all, why should she hold herself aloof? She was a working girl now like the rest. Moreover she was hungry, and this was true kindliness. So she reached out her hand with a sudden smile.

"Thank you!" she said heartily. "That looks wonderful!" She ate the pear gratefully, and then wrote the faster to make up for the brief loss of time. But a queer thought came to her while she was eating. Did God send this job to her? It wasn't a very big answer to her prayer, of course, but it was something. And did He send the pear? It seemed almost irreverent to think such a thought, but there was a warming of her heart, a stealing in of a bit of comfort like a warm ray of sun. And it certainly was good to have eaten that pear, for in case the work lasted another day they likely wouldn't pay her till it was done, and there was only one cracker left in her room for dinner tonight. How long could one live and go on working without food?

But the manager came to her just before closing time, and smiled.

"You've worked well, Miss Disston," she said. "It really was quite important to get off as many of these as possible. I thought perhaps you'd like your pay tonight for the day, but we'd like you to come back in the morning if you will. Some new lists have just come in by the late mail, and there is a prospect that we shall have work for you for several more days."

Diana's face lighted up.

"Oh, I'm so glad," she said earnestly. "And it is good of you to let me have today's money now. I really need it."

"That's quite all right," smiled Miss Prince, "and I'll see you in the morning."

It wasn't a large sum of money that she carried away with her, but it meant all the difference between starvation and life. Diana went at once to a restaurant, the cheapest decent one she knew, and ate a real dinner. To be sure its price was very small but she chose wholesome things that would sustain life a long time. She mustn't allow herself to get so near to nothing again. She recalled the sinking feeling she had in the pit of her stomach at noon before that girl gave her the pear. And how dizzy her head had been! Sometimes she could hardly see what she was writing. One glass of milk couldn't keep one working all day. She must provide a lunch!

So while she was eating she studied the menu and on her way out purchased the cheapest sandwich they had, and two nice red apples, then at the little grocery near her room she bought a pint bottle of milk and a box of dry cereal. Now, she was provided with food for breakfast and a lunch like the others, with an extra apple to repay her friend for the pear, and she had money left to keep her, if she was careful, for a couple of days longer. Not that she could live very expensively of course, but she had demonstrated by this time that a fifteen cent plate of soup and a few crackers would keep one alive for quite a length of time.

When she reached her room she put her bottle of milk in the open window with a wet cloth about it to keep it cool, stowed her sandwich in a small tin box she had, put the bag of apples beside it, and then looked around her room with a deep breath of relief. She wanted to cry, but she wouldn't. She had had her first success and she was grateful. It wouldn't do to sit down and think from what an estate she had fallen, nor to sit and blame her poor father. She mustn't let herself think about her troubles or she would give way, and one couldn't work well if one cried half the night. She had tried trusting in God that morning and wonderful things had happened. She must keep on trusting.

Before Diana had left her home, in fact that last morning when she went down to the village to telephone the moving van, she had stopped at the postoffice and asked them to hold her mail, after that afternoon's delivery, until she should send them another address. She had even left money for forwarding second-class matter. Not that she had so much mail, but she dreaded to have anything that belonged to her fall into Helen's hands. There was Bobby Watkins for instance. Suppose he should take it into his head to write her a voluminous letter as he had done more than once, and try to argue with her about her attitude toward him? He had called up twice during that last day to berate her for the way she treated him going down the drive, and to try and explain how much he loved her. She no longer wished to protect Bobby Watkins from Helen's mocking laughter, Bobby could take care of himself, but she couldn't bear the thought of Helen's opening letters and reading *anything* addressed to her, and laughing over it as she would laugh. For she knew Helen would have no scruples against opening her letters if she chose to do so. She had seen her do it several times.

Also, there would be invitations, and a few letters from her girl friends. Nothing that would amount to anything or that she really cared much about, but she did not want Helen reading them and destroying them.

So now that she had a job, at least for a few days, she sat down and wrote an order to the postman at home to forward her mail. The postoffice was not allowed to tell others her address, so she felt she was perfectly safe in doing this. Of course by and by she would write to her father as she had promised to do, but not until she was sure of a job that would pay for her food and room. Never should he be allowed to think that he could break her resolve by holding back her money. Her heart was full of bitterness toward him as she thought of what he had done, although there was more grief at having lost his love and her feeling that he trusted her, than bitterness. And if she could have known what anxiety he was suffering about her she would have forgotten to pity herself and would have somehow managed to get in touch with him at least to let him know she was safe. She felt that he had Helen and that was enough for him. Not for an instant did she take as sincere what the banker had said to her about his anxiety to know where she was.

His refusal to come to her when she pled with him, or to have any discussion with her before it was forever too late was still strong in her mind. It had cut her to the heart.

So she wrote her few lines to the postmaster at home and then, because the postbox was only a block and a half down the street, she went out and mailed it. It would get there in the morning and perhaps by tomorrow night she would have some mail. It would be more like living to be getting something of her own, even if it was nothing she cared about.

Out in the street with its dismal half-lit shadows she almost repented, but hastened her steps into a run, deposited her letter, and flew back to safety. She did not notice a lank awkward young man slouching against a closed grocery doorway across the corner. She did not see him look up and peer across at her, nor know that he had followed her noiselessly on the other side of the street, keeping in the shadows and hiding in a deep doorway till he saw where she went in, and that later he walked by on her side of the street and studied the house, taking note of the number before he melted into darkness again and went on his unknown way.

Diana went upstairs, locked herself into her haven and went to bed. But before she slept she tried to pray.

"Oh, God, if you really care, and have helped me today, I thank you!" she said softly into her pillow. "Oh, God, if you really do care I would be so glad!"

15

DIANA worked in the publishing office for nearly a week, and then one morning the manager came to her just as she had begun her work for the day and asked her if she could run a typewriter. Diana looked dismayed and told her no.

"I'm sorry," said the manager. "I hoped you could. This work you have been doing is about finished. It won't last longer than today. I thought if you were a typist we could use you right along, for one of our girls is getting married next week."

"I could learn," said Diana with a desperate look in her eyes.

The manager shook her head.

"We need experienced typists, you know," she said. "But if you will leave your address we'll promise to send for you whenever we have any extra work that we think you could do. The editor was very much pleased with the way you took hold of things. I'm sorry," she said again with a pitying smile as she walked away.

Diana sat and worked all day, her heart as heavy as lead. She did not go out to lunch as she had been in the habit of doing. She said she had a headache when one of the girls asked her to go with her. In reality she was frightened. She wouldn't waste even fifteen cents to buy lunch. The money she would get tonight would not be enough to carry her many days and here she was plunged back into the blackness of despair again, with visions of that awful restaurant in her mind. Perhaps she would have to get a job like that yet. Perhaps she wouldn't even be able to get one like that now, for likely that was gone long ago.

She received her pay envelope and the kind words of the manager that night with as brave a look as she could summon, but her feet dragged heavily as she went on her way home, and instead of stopping to get a good dinner she bought bread and cheese and went on to her room. Why waste money on a dinner that she could not eat? Oh, why did she have to go on living? Where was the God in whom she had been trying to trust? Had He forgotten her? No one cared any more. Her father seemed to be making no further move to try and find her. Helen doubtless had told him that she would come home when she got good and tired of wandering around without money, and likely he had believed her. Oh, God, God, God, do You care at all? How could You care? I'm just nobody!

The tears were in her eyes as she rounded the corner to the dismal rooming house, and all her life looked drab and dreary before her. Would there ever be anything ahead to make her feel happy again?

But as she came to the steps of the house she saw that the door stood open and a postal delivery car was at the door.

"Here she comes!" said the landlady grimly. "Let her sign it herself. I've got too much to do to bother. I smell my dinner burning!"

Diana stared at the landlady and then at the postal delivery, and then she saw a large parcel lying on the hall chair. In the dim light permitted in that dismal place she could not read the name clearly, but the boy was holding out a card and pencil to her.

"Sign here," he said and thrust the pencil into her hand.

Diana, filled with wonder, signed her name, and the boy vanished. Then she turned to take up her parcel and came face to face with her landlady again.

"That's from a florist's isn't it?" she asked belligerently.

Diana gazed at her, astonished.

"I don't know what it is," she replied. "I haven't opened it yet. I wasn't expecting anything."

"Well, if you're gettin' that many flowers in your position I think you oughtta be payin' more rent fer your room."

Diana laughed. It struck her as remarkably original logic.

"Just how do you make that out?" she tried to say it pleasantly, trying to remember that this was only a poor ignorant woman in a semi-tenement. "I couldn't really help it, could I, if someone chose to send me some flowers by mail? It wouldn't make me any better able to pay more rent, would it? Unless you think I might sell them to somebody." She laughed with a little tremble in the trail of it that gave a strange pathetic sound even to herself.

"Is he your steady, or is he just a pick-up?" asked the landlady fixing her with a cold eye. There was a strong smell of fried potatoes and onions burning that almost stifled Diana, but she paused with her foot on the lower step of the stair and stared at the woman.

"What is a steady?" she asked, mildly interested.

"Ef you don't know it ain't likely he is. Well, then, I

thought mebbe you wasn't so awful respectable after all as you set up to be."

"I really don't know what you mean," said Diana almost ready to cry.

"You must be awful dumb then. I'm askin' you ef the flowers you got in that there package is from a regular sweetie you go with all the time, or just from some bum you picked up at a night club? I liketa know what kinda character my tenants has. This has always been counted a respectable house. It looks kinda suspicious you havin' all that furniture, and now gettin' a stack o' flowers."

Diana suddenly froze into dignity.

"Really," she said, "I'm sorry but I can't answer any more questions. I haven't opened this package yet, and I haven't the slightest idea where it came from or what it contains. But if renting a room from you gives you a right to pry into all my private affairs I shall certainly move out tomorrow!" and she sailed upstairs carrying her big parcel with her, and suddenly remembered as she rounded the head of the stairs and prepared to ascend the next flight, that she had no job, and almost no money and if she were to move out tomorrow she could only do so by dragging her furniture to the window and flinging it out in the alley with her own hands, for she certainly couldn't pay a mover, nor rent another room, not until she got a job.

She was so filled with shame and distress by the time she reached her room that she locked the door and flung herself down on her bed without waiting to open her unexpected parcel, and had a good cry all in the dark by herself. That awful old woman, and her horrible room! Oh that she might take her precious possessions and fly to the ends of the earth away from here! Anything, *any*thing would be better than this!

Then suddenly she came to herself. No, *any*thing

would not be better than this! It would not be better in any way to go back home and have to live with Helen. She had come away from something infinitely worse than just an ugly room with an ignorant landlady. This was really a haven and she must be glad for it. She must! She must ignore the poor creature downstairs and live above it all. She must have courage, and trust. She would go and get a job in some little dirty restaurant if that was all there was to get, she would do anything, but she would not let circumstances conquer her. That was what Helen had thought would happen, that circumstances would be too much for her and she would come meekly home and succumb to her will, and it *should not be!* Besides, there *was* Someone who cared. She had determined to believe that little tract, and it had seemed almost as if it was so, until she lost her job. But she would not let go so soon. She would trust in the One who had suffered Himself, and understood.

Suddenly she sat up and wiped her eyes, looking about her room.

She could dimly see the parcel there on the chair where she had dropped it when she came in and all at once an overwhelming curiosity came over her to know what it was and where it came from. Of course it couldn't be flowers. Who would send her flowers? Even Bobby Watkins didn't know her address. This was probably a parcel belonging to someone else, and it might be anything but flowers. She ought to have looked at the address carefully before she came up. Now she would likely have to drag it downstairs and take it back to the postoffice.

She got up and turned on her glaring bulb, that with all its unblinking blaze barely made light enough to read by.

Yes, there was her name written clearly, but not by

any hand she knew. Bobby Watkins wrote in a round childish script as if he had never grown up. Moreover the address was written in a different hand from the name. Ah! the address was probably in the postmaster's writing. It must have been forwarded from home, and now she thought of it she had not as yet received any mail since she had sent the postmaster her address. But what on earth could this be? It couldn't be anything from her father, it wasn't his writing. Nor Helen's either. And that was a florist's label on the outside of the box. The landlady had some ground for one of her assertions at least. Well, if she found Bobby Watkins' card inside she would throw the flowers down in the alley. Even if they were gardenias!

And what was more, if Bobby Watkins had found out where she was she would move tomorrow morning even if she had to go and leave her things behind her. No, she couldn't do that! She could not leave her beloved things. But she would find a way to get them out of this house at once. She would, even if she had to mortgage the job she hadn't got yet to move them!

With a hysterical little laugh she picked up the parcel and tore open its wrappings.

Yes, it was a florist's box, a florist back in the home suburb!

She found her fingers trembling as she lifted the cover of the box and turned back the wax paper wrapping. Ah! A breath from a heavenly land was wafted into her face and her weary senses drew it in with sheer delight! Suddenly the sorrows of the last two weeks dropped away from her and a soothing perfume wrapt her about. She looked, and her eyes were wide with wonder. Carnations. Myriads of them! Her mystery flowers had come to find her!

For a moment her eyes swam with tears and she saw

the delicate seashell pink of the blossoms as if they were in a heavenly vision. She bowed her head, buried her face in their loveliness and drew in deep breaths of their perfume. It satisfied her heartbreak and loneliness as a life-giving draught will quench a great thirst. Her heart was overflowing with tenderness. All her joy in the single flowers that she had found upon her pathway back at home rushed over her, and more. There was something deeper than mere sentimentality. It was not a fancied lover, casting admiration in her way, it was a great overwhelming love offered to a soul that was starving and alone. It did not seem to matter who had sent these. It was not Bobby Watkins, she was sure of that. Bobby had no delicate sensitive romance about him. Bobby brought his flowers himself and gloated over you while you opened them. Bobby could never forget himself long enough to drop a flower anonymously, for genuine love, that cares to bless without receiving recognition or praise. It might be some woman, old or young—whoever it was it seemed like an angel to her now, more than ever, a messenger from God.

Presently she lifted her face to search for a card, almost dreading lest she should find one, yet longing, too. She could not bear to have her delight destroyed, her illusion dispelled by cold facts. She wanted to feel that it was a gift from one who knew God.

But there was no card. Just those dear flowers, so fresh and lovely that it was almost unbelievable they had not been picked but an hour before.

When she had satisfied herself that there was no message she put her face down to the flowers again and began to talk to them softly.

"You lovely things! You beautiful mystery flowers! God sent you! No matter how He got you here I am going to believe God sent you to show me that He is caring for me!"

Then softly she slipped down upon her knees, the flowers still in her arms, and with her lips against the fringes of one big blossom she began to pray:

"Oh God, I believe You *do* care. I don't see why You would, but I *believe* You do. You wouldn't have sent me these flowers just when I needed them so badly if You didn't care a little bit. Dear God, it doesn't matter who You told to send them, I believe they came from You. And if it was anybody like Bobby Watkins You used, please don't let me find it out. Please let it seem just You unless it was somebody *dear.*"

She knelt there for some time, her face among the flowers, and then as memory went back to the cool, quiet, shadowed spot where she had found those other single blossoms, slowly she began to remember. She stood once more against the tall hemlock hedge, leaning against the resilient boughs, thinking of their perfume, hugging the thought of them to her sad heart, and a voice spoke again. How long ago it seemed since she heard that voice praying. What were those words? How the days that had come between had almost blotted them out. She had written them down. What were they? Then they came flocking back like birds to her call:

"We thank Thee for the care of the day, and for these gifts for our refreshment," how the words fitted her own case! She paused to wonder, and then memory went on:

"And Lord we would ask Thy mercy and tenderness and leading for the people up at the great house."

Had that prayer been for her father's house? If it was had it been at all answered? Mercy and tenderness and leading. Had she had those since she had left home? Would the blessings have followed her away from the house? Mercy and tenderness and leading. Perhaps there had been a degree of all. Terrible things might have happened to her. It had seemed that they did, but now she wasn't quite sure. Perhaps there was a degree of leading in it all.

"Perhaps some of them are sad," went on that unseen voice, "Lord, give them comfort!"

Well, here were the flowers, right out of the blue, and they did seem in a degree to soothe her soul.

"Perhaps they need guidance."

Ah, didn't she?

"Do Thou send Thy light—!"

Oh, why hadn't she stayed to hear the end, stayed at any cost?

Yet the memory of the prayer was there fresh in her heart. Perhaps the answer was following her about. Perhaps these flowers had come to foreshadow some kind of light. They were comfort. Oh, for the light—!

Then at once it came to her that the light might be found in her little tract and in the Bible to which it had directed her. Was that possible? If she would diligently seek would she find the light and some way out of this dark maze in which she had lost her way?

If she only could find the person whose voice had uttered that prayer! How many questions she would ask him! Perhaps, in some church there would be a minister who was like that one. If she went the rounds of all the churches she might find one to whom she would dare go and seek advice. But no—that would not do. She would see old friends perhaps, they would ask her uncomfortable questions. She could not face the old world in which she had moved. She would seem to be criticising her father, yet she could not explain her absence from home in any other way. No, she could not go searching among the churches. But she would search in her Bible, and now that the flowers were here they would help her. They would comfort her. She was beginning to have assurance in her heart that God cared. Dear flowers, dear mystery flowers!

Her job was gone, but she had the flowers! The flowers would rest her, and tomorrow she could go out and get her a job!

The morning brought her letters, just a few, and her heart leaped up. Perhaps there would be one to explain the flowers! And yet she almost dreaded lest there would be. If it should be that they came from some common-place source would it destroy her new found faith that God cared?

She hurried back upstairs to read them before she went out. If she sat down in the hall to do so that terrible landlady would come out and question her again. She was so glad that she had met the postman just at the door.

Two of the letters proved to be bills for small pur-chases made at the little local stores at home. One was an advertisement of an entertainment to be given in the village, one was a brief and disagreeable note from Bobby Watkins asserting that it was high time she apologised for her strange actions the night he called, and the fourth was a short note from an old schoolmate who lived in a suburb of the city.

Edith Maythorn had never known Diana in her home surroundings, only in college. Her home until a few months ago had been in a far city, from which she had occasionally written Diana, who for a short time had been her roommate. She had only recently come to this city to live and was not acquainted with Diana's circle of friends. The letter was an invitation to spend the week-end with her at her new home and attend a small house party among whom were two girls who had been in college with them. When Diana read it first she shrank away from the thought of attending such a festivity.

Then it occurred to her that these people did not know her circumstances at all, and were not likely to come into touch with her old friends. Why not go? It was only over Sunday and as others were to be present there would be little time for intimate talks with questionings. Why couldn't she go and get a little breath of real living again? She had plenty of pretty clothes, and no one need know that she was contemplating taking a job in a very common restaurant. None of these girls frequented restaurants of that character. Why not just have a little let down from the strain of sorrow and loneliness? Incidentally she would save money on her meals for two days and that meant a great deal. Her cheeks burned as she remembered what sordid thoughts and impulses had come to move her now. But it was an item worth considering. And of course it was supposable that sometime in the future she might again be in a position to ask Edith to visit her somewhere somehow. Monday morning she could quietly say good-bye and drift out of Edith's ken again and that would be that, but it would give her a much-needed rest, and wholesome food without cost.

As she hurried down the street in search of that job she was weighing the possibilities, pro and con. Of course, if she went she should call up and accept. Yet suppose she found a job and had to go on duty at once? Well, in that case she would just have to call it off of course.

But strangely enough she came on a little eating place late in the afternoon that wanted a waitress to come on Monday morning. It wasn't a cheerful place, nor overly clean, and the food as she swept the room with a comprehensive glance did not look attractive, but she was deadly tired, and it was a job. Perhaps she could do better later. It gave her such a panicky feeling to have no job and her money melting like snow on a hot day that she was ready to take anything no matter how unattractive. She would have her board here, and an infinitesimal wage, together with "tips," how her soul loathed the thought of them, but she was in no situation to be fussy about such matters. She took the place, dropped into a chair by a vacant table to eat an unattractive sandwich and drink a cup of tea, then she went to the telephone with sudden resolve and called up Edith. She would go to Edith's house party and have one day of friendliness and enough to eat before she started in at her obnoxious job in that odious little restaurant. The girls needn't even know that she had left home. Edith knew only that her mother was dead, and if she told her that she had been away when her invitation came that would be excuse enough for her delay in replying.

So she called her friend and found an eager welcoming voice at the other end of the wire which warmed her heart and helped her to keep her resolve not to think about that awful restaurant until Monday morning.

As she unlocked her door the breath of the carnations met her and she felt a sudden reluctance to leave them. But it was too late now, she had given her word that she would come, and she could wear a good big sheaf of the flowers and put the rest safely in their box sprinkled and find them quite fresh and nice on her return.

So she hurried with her dressing, put some of her prettiest things in her overnight bag, fastened on some flowers and departed.

It was dark as she went out of the door and she hurried a little as she noticed a skulking figure across the road in the shadows. Diana found it hard to get used to her surroundings and was just the least little bit afraid every time she went out into the dark ugly street alone at night. She wished she had got started earlier. Well, she was off for a whole day, and she wouldn't remember that Monday was coming and she would have to serve smelly meals to an unwashed throng of common people. She would try and feel happy like other girls just for one day at least. After that she would have to disappear, drop out of sight. Her job would claim her inexorably. She must remember that in talking with whomever she met to-night, she must be exceedingly hazy about her future. She had engagements which would keep her away from home indefinitely. That would be a good explanation to give, and she wasn't quite sure where she would be, but the home address would reach her.

She drew a breath of relief as she settled this matter in her mind, and climbed into the nearest bus that would land her at her friend's new home. She did not notice the man who stealthily slipped into the crowded bus behind her, and kept in the shadow with his hat brim down, nor notice that when she got out, he dropped off into the darkness also. She even approached him a moment later as he stood in the shadow of a hedge and asked which way the numbers ran on that street, and where would be number three seventy-two. He pointed indefinitely off to his right, and shuffled away in the darkness like a wraith. She went on her way, presently finding that he had been wrong in his direction, but arriving at her destination safely in spite of it, and meeting a warm and eager welcome.

Just for one day she would forget!

16

THAT same evening at the Disston mansion a party was going on. It was not of the master's bidding, but he was there figuring in the capacity of happy bridegroom, albeit with a weary look and a heavy heart. If Diana had started out to punish her father for what he had done she could have taken no quicker or more effective way. Though Diana would have been aghast if she had known how heartbroken he was. Diana was only hurt. She never dreamed what her going would do to her undemonstrative father.

Secretly for several days he had been going about silently, cautiously like a sleuth, while his wife was off somewhere shopping, playfully resenting the pressing business which he professed to have.

He had telegraphed to Aunt Harriet, and when he found no trace of his missing daughter even though he carefully hunted out and telephoned a number of friends, he was really frightened.

Then he had tried to find Diana's list of correspondents but all Diana's personal belongings were gone. He had contacted every person he could think of to find out if she was visiting them, doing it cautiously and skillfully lest they should discover that her own father did not know her whereabouts, just a casual telephone message to know if she were calling there, because he wished to speak to her about an important matter, but nothing came of it. He had written scores of letters, some addressed to her friends in various places, and some to herself in their care, but had found no trace of her. He could not eat nor sleep as the days went by and there was still no word from her. His imagination pictured her in all sorts of predicaments and perils, until it seemed to him that he would lose his mind.

Through all this Helen watched him warily, a little amused twinkle in her eyes, and a sweetly sympathetic note in her voice. At last, having possessed herself cleverly of the facts about how much money Diana likely had with her, and how much more she could get hold of without applying to her father, she asked just how much power the father as trustee had over Diana's inheritance. Then she suggested cautiously, almost deprecatingly as if she did not wish to intrude into affairs not her own, that her husband cut off his daughter's income for a time. That would bring her back in a short time she felt sure. Ah, she went about it all in a masterly way hesitating and yet insistent, making it quite plain that Diana must eventually apply to him for money. And the poor man caught at the suggestion as a drowning man might catch at a straw. Indeed he insisted on telephoning his banker at once, though it was quite late at night when Helen suggested it.

The banker had been surprised, a little shocked, Mr. Disston felt. He did not try to explain except to say that Diana had gone away visiting and had not chosen to say where she was. He was taking this method of finding her. "You know young people today are getting a little highhanded and independent," he added as his sole explanation. But it had hurt him to say such a thing about his girl, who had never been anything but docile and loving to him before in her life, and he had suffered acutely ever since. He had waited all day with tense body and agonizing mind. His little girl, Diana! What would her mother think of him for having gotten Diana into a position like this?

He had heard nothing from his banker until late in the afternoon, and he had not been able to settle down to just waiting for some word. But the word when it came did not give him much comfort. Mr. Dunham reported that Diana had just been in to see him about getting some of her next month's money ahead of time and when she heard that her father had cut off her allowance, had walked out like a thoroughbred with her chin in the air, without even cashing the few dollars that remained in her own account though he told her there would be no objection to that.

"I think she'll come to time pretty soon, I really do, Mr. Disston," added his friend the banker. "I hated like sin to tell her what you said I should, too. Pretty little kid. Real thoroughbred! But of course I was certain when she got up to leave my office that she meant to go right home. I never had a question until I saw her turn and walk out, and then something in her manner made me uneasy. I got to thinking over what she had said and I realized she hadn't actually *said* she was going home at all, just walked out on me and left me to think what I would. Then I went to the door to see if she cashed her check and she wasn't there. She must have gone out the side door opposite my office I guess, but when I looked out that she wasn't in sight anywhere. You say she hasn't come yet? Oh, but I'm sure she will soon. Sorry, no, I didn't think to ask her address. I tell you I supposed of

course she meant to go right home. But I'm sure she'll
turn up tonight or tomorrow. I wouldn't worry if I were
you. She looks as if she could take care of herself. And
of course she's proud. She wouldn't be your daughter if
she wasn't."

"That's the trouble," said the father anxiously, "I'm
afraid she'll never come back for money, not if she
starves to death. She's terribly proud. Just what did you
say to her?"

"Well, now look here, Disston, *I* didn't get this up,"
said the banker, "I said to her just what you asked me to
say!" and the banker went carefully over again the
conversation he had had with Diana. But somehow
Diana's father shrank from the words as if they had been
blows dealt upon his own heart, for now suddenly he
saw how they must have seemed to Diana, and he
wondered why he had been willing to send her a word
like that. Why hadn't he known how those words would
hurt her? Yet when Helen had suggested them the whole
thing sounded so right and reasonable and kind! And
now it seemed so brutal! The father hung up the receiver
at last and sat back groaning in spirit. Then he remembered his position as host at a party and hastily slipped
out into the other room and took up his duties again,
aware subconsciously of Helen's dissatisfied eyes watching him, aware that some of the guests were looking at
him and Helen, comparing their ages and wondering
how she came to marry him. Of course, this lovely
house—and he could see them look about upon the
luxury which even in these few days since Helen had
come there to reign, had become almost garish. He felt
very old indeed that night.

The evening finished disturbingly for the master of the
house. Some of the guests were too hilarious for his
liking. Helen too was gayer than he had ever seen her

before, her face a sparkle of pleasure and interest, in contrast to his own haughty expression. He looked about upon the guests Helen had assembled and decided that he didn't like any of them. He would introduce Helen to his friends of course, and gradually wean her from such companions. Poor child, she had not had a mother or father to guide her for years, and of course she wasn't wise in discerning character. But she would listen to him. She always had.

But when the last guests had left and they turned back to the quiet of the home again, Helen made the first attack.

"Well, and is that the way you are going to treat my friends when I have a party?" she asked in a biting voice. "If I had supposed you were going to act like an old grouch I certainly wouldn't have invited them. What do you suppose they thought of you?"

He turned upon her with dignity. He had meant to be very tender in his remonstrance with her but her stinging tones roused his tormented spirit.

"I didn't like the people you had here!" he said sternly. "They were coarse and ill-bred. They are not the kind of people with whom I want my wife to associate!"

"Oh, really?" said Helen petulantly. "So you are going to hide your own behaviour behind a grievance, are you? Well that won't get you anywhere. You remember you told me I might have a party, and you gave me permission to have it just as I wanted it. You said you didn't care who I invited, and now you're objecting. If you think that is being fair I don't. As to my friends, if you don't like them you know what you can do, don't you? Just stay away from my parties! For I give you my word I'm not going to give up my friends! All the people I know are like that, gay and free and easy."

"Then it's high time you knew another class of

people," said Mr. Disston sternly. Then his voice softened a trifle. "I suppose you haven't always had the opportunity to know the right kind of people, dear, but now that you are my wife I shall want you to know my friends, and move in the best circles. It's your right as my wife."

"Indeed!" said Helen flashing her beautiful eyes, "I prefer to move in circles of my own choosing. I'm not an old fogy yet, if you are, and I want to see a little gaiety and life. I don't want to sit by the fire in beautiful domesticity and go to bed at nine o'clock. If that's your idea of married bliss you can count me out!" And Helen flouted out of the room and upstairs closing and locking the door to their room.

Then the master of the house turned out all the lights and locked himself into the dark library and sat down by himself and groaned in spirit. Was this the married bliss he had expected to have? He sat there till the morning dawned. He then came to breakfast alone, and was told his wife did not wish to be disturbed, so he went his way to the office in deep sadness of heart.

To Diana it was almost like entering heaven from the darkness of the pit to enter that bright home of luxury. It was as if some magic had touched her with a fairy wand and she were Cinderella at the party.

The door swung wide and well-trained servants took charge of her suitcase and overnight bag. She was led to a chamber bright with airy organdy hangings and frills of delicate lace and ribbon, costly trifles scattered everywhere with lavish hand. Softly shaded lamps of unusual design, a picture or two that caught the eye, just a lovely homelike room. It almost took Diana's breath away, that first glimpse, it reminded her so of her own sweet home, a little more lavish, perhaps, but still with the touches that spoke of taste and culture and plenty.

As Diana entered she had a swift vision of Mrs. Lundy's rooming house and the third story back where her own treasured furnishings were waiting. The contrast brought quick tears to her eyes. Oh if she might just take them and go home again to the place that had always been home to her!

Then came Edith rushing with open arms to greet her. Edith in bright rosy garments and her hair done in the latest thrill, jewels sparkling about her neck and wrists.

It was delightful to have to hurry and get dressed for dinner, and put away all unpleasant thoughts. That was what she had resolved to do, not to think of her own troubles, neither past nor future. It would be the only way she could possibly get through this evening without everybody knowing that she was in some great trouble. And that must never happen. She simply must carry this off and never let anyone, even Edith, suspect.

So Diana put on a diaphanous dress of delicate green, almost the shade of the taffeta of years ago that Helen had so gracelessly borrowed. It was a color that Diana's mother had loved on her, and the dress was one she had ordered during her illness, with loving eagerness to have her girl go out among her friends.

While she was getting into it she was recalling little things her mother had said about the dress, and how it became her. Precious things, but she put them away in her heart for the tears were too near the surface to trust such thoughts, and she must hurry. Edith had said that dinner was about to be served.

She looked at herself in the mirror when she was ready, startled to see herself looking so well. She had been through so much during the past two weeks that it seemed to her her brow must be seamed with care, and her eyes dull with weeping.

But the excitement of the moment had brought a soft flush to her cheeks and a sparkle to her eyes and she scarcely knew herself. As a last thought she remembered her flowers and took them from their wax paper wrappings, fastening a great lovely mass of them at her shoulder, then turning her face toward them and touching her lips to their fringes caressingly. Dear flowers. They seemed somehow to give her a kind of moral support, or background, perhaps it was background. They had come from home, somewhere, somehow. When she looked at them she could think of the tall pines standing guard among cool shadows, and a single blossom smiling up at her from the dewy grass. It seemed as if those flowers acted as ballast to keep her soul steady during these hours that were before her, as if just touching them with her cheek, breathing in their perfume, would calm her and give her courage if it all seemed too much for her.

Edith came back for her and they went down the wide deeply carpeted stair together, their arms about one another as they used to do when they were school girls.

"How darling you look!" gushed Edith, and Diana for an instant felt warmed in her soul. This was going to be pleasant after all, meeting Edith and being in things again.

Then came the other three girls whom she had known in college, and Diana began to revive in her spirit. A little smile lurked in the corner of her mouth as inwardly she compared herself to a wet kitten that had been out in the storm, and had crept in to find food and comfort and a place by the fire.

Edith's mother was large and comely, well groomed and pleasant. She accepted Diana as one of them, called her by her first name as if she had been with them always. Diana liked it and was glad she had come. No one said anything about Diana's home or her condition in life. They were all talking gaily about trifling things, laughing a good deal, cheery. Oh, it was good to be there! To get a few hours surcease from the awful loneliness and incipient fear of the future, and dread of the past!

Some young men arrived after dinner and Diana liked them all well enough. There wasn't one among them like Bobby Watkins. But she couldn't quite imagine any one of them dropping a single flower in the grass day after day. Her mysterious donor was probably only a woman. But no, she would not limit those spirit flowers to any earthly means. As long as she could she would think of them as having come straight from God. It might be that God had somewhere a young knight who would love a lonely girl and woo her with flowers, but she did not know such a one. She could please herself by thinking of it all as romance in the form of a fairy tale, but she felt a growing conviction that behind it all was God, calling to her, trying to let her know He cared, and the belief comforted her.

The young men flocked around her as they did to the other girls. She did not feel left out. One especially seemed drawn to her, Jerry Lange. He called her Diana as soon as they were introduced.

"Diana, you for mine!" he said engagingly as they paired off for the fun of the evening.

And Diana liked it. Yet as the evening went forward in the usual amusements she had a feeling that they were just children, playing at life, not really in earnest at all, and she alone of them all had grown up. What they were doing so eagerly soon palled on her. Was that what trouble, and loneliness did to your soul, made it suddenly grow old and satiated? Though she had never had a great deal of gaiety in her life, yet it seemed so trifling now. She thought of her dreary crowded third floor room in the unkempt street. She thought of the restaurant where she was going to work on Monday. She thought of her home, now her home no longer, and then strangely she thought of God. Was He caring for her, here, now in the midst of this bright laughing scene? Was He standing unseen behind her here and caring? What a strange thought that was to come into the midst of her outing!

She looked around upon them all, she looked into Jerry's laughing eyes as he tried to tell her how he had just been waiting all his life to find her, and called her "Beautiful" and "Darling" in the parlance of the day, laughing and giving her charming courtesy, that didn't of course mean a thing. Just gaiety. And she wondered if Jerry knew God. If God cared for all these here. Of course He did for that verse had said "God so loved the world!" Nobody would claim to be left out of that. God was caring for them, but they—were *they*—? No, they were obviously not conscious of Him. Not at the moment anyway. And it was altogether likely that none of them ever thought of God at all. They were all as she had been before her trouble came.

She wondered idly as she watched the handsome youth beside her, talking brilliant nonsense to her, what would be his reaction if she should ask him about it? What for instance would he say if she were to ask, "Do you know God, Jerry?" Of course she would not do it, but she could almost feel the chill silence that would ensue for an instant, the blank surprise with which he would look at her. But it would not be for long, likely. He would have ready some flippant reply, some brightly funny answer, and suddenly she knew she would not want to hear it. It would hurt her sense of reverence for the Lord who cared for her. What had happened to her?

It couldn't be all merely sorrow that had done this. But if it was it had certainly done something definite to her. She never used to think about God before, any more than they did. But now she realized that she had become God-conscious.

She was glad when they turned from the games and the dancing for she somehow felt very little interest in them, and voted to go for a drive in the big open sports car that one of the young men had brought. They put down the top of the car, for there was moonlight, and besides, the night was unusually warm. All eight of them piled into the car noisily, and Jerry sat by Diana and tried to hold her hand. She had some ado to keep it to herself, for now and again he would catch it up impulsively as though they were children at play. But on the whole the ride was a lovely experience, crowded cheerily together under that great white flood of moonlight, flashing out through the city streets, rushing traffic lights, barely missing pedestrians and smaller cars, and sweeping out a wide silver road into less populated regions. The sultriness of the evening was gone.

As the soft summer breeze played in Diana's hair, it seemed pleasant to have Jerry beside her, saying bright nothings, seeing to it that she was supplied with candy, and that her wrap was adjusted when the breeze grew a bit chilly as they swept into the countryside. This was the life she was born to, good fellowship and fun and friendships like this. This would have been hers as a matter of course if her mother had lived. They had often talked about how she would go out to parties and enjoy herself when her school days were over. And then—they had never been over! They had just stopped!

All at once Diana realized that the road they were traveling was familiar. Her heart stood still. They were on the highway that led directly to her home! Oh, why had she come to this party? Why had she come on this drive? She nestled her frightened face down into the knot of fringed blossoms on her shoulder as if they would somehow help her through. She felt herself growing weak with the thought of the nearness of the spot that had always been the dearest on earth to her.

Then she tried to rally her forces. None of this crowd knew where she lived, except Edith, and it was to her only a name, only a postal address, she had never been there. She perhaps did not even know where they were. She had only so recently come to the city and was not familiar with the roads.

Diana felt as if she must do something to still the wild beating of her heart lest the others should hear it. How silly she was, she told herself. Even if Edith recognized the place and spoke of it, she need only be quiet. It was not likely they would ask her questions. She could just act as if it were a matter of course. If Edith should suddenly cry out as they passed the town and she saw the name somewhere, "Why, Di, isn't this where you live?" she could just say, "Yes, it isn't far from here," and be very vague about it. Would she be able to keep her voice steady to say that, she wondered?

And now they were rushing through the village. The lights were bright along the way. The village shops were blazing with display windows. There was the electric shop with its big white refrigerators, and ranges and lamps. There was the postoffice, and the drug store. There was that new florist's shop, the window filled with gorgeous blossoms with tall tropical ferns in the background. Her flowers had come from there. Her heart gave a wild little thrill and she put her face down close to them, her lips upon them, as if she would hush their very perfume lest it should call attention to where they came from.

And now they were passing the bank with the name of the town in great stone letters across its white front, a flood light bringing it out like a picture. It was a beautiful building and it was new. The town was proud of it. But Diana trembled as they shot by it, and then drew a breath of relief as they passed on up the wide avenue into the region of high hedges and estates. In a moment more home would be in sight! Could she get by it without sobbing?

There, there it was, its whiteness gleaming against the dim green of the dark pines in the background. She wanted to close her eyes till they were by, but Jerry was looking down into them and he would ask her why she was doing it, "Beautiful?" if she did. No, she must keep them open and smile back to what he was saying, though she hadn't heard a word of it. She must laugh and not seem to be interested in anything along the way. Soon it would all be past, and none of them would know that it had taken the heart out of her to pass that way, so near to home and Father, and not know what was going on, not have him know that she was there! Oh, why had she come on this party?

Then suddenly one of the girls cried out, "Oh, see that lovely mansion, boys and girls, isn't that just ideal? See the way that lawn curves up to the terrace! And aren't those pines simply ducky behind there. I'll bet they have a swimming pool and a sunken garden back of that. My, I'd like to go there and visit. Pity we haven't any friends around here to scrape acquaintance with whoever lives there. Where is this, anyway? I want to remember it."

Diana drooped her face down lower and held her breath. Now it would come! Somebody would be sure to know the name of the suburb and then there would be an outcry and Edith would say, "Why, Diana, isn't this where—?"

She could see the lights of her home now, flung out like a banner to challenge the moonlight on the lawn. She could identify each light. The front door was flung wide, just as it had been the night she went away. And was that Helen standing in the doorway talking to a man?—not her father, she could see that, he was too short for her father.

But then the hedge and a group of trees swept in and hid the house from view for an instant, and the identity of the place had not yet been discovered. Oh, would they never get by? Why were they slowing up?

Here was the stone cottage at last, dear little stone cottage where she heard that prayer. She gave it a hungry fleeting glance, and then looked again, for the door was suddenly flung open and a young man came and stood in the entrance looking out. She looked again. Could that be the man who had prayed? How she wished she knew!

Then as if in answer to her wish their car suddenly swept up to the curve and stopped dead with a startling abruptness, and Diana's heart simply stood still. What, oh, what was going to happen now, and what should she do? Jump out and run away?

Her frightened heart seemed to be beating in her ears like a drum and she dared not look up. Why was she so frightened? Nothing was going to happen. Nobody was looking at her. Or, were they? Perhaps they had somehow got a message from her father and were taking her home for a joke! Oh—!

Then the driver called out and broke the awful spell that held her.

"Hey, Brother, which way to Windham Road?"

The young man in the doorway came down the step and stood in the moonlight answering. His voice had a pleasant accent:

"Straight on two miles and turn to your left. Filling station on the corner. You can't miss it."

"Thanks a lot!" said the youth who was driving. Then he shot on down the road so that it seemed they had scarcely paused.

It was all over as quickly as that, and the white mansion with its grassy slope and its background of dark pines was gone, gone the little cottage with the tall young man in the doorway. But the voice that had answered their question lingered in Diana's heart.

For that was the voice that had prayed: "And Lord we would ask Thy mercy and tenderness and leading for the people up at the great house. Perhaps some of them are sad. Lord, give them comfort. Perhaps they need guidance. Do Thou send Thy light—"

What a prayer! And how its accents came back with the sound of that voice. That voice so strangely familiar! Where had she heard it before? *Had* she really heard it before the prayer, or only in her dreams? And his face as he stood there in the moonlight, a fine face, strong and trustworthy and yet tender—a face that matched the voice! It thrilled her to think of his face as he stood there in the moonlight looking at them all so interestedly, and speaking with that pleasant voice. Who was he? Where did he come from? Was he just a visitor there?

And suddenly she knew where she had heard that voice before! It was the voice that had spoken in the darkness when Bobby Watkins—

"What is it, Beautiful? What are you thinking about? I've asked you the same question three times and you haven't heard it yet!"

"Oh, did you?" she said rousing with a little laugh that somehow seemed to have a new lilt in it. "Do excuse me! Ask it again. I was so taken up with the beauty of the night that everything else was just a dream!"

He asked his question and she answered it superficially, keeping up her end of the cheerful banter skillfully, with only half of her mind upon it, for deep down in her heart she was hugging to herself the thought that she had seen the man who had prayed for her house. And was it conceivable that he was still praying for them, and was she possibly included in that prayer? How she wished that sometime she might meet him and ask him some of those throbbing questions that had been roused in her mind by the little tract given her in the railway station, and her reading of the Bible!

There was more gay banter as they swept on through the moonlight; singing too, rollicking songs, love songs, and shouting out of their youth and high spirits. It was all like a dream after that to Diana. She went through everything, smiling, gracious, yet pleasantly distraught.

They stopped by the wayside and had ice cream. Then they went back to the city house again and sang more songs and played more games, but at last it was over, and in the small hours of Sunday morning Diana found herself at last alone in the lovely guest room lying in the cool darkness dropping off to sleep, with one sweet carnation lying against her cheek on the pillow, and the sound of a voice praying, a voice that presently blended with her dreams and prayed for her by name with great gentleness. And so she drifted off to sleep.

17

DIANA went back to her hot third story room in the city early Monday morning before the rest of the week-end party were awake.

She had had much ado to prevent their taking her wherever she was going, and had had to resort to strategy to keep them from knowing her present place of residence. She was utterly aghast at the thought of Jerry or any of the others escorting her to that awful rooming house, with the consequent explanations of her present situation if she let them do it. Even the girls had insisted they would take her to her train, for she had told them she had an engagement for the day in another part of the city. So in the very early morning, quite before any of the servants were stirring in the great beautiful house, except perhaps a sleepy cook down in the kitchen, she arose, wrote a hasty note, slipped it under Edith's door, and went silently down the velvet shod stairs and out of the house without disturbing anyone.

The note said:

Dear Edith,

I'm dreadfully sorry to run away this way without seeing you again, but in thinking it over I find I must get another change of garments before I go on my way for the day's engagement, so I'm just running off without waking you. I know you will forgive me. And I shall hope to see you again soon. I'm not just sure where I shall be the rest of the summer, but if I ever do get home again I hope I can have the pleasure of a visit from you. I've had such a lovely time! Thank you for asking me.

Lovingly,
Diana

So Diana had slipped around the corner from the house and waited in the next street for the bus, while the morning dawned in rosy glory, and most of the city was still sleeping.

Diana had gone through the Sabbath as in a pleasant dream, taking as little part as possible in the hilarity and fun that was the atmosphere of the gathering, smiling sweetly at everybody, but in reality not absorbed in what went on.

The young men arrived again early in the day and Jerry was as devoted as ever, but failed to get the overwhelming interest from this girl that was usually accorded him everywhere. Diana was a nice good comrade, but she seemed somehow remote. He couldn't quite understand it. He looked for an engagement ring, but there was none. And perhaps her attitude only intrigued him the more, for he was most devoted all the day and evening, and quite insisted that she let him come with his car in the morning and drive her home. She had succeeded in putting him off at last by saying her plans were not fully made yet, she wasn't sure just what time she would be going, and so he said good night with a warning that he would be back early the next day to be ready for whatever plan she made.

So Diana escaped them all and went to the rooming house to change from her gay garments into the plainest black dress she owned.

She had ripped off the only pretense at decoration it had, and cut the sleeves to the elbow, with just a plain hem, but even so she had a stylish look as she surveyed herself in the glass before leaving for her day's work. Even when she enveloped herself in the big white apron she had bought, she looked a thing apart from that restaurant. Not a ring on her finger, not even a string of beads about her neck, nor a pin at her throat to fasten the plain white collar, yet there were "lines" unmistakable to the simple dress that showed it well cut and tailored, there was a trimness to her plain black pumps and a delicacy of face and figure that showed she was not the usual waitress in a cheap restaurant.

Even her watch had to be left in her room. It was a pretty toy, platinum set with diamonds about its face and in the delicate links of the bracelet. It would never do to pass ham and cabbage and baked beans with such a wrist watch. She would be suspected at once, as well as being a prey for thieves.

So she locked her watch into her bureau and went her way through the noisy waking streets, dreading what was before her, yet not thinking about it as much as she had expected, for in her mind there lingered the memory of a voice, and a strong face with wonderful eyes, and a prayer, that seemed following her out into this new unknown world which she was to enter today.

And she had prayed herself, before she left her room, a little trembling prayer, shyly, as if the man who had once prayed for her were there before God with her, and listening to what she said. Just a shy claiming of God's guidance, and an affirmation that she was trusting and then, after a pause, an "I thank You!" She didn't say for what, but in her heart it was that she had seen the one who had prayed that night and whose words had lingered all these days in her heart. It seemed to her that the earth did not reel quite as much under her untried way as it had on Saturday, nor was the way quite as dark and empty and long, since she knew there was a man like that, and he had prayed for her, even but once.

So she entered her new world and was suddenly faced with all its sordidness anew.

The other waitresses were coming in, yawning, heavy-eyed, loud voiced, discontented. She heard them telling one another where they had been the night before and how late they had been up. She heard their half-finished confidences, their bitter laughter. Their faces were painted, their garments were cheap but gaudy, and most of them had dark circles of unhappiness and exhaustion under their eyes. Looking at them it suddenly occurred to Diana that these were all a part of God's world as much as she was, that He must love them, since He died for all, and the thought was startling. It made her look at them from a new standpoint, so that their commonness and coarseness and lack of culture did not stand out to her gaze as they otherwise would have done. They were dear to her God, she must not turn from them as her natural instincts would have had her do!

But those girls had no such common bond to bind them to her. They looked at her with hostile eyes. She was an intruder from another world. She had once been rich, they could see that from the very way she wore her clothes, from her walk, from the delicacy of her lovely hands that showed no sign of having worked. They called all such girls snobs, and hated them. They resolved to make it too hot for her so that she would have to leave and make room for one of their own kind. They began at once, drawing away from her, whispering with furtive eyes upon her, aloof and cold.

It had not occurred to her that she would have to have much to do with the other waitresses, but she found at the start that she was somewhat dependent upon them. She approached one girl, the least disagreeable-looking one of the lot and asked where she should put her hat, and the girl shrugged her shoulders, with a wink at the others and said "Ast the boss! I ain't got time ta show ya." Diana stepped back bewildered, feeling as if she had been slapped in the face.

Later she discovered that her very voice was an offense to these girls who had very little education. Most of them had left school to go to work even before the law allowed.

She approached the boss for information and found a beetling brow and an ugly jaw. He scarcely glanced at her.

"Ast one o' the girls," he growled, "I ain't got time! Here, you Lily, you show this new number the cloak room. Mame, whatcha standin' round fer? Dontcha see that customer over ta the corner? Get a hustle on ya. There's plenty other girls ef ya don't find it convenient ta worruk taday!"

The girl gave a frightened glance and started toward the table over in the corner where the waiting customer sat, and Diana learned a startling lesson. She stood a second waiting uncertainly for the Lily girl to show her the cloak room, but Lily had hunched her shoulders and vanished into the kitchen.

Diana shrank from asking any of the others who so obviously considered her an intruder. Then she saw another girl hurrying in out of breath, taking her hat off as she came. She resolved to follow her and ask no questions.

"Hey, you, Ruby! This is a pretty time o' day ta be comin' ta worruk!" roared the manager.

"Oh, is it late?" panted the girl turning and almost colliding with Diana, "I—you see—my grammother was sick!"

"Yeah? Yer grammother again! Ain't it so? Ya can't put that over on me! Don' let it happen again!" he snapped. "Get a hustle on! Make it snappy!"

Diana shrank into the shadows of the back of the room and disappeared after Ruby. Perhaps Ruby would be kindlier than the rest. She might ask her what to do.

But Ruby had slung her hat on a hook and dashed out again tying on her apron, and Diana perceived that she had better do the same. As she went out she reflected that she couldn't have that terrible man roaring her name out everywhere. What should she do? Take another name? Her middle name was Dart. She had registered as Miss Dart. But apparently that man would never call her Miss Dart. Well, let him call her Jane.

Her decision was none too soon, for he met her at the door of the cloak room with a card and pencil.

"Write yer name an' *ad*dress," he commanded, "an' be quick about it! Then take a tray an' get ta worruk! There's a customer comin' in now. The menu's on tha wall, but some of 'em can't read. Ya'll haveta memorize it as ya go. Getta hustle on! And don't bother me with questions. Use yer head!" He glanced at the card and added, "Jane!"

Diana gave him one quick startled look, caught up a tray from the frame beside her and went over to the table in the corner.

The man sitting there was rough and uncouth. He had

a deep stubby growth of hair on his face, and his eyes were bleared and fierce-looking. She glanced away toward the menu on the wall as she approached him and then turned beside the table to see his hateful eyes fixed upon her. She controlled a little shiver of horror and forced herself to look at him steadily and impersonally, and suddenly that same question came to her again. Did God love this man, too? Did He die for him? What a strange world she had come into! She had never questioned that before about anyone. The people she had known had been on the same social level with herself, and her contacts had been carefully guarded. She had never thought about people like this, and here she was serving them! But why should she resent them? The Son of God died for them!

But his first words and his offensive glance made her shudder again.

"You a new un, ain't ye?" he said, and his voice was offensive also.

She gave him a frightened glance.

"I beg your pardon," she said with the least little bit of haughtiness in her voice.

"Whatcha beggin' my pardon fer?" His eyes narrowed and seemed to be boring into her soul like gimlets. She gave a swift glance toward the manager and saw him watching her with an amused grin on his ugly thick face, and instantly she rallied. Here was her testing. She must not fail.

"Will you have ham and eggs, sausages, or liver?" she asked in a voice that sounded even to herself as if it came from very far away.

"H'm! Snooty are ye?" said the man contemptuously. "Wal, make it hot cakes and sausage, with plenty o' syrup, and a pot o' coffee, an' *scram,* fer I'm in a hurry!"

Diana didn't know what "scram" meant but she fairly

flew, lifting her tray above the mulling crowd of customers that were beginning to pour into the miserable little eating place now in numbers too many for the accommodations, lifting her highborn chin a bit haughtily. She was here to serve, and if she lost her job she would have to get another, perhaps worse than this. If God had died for all these dreadful people and loved her too, He could surely protect her. And of course mere words, nor looks, could not really hurt her. She had read something in her Bible the other day about being kept by the power of God through faith unto salvation. She hadn't known what it meant at the time, but now a dim vision of what it might mean came to her. She couldn't see any keeping hand, nor any guiding hand. It all had to be done by faith, faith that God loved her, had sent His beloved Son to die for her, had thought her soul worth saving. It was therefore inconceivable, since all that was true, that He would let her be hurt or lost in any way, since He was all-powerful, all-seeing, and *cared!*

While she was waiting for the hot cakes and preparing the tray as she saw the other girls do she was thinking these things, and a memory of the man last night standing in the bright doorway of the little stone cottage by the home gate came to her. It lifted her out of her fright and gave her a kind of peace to think that a man like that had been praying for her. She liked to think that perhaps he was doing it now.

Inside the breast of her plain black dress she had pinned a single carnation, as a kind of talisman. Its breath stole up faintly like the far fragrance of another world and comforted her.

The manager was watching her. When she brought her tray back so swiftly he seemed surprised. She was not clumsy as some of those other girls had been at the start. Her fingers were deft and worked quickly. As soon as she had learned where the knives and forks and spoons were kept, and where to fill the glasses with water, her tray was arranged by the time the food was ready, and she carried it without slopping the coffee too, not that the manager cared so much about that, however.

Before the day was over the manager had learned that even though she was "classy" she seemed to have a better mind for her work than some of the others. Moreover she didn't dally, and there wasn't a lazy hair on her attractive brown head. The manager decided he liked her, and he saw to it that she had a chair at a table when she ate her swift meals. The other girls noticed this and hated her for it. The manager knew that she was worth more than some of the others, when she got in training, and he called her for some of his best customers, "Jane! Take that number, Jane!" and the other girls would pause and cast malevolent glances. He was giving her some of the people who gave the biggest tips, and they hated her more. They talked about it as they passed one another, or when they lingered at the counter waiting for their orders.

"Next he'll be takin' her out ta a movie," they whispered, "an' what'll Gwendolyn think o' that?"

But Diana went on her swift way not noticing either them or him, intent only on doing her work and not getting fired, though she was weary and footsore, with aching arms unused to lifting heavy trays, and tired back that rebelled at the unusual strain put upon it. At lunch she ate a small portion of the unattractive greasy food that was given her, but when dinner time came she was too tired to swallow but a few mouthfuls. The long hurried hours were telling on her. Would the day never be done? And there would be other days, succeeding one another, day after day, working like this for her existence. And there was no end ahead. It would go on and on and on, unless God did something about it, for she had no home any more, only that room that she must keep or be put out on the street!

She was on her way out at last when the manager stood up from his table where he was counting a heap of small change and tapped her on the shoulder.

"You done purty good, Jane, fer a first try."

She thanked him wearily and with his words of commendation in her ears went on her way.

The breath of her flowers smote across her consciousness as she entered her room. Poor flowers, condemned to brighten this dim room alone. Yet the very consciousness that they were here in this quiet place that was all hers, made it possible for her to keep on through the day. She stooped to caress them and the healing balm of them as always soothed her. But she was too weary even to think about them tonight. She flung off her garments and got into bed, drowsing even in the act. She had never before known what it was to be so tired, and the blessedness of sleep came down upon her like a curtain. She roused only to wind her alarm clock, mindful even in her weariness of the ugly warnings those other girls had received at being even a second tardy.

Morning and the sharp insistent shriek of the little imp of a clock by her side, and she roused to the bitterness of her new life, languid, sore in heart and muscle, and dragged herself up to go through another day like the first one. Was it humanly possible for her to keep this up? Her gains through tips the first day had been so pitifully little, less than a dollar all told, and the starvation wage would not come till the week was up. That was the whip her employer held over the heads of his help. Of course she had food such as it was, but no appetite for it. It seemed to her sick senses as if it was something that her soul had wallowed in for centuries, when she came to eat that food. Its strong, greasy, scorched aroma had filled her lungs and nostrils till they were sated. Why should anyone want to eat anyway? Why should they have to?

Even Sunday brought only half-day relief, for the arrangement was that the girls took turns getting a full Sunday off. Jane was told that hers would come in four weeks, as she was a newcomer and must wait her turn. In consternation she looked forward to four steady weeks of this toil, broken only by that half-day once in seven! And when the seventh day came and she reached her room she had no wish but to lie down and sleep again. She did not even stop to caress her drooping flowers. What did it matter? Someone had cared to send them, but she was too far gone in weariness to give them the attention they demanded. Well, they were dying and she would soon be dead too, perhaps.

She had tried to read her Bible nights when she came home, but found herself so utterly fagged that she could not take in the meaning of the words. She was gradually comprehending the life a large part of the world was living, and she wondered if God cared? Did He truly care? Oh, she wanted to believe it, but somehow that first Sunday afternoon after she became a waitress in that awful restaurant she could not quite feel sure any more. She was just sick with weariness. Perhaps, later, she would become accustomed to such hard work, and wouldn't mind it so much, she told herself as she put her head down upon the pillow that first Sunday afternoon without the ceremony of undressing and was immediately drenched with sleep.

It was Mrs. Lundy who wakened her, just at early evening, knocking at her door. She had a large box in her arms and she was quite insistent.

"These here come las' night but you wasn't in yet. I told Lottie to bring 'em up when she heard you come in, but she didn't bother, and when I come up this mornin' you was gone. I guess it's more flowers. Say, he must be a reg'lar guy, sendin' 'em oncet a week."

Flowers? Diana looked up with her sleep-laden eyes. Her heart leaped up and she came awake at once, a soft color stealing into her pale cheeks. The flowers! They had come again! Not just once, but at regular intervals, just as they had been at home, only now by boxes instead of by blossoms! Wonder of wonders! And she had doubted her God's caring!

Of course the Bible said nothing at all about God's sending carnations to show His loving care, but somehow in spite of common sense those spirit-flowers seemed connected in some way with God.

"I said he must be a regular guy, sendin' 'em oncet a week!" repeated the landlady looking at her curiously.

"Oh, yes," said Diana, a light coming into her eyes. "Yes, it does seem that way, doesn't it?" and she swept an upward glance at the curious old woman with a smile that suddenly wiped away all the weariness from her face. "Yes, it does!" she lilted. "He must be!"

"Well, if he's such a swell feller, why doesn't he come across an' give ye enough ter pay yer rent on time?"

"Oh," said Diana quickly, apologetically, a flush coming to her cheeks. "I have it right here, Mrs. Lundy. I meant to give it to you last night but it was so late, and your room seemed to be dark—and I was so tired—!"

Mrs. Lundy, with a mollified manner, swept her another curious glance.

"Seem like ef he can afford ta send a lotta flowers like that he might do somepin' ta keep ya from workin' sa hard!"

Diana cast her a superior smile from a cool distance.

"But you see I wouldn't let anyone do that, Mrs. Lundy!" she said proudly.

"Oh!" said the woman significantly, and then after a pause, "Wal, some does that way o' course, but I say it don't pay ta be too pertikelar in these days! Ya gotta live, ya know!"

"I'm not so sure," said Diana, counting out the change, and Mrs. Lundy went on her way.

Then Diana locked her door and turned back to her box, thoroughly awake now, her cheeks flaming crimson, her breath coming quickly as if she had been running, her eyes starry bright.

They had come again! Her dear mysterious flowers. She did not care where they came from, they had come. God had let them come. Perhaps she would never find out who sent them, but she knew they came from God.

She opened the box, and suddenly saw a white envelope bearing her name, lying right on the top of the wax paper that veiled the flowers, and her breath almost stopped. She sat back staring at it for a full minute before she put out her hand to touch it.

Was that the same handwriting that had been on the outside of the first box? No, it wasn't! She reached down in the corner and picked up the first box where she had hidden it behind the bureau. No, it was a different hand! It was a fine clear strong hand. A man's hand? Or—could it be a woman's? No, not possibly, and yet some women—nowadays—wrote in quite a masculine way. But the woman, if it was a woman, who would conceive the idea of putting flowers in the way of a troubled girl would never be one who would write a masculine hand. It wasn't thinkable.

These thoughts raced through her brain while she sat staring at the envelope, quite forgetful of the flowers whose perfume reached delicately out to enwrap her soul again.

How silly she was to sit there staring when she had

only to open that envelope and the secret would be revealed, likely, the mystery solved. Yet she dreaded knowing the truth, now it seemed within her grasp. She could not bear to have her one little romance stripped of its mystery and brought out in the open commonplace of day.

Then at once she could stand it no longer and she opened the envelope with trembling hands and read what was within:

> Dear Flower Girl,
>   I found your precious note. I am glad the flowers helped.

That was all! No name signed, no address nor date, nor anything!

And the mystery was still unsolved, yet very precious, but now there was a definite person connected with them, a real intention of sending them.

She arose with her flowers, knelt as before, and thanked God for sending them. Then she arranged them in a lovely jar and sat down before them to enjoy their beauty and fragrance and think over and over again the words of that message.

"I found your precious note"—"*Precious*"—! It thrilled her just to think it over. Precious! Somebody cared! God cared at least. And He must have let *somebody* else care too, but not in any foolish way. In a wonderfully tender way, with more of heaven than earth in its quality.

Flowers! *Precious* flowers!

18

AT the Disston mansion the servants had reigned for a week only, ordering what they liked and keeping high carnival. Helen had not bothered to look up their references. She said they were smart-looking and knew their way about. She wanted them because they had served in fashionable circles, or professed to have done so. But when she chose to insist upon week-ends at the shore or mountains, and spoke of whole weeks away, with the house running and ready for immediate occupancy, they looked forward to time on their hands and carte blanche to do as they liked. If the master of the house protested at such waste Helen silenced him at once with the suggestion that Diana might choose to come home at any time, and he wouldn't want her to find a closed house, would he? And the master said no more.

He was more and more worried about Diana, waiting daily, expectantly, for word from her which did not arrive, depressed beyond rallying after the mails would come and still no word.

He and Helen had come home at his insistence. He must look after his business, he said. And indeed it had been sadly neglected, his mind being on other things. There were plenty of things about his business to worry about if he had only chosen to remember it.

They came home about the middle of the morning just after the mail had arrived, and then trouble descended upon them.

Helen looked up brightly from her sheaf of letters and invitations.

"Listen!" she cried, an open letter in her hand. "Max Copley has invited us to a house party! It's to be the end of this week. Isn't that swanky? I must get a couple of new dresses for it. I might go in town this afternoon and look around."

"No!" said her husband sharply, "not with any idea of going to a party at that man's house. I want nothing to do with him or any crowd in which he moves. He isn't fit for you to speak to!"

"Oh, really," said Helen with lifted brows, "now that poisonous mind and tongue of yours is going to give us another exhibition, is it? What a veritable old crab you are getting to be, and so soon after we are married! Well, I supposed it wouldn't last, but I didn't think you would change so soon. However, do as you like for yourself. I'm *going!* Get me? You can't tie *me* down to your age!"

The gray look that was getting to be habitual on Mr. Disston's face suddenly descended.

"Not my age, perhaps, Helen, but to my station at least, surely."

"No, not to your station either, not if you are determined to live in a past generation. I'm stepping out, and you can go with me or stay behind for all I care. It's entirely up to you, darling. But you can't tie me down for I won't be tied! And I'm going into town to get a few new clothes! I'd like some money if you don't mind.

You'd better give it to me now so I won't be delayed about it after lunch. I want to get an early start."

A still grayer look came over Mr. Disston's face.

"I'm sorry," he said after an instant's hesitation, "I can't give you any now. In fact I'm afraid I can't give you any more till the first of the month. We've been spending a good deal more than usual and I find I am running a little short." He said it in an apologetic tone, but Helen's face flushed red.

"Really?" she said with a touch of scorn on her lips. "Well you certainly have got to the end of your resources in a hurry. We haven't been doing very much for a honeymoon. Just a few week-ends."

"We've been to the best hotels always, and you've wanted all the extras. Besides, we've had a great deal of company. You've no idea how that counts up. Of course you haven't had much experience in housekeeping yet."

"Oh, I suppose your model daughter would have done better!" flashed Helen angrily.

"I didn't say that, Helen," said Mr. Disston sadly, "but of course those new servants you got did bring the bills up a great deal. I was rather appalled at the bills. They all came to the office yesterday. And coming just now when business is at the very lowest ebb, it makes it pretty hard."

Helen stared at him with vexed eyes, and then flounced up from her chair letting fall a sheaf of letters to the floor, and went and looked out of the window.

"Oh, well," she said, still offended, "of course I can always charge things, but I hate to be hampered this way. When you are married you naturally consider that you can have a few things the way they ought to be. Well," with a sigh, "never mind, I can charge things."

Disston glanced up with a look in his eyes that was almost frightened.

"No, Helen, please don't do that either. I've had several insistent letters from the places where you have been buying. It seems you have already been charging things, and I thought I had given you money enough in all reason for the things you said you wanted to buy."

"Oh, my goodness!" snapped Helen, "have I got to be watched and spied on? I hate a spy! And I hate a tightfisted man. I supposed of course you wanted your wife to appear as well as she could. I only got what I absolutely had to have."

"Helen, you distress me, dear. Come and sit down and let me explain to you."

"You distress me too," said Helen bitterly. But she came and sat down.

"Well, it's just this way. I don't want to trouble you with my business affairs any more than is necessary, but just this last week a situation has arisen which makes it necessary that I save every penny possible, for a short time at least. You will remember that I have been much away from the office during the past month, and it seems a number of critical situations arose during my absence that had to be met by my subordinates. They did the best they knew, but it was not what I would have done if I had been there, and therefore things have got into a serious tangle. Of course I am hoping that I shall be able to right matters soon, and all will yet go well, but just for the present, until I tell you further, I shall have to ask you to spend just as little as possible. You must know that this is mortifying to me, just after our marriage, to have to say this to you, but I am sure you will cooperate with me in this matter until we have clear sailing before us again."

He looked at her wistfully, but she regarded him stonily.

"I suppose," she said in a hard voice, "that what is really the case is that you have made such a fool of yourself over this matter of Diana's going away that you aren't fit to put your mind on your business. Oh, you needn't talk to me. I have eyes. I can see. You care far more for Diana than you ever did for me. I ought never to have married you. I might have known you were too old to give up your life habits!"

And suddenly Helen let fall two enormous well-calculated tears straight down into her lap splash on her diamond engagement ring, which twinkled at her troubled husband enormously and expensively, and reminded him that it was not yet paid for, as also were several other things that Helen had lately acquired at her own insistence.

"There, there, child!" he said coming over to her and laying his hand upon her head, as he might have done to Diana, "I didn't mean to trouble you. I'm sorry. I'm only asking you to be a little careful, for a few weeks at least, till I can get things in hand again. You know I do not want to spoil your pleasure——"

"Oh, yes, you do!" sobbed Helen adroitly, "and I'm not a child! I'm a grown woman, and I know what I want, and you said you were going to make me happy!"

"My dear! I certainly want to make you happy. Just as far as I am able. And I confidently expect soon to have everything in shape so that our good income will be assured again. Come, Helen, be reasonable——I can't give you anything more just now."

"But now is when I need it," pouted Helen. "Why can't you put a mortgage on this house, then, and get some more money? People do that. I know they do. Max was telling that his house is mortgaged up to its full value. Or why can't we sell the old thing? I just hate it anyway. I want a house over on the west side where all my friends live. There's a darling house over there we could buy for a little more than the value of this. In fact I've already got a buyer for you!"

Helen's tears were forgotten now and her impish gay smile bloomed out like April sunshine. "He's a friend of Max's and he's coming out some time today or tomorrow to look at it."

Her eyes were bright with the few recent tears, her cheeks a lovely rose. She had a mischievous beauty all her own, and her troubled husband looked at her hopelessly, a stern weariness overspreading his face, with a kind of gentleness about his eyes, as when one tries to explain serious matters to a lovely child.

"My dear," he said, "that would be quite impossible."

"There! I thought you'd say that!" stormed Helen stamping a costly little shoe and biting her lips until the tears appeared on the horizon again.

"Well, my dear, it is impossible. This house cannot be sold nor mortgaged either."

"Just why, I'd like to know?" demanded Helen, whirling upon him, a fierce light in her eyes. "That's silly! Of course it can. Any house can be sold or mortgaged. Why can't this? I've always hated this house, and I won't live in it. I *won't,* do you hear me? Not another day! Won't you sell it for me?"

She suddenly dropped into her sweetest wheedling tones.

"I cannot," said Stephen Disston. "Helen, this house is not my own."

"Not your own? Have you already sold it or mortgaged it then?" she asked, looking with startled eyes at him. "You have done that and did not tell me?"

"No, I have not," he said sadly. "I have no right either to sell or mortgage it. This house belongs to Diana. Her mother left it to her!"

"To Diana!" cried Helen indignantly. "The perfect idea! If that is true how do you happen to be occupying it?"

"I have the right of residence during my lifetime," said Stephen Disston gravely.

Helen stared for a minute and then her shrewd eyes narrowed on her husband's face once more.

"But how could Diana live in a house like this without money?" she asked contemptuously. "If you refused her money she could not keep it up."

"Diana has money," said her father quietly. "She has enough to keep up this place and live in comfort here. She will come of age in a few weeks now."

There was silence while Helen took this in.

"But you are her trustee and guardian," said Helen with assurance. "You could easily persuade her to sell this house."

"No," said Diana's father, "that is one of the provisions of the will, that the house shall not be sold during Diana's lifetime. If she has children it will pass on to them."

Helen's brows grew black.

"That's a raw deal for you!" she said icily. "A nice thing for Marilla to do to you."

"It was my wish!" said Stephen Disston quietly. "I knew that the house was given to Marilla with that idea in mind, of making it a family homestead from one generation to another."

There was an ominous silence in the room for several minutes, and then Helen whirled gaily about from the window with one of her lightning changes of mood.

"Well, then, let's get out of it!" she said. "You couldn't hire me to stay here any longer. You knew what you were bringing me into when you married me, now you've got to do something about it. Come on, let's pack and go to the city to a hotel. We'll stay there till we can find a new house. If this is Diana's that's probably why she left, till we got out."

"No, Diana is not like that!" said her father sadly. "Besides, Diana does not yet know that the house is hers. Her mother did not want her to know until she came of age."

Helen turned and faced him, giving him a long significant look, and then said, "Oh-h-h-h-*oh!*" with lifted brows. Then after a minute she added:

"Then you *could* do something about it. Right now you could, before she comes of age, and you owe it to me to do it too! Those things can always be managed. A good lawyer will find a way out of it, and Diana will never make a fuss about it anyway. *I* know Diana! You can just tell her that it seemed best for you to sell, you had a good chance. I think I can make this man that wants to buy pay a little more, enough to get the other house I want. I'm sure I can."

Mr. Disston arose and faced his wife, amazed consternation on his face.

"Helen!" he said sternly, holding her glance with his eyes, and said no more, but it was as if he had said "Get thee behind me Satan!"

Helen faced him unflinchingly, but her own eyes narrowed for an instant, and grew shifty. Then came one of those sudden changes. She was a little innocent thing misjudged.

"Now, what have I said? What can I have done?" she quivered like a hurt child. "Wouldn't that be perfectly proper for you to do if you thought it was best for Diana? But anyway, I only meant it for a joke, and you took it seriously."

Stephen Disston was an honorable man. It went deep to have his wife suggest something dishonorable, and it was some time before Helen could finally convince him, or partly convince him, that she had meant nothing dishonorable by her suggestion.

But having at last won him back to his usual gentle self, she went upstairs with averted face, and furtive eyes in which there dwelt a degree of triumph. She had won him over to say that he would take her away, at least for a few days. He would have to go to the office perhaps every morning and stay all day, but she could do what she pleased. So she hurried upstairs to pack.

As they drove away from the house late that afternoon Stephen Disston turned his eyes regretfully back to his home and sighed. Then he looked at his wife apprehensively. He dared not even sigh in these days, things were in such a precarious state. He spoke quickly to cover his sigh.

"You will remember what I said about spending money, dear, won't you? It really means a lot to our future."

"I'll try," said Helen meekly, though there was a sullen gleam in her eyes. "It's awfully hard to meet that though, right at the beginning of my married life, when everybody thinks I've done so well. I didn't suppose when I married you that I would have to go on scrimping all the rest of my days."

Her red lips were pouted prettily, and Stephen Disston foresaw another bout of weeping and complaint, so he hastened to say:

"I hope it won't be for long, dear. I hope soon to get things straightened out. If we could just find Diana and my mind were free I am sure I could easily work things out."

"There it goes again!" sobbed Helen suddenly. "You don't care for me. You only want Diana! It's nothing to you that I am here with you all the time, giving my youth to keep your days happy! You just want Diana! And that's what I told you would happen! I told you you would tire of me and want to please her! I told you she

would resent my coming! But you said, no, no, it would
be all right and we would all be happy together! You
don't c-c-care for me any more!"

Stephen Disston cast a distracted glance toward the
taxi driver, and another out of the window at the people
they were passing on the street, for Helen's voice was
high and shrill, and her sobs were unmistakable.

"Darling!" he said with quick eagerness, "don't do
that! You know that is not true. You know that you are
very dear to me!" and even as he put out his hand to lay
it on hers he was suddenly filled with a great question,
whether what he was saying was strictly true? Was she
after all so dear as he had thought?

He put the idea from him at once. He was an honorable man. But it hung around and haunted him, made
him unnatural in his efforts to soothe Helen. He groaned
within himself at the new trouble that beset him. Would
he never get this thing straightened out, this hasty marriage that he now saw Helen herself had really persuaded
him into? Oh, if he had only taken a little more time,
and talked it over with Diana, he would have been
assured of her usual sweet cooperation. He should have
talked everything thoroughly over in a reasonable way
with them both. With everybody cooperating, surely
things would have gone all right!

It seemed to Stephen Disston that it was a hundred
miles into the city, but he finally managed to placate
Helen in plenty of time for her to get out of the taxi and
into the hotel in radiant form. Helen never showed her
tears afterward, and that was a thing that came to puzzle
her husband in thinking it over.

She made him take her to a concert and was charming
all that evening, and irresistible next morning when she
pled with him to stay with her, take her down to the
stores and let the old business go. She knew he wouldn't

stay. In fact it would have greatly upset her plans if he had, but she created an impression that she was inconsolable without him. Then as soon as he was gone, she flew around frantically to get ready to go out.

She had made a careful study of the business directory of the telephone book and then she went down a little back street in the lower part of the city and made a few purchases. Returning to the hotel she changed her garments, stowed her purchases in a soft blue tooled leather bag that was capacious, yet artistic to carry, and went out again, a look of impishness dancing in her eyes, her face all a-sparkle with determination.

Down in his office Stephen Disston was opening his mail, scanning eagerly every letter, hoping that there might be one from Diana, sighing as he laid each one aside, only half taking in its message. But suddenly his thoughts were brought to a sharp focus by a letter that involved a large sum of money owing him which he had hoped was soon to be paid. The letter said there was no immediate hope of getting anything out of it. If that were literally true then it spelled ruin for the Disston business, an old and respected firm, originally started by Stephen Disston's father, and later continued by the three sons. The other two sons had died within the past ten years, leaving Stephen Disston the sole remaining member of the firm.

He had thought that the business was on a solid foundation until a year before, but even then he had made hasty retrenchments, and had sold off some of his land which was by his wife's will left to him, clearing all indebtedness and giving a fair outlook for the future. This contract which involved so much money had seemed no risk at all, but the man who had guaranteed it, a lifelong friend in whom he trusted, had been killed in an accident a few months ago, and his profligate son was managing his affairs. The result was that a small technicality that under the father's regime would have been entirely safe, had proved a loophole through which the unscrupulous son had slipped and taken with him the money that would have meant security to the Disston business! The result was crushing.

Stephen Disston lifted a ghastly face from the letter he held in a trembling hand and stared across his office at the blank wall, and for a moment everything in the room reeled.

19

LITTLE by little he took in his situation, and what it was going to mean, not only in the business world, but also in his home. *Home!* Did he have a home any more? Of course there was a place there in the old house that was Diana's, where he might stay all the rest of his days, but could he, with Helen? He was bound to Helen now, and how was he going to support her? And what of Diana, his precious daughter? Oh, what a fool he had been! If only this blow had come before he involved Helen also.

If it had been only himself and Diana how simple it all would have been. He could perhaps have enough to pay off his debts. There were not many. He had been careful until lately. And then Diana would have had enough and to spare for them both.

But feeling as she did about Helen, and as Helen was growing to feel about Diana, he couldn't of course let Diana do anything for them. And what was going to become of—*everybody?*

He put his head down on his desk and groaned aloud.

Ten minutes later his secretary coming in roused him to actualities, and he realized that there was much to be done, and necessity of haste in the doing. He must not let everything slip from lax hands without making some attempt to rescue a part at least of what was his own. He sent for his lawyer, and they spent the morning together going over everything. He dictated sharp crisp sentences to his secretary, and concentrated on his business as he had not done for two months. His lawyer looked at him with eyes of admiration. He was rallying splendidly to the situation. If anything could pull the old Disston firm through this crisis, this attitude on the part of its head would. He roused himself to keep up a state of good cheer, and started so many little side lines of battlements to fight the coming disaster that Stephen Disston was cheered and given heart of hope. Of course time would tell whether all their work was vain or not, but in the meantime it was good to feel a little hope, since they must go on and do these things whether they succeeded or not. And so with his lips in a firm line of determination and his eyes stern, Stephen Disston faced the facts and took the reins in his hands. He must drive through or all was lost, and that he would not consider—not yet at any rate.

And for all the rest of that day it is safe to say he did not once think of the unscrupulous sprite of a woman he had married, not even while he was eating a hurried lunch he had sent up to his office while he worked.

It was a strenuous day. Drastic measures had to be taken, daring methods adopted, innumerable telephone calls made, telegrams sent, sheafs of letters written. The lawyer stuck by him like the friend he had always been and they worked till the world outside the office grew dark. Then the lawyer rose.

"There, Steve," he said rubbing a large capable hand over a weary kindly face, "I guess that's about all we can do today. Now we've just got to wait and see the result of this. We ought to be hearing from these things about day after tomorrow. And, in the meantime, let's go home to dinner."

Then Stephen Disston suddenly remembered that he had no home but a hotel tonight, and nobody he dared confide in when he got there. He must adjust a smile and keep it on for the evening. He thought with a stab of pain of the daughter who had left him. Where, oh, where was Diana? Diana who always knew when her father was troubled. She never bothered with questions, but crept near and stole a quiet hand in his and smiled her comfort. Oh, how had he allowed himself to do anything to alienate Diana?

But when he got to the hotel weary and sick at heart he found a note from Helen. She had gone to Max Copley's apartment to help him plan for his house party, and she demanded that he follow her as soon as he arrived. Helen in that man's apartment, planning follies for a party! He frowned and sighed and sat down with his head in his hands. How were the troubles multiplying about him! He seemed to himself like one caught in a net from which it was hopeless to try to escape. Helen in that disgusting man's apartment, and he had no power to keep her away! Of course she couldn't realize what he was, but why wouldn't she listen to him, her husband? Why wouldn't she take his word for it that the man wasn't a fit associate?

And now she was demanding that he come also. Three times this had happened already and twice he had yielded and gone, only to find that his presence was scarcely noticed by the gay crowd, least of all by Helen who was wholly taken up with others, and expected him to find his own amusement. He had gone to protect her by his presence, but he had found that his presence did not protect her from the things to which he objected.

He told himself that of course she was innocent and did not in the least realize what kind of people these were with whom she was finding her pleasures. He had planned to give her other and better pleasures and wean her from these people, but he found to his dismay that she did not enjoy the pleasures he planned for her and was only eager to get back to her crowd again.

And Diana was gone, dear Diana, and there seemed no way at all to get in touch with her. What should he do? His life was going into a slump, financially, socially, domestically, and there was no way out.

So he put his head down and groaned.

He would not go after Helen this time. Let her stay until she realized what she had done. He would wait here for her coming. It did no good to go.

He felt old and tired. He was hungry too, though he did not realize that. It was long after dinner time but he did not know it. He was trying to think back over his past life and see just where it was that he had got off the beaten track, just where he had diverged from the path which he had trod so successfully all the years till now. Money gone, daughter gone, wife gone, home gone— was there anything more missing? Yes, his religion seemed gone too.

He recalled how he always used to have family worship in the old days when Marilla was living. How they went to church together and tried to order their lives in a Christian manner. He was a Christian man, respected, for a long time an officer in his church—where, how, had he gotten away?

Suddenly he slipped down upon his knees and prayed aloud:

"Oh, God, I'm a sinner! Set me right. Show me what to do."

A long time he knelt, and then arose and dropped into

the big chair again. Helen found him sitting there with his face bowed into his hands and a look of utter dejection upon him.

She stood poised in the doorway for a moment surveying him with narrowed eyes, then she closed the door behind her and swept to the other end of the room assuming her battle array.

"I love the way you leave me to run around alone!" she said sweetly, tapping her hand on the arm of the chair. "And you needn't think you can sit and mope and get away with it, either. We might as well have this out now as any time. When I leave a note for you to meet me somewhere I expect you to do it, see? I don't like being deserted that way and it certainly is too early in our married life for you to act like an old grouch."

Stephen Disston lifted his haggard face.

"Helen," he said in a weary, husky voice, "you'll have to understand that I cannot have anything to do with that man, and I do not want you to be seen with him, much less go to his apartment. I am grieved to the heart that you should persist in this. I have explained to you that the man is not fit for you to wipe your shoes on. If it is necessary for me to go into details I can do it, but I wish you would take my word for it. You are young and innocent, and have no idea what kind of a man this Copley is—!"

He was interrupted by an impish chuckle.

"Oh, I like that! I don't know what Max is, don't I? Ask Max that one. Ask him if I don't know all about him and see what he says. So, I'm innocent, am I? Well that's a good one."

She laughed immoderately and then suddenly sobered and put on a haughty dignity.

"My dear, you certainly are rare! You think I am a babe in arms like your little Diana. But remember that I was left alone at a tender age, and had to rub elbows with the world. I am beginning to suspect that I really am wiser in the wisdom of the world than even you, who seem to think you know all there is to know of evil. However, you might as well understand right now that I know my crowd from A to Z, and I like them just as they are, and I intend to stick to them. And what's more, if you want to keep me you'll have to like them too, *and like them a lot!* For we are going to run around with them from now on."

"Never!" said Disston sternly, rising and pacing up and down the room. *"Never!"*

"We're going to Max Copley's house party the end of this week," went on his wife calmly, just as if he had not spoken, "and then early next week we're going on a yachting party with Max's friend Count De Briscka. He invited us informally today, and he's sending a written invitation tonight lest you would stand on ceremony. The yacht is one of the finest on the water, it cost a mint of money, and is perfectly spiffy. Its name is *Lotus Blossom.* Isn't that precious? Everybody I know is crazy for an invitation. If it hadn't been that we are Max's most intimate friends we wouldn't have been invited, but he's just crazy about Max. And do you know, Max says if you get intimate with the Count he'll put you on to some good investments that will pull your fortunes back into line and make you rich in no time, richer than you've ever been before. Max says—"

"Helen! Have you been talking my affairs over with that viper?"

"Why of course I have," pouted Helen. "Why not? Max has made some awfully good plays on the market lately and I knew he would give me some pretty good hints. I was awfully down you know because of what you told me this morning, and so I suppose he saw I was blue and he naturally asked me what was the matter, so of course I had to tell him. And his answer was to call up Count De Briscka, and a half hour later he came in and we had such a jolly time, and he gave the invitation before we had been talking five minutes. Max says that's what he does when he wants to show the crowd a good time, just invites them over and calls up the Count and the Count always takes the hint and invites them on a yachting trip. He says the Count likes it. So you see, darling, it's quite up to you to change your ideas and get to liking my crowd. For that's who I'm playing around with the rest of the summer."

"Never!" said Disston severely. "Never! Helen, I don't know how to express myself in suitable words to show you my disgust and dislike of these people. Never would I consent to dining with them again or attending their parties, or going on any trips whatsoever with them. Most certainly I will not accept any invitations from any of them, and you will not do so either, not with my consent."

"Oh, dear me, darling," laughed Helen amusedly, "that's just too bad! Because you see I've already accepted and I intend to go! If you won't go with me, why then, tra-la, Max always has plenty of interesting men friends for me to pair off with."

She looked at him archly with a significant smile, but she met a grave, sad expression that had almost disillusionment in it. He looked at her steadily for a moment and then said:

"You cannot do a thing like that, Helen, and remain on a friendly footing with me. You cannot go to a party like either of those you are proposing without bringing disgrace on my family. Those men who have invited you are notorious drinkers and gamblers. In a fashionable way, I admit, but nevertheless a disgraceful way, and I cannot allow you to get your good name and mine besmirched by having anything more to do with them. I shall have to ask you to refrain from further friendliness with them."

Helen looked at him with angry eyes for an instant and then her eyes began to dance with impishness.

"Oh, isn't that too bad!" she said with a giddy little laugh, and then she turned and flouted off into the bedroom and locked the door.

All night Stephen Disston sat bowed in that big armchair in the sitting room of his hotel suite, his face in his hands, his soul borne down by heaviness; while a few miles away in the suburb that had been his home for years policemen and firemen and friends and neighbors were keeping the telephone wires hot with calls, trying to locate him, to tell him that his house was on fire. They even found his old friend the lawyer with whom he had spent the day, but he could give them no clue to his whereabouts.

20

THAT afternoon Gordon MacCarroll had reached home in the early twilight and found his mother out in the driveway sniffing the air and looking up toward the great house.

"What in the world are you doing, Mother?" he called out, stopping his car by the garage and jumping out.

"Why, Gordon, I've been smelling smoke all the afternoon. At first I thought it was someone's bonfire, but I couldn't locate it, and the last half-hour it has been growing stronger. It seemed to come from the back of the house so I looked up toward the big house and I thought I saw a thin wisp of smoke against the sky coming from that far corner. It worried me a little because the caretaker hasn't been around today at all. I thought maybe some tramps had been tampering with the wood pile back of the house."

"Maybe the family have come home and built a fire in the fireplace to get rid of the dampness," suggested Gordon.

"No, the family didn't come home," said his mother

positively. "I've been sitting right by the window almost all day sewing. I wanted to finish my dress. Even when I ate lunch I brought a plate to my little sewing table and ate while I sewed. The new Mrs. Disston came about half-past twelve for awhile, but she didn't stay. She arrived on the bus and walked up the drive, and in about three quarters of an hour she came back again and stood out there on the street waiting for the next bus. There hasn't been anybody else here all day."

"Are you sure you would have noticed?"

"Yes, I'm positive. I was watching. You see when she arrived first she had a blue leather bag over her arm, with some bulky packages in it, as if she had been shopping, and I thought perhaps they were coming back to stay and she had been to market. But when she came out again and went away she hadn't anything in her hand but her purse. I suppose I noticed the bag because it was exactly like that one that Cousin Lucy brought back from her Mediterranean trip. Do you remember that? You admired it so much. It was soft blue kid tooled in gold. I know you said it would make a wonderful cover for a Bible. And when I saw her go in I couldn't help noticing it because it was exactly like Lucy's.

"So of course I kept looking up that way to see if there were any signs of her, and pretty soon she came out with just her purse. I was hoping she had come to stay, and maybe all of them would come. You know I always feel sort of responsible for that house when they are all away. It's so far back from the street none of the other neighbors can see it very well. I thought she might only have gone to market. But she didn't come back. And about an hour ago I smelled the smoke getting stronger, and just now I thought I saw a sort of a glow in those windows over on the left, as if there were a fire in the room. She surely wouldn't go off and leave an open fire in the house, would she?"

Gordon's eyes went quickly to the windows his mother indicated.

"I'd better take a look," he said. "It's probably only a bonfire at the back. Maybe the caretaker came a back way or something, but I'll feel better if I just run up and see. You stay out here where you can see the end of the house, and if it's anything serious I'll come out and wave and you can telephone for the fire company, but I don't think it's anything."

Gordon walked rapidly up the drive and disappeared around the end of the house. But only an instant later he appeared again waving his arms wildly. His mother waved back and turned running into the house to call the fire engine.

Gordon hurried back to see what he could do before the firemen arrived. He found a door into the tool house ajar and looking in discovered the garden hose.

The smoke was pouring out of an open cellar window, and flames were beginning to lick up like hungry tongues out of two of the windows at the back. The whole back corner of the house seemed to be involved, all the way to the roof, for wisps and feathers of smoke and flames were darting out of an upper window, tentatively, as if they were searching out the best place to really take hold and devastate. He hadn't arrived an instant too soon.

It looked to MacCarroll as if it had been a slow fire, perhaps started by a match or cigarette, smoldering through rags or rubbish in the cellar till it gained a footing. Then creeping upward it must have made a passage for itself, and had only now begun to leap upward.

But there was no time for thought. Gordon dashed

out of the tool house dragging the garden hose, searched blindly through the smoke which was becoming dense now, for the outlet. Finally he succeeded in locating it, screwed on the hose and turned on the water.

But it was such an inadequate little stream that poured out after he had done all he could. He turned it to its utmost and played it upon the house, but even in the minute that it had taken to get the water started, the fire seemed to have gained the ascendancy. It had crept underneath and roared up the wall of a small annex, perhaps a laundry or out-kitchen, and now the flames were feathering upward from the roof, cutting it in half, and roaring in triumph. It would not take long to reduce the annex to ashes if this could not be stopped. And meantime the main house was in grave danger. The flames were shooting out now through one corner of the roof. Would the fire company never get here?

There was another water outlet the other side of the back porch. Gordon wished there were two of him. There was a large bucket standing under it. He could draw water and throw it on where it would prevent the spread of the fire, if he could only fix up something to hold this hose so that it could work while he was working elsewhere.

But even while he was casting about in his mind what to do his mother appeared and took the hose from him.

"I'll hold this, Gordon. Do you see what else is to be done. The fire company are on the way and I've telephoned the neighbors. Here's the axe, too, I thought you might need it."

So the two worked valiantly, breathlessly, on the fire that had now leaped up into a mighty conflagration, threatening to devastate the whole house.

Neighbors came running across the fields now, and cars dashed up the drive and parked on the lawn to make room for the fire engine, and then the fire company arrived, with chemicals and a great hose running back down the drive to a hydrant in the street.

A neighbor volunteered to try and reach the owner by telephone. The police arrived and took a hand also, and the fire roared high and reached forth arms of flame greedy to envelop the whole back of the house and one end, licking out now and then tentatively around the corner to the beautiful white front with its fine lacework of vines.

As soon as the firemen arrived Mrs. MacCarroll went home and made coffee in a great white preserving kettle. It was near dinner time and the chances were that the men would be working there for hours yet. Some of them at least would have to stay around and be sure that all was safe, even if they succeeded in saving the main part of the house. So she went to work quietly to help in the only way she could see herself of any use. She spread bread and sliced ham and made a lot of nice sandwiches, and putting them in wax paper in a basket, she packed another basket with cups and saucers. Then taking the kettle of coffee herself, she got a couple of boys from the rabble drifting up the drive to carry the baskets, and so she established refreshments for the firemen over by the tool house.

Gordon MacCarroll was in the thick of the fight all the way through. It was a volunteer fire company and they were glad to get such efficient help, though everyone was so busy during the worst of it that no one had time to question who was working and who was not. So it happened that when the fire was finally under control, it was Gordon who climbed down into the cellar first, stepping knee deep in water. He was in utter darkness except for his flashlight, which peered through the smoke and murk sending a sharp inadequate ray cutting the gloom and locating stairs, chimneys, and charred doors to storerooms and preserve closets. It was Gordon who lifted a dripping something floating on the water, turned his flash on it for a brief second and then flung it far up the cellar stairs into the corner of the top landing out of sight. He came up out of the cellar window a few minutes later with a thoughtful look upon his face and his lips closed firmly.

"All safe below!" he said cryptically. He didn't mention what he suspected. There wouldn't be an investigation till the water had gone out.

That night, quite late, he came home and took a bath and ate his supper. His mother hovered about and saw that he had all that was needful and a good deal that was not. She did not talk. She was a wise woman and noticed how tired his eyes looked and how his cheek was bruised where the big hose had hit him when it was flung out by a careless amateur, how his hands were torn and bleeding. He had worked hard and been in dangerous places she knew, but she was too well trained to notice a little thing like that. Only one question she asked when he came in.

"Is it all safe for the night now, or will you have to go back?"

"All safe!" he answered. "They've left a couple of watchmen there for the night."

Then she brought his dinner, hot and tasty, and he fell to eating. But when he had reached the cherry pie he took one bite and then looked up.

"Mother, what color did you say that bag of Cousin Lucy's was? Blue? With gold stampings?"

"Yes!" said his mother with a startled look on her face. "Gordon! You've found it!" It was rather a statement than a question.

He didn't look up. He didn't answer.

"It was down cellar!" his mother said with conviction. "That means—" She shut her lips on the rest of the sentence. Then after another silence he answered that half question.

"Not necessarily, Mother."

The next silence was longer till she asked:

"Did anybody else see it, son?"

He shook his head,

"And did you—leave it—put it—*hide* it?"

"No," he said, "I wasn't sure I should. I flung it to the top of the stairs. It won't mean so much there. Perhaps— in the morning— But there may be no opportunity. There wasn't time then to do more than I did. Perhaps, after all it may not be significant."

Mr. Disston did not get the word until he reached his office next morning, whither he had gone very early, before Helen had shown any sign of being awake. He did not wish to wait around to be scorned and scoffed at. Helen must understand that he meant what he said. There was no point in repeating his words, or in staying to argue further. There was a point at which dignity must stand. If he had been at home it would have been different. In his own place he could speak with more force, but this was not home. So he went down to his office.

The elevator boy was just going on when he arrived.

"Did they get ya last night?" he asked.

"Get me?" asked Stephen Disston in a weary voice. Something had got him very badly. Was there more?

"Yeah. They said yer phone rang an' rang, and yer secretary was wild ta know ef you was in the building, but I told 'em I took ya down. Then a lawyer man called and wanted ta talk ta me, and he asked did I know just what time it was ya left, and whether ya cum back last night at all, and I said ya hadn't when I quit at six o'clock."

A sudden thought came of Diana. Perhaps it had been Diana. Perhaps something had happened to Diana. Then all the other worries suddenly melted away and Diana became the only anxiety in the world. Oh, if he could only find Diana and know she was safe!

It was after nine when word finally came over the wire about the house being on fire, and his heart seemed so heavy he could hardly drag himself up out of his chair after he hung up the receiver.

"It's all out, that is, some's smoking yet," said the fireman who called, "but ya better come out and see whatcha want done. We had a watchman on the job all night, but the burned place had oughtta be closed up fer safety ef ya ain't comin' home ta stay. Yep, we got on the job right soon, but ef it hadn't a been fer the party that lives in that there stone house at the gate she woulda gone up in smoke afore we ever heard. Yep. That's him, tall, curly hair, a nice eye! He helped a-plenty. All by his lonesome till we got there! An' he done good work too. Yep! Ya better come out soon's ya can. So long!"

When Stephen Disston arrived at his home he found Gordon MacCarroll just starting up the drive. He had gone early to his own office, and then driven back by way of home to make sure that all was well at the scene of the fire. He looked relieved when he saw the man of the house coming behind him.

"Oh, I'm glad you've come, Mr. Disston," he said, turning about and walking up with him. "I felt as if I ought to hang around and see that there was an adequate guard until you were here to give orders. You see the house is practically open to the public and it seems impossible to keep the rabble away. The children have been swarming all about. I got in and locked a few doors so they can't penetrate far, but I certainly am glad you've come. Here are the keys I took. This one fits the door where the most damage has been done, servants' dining room perhaps, and that opens into the hall."

Disston thanked him gravely and took the keys.

"They tell me you rendered swift and marvelous assistance. The Fire Chief said you practically saved the house."

"Oh, I did very little," said Gordon lightly. "I'm only sorry I didn't get home sooner. Mother had been smelling smoke for an hour. By the time I got here there was a glow in some of the windows. I found her out in the driveway looking up toward the house. She didn't know whether anybody was at home or not. She said your wife went in about noon, but didn't stay long."

"Oh!" said the master of the house turning startled eyes on his tenant. And then a forced, "Oh yes. She—we—were away—last night!" But his face wore a confused, troubled look.

"How—do you think—that is, what is your opinion of how—where—the fire started?"

"In the cellar," said Gordon quickly. "It almost looked as if it had been *started,* though you can't tell surely till the water subsides. Had you any servants you had reason to distrust?"

Stephen Disston turned his tired eyes on the young man.

"Yes," he said, "there were some new servants. We didn't keep them long, but I don't see what object they would have in setting fire to the house. They were quite adequately paid. They knew we were going away for a time—" He walked on thoughtfully, his eyes upon the ground as if he were studying it over.

"What made you think it was started?"

"Well, there seemed to be a pile of debris over in the

corner where the fire raged the hottest, as if things had been piled up there, and there were a few rags floating about on the water, that evidently had been too far away to ignite, that were soaked in kerosene. But the corner looked as if combustibles had been piled up where the flame would easily reach the beams of the first floor. That was what actually happened I think, the fire evidently was a slow one, but by the time it reached the corner it had gathered force enough to eat through the floor and run right up the wall."

The master of the house turned another startled gaze upon Gordon and they walked the rest of the way in silence.

"We'll go in the front door," said Disston as they reached the terrace. "I'd rather see the worst before I face the rabble out there."

"Sha'n't I just wait outside?" offered Gordon.

"No! Come! I'm glad to have you with me!"

Gordon thought to himself that he had often hoped to see the inside of the great house sometime, but had not expected to enter under such circumstances.

Disston unlocked the door and they stepped into the beautiful hallway, with its wide staircase, and lovely vistas of rooms on either side.

"Oh, I'm glad this part didn't get hurt!" he said with quick eager exclamation.

"Yes!" sighed Disston as if the sight of it were very dear indeed.

They walked through to the kitchen, and the master went to the cellar door and fitted in the key. Then Gordon remembered the blue bag and wished he had left it in a corner of the cellar. But perhaps it would not be noticed!

Disston unlocked the door and swung it wide and the morning sun from a big window over the kitchen sink flooded across the landing. There lay the blue kid bag, its lovely gold tooling stained and spotted with water and grime from the fire! Disston saw it and stared as if he had seen a ghost.

Gordon tried to look away, but he caught a glimpse of the man's face and it was pale as death. His eyes were staring wildly.

"What is that?" he asked huskily. "How—how did that—get here?" He was too distraught to realize that he was showing his emotion before this stranger.

"It was floating on the top of the water," explained Gordon trying to speak in a matter-of-fact way as if he saw nothing out of the ordinary in the occurrence. Perhaps this was after all the best way to let Mr. Disston know without making it appear that it had any particular significance to him. He had been so troubled whether he should tell about finding the bag or not, and now here it was made plain and easy for him.

Stephen Disston stooped and picked up the bag by its dripping leather strings and held it a moment looking at it closely. Then, as if his conscience drove him and he were not in the least aware of the presence of another, he felt of it, then turned out upon the floor what it contained and stood there staring at it. Gordon could not help seeing what was there.

Then Stephen Disston came awake and looked up in consternation at his companion.

But Gordon stooped and picked them up.

A piece of punk, a wire coil, a couple of candles and a box of matches! And the whole smelled unmistakably of kerosene.

He put them carefully into the bag as if he were not noticing what they were and handed the bag over to the master of the house.

"You'll want to put those away out of sight, won't

you? At least for the present? No need to have reporters poking around trying to find leads for headlines."

He tried to say it carelessly as if it were not a thing that mattered so much. Then his eyes met the unhappy eyes of Disston and he saw the other fully understood. His face was still very white.

"Thank you," said Disston. "I'll take your advice—for the present,—at least until I understand what this means."

A newspaper lay on the kitchen table and Gordon proffered it.

"Wrap it in that and put it away somewhere till things clear up a little."

"You're being very kind," said Disston, visibly getting his emotions in hand.

"Not at all," said Gordon. "I wish there were something really worth while that I could do for you."

"You have done a great deal," said Disston slowly, "and—I shall not forget it."

Their eyes met and a smile of friendliness flashed between them. Then Disston silently unlocked the door that led to the scene of ruin and they stood for a few minutes studying the probable course of the fire.

"This wall ought to be closed up at once," said Gordon. "When the police leave it will be practically impossible to keep out the swarm of small boys and curious people."

"Yes," sighed Mr. Disston looking about with a hopeless sadness in his voice. "I suppose I ought to send for a carpenter at once."

"I was going to suggest," said Gordon thoughtfully, "that there are some boards out there in the tool house. If you are willing I could bring them in and nail them up over the largest break in the wall. That would do temporarily until you have time to get your mind on what should be done."

"Oh, I couldn't think of troubling you any more," protested Disston.

"Nonsense," said Gordon eagerly. "We're neighbors you know, and besides my mother and I have taken a deep interest in our landlord's house." He smiled a deep warm smile that comforted the heart of the sorrowful landlord. "You'd do the same for me, I'll warrant, if I were in trouble."

"I'm not sure I would know how," said the elder man humbly. "But where is this lumber you speak of? I ought to know of course, but I've never had much time to look after details about the house. If I could just get this place closed to curious eyes for the time being it certainly would be a great help."

They went together to the tool house and brought back planks, Gordon handling them capably and taking the heavier part of the labor.

"Now," said he, when they had enough of the planks to cover the great gap in the wall that the fire had made, "I wonder if you happen to be able to locate a hammer and some nails? I think I saw a ladder in the cellar stairway. It won't take long to make this secure."

He went capably to work, and in a very short time the room that had been gutted by fire was closed to the eyes of the countryside who continued to straggle about all day to look and wonder and say who they thought had done it, or how it had got on fire.

"Now," said Gordon, coming down from the ladder after driving the last nail, "you'll come down to the cottage and have a bite of lunch with me won't you? You look white and tired. I'm sure you need it. Yes, come, I'm sure Mother will have something ready."

So, comforted by the friendly smile, and the insistent

hand upon his arm, Stephen Disston walked down to the stone cottage with his tenant and they had lunch together. Such a comfortable quiet lunch in that sweet little home wherein there seemed to be no perplexities nor hates nor problems. Such a home as he used to have before Marilla went away. Yes, and even afterward when he and Diana comforted one another together. Would life ever unsnarl itself and things go right again? Who had started that fire? And was that bag Helen's? Could that be the one he had seen lying across the end of the couch night before last in the hotel? Or stay—wasn't it really Diana's, the one that someone sent her from abroad? How had Helen got it? And where, oh, *where* was Diana?

"Your daughter is not at home just now?" Mrs. MacCarroll was asking him pleasantly. "I thought she was such a sweet girl. I miss her going by."

Diana's father looked up with a heavy sigh.

"No, she is not at home!" he said, with infinite sadness in his eyes and voice.

Where, oh, *where* was Diana? If he could only find Diana!

21

DIANA had been working hard in her restaurant, day after day. Sometimes it seemed to her that she had been here a year serving uncouth uncultured people. Sometimes it seemed to her as if almost all of them were animals, just animals feeding, with no resemblance to humanity at all, at least not to the lovely refined humanity that she knew. She shuddered as she crept wearily into her bed at night, at the thought of another day that would rush upon her oh, so speedily in the midst of her heavy sleep and drag her back to her duties again.

And her pay was so pitifully small, her tips so trifling and scarce. People of the sort she served had not much to spare for tips, greedy hard-eyed people, all but those few who appraised her eyes, her hair, her smile, her figure, and gave only when they could win her notice. From those she shrank most of all. Some were half drunk when they came in. How she loathed them! It was only through trying to remember that God must care for them too, that Christ died for them, that she could make herself wait upon them.

How the days loomed ahead of her, each one worse

than the last! How she dreaded each one as she went forth, and came home so deadly tired that she could take no comfort in the quietness and peace of even that little third story back.

The only oasis in the dreariness of her life was the box of carnations. Twice they had come on Saturday nights. Would they come again? The hope of them made one little sweet thing to look forward to. Somehow her heart rested down on those mystery flowers as if they were part of her religion, and as if they came fresh each week from God to let her know He cared. Her faith grew little by little as she breathed in their spicy breath. They were such frail lovely things, and yet so sturdy and healthy and long-lived. For each instalment had lived and glowed and been beautiful until the next arrived. And it comforted her sometimes on her hardest days to think of them back there in her little high lonely room glowing and waiting for her, a rosy breath of love and sympathy, from someone, whom she would probably never know except vaguely as God's messenger.

It had been a hard day, harder than usual, because it was a holiday and Saturday again. There had been a tougher lot of people in the restaurant than usual. The place had been crowded from early morning on, and Diana had been greatly rushed. Moreover some of the other girls, who had never really recovered from their resentment at her finer ways, had made it more than usually uncomfortable for her, maliciously upsetting her tray when it was all ready to take to a customer in a hurry, spilling a glass of water over the food she had prepared to take to another, tripping her as she passed with a heavy tray lifted high above her head, and almost bringing her down among broken dishes. It was not their fault that she had been able to avert the catastrophe by an almost superhuman effort, and recover her balance with only a broken plate, and the loss of an order—which of course she would have to pay for. She discovered as the day went on that she had also wrenched her back, and her head was throbbing wildly. By three o'clock in the afternoon she suddenly began to feel that she actually could not go on any longer. Her feet were aching in sympathy with her back and head, and a great despair was surging over her soul. She was being beaten, beaten by this job. She could not go on any longer. Yet she knew she must or give up utterly. Because if she lost this job where would she turn for another? Beaten! What could she do? Would she go home? Never! The thought of Helen still loomed as a positive barrier. There was no relief there. And if she gave up her job and was sick in the bargain where would she go? Who would take care of her? Suppose she had a fever? She was burning up now. It probably was fever. Would they take her to a charity hospital? Well, there might be even worse fates than that. Perhaps she would die and then she would be out of it all. If God cared for her then she would go to be with Him!

In the wildness and flurry of the sordid atmosphere the thought of going to God seemed only a thought of quietness and peace. Nothing else seemed to matter if He cared enough just to set her free from all these worries of the world into which she had wandered, where there were no open doors to go back to home and safety and peace.

It was in this state of mind, and while she lingered an instant standing by a shelf in the kitchen, trying to swallow a cup of weak coffee that was not even hot, that she heard her name shouted by the manager.

"Jane! Here! Customer calling for you, Jane! Make it snappy!"

Her hand trembled as she set down the distasteful cup

hastily, caught up her tray and hurried away, praying as she had of late fallen into the habit of doing, "Oh, God, help me to get through this one more."

She was almost up to the table the manager had indicated before she realized who the customer was that had called for her. It was a man who had been there three times before that week. He was a large sensuous brute, with thick lips and a cruel face. She remembered his fulsome flattery the first time he had come in, his little pig-eyes upon her had seemed to soil her very soul. She had avoided waiting upon him several times since that first experience, but now it was too late for that, and she had been ordered by the manager to wait upon him.

She gathered all her dignity and went forward, a shudder of horror passing over her slender shoulders in spite of her best efforts, and when she reached him she found that he was drunk!

Frightened, she paused, keeping the table between them, but he reached out a burly arm and grasped her wrist, trying to draw her nearer.

"Come over here, sweetie," he demanded in a loud tone that everybody in the room could hear! "I need sympathy! That's why I sent for you, Jane! Come clost an' tell me whatcha got ta eat—!"

But Diana, more frightened than she had ever been in her life, struggled with all her might to get her wrist free from that terrible, contaminating grasp, and suddenly she felt a stout arm about her waist, and a familiar voice towering over her.

"Hey, you Mortie Matzan, you lay off my gal! She's *my* sweetie an' I don't want nobody else buttin' in. Scram there! Hear what I say? This dame is mine. Ain't you, sweetheart!"

The voice was not loud on account of the roomful of

customers, but the manager's hideous face loomed over her in a possessive leer that almost took her senses away.

Diana gave one terrified sound like a wounded animal, and tearing herself loose from the hateful arm she suddenly raised a glass of water from the table before her and flung it full in the proprietor's face. The glass falling where it rolled heavily down on the drunken man's foot brought a howl from him to add to the confusion. But Diana was not there to see. She was madly dashing down the room toward the kitchen, colliding with another waitress in the doorway, leaving a shower of tray and dishes in her wake, flying through the kitchen and out the open door into the alley at the back, barely escaping a fall over the great garbage can that stood in her way. She rounded the corner into the transverse alley, went blindly up one street and down another, through any alley that presented itself in her way, only so that it lay in the general direction of her own little third story room.

It was only about two o'clock, and people all about her everywhere, but she dared not look behind her. It seemed to her that the whole restaurant, proprietor, employees, customers, drunk and sober, must be following. She did not remember that she had left her hat and jacket. Even her purse was of no moment to her now. They were in her locker and she wore the key about her neck but she would never go back for them, not if she starved to death. There was only fifty cents in the purse anyway, and what was fifty cents now?

She was panting and frightened, more frightened than she had ever been in her life before, and the tears were rolling down her cheeks, though she did not know it. She turned at last into her own street, and fled up the block like a shadow.

She did not see the shabby form that lurked across the

street in the narrow arched court between two houses, all unsuspected, watching for her arrival. Having nothing to do for the time being, and having a hunch it might be useful, he had stationed himself there to discover if possible her comings and goings; and now she came so startlingly, flying through the street hatless and fairly flinging herself at the door with the latch key in her trembling hand, that he had to look carefully to be sure it was really she. He had never seen her before without a hat on, not since she had been a little girl in school, but there was something about her lithe way of running, even in her fright, that made him sure of her, and so he stood there watching till she had disappeared from sight and the grim door had slammed behind her. Then he slowly disengaged himself from the shadows of the archway and slithered down the street and around the corner, skulking close to the houses, skirting the block till he disappeared into the alley behind the house which she had entered. There he took up his stand to watch for a possible vision of a girl in the third story back window.

But Diana was lying face down across her bed weeping her heart out, and he presently stole away to refresh himself with a glass of something heartening. It was not the first time he had watched in the alley under that window.

Earlier in the day Stephen Disston had gone in desperation to his bank and had it out with the bank president. He had spent three lonely nights in the damaged house with no word from his recalcitrant wife, and three grilling days in his office waiting for results that did not come, and there had been ample opportunity to think about his lost child. There had come no encouragement as yet from the private detective whom he had hired several days ago to hunt for Diana, and he was almost in despair. But he gained nothing by his anxious questioning of the bank president except an added load of anxiety. And finally Mr. Dunham, growing weary of the interview in the midst of his busy morning, had politely suggested to his friend that the best way to find his daughter was to page her on the radio. The idea was shocking to Diana's father. It seemed as if he would be descending among the criminals of the world to seek her. As if he thought that Diana had run away and got married, or done some sensational thing that should not be blazoned to the world. But the more he walked about the city and saw the lurking humanity on every hand, with faces of might-be criminals, the more his tormented soul entertained the thought that something terrible must have happened to Diana or she never would have kept this long continued silence. It did not occur to him to wonder what her reaction had been to his withdrawal of her money. That seemed a simple matter. He did not realize how it had stunned her to have her beloved father take such drastic action against her. What did occur to him, and worried him beyond expression, was the fact that she had no money. He was a man who had had money all his life and plenty of it, and he could not conceive it possible that his daughter out in the world alone could get along at all without it. He had been entirely convinced when Helen suggested it that Diana would come home at once when she found she had nothing wherewith to buy food and shelter.

But Diana had not come home! What had she done? Had something terrible befallen her? He could think of no friends or relatives with whom she might have taken refuge whom he had not already questioned, and now it seemed to him that he should go crazy if there was not some immediate way of finding her. And added to all the strain and worry he had dreamed for three nights in succession now, alone in that house where he had lived so happily with his first wife, that Marilla had come to him and stood beside his bed looking at him with mournful eyes and had reproached him. "Stephen, what have you done with our little girl?" Just that question and then she would vanish with his sleep, and leave him to the long wakeful hours before the dawn.

Back in his office alone again after the interview with the banker he thought of his advice, and at last surrendered to the idea. He would trail his pride of family in the dust and descend to broadcast his anxiety. If that was the only way to find Diana he would try that. He would leave no stone unturned.

And now he wondered that he had waited so long, and sat with trembling fingers, writing feverishly, the words that were to go on the air: "Paging Miss Diana Disston, who left her father's house several weeks ago to visit relatives and has not been heard from for ten days. When last seen in this city she was dressed in—" the hurried pen paused and the father tried to conjure up a vision of his sweet young daughter, the blinding tears filling his eyes and falling on the page as he recalled her, straight and slender in her dark dress. His description after all was vague, not helped much by the banker who had given mainly his impression of her lovely eyes shadowed by sorrow, her noble bearing, her proud little chin. No, one couldn't put those things on the air, not even to find Diana!

But a few minutes later that afternoon, just after Diana had fled the restaurant in the noisy little plebeian street, an announcer startled suddenly into the midst of a musical comedy program of the afternoon: "Paging Miss Diana Disston, five feet two inches, slender, dark hair and eyes, weighing one hundred and ten pounds, dressed in black—"

The voice of the announcer boomed out solemnly as

though he were pronouncing a requiem on the dead. One more unfortunate dead! And Stephen Disston sat in the far corner of the stuffy recreation room of a strange downtown hotel where he had never been before and knew nobody, and listened. His hat was drawn down over his eyes, his open paper flung up in front of his face. He listened while the blood stole shamedly up into his haggard face, suffusing it with a kind of purple shadow, and then receded, leaving his face white and drawn. To think it was his daughter, his little Diana, whose precious name was being called out that way to the world! And it was his own act, his hasty words, his refusal to listen to her pleadings that had sent her forth from home and him.

Several miles away across the city in an uptown apartment where a gay throng of Helen's friends were gathered playing bridge with the radio going full blast to drown their quarrels, Helen heard the words boom out, and looked up with a laugh, saw no one was noticing and hurried to turn the dial to another number. But on her way back to her seat she laughed. With no apparent reason she laughed immoderately. But no one looked at her curiously. It was a free and easy party and no one thought anything was strange. The stranger the better! They were combing life for thrills. It was the thing to do.

Edith Maythorn and a few of her friends spending a gay pleasant afternoon together, heard it and looked up at one another startled.

"Oh, that's not our Diana," said Edith carelessly after listening for a minute. "She was here just a short time ago, and besides, she never wears black, not that I ever saw. But isn't that strange? Two people of that unusual name. I'll have to telephone Diana about it. Won't she be amused? That's almost as funny as when my brother Jimmy saw his name in the papers as having won in a prize fight!" They chattered on and presently forgot all about it.

Standing at a bar in a fashionable hotel Jerry Lange heard it as he tossed down a cocktail and paused thoughtfully. Diana Disston! Where had he heard that name? Wasn't that what they called that quiet little girl at Maythorn's? But it was probably not the same name after all. He never remembered names very well. He always thought of her as "Beautiful," somehow. Of course it wouldn't be the same name. Still you couldn't tell these days. Things were happening! So he ordered another highball and tossed it down and went on his way whistling.

Mrs. MacCarroll heard it as she sat darning Gordon's socks and setting neat patches in partly worn garments. She heard it and gathering up her work stuffed it into her sewing basket summarily and went to the window to look out up to the great house. Oh, poor poor man! What was coming now? And where was the sweet little girl? Had something awful happened to her?

Maggie, in her sister's neat parlor, entertaining the baby while her sister went to the store for a spool of thread, heard and went to the window again and again hoping her sister would return. Hussy or no hussy she must go to the master as soon as Mary came to care for the child. And Diana! Poor wee thing, where was she, and night coming on again? Maggie's cheeks grew redder than their wont with excitement, and her blue eyes were drenched with tears, as she stood by the window looking out and wiping her eyes with the corner of her neat white apron.

And down in the cellar of a miserable rooming house where the scum of the city found refuge, Bill Sharpe sat at a sloppy wooden table guiltless of even an oilcloth cover, and slowly drank a glass of vile beer, while a cheap radio over in the darkness whined out whatever came along on the air. His eyes narrowed cunningly as he listened, put down his glass, and stared at the corner from which the sound came. He sat listening to the end of the announcement. Then lifting his glass he gulped the rest of the beer and wiped his mouth on his ragged sleeve as he slunk off from the table with a motion between a slouch and stealth, and vanished up the cellar steps. Down the dirty street to a little dirty shop with dusty windows where children bought all-day suckers for a cent, and their elders found salacious literature, he went. He purchased a sheet of paper and an envelope for two cents and stole away to a shelter he knew down by the river where a box would afford all the writing desk he needed, and there in the late afternoon he wrought out a communication, brief and to the point. He needed no study nor thought to distort the spelling almost beyond recognition, for he came by bad spelling naturally. And while he wrote with his stub of a pencil on the cheap paper that was by no means fresh, did he have a vision perhaps of a little girl with brown curls and golden lights in her brown eyes, wearing a fresh white dress, sitting at a far desk in the same room at school with him? For a few days only, it was, until he graduated backward into the grade below, and she passed on out of his horizon entirely.

The note when it was finished read:

> Yor doter is huld fer ransum. Putt fifty thousand dolers under the big stun in yor springe howse tanite an she will cum bake tanite otherwiz she will be kilt. dont tel tha perlise ore yor lif wil not be wuth 6 pents.
>
> yors DESPRIT

He addressed the letter and stole away out of the precinct, and just before the sun set he emerged cautiously from the woods around the little creek that ran below the garden at the big house. Stealthily he approached from shrub to shrub, till he stood hidden behind the bushes that fringed the top of the terrace, and from there reached forth a ragged arm with one quick motion and hung the letter by a dirty string to the door knob. Then he melted back into the shadows and was gone, and not even Mother MacCarroll, keeping her steady vigil from window to window, caught a glimpse of him.

A few minutes later Stephen Disston swung himself stiffly off the bus and walked slowly up the drive. He walked like an old man, with his head bent down, and Mother MacCarroll watched him from the window, and longed to run out and try to comfort him, only she felt that perhaps he would not like it, so she stood there at the window watching him and praying for him. Poor sad lonely man! And where could the new wife be? Had Maggie been mistaken perhaps? Maybe there wasn't any new wife after all.

She watched him until he reached the front door. There was just light enough for her to make him out standing there fumbling with the lock. How long it took him to open the front door!

Then the telephone rang and she had to go.

It was only a wrong number and she was soon back, but she couldn't see the master of the house any more, and the door was shut. He had probably gone in and the light would spring up in a moment. She had watched him for three nights now and it always did, but though she watched for five minutes there came no light, and— was it fancy, or was there something dark lying on the white steps?

Fancy of course. She would better go about her business instead of watching her neighbors. But poor man, poor man!

So she turned about and flashed on her own lights, hurrying to get dinner ready. Gordon would be coming home hungry soon and she wasn't ready. She had been mooning for the last hour. But she cast an anxious glance out the window now and then and still there was no light in the great house!

22

DIANA lay upon her bed and wept her heart out, wept until exhausted nature took revenge and sleep fell down upon her. Just a locking of her tired senses in oblivion for a little time, a fitful sleep wherein the terrors of the day were for a moment forgotten. Then suddenly somebody slammed up a window across the alley and loud angry voices broke upon her quiet release, mingled with a sudden sharp whine of two radios of different themes. The usual suppertime pandemonium had broken loose on the neighborhood, and Diana, not used to it at this hour, awoke with a start and sat up looking about her.

Then it all came back like a flash what had happened to her and she sat there shuddering with chill and fright as memory furnished each scene of the day with vivid flashes.

But the brief respite had done her good, nevertheless, and she was able to think now more connectedly. She told herself that her door was locked and no harm could come to her. She must calm herself and try to think her way out.

Her job was gone forever, of course. And she was

glad, *glad!* It would have been wrong to give it up, just for sheer weariness, but this had been something she could not stand, not even if she starved to death! So now she might rejoice.

But quickly there came the fear that that awful man might follow her, that manager! He had her address and there was no telling what right an employer had over his employees who left without a week's notice. Perhaps there was some law by which she could be made to go back to finish out her month! Well, she wouldn't! Never! Not if she had to lie down and die, she wouldn't! But perhaps she ought to get out of here and disappear where he couldn't find her! Could she do that without money? It would cost a lot to move, especially if she put her goods in storage again. Storage would have to be paid in advance. And then where would she go? How live? Boarding was out of the question, anything she could afford. Afford? She laughed. She couldn't afford anything. She had barely enough hidden away in her trunk to pay Mrs. Lundy, and this week's wages would never be paid now because she would never go back for them. They were due tonight, but the manager would be so much wealthier. Even her fifty cents in her purse was gone. And her hat. Well, of course it didn't matter about the hat. But what was she going to do now? Her way seemed blocked on every hand. And where would she find another place as cheap and tolerable as Mrs. Lundy's? It was bad enough, but there were others worse, and she shuddered at the thought of going out to hunt one, and another job! Oh, did God care?

Suddenly she slipped down upon her knees beside the bed and began to pray.

"Oh, God! I'm yours. You died for me and I believe it, and I'm yours. I take you as my Saviour. Nobody else seems to care for me. Will you take me? I can't take care of myself. I don't know how. I've tried and I've made a miserable failure. Now, I'm going to trust you to look after me, to show me what to do. Guide me, please. Give me that light that other prayer spoke of. Please, I've nobody else, and I'm leaving me with You!"

It was not like any prayer she had been taught, but she got up with a strange feeling of peace upon her. She had taken her trouble to God, and He would show her what to do. She was going to trust it with Him.

She stood for a moment looking about her room, wondering how the Light would come, and then she went to work. She was not going to be afraid any more. But she must get ready for whatever might be coming.

Almost feverishly she began to put her things away in trunk and bureau drawers, just as if she had received definite word that she was moving. She gathered her pictures and small trinkets together and packed them carefully. She took down her garments from the closet and folded them into her trunk. Her fingers flew silently, rapidly, and in a short time her pretty room was stripped of its decorations. Quite definitely she locked them up, leaving out such things as she would need to wear away. She almost laughed at herself while she did it. Where was she going? She did not know. But at least she would be ready.

There were tears on her cheeks while she worked, yet they were no more conquering her, and the weariness of the day had passed away in the excitement of the moment. She wondered, was it just her own spirit that had worked herself up to this pitch of a false peace, or was it really God who was there helping her?

She paused beside the vase that held her carnations of a week. Their edges were brown now, and they would soon be gone. It was Saturday night and no more had come. Was it too late? Were they perhaps downstairs as they had been once before? Should she go and see? She paused with her hand almost out to the door and then decided against it. She dreaded going out of that room again until she knew what to do. If the flowers were down there they would keep as they had done before. She hoped they would not come after she was gone. If they were God's flowers He wouldn't send them too late!

Then she smiled at herself again. Was she losing her good sense, talking fairy tales to herself? Perhaps it was dear old Maggie who had sent them. Perhaps it had somehow been Maggie all the time. But anyhow it was God.

Suddenly she knew that she was very hungry. She had scarcely eaten anything all day. She ought to go out and get dinner. But to go down and out into the darkness of the street again tonight after all that had happened seemed an awful undertaking. No, she would rather stay hungry. She had taken off her old working dress and slipped into the one she had left out, but the outside world seemed too beset with enemies lurking in the dark.

She went over to the tin cracker box on her window sill where she kept her supplies. There were only two small salt crackers left in it, and a tiny piece of cheese less than an inch square. Well, she would eat those. That would be plenty. She took the box and turned away from the window and as she did so her profile was silhouetted for an instant delicately on the white window shade. And down in the alley a shadowy form looking up caught the vision and slid like a gaunt rat to a drug store not far away. He slunk unobserved into the telephone booth and called a number. As soon as he recognized the voice at the other end of the wire he spoke guardedly:

"It's O.K. by me now fer the machine, Spike! Park her on th' dark side the street. Say ten minutes to a half-hour. S'long Buddy! I'll be seein' ya!"

But up in her quiet room Diana sat sadly and ate her frugal meal, the dying flowers beside her on a little table, their withering beauty seeming to mock her, yet she closed her eyes on the tears that would persist in rolling down her cheeks, and kept saying over and over to herself:

"I will believe! *I will* believe!"

Back in the stone cottage Mrs. MacCarroll had dinner started so that it could be served at a moment's notice, but Gordon had not come. It was growing duskier all the time and she kept going to the back window and gazing uneasily toward the great house, for still there was no light, and still she seemed to fancy there was something dark and bulky lying on the steps. That was purely fancy she told herself. She could not possibly see so far in this failing light. She had almost reached the point in her uneasiness where she was ready to venture up the dark drive alone just to still her fears, when Gordon arrived.

"Oh, son, I'm so glad you've come!" she cried out with relief.

"Why, Mother! You surely weren't frightened about me tonight, were you? It's not late."

"No, not about you, Gordon," she said with a catch in her breath, "but I've been worried about things in the great house. Do you know—did you hear? No, of course you didn't. You don't get anywhere near a radio, do you?"

"Well, no, not exactly," laughed Gordon, "I have more important things to do than listen to the radio, though I'm glad you've got one to while away the hours with. But what's happened at the great house?"

"Why, Gordon, the little lady's been paged on the radio!"

"What?"

"Yes, this afternoon. It said how tall she was and how she was dressed, and the color of her hair and eyes, but it didn't say what a lovely smile she has, nor how she walks like a feather in the breeze, nor any of the things that would make folks really know her when they saw her. But it made my heart stand still with horror, to think what may have happened to her, dear child! I couldn't help thinking what if she had been my child how worried I would be! And I thought of her poor father, and wondered where he was. He's come through a hard place to be willing to broadcast his troubles to the world. For he's a proud man. You could see that just to look at him. And while I was pitying him he came walking in the drive. He'd got off the bus, and almost fallen as he got out, and he looked old and sick. I almost ran out to offer him a cup of tea, and then I thought perhaps he wouldn't like it just now. Perhaps he'd rather suffer alone. So I let him go on by. But I watched for him to go in the house. I saw him get to the door and reach over as if he was putting the key in the lock, and just then the telephone rang and when I came back he wasn't there any more and there seemed to be something bulky and dark lying on the step—only of course that must have been imagination. It was beginning to get dark, and I don't trust my eyes any more. But I've watched and watched and there hasn't been a light yet."

Gordon's eyes were fixed on his mother's face with a disturbed startled expression in them.

"I'll go right up and see, Mother," he said.

"Take your flash light along and signal me if you want me to come," she called after him as he turned toward the door.

"Oh, it won't be anything like that!" said the young man as if he were trying to convince himself, "but I'll take it. It might come in handy." She could see that he was worried, though he was trying to laugh it off to calm her fears.

She stood by the window watching him disappear into the darkness of the driveway, and then, before the sound of his footsteps had scarcely died away, there came a tap on the door, the back door. How strange! She hastened to open it, and there stood Maggie in her Sunday best, her blue eyes red and blurred with tears, her best hat awry because she had put it on so hastily, her Scotch tongue fairly tumbling over itself in an attempt to talk while she was still out of breath from hurrying so fast.

"I hope I didn't fright ye," she burst out, pantingly. "I glimpsed the licht in the kitchen an' guessed ye wad be here. I'm that worrited aboot the master's family I hadta coom an' see. Did ye happen ta be listenin' in on the radio? Did ye hear them callin' fer the little lady?"

"Yes, I did," said Mrs. MacCarroll. "And I've been worried ever since. But don't you know where she is? I thought she promised to write you."

"Yes, she did, but I've had niver a word yet," said the old servant. "I was worrited, but I thought of course she'd writ to her feyther. Now it must be he's niver heerd neither. I wonder if he's up at the hoose? It seems ta be all dark. I thought I'd juist step in an' see if you'd heerd aught? It goes sair against me ta be seen there ef the new mistress is hame, but I'd go ef I thought I could help the master only. You don't happen to have noticed if he went in?"

"Yes," Mrs. MacCarroll said in an anxious voice, "I saw Mr. Disston go up the drive over half an hour ago, and I've been waiting ever since to see a light in the house but there isn't any yet, and my son just came so I sent him up to see if anything was the matter and—there! There he is now waving his flash light! I promised to come right up if he gave the signal. You'd better come with me—!"

The two hurried out the door and up the drive, walking so fast they could scarcely talk.

"Is—the—*hussy* home?" puffed Maggie taking two little quick steps to Mrs. MacCarroll's one longer one.

"No, I don't think so," said the older woman quietly. "I saw her go up the drive several days ago, but she came back within the hour and took a bus off. I haven't seen her since."

"That's good!" said Maggie fervently, puffing along.

"There! There's a light!" said Mrs. MacCarroll, hurrying on the faster as a light streamed out from the open front door.

They rounded the drive beyond the last group of shrubbery, and saw a dark form lying across the top step in front of the door.

"Oh, it's him!" cried Maggie with tears in her voice. "It's the puir master! Oh, I knew I should never have left him ta that hussy's care. I should 'uv bided whatever she said. I mighta knowed she'd soon hang herself ef I'd give her the rope. Oh, the puir mon. The puir silly mon! An' I promised his first wife I'd look after him weel."

It was a kind of croon she uttered as she brisked along panting, talking more to herself than to her companion.

As they came up to the steps Gordon was just lifting Mr. Disston in his arms.

"He's had a fall," he explained to his mother. "I wish we knew who their doctor is. No,—I think he's only fainted. His pulse is weak but it's there."

"It's Dr. Brownell," panted Maggie, "I'll just run in an' phone him!"

"This is Maggie, their old servant," explained Mrs. MacCarroll.

"That's good!" breathed Gordon as he lifted the older man and bore him inside the house.

"Lay him on the couch in the lib'ry—," said Maggie, capably swinging open the door and plumping up the pillows. Then she pattered away to the telephone in the hall. Mrs. MacCarroll penetrated to the kitchen and brought water, and Maggie emerging from the telephone booth hurried to the medicine closet for restoratives.

"He's coomin' at once!" she reported a moment later as she came puffing back with aromatic ammonia, her hat awry, her cheeks blazing red with excitement. There were still traces of tears on her cheeks.

Their efforts were presently rewarded by a long drawn sigh from the sick man, and fluttering eyelids opened vaguely upon them.

The two women retreated to the shadows of the hallway, leaving Gordon only for him to see.

"You're feeling better now, Mr. Disston," said Gordon in his quiet voice of assurance. "You got a bit dizzy, didn't you? I am glad I was here. Take another sip of this water. That will help. The doctor will be here soon and in a minute or two we'll have a cup of tea for you. I suspect you didn't take much time for lunch today and got a bit faint, but we'll soon have you fixed up."

Stephen Disston looked at him gravely for an instant and tried to smile. Maggie hurried away for the cup of tea and Mrs. MacCarroll was preparing a tray, knowing instinctively where to find the tea things.

"Ach! The puir mon!" said Maggie brushing away another stray tear. "I juist kenned that feckless hussy would never give him the proper food."

"I wouldn't try to get up just yet, Mr. Disston,"

Gordon was saying, putting out a protesting hand. "The doctor will soon be here. He is on his way. Unless you would rather I would carry you up to your bed? I can easily do that if you will like to be in bed before he gets here."

"Oh, no," protested Stephen Disston, making another ineffectual effort to rise, and falling back again, "I must get right up! There is need for haste!" and he lifted a crumpled paper held tight in his hand! "This—" he said and looked at Gordon with anguished eyes—"I've just had a letter—What time is it?" and his eyes sought the clock.

"It's not late," said Gordon cheerfully, "but if I were you I wouldn't try to do another thing tonight. Just rest. What is it you have to do? Couldn't I do it?"

Disston's troubled eyes fixed on his face for an instant and then he groaned.

"No," he said despairingly, "you couldn't! Nobody could! I don't see how I can do it myself, but I've *got* to *somehow*. I can't let them murder my little girl!"

"What?" said Gordon with horrified tone. "What can you mean? Nobody is going to do anything like that!"

"They're threatening to," said the sick man tonelessly. "They've kidnapped her and are holding her for ransom! They want fifty thousand dollars put under the stone in the spring house tonight—see!" and he lifted the paper again.

With horror clutching at his heart Gordon took the ransom note and read it.

Could this be possible? His heart went up in instant prayer for needed strength and guidance. He needed to know what to say to this anguished father. And after an instant his voice was steady and he spoke:

"That may not be genuine you know," he said in a

quiet businesslike tone. "And even if it is there will be a way to protect her."

"But I haven't any money to put out there under the stone!" His voice was piteous. "And I don't know where I can get any! I was going to telephone my bank president, but I'm afraid it's too late to catch him now. He always—goes away—over week-ends. And I'm not sure—he would do it for me—even if I got him. My—money is—*gone!* I'm on the verge of *bankruptcy!*"

"Well, God isn't!" said Gordon with assurance. "You lie there and pray to Him and I'll see what can be done. Where did you find this note?"

"Tied to the doorknob as I was trying to fit in the key. I stopped to read it, and I must have got dizzy! I fell and struck my head." He put his hand up feebly and Gordon looking found a great lump and a gash where the blood was seeping out and matting the hair.

"So you have! Well, we'll soon look after that." Gordon motioned to his mother who came in just then.

"Mother, we need some water and clean cloths. I wonder if you could rustle them together. Tea! That's good. That will hearten you, Mr. Disston. Let me give you a few teaspoonfuls before you try to talk any more."

"But I must get up!" said the sick man. "The time is going! I cannot stop to drink tea."

"Look here, Mr Disston, will you trust me with this thing? I'll do my best. I'll do whatever you want done if you know what that is, but anyhow I'll do something. I'll search for your daughter as if she were my—sister," he added. "Now, drink this tea!"

He slipped his arm under the man's head and lifted him slightly so that he could drink from the cup he held.

Stephen Disston drank, and looked at his young comforter with his heart in his eyes.

"You have been a good friend to me. I shall never

forget it," he murmured, "but I could not let you undertake all this for me. But, oh, I don't know what to do! Where can I get the money? I never thought I would get to a place where I would have *nothing*, no means to rescue my child!"

He covered his face with his hands for an instant, and then making a supreme effort he raised himself to a sitting posture and tried to rise to his feet. But suddenly he dropped back again, his face growing white.

"I *can't*—do—it—!" he said, and then, "but—I—*must!*"

He tried to rise once more but Gordon caught him and made him lie down again.

"Now look here, friend," said Gordon, "you'll only complicate matters if you lose consciousness again. We *need you* if we are going to clear this thing up. I take it you have had no time to call the police?"

"Do you think—I should? The letter warns against that you know."

"I think the police are better fitted to cope with a thing like this than you and I are, and the quicker they know about it the quicker they can do something. I think they should be the ones to deal with the matter of what is put under a stone—if any."

"Perhaps you're right," said the sad voice and the lids dropped over tortured eyes.

"Does Maggie know where that stone is located?"

The man opened his eyes again.

"Is Maggie here? Oh, that is good! Yes, she knows. You can trust her absolutely."

"I thought so. Well, I'll have an interview with the police. Shall I take the letter? And then I'm going out to find your daughter! You be resting—and praying!" he added.

A hopeless look swept over the face of the sick man.

"You can't find her," he said despairingly, "I've had one of the best detectives in the state out hunting her for three weeks and there isn't a trace of her."

"That's all right. I'm asking the Lord to lead me to her. Will you ask Him too? You know Him, don't you?"

Disston nodded diffidently as if he were embarrassed.

"I haven't been—much—along that line lately!"

"Then get back to Him," said the young man cheerfully. "Your strength is in Him, you know. There comes the doctor! Is there anything else I should know?"

Gordon gave a brief explanation to the doctor of how he had found the sick man and the doctor looked troubled.

"He has a rather serious heart complication," he said in a low tone, "a shock like that is bad. We should have a nurse, and I'll stay here tonight as much as possible. Can you stay?"

"I have to go out for a little while on an errand for Mr. Disston," explained Gordon. "I'll be back as soon as possible."

"That's good. We may need you. If we could only get hold of Diana that would be the best medicine possible," said the doctor anxiously.

"I'm going out to get her!" said the young man with assurance.

"Maggie's got a nice little bit of supper for you," whispered his mother as he came down from the bedroom whither they had carried the sick man.

"Sorry, Mother, but I can't stop now. I'm going after the little lady. You and Maggie will have to carry on here till I get back. We've sent for a nurse and she ought to be here soon. Mother, Mr. Disston had a note saying his daughter was being held for ransom. I'm taking it to the police, some of them may be here soon, probably not in uniform. Where is Maggie?"

"Here!" said Maggie from the shadows.

"Well, Maggie, can you show the police where there would be a stone in the spring house where ransom money could be put? They'll want to know."

"I can, sir!" said Maggie eagerly from out a shower of anxious tears.

"Well, that's all. Don't get frightened, and *pray!* all the time!"

"That we will, sir," said Maggie with a strong look in her blue eyes.

"But won't you take just a bite, Gordon?" urged his mother.

"No time, Mother dear!" He smiled at her. "Plenty of time to eat afterwards."

He walked briskly away into the night, and his mother heard the little flivver cough and start on its way.

The night went on, and all was quiet in the great house. The nurse arrived and fell into her place in the scheme of things, several policemen arrived silently and entered the house rubber shod. They conversed very little. They peered out into the darkness in the direction of the spring house and prepared a neat bundle. They asked Maggie a few keen questions, and she answered them as keenly. Presently one of them was missing, and a shadow drifted out behind the house as if he had been a wraith. By and by another one was missing from the dark room at the back of the house where they had chosen to sit, and then another, till there were only two left inside on guard. At their direction all but the lights in the sickroom were extinguished, and Mrs. MacCarroll and Maggie went and sat side by side on the couch in the dark living room, silently, sat there praying, and visualizing what might be happening off in the vague distance where Gordon MacCarroll had gone. And Gordon's mother tried to keep her fears back, tried to rest her faith on the Almighty God, and did succeed in keeping back the tears. "Oh, God, keep him. Don't let him do anything rash! You've always guarded us. Keep us now! Raise up the sick father and help Gordon to find the little lady." Over and over she prayed. So they sat there and listened with ears attuned to the darkness outside and the meadows down behind the spring house. That would be where the kidnappers would steal up sometime in the night to get their money. They wondered what had been demanded, and whether the father had had enough, or what was it that the grim policemen had done up in a little bundle? They were glad of the presence of those silent policemen. It made it easier to breathe.

The hours crept slowly by, silent save for the moaning of the sick man overhead.

And sometimes Mother MacCarroll would glance out of the window down across the lawn to where her own little kitchen light glowed, and take heart of hope. Gordon had left that light burning for her. It seemed to reassure her.

23

DIANA had just finished her second cracker when she heard footsteps coming up the stairs. She sat staring at the door. It was locked she knew, but the thought of the manager of the restaurant came to her. He could break down a door as easily as he would crush an egg shell if he cared to. Of course she was crazy to think of him. He wouldn't leave the restaurant and come after her, but if he should, what should she do? She had no one, *no one* to protect her.

Then like a flash came a verse that she had read only that morning before she went out to her work.

"The eternal God is thy refuge, and underneath are the everlasting arms."

That was it. She must trust in that. "God, help, *help!*" she cried out in her heart even as the tap sounded on the door.

She hesitated a moment and then said:

"Who is it, please?" Her voice sounded frightened even to herself, and she was suddenly conscious of her eyes that were heavy with weeping.

"It's me!" said Mrs. Lundy, and there was a pleased sound to her voice, not like her usual gruff tones.

Diana snapped off the bright light and went to the door.

There stood Mrs. Lundy with a big box in her arms.

"Well, they've come again!" she announced triumphantly, "and he's a *regular* guy. He brang 'em hisself. You ain't gone to bed have ya? Cause you better get yourself togged out in yer best. He's down there in the parlor waitin' for ya, and he seemed like he was in a hurry."

Diana's eyes were filled with quick fear again.

"I don't understand what you mean, Mrs. Lundy. There is nobody who would come to call upon me here, or bring me flowers. Those flowers that came in the past were from my old home."

"Well here they are, anyhow, and he's downstairs. And ef I was you I wouldn't keep him waitin' very long. He's some classy guy, he is. I says to my daughter as I come through the kitchen on my way up, ta see the meat didn't burn, I says, 'Tilly, I always said that third story back was different, and now I know it.'"

"But really, Mrs. Lundy," said Diana drawing back and brushing away the dampness from her eyelashes, "I don't in the least know who this is, and I'm afraid there's some mistake."

"Well, have it yer own way," said the landlady grumpily. "It's your mistake, not mine, anyway. And I must say I don't see the point of you keeping on saying you don't know him. I got eyes in my head, ain't I? Whether you know him or not you march down there and settle it with him! I gotta cook my meat!" and Mrs. Lundy deposited the box on the floor with a thump and sailed away downstairs.

With her heart palpitating like a trip hammer Diana picked up the box. With excited fingers she tore open the wrappings, lifted the cover, and that heavenly fragrance of spicy sweetness was wafted through the room.

The flowers had come again! The mystery flowers. God sent them every time in her need! But now must she go down there and have the mystery and beauty torn from them by having the giver turn out to be somebody she didn't like?

She dashed cold water in her face, smoothed her hair, and then with sudden impulse she scooped the flowers from their box and took them in her arms, carrying them in a sheaf before her, to shield her.

Downstairs the doorbell was pealing through the house once more, and Mrs. Lundy ungraciously left her meat again to answer it. She eyed the creature with disdain who slid inside before she could stop him. His hair was unkempt, his face and hands were dirty and his clothes were ragged. Mrs. Lundy herself was not beyond being untidy, but this creature was of another world than even hers.

"What you want?" she frowned at him.

He blinked in the flickering light of the hall like a creature at bay and demanded:

"I wantta see the party on the third floor back."

"Whatcha want her for?" demanded the landlady.

"That's my business!" he growled.

"Awwright, you c'n stand there. She's comin' down in a minute!"

The man lifted his little unholy eyes toward the stairs, his mouth stretched in a diabolical grin that showed spaces between the rotten teeth where some were missing, and he kept one hand in the pocket of his tattered coat.

Diana came on slowly, rounding the head of the stairs on the second floor, her flowers before her.

"God! Take care of me!" she breathed as she stood a

minute dreading to go on. Then it occurred to her that the manager of the cheap little restaurant where she had worked would never bring her gorgeous expensive flowers, and she had really nothing to fear in that way. It must of course be some one of her old friends who had found out where she was and had taken this tactful way to show her homage.

So she gathered courage and came on, dreading most of all to have the romance taken from her lovely spirit-flowers. Well, whatever came she would always say that God sent them, anyway.

Her sweet eyes were heavy with recently shed tears and there were dark circles beneath them, but she was startlingly lovely as she came down that last flight of stairs.

The cringing man at the foot gazed up at her for an instant, his hand gripping that something inside his pocket. Then he lowered his head with a Uriah Heep motion and spoke in a whine:

"You're Diana Disston!" he charged as if it were a crime.

Diana stopped, startled, new fear coming into her eyes, her heart suddenly sinking. Was this creature the sender of her wonderful mystery flowers? Her arms grew suddenly heavy, like lead, and the flowers slid from her grasp and fell in a heap before her on the step. Her knees were weak. She felt as if she were going to sink down with the flowers. But she must not give way. She must not!

"I useta go ta school 'ith you. You member me?"

"NO!" said Diana from a throat that was dry and lips that were trembling. *"NO!"* She tried to scream it, but the sound was only an anguished whisper.

"My mother useta sew fer your mother," he whined on. "I got her outside now in a taxi. She's on her way to the hospital fer a noperation an' she wantsta see ya. She's got somepin' ta tell ya ta yer advantage. 'Cause she may die, that's why she wantsta tell ya. You come out ta the taxi an' talk ta her."

Diana gripped the stair railing and tried to back away. She must not fall! She *must not!* Oh, if Mrs. Lundy would only come, or somebody.

"But I *don't know* you!" she pled with that note of fright in her voice. "I *can't* go out there now!"

"I'll teach ya ta know me!" said the man, low menace in his voice now, and whipped out an ugly gun, pointing it up at her. "You scram down here right quick! Make it snappy. I ain't waitin' round any longer, see? Come on ur I'll shoot the pretty feet out from under ya! Keep yer trap shut an' come on ur ya'll be a dead 'un!"

Diana stood there powerless to move, and when she tried to scream no sound came from her frightened lips.

Then suddenly from the dim recesses of the unlighted parlor, without warning, the legs of one of Mrs. Lundy's parlor chairs crashed down upon the man's wrist, his hand fell limp at his side and his gun dropped to the floor and went off with a loud reverberation.

Simultaneously the kitchen door at the end of the hall swung open and a big burly policeman, Mrs. Lundy's brother, dropped in for a bite to eat, came stalking forth from the kitchen a big wedge of apple pie in one hand and an ugly gun in the other.

Now the best thing the creature in the hall could do was to run, and he had taken care that the door was on the latch before he began his performance, so he proceeded to put himself into action. Like a rat he turned and would have been gone into the shadows of the street but the policeman, even while he stuffed the last gigantic mouthful of pie inside his enormous lips, brought his ugly gun into action with a tiny motion no more than the turn of a wrist, and a bullet went neatly into the foot of the intruder. With a howl he dropped at the foot of the stairs as the policeman came on with a mighty stride and grasped the little human rat by the back of his ragged collar.

Then turning about to the young man who stood in between the flowered chenille curtains of the parlor doorway, the man of the law said:

"Good work, buddy! I don't know who you are, but you certainly did lam him one just in the nick of time, and if you should ever want ta get on the p'lice force I'll write ya a recommend."

"Thank you, brother," said Gordon MacCarroll coming out into the brightness of the hall and looking down sternly at the cringing, whining creature on the floor. "I'm not applying just now, but I'll take it as a favor if you'll see that this man is fingerprinted. I think he's connected with a kidnapping affair, and if I'm not mistaken it was about to take place. Please don't let him get away till you hear from me."

"I'll not let him get away," swaggered the policeman. "We got him fingerprinted already. We got plenty on him without no kidnappin' as far as that goes, but we'll hold him alrighty. I been layin' fer this bird fer three weeks, an' he slipped me every time. Now, I'm goin' ta keep him."

He snapped the handcuffs about the man's wrist, swung the door open easily, put his piercing whistle to his lips, and an instant later a car rolled up to the door. Strong hands lifted the crippled prisoner into it.

The door closed on this scene, leaving a huddled audience of open-mouthed Lundy relatives in the kitchen door, commenting with satisfaction on how "Uncle Bill give the bum his medicine." Then they suddenly melted away and there were only Diana, sitting white and shaken on the stairs with her great sheaf of carnations at her feet and Gordon MacCarroll standing stern and relieved between the chenille portieres.

"I ask your pardon," he said looking toward the drooping girl. "There didn't seem to be any other way."

"Oh, thank you!" said Diana, struggling with the silly tears which, now that the danger was over, seemed to insist upon raining down her cheeks. "I—was—so frightened!"

"Well, you needn't be frightened any more," said Gordon with a lilt in his voice. "I've come for you! But—I'm forgetting—you don't know me any better than you did the other fellow."

"Oh, yes, I do!" cried Diana, her eyes shining through the tears. "You are the man from the stone cottage. You prayed for me once—at least I hope the prayer was meant for me. I've carried it with me ever since the night I went away. And I saw you again when we drove up to ask the way somewhere—"

"That's nice!" said Gordon suddenly smiling, a great light coming into his eyes. "That makes it a lot easier. Because I've come for you, and I'd like you to come as quickly as possible. I don't want to frighten you but your father is sick and is calling for you. I promised him I would bring you at once. Can you trust me to take you home?"

Diana's eyes were wide with consternation.

"My father is sick? Oh, what is the matter?"

"Suppose I tell you on the way. We haven't any time to waste. Your father is in great anxiety about you. Every added minute is torture for him."

Diana turned and fairly flew up the stairs.

She was back in a couple of minutes. She had caught up her suitcase, which was all packed for going somewhere, taken her hat and her purse in her hand, and come. Gordon had gathered up the flowers and she took them from him as one takes something very precious.

"My father is sick!" she explained breathlessly to Mrs. Lundy, who stood in the kitchen door staring. "I'll be back!"

The big policeman was at the door when they went outside and Gordon paused to say a few words in a low tone and hand him a telephone number he had written on a card. Then he put Diana into the car and they started away.

Diana sat there tense, the flowers clasped in her arms, her face white with anxiety like a little ghost above the blossoms.

"Now, please, tell me about Father," she implored.

"Your father had some sort of a collapse this evening following a shock. He fell and cut his head. I do not know just how serious it is. I understand there is a heart complication. But the doctor felt it was important I should bring you as soon as possible."

His voice was tender and sympathetic.

"Shock!" said Diana with trembling lips. "What kind of a shock?"

"He found a note tied to his doorknob this afternoon saying you were being held for ransom and would be murdered if a large sum of money was not forthcoming tonight."

"Oh, how dreadful!"

"He seems to have fainted and fallen. He was unconscious when I got there."

"Oh, you saw him fall?"

"No, but Mother had watched him go up the drive. She felt so sorry for him. It was just after the radio announcement that you were missing."

"*Radio?*" said Diana in bewilderment.

"Didn't you know your father had you paged on the radio?"

"Oh, *no!*" said the girl shrinking back in horror. "Oh, poor Father!" There was the breath of a sob in her voice.

"He had been under a terrible strain of course, had employed a private detective with no results, and was desperate about you, you know."

"Oh! And did your mother see him fall?"

"No, it was growing dusk, but she saw him standing at the door and then he seemed to disappear, and she watched for a light to appear in the house, but none came, so when I got home a few minutes later she sent me up to see if all was well. I found him lying on the steps with a cut in his head. Mother came up and an old servant of yours named Maggie who had heard the radio call, and we got him into the house. Your Maggie called your doctor. The doctor got a nurse."

"And—was Father—?"

"Yes, he was conscious. He tried to get up. Said he must do something about the ransom, but I persuaded him to put it into the hands of the police, and told him I would go and get you."

"But how did you know where I was?"

"I didn't."

"Then how did you think that you could find me?"

"God knew where you were." He said it reverently, and added, after an instant, "And my flowers knew!"

"Oh!" said Diana with awe in her voice. Then after a moment of silence:

"But how could you send the flowers in the first place if you didn't know my address?"

"I called up the florist on the telephone, told him you were away and I hadn't your present address, but would like to send you some flowers occasionally, incognito, if he could get them through the mail to you, special delivery. Of course the postoffice isn't allowed to give out addresses, but they themselves will put on the address. He said he could get the flowers to you. He had a brother-in-law in the postoffice who would fix it up and rush the flowers through. Of course your receipted special delivery cards came back to the florist in due time, but he couldn't send them to me because he didn't know who I was, though he always told me when I telephoned again, that they had come. But that didn't do me any good tonight of course, so I just prayed all the way to the florist's, and when I walked in I said: 'Have my flowers gone yet?'

"He knew my voice, and he looked up apologetically and said: 'No, I'm sorry, but I'm just getting ready to drive into the city and take them. I was off to a funeral and my son forgot to take them to the mail. But here they are, all ready done up and addressed.' He shoved the box over to me and there was the address written plainly, and the way was made plain for me. So I told him that was all right, that I was calling on you tonight and would take them in this time myself. That was easy, you see."

"Do you always get answers like that when you pray?" asked Diana in wonder.

"The answers are not always alike," said the young man thoughtfully. "I always know there'll be an answer if I pray in the right way, with faith, with a yielded will, with a desire to be led."

Diana was still for a long moment after that. Then she said earnestly:

"You've taken a great deal of trouble for me." And then after a pause, with her lips down among the flowers, quite irrelevantly:

"I should have brought the box for these. They will get all crushed. But I was so excited I didn't think of it."

"That's all right," said Gordon, a jubilant note in his voice, "they have accomplished their purpose, haven't they?"

"What do you mean?" she asked.

"Why, they served to introduce us. I was half afraid I might have trouble getting you to go with me after I got there. I brought these along hoping you would understand and not be afraid of me."

"Oh!" she said thoughtfully, "I suppose they did. I suppose I would have been afraid of you after what happened with that awful creature. You know I couldn't see you very well, down in the shadow of those curtains. And I'd only seen you once or twice in the dark."

He gave her a quick startled look.

"But do you know," she went on gravely, "it's just come to me who that man was. It must have been Bill Sharpe. His mother did plain sewing. He was a bad boy and ran away several times. That's all that I know about him. But I am sure his mother is dead. She died two years ago. I remember the charitable organization gathered money to bury her. I never heard what became of the son. But now I am sure that was he!" She drew a deep breath of horror like a shudder and closed her eyes.

"Oh! if it hadn't been for you I might have been killed!" she went on. "How can I ever thank you for what you have done for me !"

"Don't try, please!" he smiled.

They were getting near to home now, and Diana, glancing out, shrank back into the car again. Presently she asked in a small scared voice.

"Was my father's wife—there?"

"Oh!" he said. "Why, no, I don't think she was. I didn't see her anywhere. At least—she hadn't come when I left. And—I don't think anybody remembered her! We should have sent word to her, shouldn't we? But of course we didn't know where to send, and your father said nothing about her. He was only concerned about you."

"Oh!" said Diana gratefully. It soothed her soul to know her father cared for her.

"Would you know where she is?" asked MacCarroll.

"No!" said Diana quickly, a little sharply. "I went away because—that is, I thought it would be best—She is—we don't—!"

"I understand," said the young man, deep sympathy in his voice. "It must have been very hard for you."

Diana tried to answer but she choked over the words and all she succeeded in saying was "It was."

"But perhaps—I was wrong—" she added a moment afterward. "I didn't think my father—would feel it so! I should have written him, anyway!"

"Well, I wouldn't worry over that now," he said gently.

They were turning in at the big gateway and Diana sat very still as they swept up the drive among the trees. They were passing the spot where Diana had found her flowers, over there between the pine trees.

"I wish—" she said softly, hesitantly, her eyes drooped to the flowers in her lap, "that you would tell me why you did it! Why you put—those flowers—there—in the first place!"

It was Gordon's turn to be silent now, and they were just coming around the last curve to the house as he answered gravely, tenderly:

"Because I love you!"

He stopped the car then and went around to open the door for Diana, and as he took her hand to help her out he said earnestly:

"May I tell you about it sometime?"

"Oh—*yes*—!" The answer was almost a whisper, but

then suddenly they were aware that the front door of the mansion had swung open and a silent dark figure was standing there looking out to them.

Gordon lifted her suitcase out and took her in. There was only a dim light in the hallway and the door closed almost at once and silently.

"Better get that car away safe somewhere, brother," advised the policeman. "We don't want any easy means for our man to make a getaway in case he turns up."

"Nothing yet?" asked Gordon.

"Not yet, though it's still early. We've got our men pretty well planted where they won't be discovered, I think."

"Well, I've a notion perhaps he's been hindered," said Gordon, "though of course there may be two of them, or even more. I'll run my car back and lock it in, and then I'll tell you about it."

But just then the nurse called down from the dimness of the upper hall.

"Is that Mr. MacCarroll? Mr. Disston wants to see him *right away!*"

"That's all right," said the officer, "I'll guard your car till you come. He's been asking all the evening if you were back yet."

Diana stood helplessly in her own home looking about her in the dimness. It seemed to her that years had intervened since she was here. The dim light, the presence of the quiet officers, the strange voice of the nurse, the possibility of Helen's presence, all made her feel as if she must turn and flee. Then Gordon MacCarroll smiled down upon her and took her hand.

"Come," said he, "shall we go up?"

It was Maggie who met them on the stair landing and took the sheaf of carnations from her.

"I'll put thae in water," she said, like a caress, and

Diana smiled and yielded them up, knowing they would be safe.

Then Gordon led Diana in to her father's room, and up to the bedside.

"I've brought her, Mr. Disston," he said, as if he had just been in the next room for her.

He put Diana's hand in her father's.

"You've *brought* her?" The sick man gripped the young hand in his, a great light coming into his face. "Is this really—my daughter—?" He peered through the shadows of the darkened room. "Turn up the light, nurse. Is this you, Diana, or am I dreaming?"

Diana stooped over and kissed his forehead.

"Yes, Father dear! I'm really here!"

"And—you won't go away—again?" he asked anxiously.

"Not as long as you want me, Father!"

"I shall always want you," he said wistfully. "But—you won't vanish while I am asleep! You won't let anybody murder you?"

"No," laughed Diana tenderly, kneeling beside him with her arm about his shoulder, her hand touching his cheek in the old familiar way.

"Ah!" he said slowly, feasting his eyes upon her face for a moment. "Now I can go to sleep! I've needed sleep for so long, but I couldn't sleep. Now I can!"

Gordon had slipped away. She could hear the car with sound muffled, coasting slowly down the drive, and she knelt there beside her father's bed, his hand gripping hers, his love about her, reconciliation—home—love—! It was sweet! Her own eyelids drooped. She was asleep with her cheek on her father's pillow.

The nurse touched her on her shoulder lightly.

"You could go to your own room now," she said. "He is really asleep at last. This will do him a great deal of good. I'll call you if he wakens, but I don't think he will."

Maggie had prepared one of the guest rooms for her. Her flowers were there in a great crystal vase, filling the room with fragrance. Maggie had laid out her night robe and turned down the bed covers.

Gordon MacCarroll came to the head of the stairs and whispered that he was downstairs with the policemen and she need not feel afraid. She was to go to sleep, and he gave her a smile that shot through her heart like sweet fire.

She fell asleep almost at once with the light of that smile in her heart and the memory of those low-spoken words, "Because I love you!"

Sometime in the night there was a disturbance out below the spring house, and several shots were fired. There were muffled sounds of stealthy feet, the clang of a police car off in the distance, one more human rat stayed in his depredations! But the father and daughter slept on and heard nothing of it.

IT was Gordon MacCarroll who met the reporters from the press next morning, and answered their questions in a quiet steady voice. He said that Mr. Disston had had a slight fall the day before, and was feeling a little under the weather this morning, so was not able to come down and see them, but he would be grateful for as little publicity as possible. Yes, it was true he had announced the fact over the radio that his daughter was missing. In these days of dreadful happenings perhaps he had been over anxious when he did not hear from her for a few days, and was not sure where she had gone. But it was all right now. His daughter was at home and safe, had merely started out to visit some relatives and friends and did not realize that her father would be anxious. Yes, it was true that some beings of the underworld had taken advantage of the radio announcement to send a note to Mr. Disston demanding ransom money, but the police had been prompt in rounding them up and putting them where they could not menace others.

It was all most courteous and quiet, and somehow the reporters found themselves bowed away with a rather prosaic story instead of the thrilling tale they had expected to extract.

One reporter, it is true, asked a few questions about the new Mrs. Disston. Wasn't there some trouble between her and Mr. Disston's daughter? He told them calmly that Mrs. Disston was away for a few days with friends. No, Mr. Disston's illness was not such as would warrant her coming back immediately, especially as the daughter was here now. Mrs. Disston would doubtless return very soon,

It was a quiet peaceful Sabbath, with Maggie getting a nice dinner in the kitchen and preparing a tempting tray for the invalid, with the nurse coming and going silently, and Diana sitting near her father's side, her flowers on the chiffonier at the foot of his bed where he could see them, and the consciousness that Gordon MacCarroll was downstairs with an officer of the law, just to make sure there were no more criminals waiting about.

It was a time when Diana could rest at last, and not even think, though there were pleasant things to consider, she realized later, when she was rested.

Monday Gordon had to go to his business, but he returned twice during the day to see if all was well, and came home early at night to get the latest news which his mother had gathered from Maggie.

Maggie in all her Scotch righteousness had met the reporters all day and stood for her family in great shape. A reporter would have had to cross her dead body before he could ever get by into the house, and curious neighbors went away baffled beyond belief.

There was just the quiet and peace that was needed for the invalid, and Diana basked in it and marvelled that she was here after her days of sorrow and hard work.

The doctor came and went quietly, studied his patient

and seemed pleased with his progress, yet warned them not to let him have the slightest bit of excitement or extra exertion.

But Stephen Disston seemed content just to lie still and watch his daughter going about the room, bringing her vase of carnations for him to see, sitting where he could see her with a book, or a bit of sewing, or just sitting, with her hands resting in her lap. But there was a sadness in the smile upon his face that the doctor hoped would disappear as the result of the shock passed.

They would not let him talk, nor let Diana talk much to him. The doctor had warned her about speaking of their separation or the kidnapping incident, so there was nothing to do but wait upon him and smile, sit quietly and love him.

It was Tuesday afternoon that they sat thus, keeping quiet company with one another while the nurse took her afternoon walk.

There had been no news from Helen, not even a telephone message, though she must have seen something in the papers if she was not otherwise too occupied. But Helen was not much given to reading even newspapers. They had not been thinking of her. Perhaps for the time she was entirely forgotten, as if she had no connection with their scheme of things.

It was then, just when she was least expected, that she came.

Of course it was because she had a latch key that she was able to enter the house and evade the watchful Maggie. Even then she got no farther than the foot of the stairs without a challenge.

Maggie, bearing a big spoon from which she had just wiped yellow batter with a capable forefinger, and from which a large drop of yellow batter was about to fall, swung open the door to the butler's pantry and stood like a glowering Nemesis in her way.

"An' where were *ye?*" she demanded. "It's high time ye put in an appearance! But yer not ta gang up the stair till the dochter gives ye permission! The master's had a fall an' a bad turn with his heart, an' he's not ta be excited. Ye'd best ask the nurse ef ye can go up!"

Helen stood there for an instant looking at the masterful Maggie, then put forth a small bejeweled hand and gave her a push backward, a push right in her ample chest that sent her entirely off her balance. Then with a laugh she ran lightly up the stairs.

She appeared in the doorway of her husband's room and stood there an instant taking in the situation. Diana was sitting quietly in a chair with her back to the door, a book in her lap and a smile on her face. Stephen Disston was dozing upon his pillow. They looked complete enough without her. There was a mirror across from Diana that showed the sweet look upon her face, that look that Helen always had hated.

She saw the sheaf of flowers near the bed, and she glimpsed through the window the nurse returning from her walk.

She stood poised an instant longer, studying her husband's face with her own hard beautiful eyes, and then she laughed, that gay bright heartless laugh.

Diana started, lifted her eyes swiftly to the mirror and met the amused contempt in the eyes of her father's wife! One instant their glances held, and then Helen whirled and went lightly down the hall, her laugh trailing delicately behind her. Down the stairs she went and put her head in at the kitchen door.

"I'm going on a cruise," she announced blithely. "You can tell them if they enquire. I'm not sure how long I'll be gone. They're getting along gloriously without me, and I never was much good in a sickroom. I hate it! Just tell them I'm on the yacht *Lotus Blossom*. Mr. Disston will understand."

She was gone before Maggie could recover her breath to reply, and Maggie dashed after her, trying to walk lightly for the master's sake, yet hurrying with all her sturdy might.

But when she finally arrived outside with the door closed behind her, Helen was far down the walk, breezing along like a bit of thistledown, and when Maggie flung herself down the path after her to give her a piece of her mind, and let her know how it would look to the world if she went away with the master sick, Helen only turned and flung back that gay childish laugh and tripped on.

When Maggie, all puffed and speechless, arrived at the gate, Helen was just climbing into the bus, and turning gave a mocking smile and a wave of her hand as she rode away.

Maggie, unable to believe her eyes, stood staring after the bus, an eloquent look on her loyal red countenance. A few seconds later she burst in upon Mrs. MacCarroll, all tears and anger and out of breath.

"Never mind, Maggie," said Mrs. MacCarroll soothingly. "You know the Lord can take care of her. Just leave it to him. He'll teach her in His own way. You can't!"

"I suppose yer richt," said Maggie snuffing back the tears, "an' I'm an ole fule ta greet, but it's a sair thing fer the likes of a young hussy like that ta carry on lightly when her gude mon is lying sick."

"Well, I wouldn't say anything about it now, not unless he asks. Maybe he didn't see her."

"I'm thinkin' he didn't!" said Maggie. "I heerd only her silly laughter, like a fule!"

"Well, leave it to the Lord. He'll bring it all out right in His own time and way."

So Maggie went back to finish her cake and nobody said a word about the new mistress of the house. For Diana had looked quickly at her father when that laugh rang out, and saw to her joy that he slept on and did not hear it. So she closed her lips and did not mention Helen's coming, wondering as the calm days went by if nobody else had seen her at all, wondering if perhaps she hadn't been dreaming herself and hadn't really seen her at all?

One evening Gordon came up to see Mr. Disston a few minutes. The sick man had had a good day and seemed brighter than since his fall, but still the doctor would not let him try to get up. They talked pleasantly on every-day topics, a bit of politics, the brighter outlook of the money market, the prophecy of a noted economist that things were looking up. Then Gordon turned toward Diana who sat quietly on the other side of the bed listening.

"Have you been out today?" he asked.

"Why, no," she said with a smile and a little shiver of dread. "No, I don't think I've been out of the house since I came back. I'm so glad to get here that I don't want to leave it."

"Well, that won't do. We'll be having you sick next. Suppose we take a little walk out now and catch the end of the sunset and a bit of the moonrise? Don't you think she should have a little exercise, Mr. Disston?"

"Yes, go, dear!" smiled her father. "I'm going to turn in now anyway, for I feel as if I might be able to really sleep tonight."

She kissed him good night and the two young people went downstairs and out into the "quiet colored end of evening." Diana suddenly felt breathless. It was the first time she had been alone with Gordon since he brought her home, and it suddenly became a momentous occasion. Why, she wondered? She had never felt like this before. It was probably because she had been through so many terrible experiences, and then been shut up in the house so long. She was just excited, she told herself. She tried not to let herself remember that sometime he was going to tell her about those mystery flowers, why he had sent them, "because I love you!" She had been telling herself that there was some other explanation to those words than the ordinary meaning when a young man says them to a girl. She had been telling herself that those were spirit-flowers and there was something above the earthly about their coming. She had fondly believed that she was thoroughly sane and sensible about the view her thoughts had taken of the whole thing, yet now this thrill of joy! Had all her fancied sanity been false?

So they strolled out into the evening with braided colors changing in the sky all about them, and the soft perfume of growing things in the air.

Gordon purposely led her about the house to the view of the meadows in the back with the spring house nestling its white stone walls by the brook, and the darkening woods standing majestic beyond. And just below them the garden, huddling in groups of dying colors, like devoted worshippers before the glory of the clouds. The breath of mignonette was there, with late pansies and forget-me-nots in close borders, and the white of stately lilies towering above tall spikes of larkspurs, flocks of canterbury bells, pink and white foxgloves, all bowing saintly heads at vespers. It was a lovely scene and the young man wanted the girl to lose that sense of horror which must be connected in her mind with the spring house. In the colored evening light, with flowers about and the brightness of the sunset on its white vineclad walls, and with Gordon MacCarroll's strong hand slipped protectingly within her arm, the spring house was forever robbed of its atmosphere of horror that Diana had felt since the night she came home. She would never again dread to look out toward it even in the evening.

And as the colors in the end of evening settled into purple and pearl and gray, they wandered slowly, reluctantly away from the hauntingly lovely garden wrapped in prayer; on through the shrubbery around the house to the drive, and so down across the drive to the tall plumy pines that grouped themselves back of the stone cottage.

They were walking across the grass now, their footsteps muffled by the turf, their step in unison. They had been talking of many things, and Diana thrilled to find that Gordon knew and loved the same poems and books and pictures that were her especial delight. How wonderful to have a friend—yes, she could dare to call him friend surely—who enjoyed reading. Not one of the young men in her crowd of friends had cared for reading anything but trash. They scarcely took time to read that.

But now as they entered within the seclusion of the pines, stepping between the two outer sentinel trees, suddenly Diana saw at her feet a starry flower!

Another carnation!

"Oh!" she cried, and stopped before it.

Then she looked up into Gordon's face with wonder and delight, and stooping reached out both hands to gather up the flower tenderly, and draw it close to her face.

Gordon stood looking down at her, a great reverence in his eyes.

She rose and looked at him again, a wonderful look, starry even through the dusk.

"You have put this here again!" she acknowledged.

"How wonderful of you! And you brought me out here to find it!"

He slid his arm within hers again. They took another step or two, and there behold, deeper in seclusion was another flower—and another—and another—a whole armful of carnations, it seemed like dozens and dozens of them, scattered broadcast there in the quiet luminous dark, with the stars beginning to look down from the sky.

He stooped beside her and helped her gather them up, and then as she stood breathless with them clasped in her arms he came and stood before her and looking into her eyes he said:

"And now, may I tell you about my love for you?"

He took both her hands as she held his flowers and looked down at her as if she were the most precious thing in the world. And Diana thrilled to the wonder of his voice, and looking up said with grave solemnity:

"But how could you possibly love me when you didn't know me? When you'd never even seen me yet?"

"Oh, but I had," said Gordon tenderly. "I had watched you day after day. Do you know where I saw you first? Right here in this spot where we are standing, kneeling down and picking something out of the grass. I found out afterward that it was violets you were picking, for after you were gone I went out and searched and found one you had missed. I have it now pressed in the pages of my Bible over a very precious verse."

"But where could you have been? I didn't see you anywhere," said Diana.

"No, you wouldn't. I was up in the window of my room reading my Bible and I looked up and saw you. Then when you were gone I knelt beside the window to pray and I prayed for you. Afterward I went out and found the violet. And every morning after that I watched you come for the violets till they were almost all gone. Then I was afraid you might not come there any more and I would miss you. So I thought of putting a flower there to see if you would find it. It was so I began to leave a flower each day for you. And each day I prayed for you, that you might know Him, my Lord, and be guarded and guided. And each day as I watched you and prayed for you my love for you grew until I suddenly knew it was a great overwhelming thing that was going to shut out the possibility of my ever loving any other woman. And I realized that you might never care for me. In fact it even might be that I would never get to know you well enough to tell you of my love. I am not a wealthy man, and you are a girl brought up to luxury. There were all sorts of obstacles. Yet I couldn't but be glad, for I knew there was something far more precious in loving you even this way, than to have a daily companionship with any other woman. So, I laid it before God and went on praying for you. The flowers were my only way of telling you, and you had not put them away from you. You had accepted them."

He paused and looked down at her with question and deep hunger in his eyes.

Diana stood with face slightly averted and spoke slowly:

"You don't know how precious they were! You don't know how much I needed them just then! Oh, it is all so very wonderful. I can see now why your prayer followed me everywhere, and drew me in spite of myself to God."

His hands were warm upon hers. His eyes were filled with wonder.

"But how could you possibly know that I was praying for you?" he asked. "You spoke of that before. I wondered about it."

"I heard you," she said quietly. "It was the night I went away. I had meant to be gone when Father brought her—his wife—home but they came before I expected them, and I had to slip out of the back door and hide behind the shrubbery. I was afraid they might follow me and stop me. I got down to the gate and stood out on the pavement over beyond your house, close to the hedge, waiting for the bus to come. And suddenly I heard a voice behind me praying. I did not know who you were, nor that you belonged in the cottage then. Nobody had told me except that a woman and her son had taken it. For some reason I thought the son was only a boy. But when I heard that prayer I knew it was the voice of the one who had protected me when I was terribly frightened. I thought perhaps it was a visitor at the cottage. But you were praying for *me*—at least I hoped that I was included. I hoped that our house was the one you meant when you spoke of the 'great' house, and I carried that prayer with me, for oh, how we needed it! 'Lord we would ask Thy mercy and tenderness and leading for the people up at the great house,' you said. 'Perhaps some of them are sad, Lord, give them comfort. Perhaps they need guidance. Do Thou send Thy light—!' And then that bus came along and I felt I had to get into it. But all the way to the city I kept saying those words over and over so that I wouldn't forget them, and when I got into the train I wrote them down. And I kept wishing I had stayed and heard the rest, even if I did get caught! Sometimes it seemed that I could not stand it because I had not heard the rest of that prayer. I almost got out of the bus and went back, only I had my suitcase to carry and I knew the prayer might be over by the time I got back. And then I was a little afraid that perhaps I might hear something more that would show it was not our house after all that you were praying for, and I felt as if I could not stand that. *I needed it so!*"

Her voice quivered, and suddenly his arms went round her and he drew her close, flowers and all, and laid his face down upon her soft hair.

"Darling!" he whispered.

She quivered in his arms and was still, and then she lifted her face to his and whispered back softly, shyly:

"Dear flower-person—!"

He laid his lips upon hers and drew her closer, and heaven itself seemed to come down and enfold them.

"I love you!" he told her in tones that thrilled her. "Can it be that you love me? So soon?"

"I think I've loved you since the first flower," she said smiling through the darkness. "I called them spirit-flowers, and told myself God sent them, but I loved and dreamed about whoever sent them. And—your prayer —God answered it! He sent me light to guide me, just as you prayed."

She told him about the girl in the station, and the tract that had helped her, and how she had begun to pray for herself, and he breathed a glad: "Thank God!"

They had so many things to tell! There were the times she had been saved from perils. There was the escape from the kidnappers. There was the way she looked when she came down the stairs in Mrs. Lundy's rooming house with the carnations held in her arms—! There was a great deal for him to tell her about that. And suddenly they realized that it was growing late.

"The dew has been falling a long time, and your feet must be drenched!" said Gordon. "This is a pretty way for me to begin to take care of you!"

But they were loath to leave the sacred place where their love had first found root, and it was some minutes before they walked slowly up the drive and entered the

house, their hands clinging together till the very thresh-
old was reached. They had said good night down among
the pines, but their fingers gave a last lingering pressure
as they entered decorously.

Maggie was waiting for them discreetly in the back of
the hall and came forward and took the carnations to be
put in water quite as if it were a common thing for young
men and maidens to go out at midnight and gather
carnations in the moonlight.

"There's a telegram for yer feyther," Maggie said in a
whisper, indicating a yellow envelope on the hall table.

25

DIANA and Gordon discussed whether it should be opened and decided to do so. It might be something about the kidnapping, in which case he probably wouldn't have to see it at all. But it might be something important that should be attended to at once. In any event they must know what it was before they dared show it to him, for the doctor had warned them so much about exciting him.

So Diana opened it carefully and read. It was dated from the yacht *Lotus Blossom*, and it consisted of just ten words.

> Having a glorious time. Don't you wish you had come?
>
> Signed Helen.

Diana looked up at her lover with startled eyes.

"It's from Helen!" she said. "She's off on a yachting cruise. What shall I do about telling him?"

"Let it drift a day or two," advised Gordon. "It will work out somehow. We'll pray about it."

She gave him a smile of wonder and awe as she put the message back in its envelope.

"I am sure that life is going to be wonderful and different now," she said looking up at him. "You make everything seem different. But oh, poor dear Father! How is he going to get well and strong with a wife like that?"

"Leave that to the Heavenly Father, too. Just trust it with Him! He'll have a way of working it out some day. Be patient!"

Maggie, lingering in the back hall filling the great vase with the carnations, kept sharp ears open to the low whispers, keen eyes furtively upon the two. She was not unaware of the starriness of her bonnie lassie's eyes, and her own lingered with approval upon Gordon's strong pleasant face, and fine height and build. Here was a man worthy of her wonderful girl!

And when he was gone and Diana had gone up to her room Maggie went and stood before the hall table looking down at the yellow envelope with eyes that could almost penetrate the paper, so keen they were of understanding, and then she said in a very inaudible whisper, more like a hiss:

"The *hussy!*"

Two days later Mr. Disston was so much better that the nurse said he could sit up against three pillows for a little while, and might have the paper to read for a few minutes.

They had given him the telegram the day before, and he had read it without comment and cast it carelessly on the table, whence it had floated to the floor. Maggie when she came in to "redd up," as she said, gathered it up and had the satisfaction at last of knowing the exact words of the message that she had read before by thought transference, or whatever it was that helped her to unravel the secrets of those about her.

So the nurse plumped up the pillows, and Stephen Disston sat up against them with the morning paper.

He thought he wanted very much to see what the stock market was doing, for his lawyer friend had been in to see him for a few minutes the day before and had brought encouraging news, but he let his eye wander over the first page of the paper before he opened to the commercial pages, and there in large letters heading one column was the announcement:

YACHT *LOTUS BLOSSOM* SINKS IN MID-OCEAN WITH ALL ON BOARD!

There were definite details about the owner of the yacht, its description, its history, speed, etc., and the accident by which the catastrophe arrived, also a lengthy discussion of why the S.O.S. did not bring neighboring ships in time, but Stephen Disston did not read them, neither did he turn over to the commercial page at all that morning. When the nurse came back she found him lying back on his pillows with his eyes closed and the paper on his lap. She told him it was time for his orange juice and his morning nap, and went to prepare the orange juice. But when Diana came in a moment later her father handed her the paper with a sad little smile and pointed to the headlines.

"Diana, I want you to know that you were right and I was wrong," he said sadly. "It is terrible when God has to send tragedies like that to teach a man sense!"

"Oh, Father!" said Diana looking at him with terrified eyes. "Don't say that! I was wrong! I know I was all wrong! Dear, *dear* Father! Can you ever forgive *me* for forcing a tragedy?"

"Dear, dear child!" said her father laying his hand tenderly on her head as she knelt beside his bed, "I thank God that he saved *you.*"

They did not talk further about the tragedy, and Diana watched her father all that day, dreading a reaction when he should realize the blow that had fallen upon him. But though he was quiet and grave, he did not seem greatly depressed.

"It is better so, little Di," he told her that night when she came to kiss him good night, and he recognized in her added tenderness an attempt at sympathy. "It is a terrible thing to have come, but, Diana, if she had lived she would not have been happy with me. I found that out."

That evening she talked it over with Gordon.

"Didn't I tell you that God would work it out in His own way?" he said gently.

"Yes, work it out," said Diana, thoughtfully, sadly. "He's worked it out for *us* of course, and made the way easy for Father and me. But I've been thinking about Helen. Gordon, I never thought about people that way before, until after I was saved. But I keep thinking that Jesus died to save Helen as much as He did to save me. God loved Helen, and sent His Son to die in *her* place, too, and I'm quite sure she never thought anything about it. I'm quite sure she wasn't saved. Gordon, I keep thinking that I did wrong to go away. I should have stayed here even if it was hard. I don't know that I could have done anything about helping her to be saved, though, because I didn't know Christ as my Saviour myself then, but there might have been a way. But now I'm practically sure she must be lost. And I can't think of her laughing to God! I don't think she laughed when the boat went down! I know she was frightened! Poor Helen!"

Gordon put his arms about her gently and drew her head to his shoulder.

"I know, little girl," he said, "but you can't tell what may have happened between her soul and God at the last minute, even in the twinkling of an eye. It does not take time to believe on Jesus Christ. I know it seems a terrible mystery, but we can safely trust our God to do right. You have seen your wrong and confessed it, now believe that it is forgiven and put away."

"Oh, do you think so?" she said, turning eager longing eyes on her lover. "Oh, I hope she is saved. I used to hate her, but now I hope she is saved. Since I have learned that Jesus loved everybody enough to die for them I can love her too. And I don't want her to be lost!"

Two days later was Diana's twenty-first birthday.

Gordon and Diana went together to Stephen Disston's room to tell him of their love for one another.

Mr. Disston was feeling decidedly better. The nurse had a surprise for them. Mr. Disston was sitting up in a chair beside the little bedside table, clothed in dressing gown and slippers, and smilingly ready to receive them.

And when Gordon had told him, Stephen Disston looked at them both lovingly and said:

"There isn't a man in the world I know or have ever seen that I would as soon trust my girl with as you, Gordon MacCarroll. And it is not only that I trust you, I love you myself, for you have been like a son to me in my deepest trouble, and if it had not been for you perhaps I should never have had my little girl back again. I can truly receive you as my beloved son, and no 'in-law' about it."

Diana's eyes were starrier than ever as she looked toward her lover, and touched to her lips the great white rose bud, one of a new flock that he had brought her that morning for a birthday token.

They stayed on in sweet converse for an hour, and then as the nurse was heard to approach and Mr. Disston knew it was time for his morning rest he reached out his hand to a folded paper that lay on the table and handed it to Diana.

"Here, Diana, is a birthday gift from your own mother. She planned before she left us that you should be given this house with a sufficient fortune to keep it up and give you a good income all your life, on your twenty-first birthday."

Diana's cheeks grew pink with bewilderment and joy.

"Oh, Father! But I thought this house was yours."

"No, Diana! It never has been. Your mother's mother gave it to her as a wedding gift with the understanding that it was to be an ancestral home, and to pass to your children after your death."

Diana looked toward her lover with sparkling eyes, but was surprised to see a new gravity upon him.

"I did not know that I had presumed to ask the hand of an heiress," he said with troubled voice. "I thought you told me that you were bankrupt, Mr. Disston?"

"And so I did," said Diana's father with a sad little smile, "and so I was—although my lawyer told me yesterday that things are coming out better than we had feared and that it will not be as bad as that. I can pay all my debts and have a small income for myself. But this should make no difference to you, Gordon. Money should not enter into the scheme of things when two people love one another. It's only something for which to be thankful when God chooses to send more than you asked."

Then Diana lifted her head proudly.

"Gordon, have you forgotten that you saved my life? Isn't that more than money? Don't I owe you all I have? Please don't feel that this house and money could put even a faintest cloud between us two."

She lifted her sweet eyes to his pleadingly and he stooped and kissed her reverently.

"I won't, sweetheart. Only—well I'm glad I didn't know it till afterwards," he said with a merry twinkle.

Half an hour later as they came out from the sickroom where the nurse was bustling about with reprimand in her countenance, to hurry her patient back to bed for a rest, Gordon said:

"What about your room over in that terrible place where I found you, dear? Oughtn't you to do something about that? You said you had some furniture there."

"Yes," said Diana, "I have some of my most precious possessions there, my mother's picture for one, and I know Father would want that back in his room. I telephoned Mrs. Lundy last night that I would be over tomorrow to pay her and see about taking my things away. I telephoned the movers, too."

"Well, I'll fix it up to go with you. I think if I do a few things this afternoon while you are resting I can get off tomorrow and stay till you come away."

"Oh, you don't need to do that, Gordon," protested Diana. "I shan't have to do much. The movers are perfectly capable, and you know it isn't as if I didn't know my way about there," she laughed.

"That's all right, sweetheart, you may know your way about but I'm not trusting you alone in that terrible neighborhood again. God has put the responsibility on me now, and I intend to care for you to the best of my ability. And how about taking Mrs. Lundy a box of bright flowers to go in her plush parlor just by way of farewell?"

"Lovely!" said Diana twinkling. "But they will have to be bright flowers, not spirit-flowers. The spirit-flowers are mine. My dear mystery flowers!"

About the Author

Grace Livingston Hill is well-known as one of the most prolific writers of romantic fiction. Her personal life was fraught with joys and sorrows not unlike those experienced by many of her fictional heroines.

Born in Wellsville, New York, Grace nearly died during the first hours of life. But her loving parents and friends turned to God in prayer. She survived miraculously, thus her thankful father named her Grace.

Grace was always close to her father, a Presbyterian minister, and her mother, a published writer. It was from them that she learned the art of storytelling. When Grace was twelve, a close aunt surprised her with a hardbound, illustrated copy of one of Grace's stories. This was the beginning of Grace's journey into being a published author.

In 1892 Grace married Fred Hill, a young minister, and they soon had two lovely young daughters. Then came 1901, a difficult year for Grace—the year when, within months of each other, both her father and husband died. Suddenly Grace had to find a new place to live (her home was owned by the church where her husband had been pastor). It was a struggle for Grace to raise her young daughters alone, but through everything she kept writing. In 1902 she produced *The Angel of His Presence*, *The Story of a Whim*, and *An Unwilling Guest*. In 1903 her two books *According to the Pattern* and *Because of Stephen* were published.

It wasn't long before Grace was a well-known author, but she wanted to go beyond just entertaining her readers. She soon included the message of God's salvation through Jesus Christ in each of her books. For Grace, the most important thing she did was not write books but share the message of salvation, a message she felt God wanted her to share through the abilities he had given her.

In all, Grace Livingston Hill wrote more than one hundred books, all of which have sold thousands of copies and have touched the lives of readers around the world with their message of "enduring love" and the true way to lasting happiness: a relationship with God through his Son, Jesus Christ.

In an interview shortly before her death, Grace's devotion to her Lord still shone clear. She commented that whatever she had accomplished had been God's doing. She was only his servant, one who had tried to follow his teaching in all her thoughts and writing.

Don't miss these Grace Livingston Hill romance novels!

Mail your order with check or money order for the price of the book plus $2.00 for postage and handling to: **Tyndale Family Products, P.O. Box 448, Wheaton, IL 60189-0448.** Allow 4-6 weeks for delivery. Prices subject to change.

The Grace Livingston Hill romance novels are available at your local bookstore, or you may order by mail (U.S. and territories only). For your convenience, use this page to place your order or write the information on a separate sheet of paper, including the order number for each book.

Please send the titles and quantities I've indicated to:		
NAME _____	BOOK TOTAL	$ ____
ADDRESS_____	SHIPPING & HANDLING	$ 2.00
CITY _____	APPLICABLE SALES TAX (IL)	$ ____
STATE_____ ZIP_____	TOTAL AMOUNT DUE	$ ____
Allow 4-6 weeks for delivery. Prices subject to change	PAYABLE IN U.S. FUNDS. (Check or money order)	
	Tyndale House Publishers, Inc.